THE UNCOMMON BOND

of

JULIA AND ROSE

Ann Williams

A Novel

Author's and cover photo by Daniel Coston

Interior image designed by Freepik

Published in the United States of America by
Floating Leaf Press, 2015

ISBN: 978-0-9969303-0-7

BISAC category: Fiction / Historical / General

To the Memory of the Real Rose,
My Muse and Inspiration

...and concerning my said old faithful servant Rose, my will is that she shall not be sold (like a brute beast) but shall be kept by my said three daughters in as easy circumstances as the nature of slavery will admit...

From the will of Annabella Morrison
March 16, 1808

LAST WILL AND TESTAMENT

In the name of God, Amen. I, Julia Campbell Henderson of the county of Lincoln and the state of North Carolina, and relict of Thomas Henderson deceased, having been supported by a kind and merciful God for sixty years, and even now enjoy a competent degree of health, and blessed with sound mind and memory, praise to God for all his rich blessings fully given unto me; and believing that I must one day die and leave earthly enjoyments and blessings, do therefore make this my last will and testament, viz: I give my soul to that Almighty God who gave it to me, and my body I recommit to the earth, dust to dust, doubting not that they will be reunited by the Almighty power of God on the glorious day of judgment. Such small worldly portion of the good things of this life as God saw fit to bestow upon me, I will, give, and bequeath as follows:

Item: I will and bequeath to my beloved daughter Adelaide Lowery, hereinafter known as Adie, to her and her heirs and assigns forever, all the goods and household furniture which I brought from my own house, and are now in the possession of the said Adie, except one mare and six silver teaspoons.

Item: I will and give said six silver teaspoons to Julia, my granddaughter and namesake, daughter of my beloved son Tom, deceased.

Item: I will and give to each of my seven grandchildren one pocket Bible, viz: to said granddaughter Julia; to Rebecca, Benjamin, and Matthew, children of my daughter Adie; to Annabella and Constance, daughters of daughter Eliza; and to William, son of my youngest child Rachel; which Bibles shall be delivered to them at such times as my executors may judge prudent and proper, unless I myself should give Bibles to them between this time and my decease as God may spare and enable me.

Item: I will and bequeath to my three beloved daughters, Adie Lowery, Eliza Wilson, and Rachel Harris, to them, their heirs and assigns forever all the residue and remainder of my estate which will include said mare and my old Negro slave Rose, to be divided among them, share and share alike, and concerning my said old faithful servant Rose, my will is that she shall not be sold (like a brute beast), but shall be kept by my said three daughters in as easy circumstances as the nature of slavery will admit, by having or keeping her about each of their homes for three or six months (each at a time, as they three *shall agree on), for their own profit, ease, and convenience. And that they, my three daughters, so divide my wearing apparel as they please.*

Lastly, I hereby nominate and appoint my trusty and faithful brother Frank Campbell, and my son-in-law Isaac Lowery, to be my sole executors of this my last will and testament, hereby revoking all former and other wills either by work or writing, ratifying and confirming this and no other to be my last will and testament. In witness whereof, I, the said Julia Henderson, have hereunto set my hand and seal, this the fifteenth day of March Anno Domini, 1860.

Julia Campbell Henderson

Signed and sealed in the presence of these Witnesses:

James McWhirter,
Frank Campbell

March, 1860

I penned these words, more or less, three days since in the office of a lawyer. I say more or less as the lawyer's clerk did the actual penning, and the flowery words and legal phrases flowed from the lawyer's lips. Had I been the writer, the opening of this decree would have been couched more plainly. I have no quarrel with its message however, as my faith is strong. The man assured me that the lawyerly parts would prevent a challenge, in spite of the fact that I have no former wills to revoke. Why anyone would challenge for a widow's mite is more than I can fathom.

It was my brother Frank – a bachelor physician of fine repute – who insisted I draft a will, and dragged me in his rig to the lawyer to attend to it. Why, I asked him, as I have nothing of significance to be spoken for, and he carried on with his newfound concern about troubling times that surely lie ahead. Frank seems convinced that we are going for a war, and that my daughters' interests should be protected should their husbands be sent to it, and – God forbid – not return. I've no idea how a mare and six silver teaspoons would accomplish such a feat. If you ask me, Frank is a worrisome old maid.

And then there is Rose. In the eyes of the law I suppose she is my property, but I cannot believe it true in God's eyes, no matter what we are told at preaching. She is a woman born into her circumstance, as I was into mine. She may do my bidding, but has demonstrated clearly that she thinks for herself. I own her as a man owns the water in the creek that flows across his farm.

After the lawyer took down the parts about the furniture, the teaspoons, and the Bibles, he asked if there was anything else to consider. The man had a manner about him as if I were wasting his time, after all, I could easily make a gift of the spoons and Bibles while I live, and the furniture is already in my daughter Adie's house, as I abide there with her. So I boldly announced my intention to make provisions for Rose, secure and irrefutable. I could see brother Frank wince as the words left my lips, for I have a reputation in the family of being wrong-headed on the matter of slavery, a reputation that Frank would rather not have trotted out and aired. But I said my piece, and could see the lawyer snickering behind his mustaches, and the clerk growing wide-eyed, pen flickering in the air, not knowing what to write. Well, the lawyer hemmed and hawed, and tossed out legal words which seemed to me to soften my position to mush, and leave Rose's fate to my executors. If Frank is right about impending war – and I am beginning to fear he has a point – and the possibility of my sons-in-law dying and being replaced by persons unknown, then Rose is truly in peril. My daughters could tell of my wishes, but being female, their opinions would carry no weight. I have learned one thing in this life, a lesson dearly bought: sheltering Negroes from the whims of men is no simple matter.

We talked at length about it, harsh words being spoken, however the lawyer reluctantly conceded to include my words, smashed between parentheses as if it were a mere by-the-by. I pray that what was written by that mousy clerk will prove sufficient to protect my poor servant. Dear Lord forgive me, for I bear shame enough on her behalf, sin I shall carry to my grave.

I suppose Frank thinks himself the victor, as I did not call for Rose's freedom. Such a petition would go for naught, as manumission laws have day by day become more onerous, and may already be prohibitive. I did consider giving Rose her freedom after becoming a widow, with no one left to object. But Rose would have been required to leave North Carolina, and I to post a thousand dollar bond of assurance. The cost was far beyond my meager means, and our separation would have been unbearable. "Assurance" only travels one direction; Negroes, even those in possession of papers or living at the North, are often captured and sold back into slavery. A free black nowadays is in far more danger than a well cared for slave.

Frank also harbors the erroneous notion that I consider Rose my equal, which I do not. I am well aware of the shortcomings of the Negro race, and know they need our constant guidance. Yet they are human beings, created so by God. No human, no matter how degraded and disadvantaged, deserves to be kept in bondage.

That was three days since, and I've had some time to reflect. I saw no need to write a will when Frank dragged me to that lawyer, but I came away glad of it for Rose's sake. I've watched her eyes and face these past few days, looking for joy or discomfort or affection, and found them all in a great pool of familiarity. Rose was mine long before I wed my dear Thomas and gave birth to my children; sometimes I feel that we are bound blood deep, that she is my extension as much as my possession.

My family may think me wrong-headed, but I purely believe that slavery is evil. I am not alone in that concept even among Southerners, although surely we are a minority. But I've no remedy to offer. The

Bible decrees that the black race descended from Ham and is condemned to serve us for turning from God. Yet all Negroes of my acquaintance have embraced God's promise of salvation. Have they not redeemed themselves? In my humble opinion a malignancy spawned by cotton, not God, perpetuates slavery. Cotton intertwines every man's livelihood, slaveholder or not. Those who own no people, whether by poverty or conviction, know that all they possess springs from cotton's wealth wrought by slaves. And those at the North who buy our cotton cannot possibly be ignorant of the color of the hands that grew it. None of us are willing to give up cotton's prodigious bounty.

Now my opining was not only about Rose, as I've done the best I can for her. It disturbed me to think I might leave nothing behind save six teaspoons, a mare, bits of furniture, and Bibles yet to be bought. So I determined to do some penning of my own and leave for my children and grandchildren a story of my life; if only my mother or father had done such a thing, I would be richer for it. I asked daughter Adie for a copybook, as I wished to keep a journal of my thoughts and experiences, and she was happy to comply. I suppose it will be a journal of a sort, for I aim to tend to it every day, yet my purpose is not merely to record daily events, but all that has accumulated in a lifetime. Tomorrow I shall begin.

Monday, March 19, 1860

I am Julia Campbell Henderson, a widow lady sixty years of age, having been born on this earth on the tenth day of January in the year of 1800 – ushering in the new century, Pa always said. (Dear daughters, I know you are familiar with many of these facts, but it suits my sense of order to set them all down, and someday, should your children read these pages, they might find the details illuminating.) I make my home with my oldest daughter Adie, her husband Isaac Lowery, and their three small children. I thank God daily that she had the Christian compassion to take me in, an old woman all alone after my dear Thomas departed this world.

I am the oldest of my parents' four offspring, and will give here an account of my interesting childhood. Pa was neither a rich man nor a poor one. He kept a middling farm of three hundred acres, more or less. When I was small he raised corn and hogs, kept a few milch cows, and grew the bounty for our table. He was assisted in this endeavor by the black family we owned, a man and his wife and their six children. As I grew into womanhood Pa began to raise the upland cotton that became so popular in the eighteen-teens, then began to flourish into grand prosperity about 1820. Our farm was located in Lincoln County, North Carolina, a few miles west of the Catawba River. It was a pretty piece of land composed of red clay hills, cool water creeks, and hardwood forests. Part of Pa's land was rich in the iron ore that could be dug and sold to a nearby foundry, Vesuvius Furnace it was called. Pa made good use of his little farm that was first tilled by his father before him. Which brings up a bone of contention.

Pa told me his father bought the land before the Revolutionary War when Pa himself was a small boy. He remembered my grandfather coming home from the war, bruised and battered, but triumphant, an American Patriot, pure and simple. Many years later when I was being courted by Thomas Henderson, some of my future in-laws claimed that Campbells were of two stripes: valiants who fought for Independence, and traitorous allies of the English king; and as my family was unknown to them, could they have been of the latter sort? Well, Pa was irate at this insult, and came near to withdrawing his blessing on my impending marriage. He had vivid memories of his father's homecoming from war, particularly of the heroic victory at Ramsour's Mill just ten miles west of our farm. There were no British on that field; Americans all, some avid for independence, others loyal to the king, brothers armed against brothers, perhaps Campbells in both camps. Brutal combat (called a mere skirmish by some!) resulted in many scores of fatalities. Pa being a child at the time did not retain details of his father's adventures, and had no knowledge of the brave man's regiment, nor any papers to reveal it.

Fortunately for me, my dear intended Thomas was an amiable and charming man who had no use for grudges and pointless conflict. He convinced Pa that it was me he was courting, not the ghost of my grandfather. Neither he nor his immediate family (with the exception of his odious mother, another contentious bone!) had a shred of doubt about the gentleman's patriotism, and even if they had, it would not matter one whit which Campbells we had sprung from. The foolish question had been raised, Thomas claimed, by some maternal uncles who had no business in the matter. I can still see Thomas speaking to Pa through his sprightly grin that I had come to love so much, "Sir, those uncles of mine ride a mite too high on their horses, if you ask me, and spend far too much time pricking at folks, checking the blueness of their blood. If anyone has something to hide, 'tis probably them." Well the whole thing came to nothing, as Pa concluded that Thomas was indeed worthy of me. The offending uncles did not live in our neighborhood, and we never again heard any more of it.

I mention this long forgotten event, as it came to me during my recent spate of mental meandering. As inconsequential as it turned out to be, it was a brief but wrenching terror for a young girl thoroughly smitten. For several wretched nights I wept and cursed into my pillow, slamming fists into the ticks, raising only useless wisps of feather dust. I vowed to fling myself into the river and endure the wrath of God should Pa withdraw his permission for me to marry. I was certain there was no one else on earth as dear as Thomas – which I still know to be true. As I have said the storm dissipated as quickly as it arose, and Thomas and I were soon wed.

Upon seeing brother Frank wince at the lawyer's office when I declared for Rose, I concluded not to be remembered as a wrong-headed unpatriotic woman. A person's life is always more complex than it would seem from casual observation, and so I set mine down, so as not to be like my grandfather whose allegiance was questioned, and who left no words in his defense.

Tuesday, March 20, 1860

Today my son-in-law Isaac is preparing the soil to plant his cotton. It is a cold windy day for late March, the fickle warmth of early spring being in retreat. Isaac frets that peach blossoms may have formed too soon, and might be harmed by a late frost that now threatens. Adie spent the morning with her children hearing their catechism, and the afternoon seeing to a ham taken from the smokehouse, scraped of mold, and put on to boil.

I was born in 1800 – as I have mentioned – and was followed three years later by Jeff, who was named Thomas Jefferson Campbell after the then-sitting president, if further proof be demanded of my family's patriotism. Frank came along in 1806, and little Jane in 1808, a year of great distress. In the late summer of that year, the season in which fevers and miasmas generally attack, our mother was taken ill. I do not know the name of her malady, only that she burned with fever that broke into sweating chills, followed by another bout of burning. During the day Pa shooed us children out of doors to shelter us from her suffering, and to protect us from her affliction. But in the night I shuddered at her racking cough that did little to relieve the gurgling in her lungs. One night her breathing became soft and shallow, less labored, and I fell into a contented sleep convinced that she was cured. I woke at first light to discover that her suffering was indeed over; my mother was dead. Pa sat stunned on their bed cradling her limp form in his lap – her face as blue-white as skimmed milk, lips gone purple, her expression at long last, peaceful.

I had barely taken in this scene when Greene, our black man, poked his head through the doorway. Knowing Ma was ill, he was not alarmed to find Pa absent from the barn at daybreak, and had come to the house to ask what chores he should attend. He gasped when he saw Ma's blue-white face and Pa's red sodden one. "I go fetch Cissy," said Greene, and in a flash was gone for his wife, for it is always a start to encounter the mask of death and a grown man sobbing. Cissy appeared in a trice with her oldest girl Mattie, and the next few days have blurred together in my memory. We children were kept out of the way while neighbor ladies came to help Cissy bathe Ma and put her in her Sunday best. Men gathered behind the shed to build a coffin which they sanded smooth as glass, then waxed into a burnished golden hue. Lastly they trimmed it with the best hardware that could be found. A stream of folks came by to see Ma laying out, and give comfort to Pa and the rest of us. In no time the entire neighborhood was gathered in the church where the preacher prated on far too long over the condition of Ma's soul. She had been a devout Christian woman, yet the man pled with God that she had been holy enough to enter His Kingdom, although none of us sinners deserve such a thing. I scrunched back tears, sad for my mother's death, still much too young to understand how long forever is, ill as a hornet at the preacher who had the audacity to question my mother's goodness and her worthiness for heaven. How dare he plead with God!

It was then that Mattie and Rose entered my world. Oh, they had always been in the cabin with their brothers and Cissy and Greene – but it was then that Mattie came to occupy our house. Pa was beside himself with grief and four small children to care for, so twelve-year-old Mattie was told to fix herself a pallet in our garret and act as our nursemaid. Rose was four and tagged along, as caring for Rose was already one of Mattie's chores. Each evening Rose went back to the cabin to sleep with her family, and each morning she joined Mattie and us children for whatever the day held. Cissy cooked our food and washed our laundry, and now with Mattie's help, took over the sewing, gardening, and house cleaning that Ma used to do. Greene and his four boys – one several years older than Mattie, the others stair-stepped between their sisters – worked with Pa at farming and digging iron ore from the earth.

Thursday, March 22, 1860

I promised myself to keep at this journal every day, but yesterday presented no time for writing. Adie went to town to shop for cloth for her children's summer wardrobe, seeds for the garden, any number of things. I expect she also needed to get in some visiting. She has little company of other women, discounting myself, between Sabbaths. I passed the day with my grandchildren, Rebecca who is ten, Benjamin eight, and little Matthew only four. Adie miscarried several times between the boys, and fears she may not be blessed with another child. I pray for her.

My sister Jane was three months old when Ma died. She had been tiny at birth, a lank child who suckled weakly. Lacking muscle tone, Pa had said. When Ma took ill, the fever dried up her milk. Pa and Cissy tried to feed Jane with cow's milk, diluted with water and sweetened with honey, but most of what was spooned into her listless mouth dribbled down her chin. Cissy tied a lump of sugar into a rag and dipped it in milk, a sugar teat she called it, but the babe was uninterested. The poor thing hardly cried at all, just whimpered from time to time, and within a month she too was dead. This time Pa was not only grief stricken, but terrified that Jane had caught Ma's affliction, and his remaining children were soon to follow. Cissy assured him that Jane had been born too small and it was a wonder she had lived at all, that the rest of us were as fit as colts. I don't know if Pa believed her, but she proved to be right. I cannot summon up Jane's countenance in my memory, but I well remember Pa's at the time, brow furrowed with worry, his mighty hand spooning milk between her wee pink lips, rocking her gently in his thick strong arms, fragile as she was. Pa made a very good mother.

Jane was buried next to Ma, a tiny lamb on her headstone, and in the fullness of time Pa was satisfied that his remaining children were in good health.

It was a cold winter after Ma and Jane died. I cannot remember if bitter weather was the cause, or simply a heart chill from death and sorrow. Mattie was no help; I mean with the sadness. She was generally awakened each morning by the rooster's crow or the sun slicing through the shutter slats of the garret. If those failed, and Pa had to shout for her, she bounded down the stairs with keen agitation, as if she had suffered a mortal failing in not anticipating the day, and might be punished. Pa took no notice. She was only twelve, and unaccustomed to her new responsibilities. If she wasn't up, he called for her, a simple inconsequential matter. Otherwise she moved blandly through her chores, showing nothing on her face. She spoke only when spoken to, or to direct us children. Each morning she came to my room with fresh water for my washbowl, pleasantly warmed. Then she would tend to my brothers, as I, turning nine that winter, was quite capable of washing and dressing myself.

I generally came down for breakfast about the time Cissy brought the food into the house from the kitchen, precious Rose bobbing behind her, clutching her coattails. Rose, having already been fed, would be settled in a corner with a scrap of bread or simple toy to keep her occupied while our family ate. Rose had a bright smile and gleeful laugh, a true joyful spark amongst all the long faces. She was only four, much too young to recognize death or to know she was a possession. I can still see her pretty head popping up from behind a chair or a table, bright eyes wide with wonder, and then disappear as she dropped to the floor in a rousing whoop and giggle, as if completely surprised to find another person in the room. Meanwhile Mattie, having dressed my brothers, solemnly served our plates, and when we were done, gathered them up and carted them off to the kitchen to Cissy's dishpan. Then she would be back to mend or dust or sweep, all the while tending us children.

Back then I had no concept of what was in Mattie's mind, although I felt awkwardness on both our parts when she, a Negro, gave me my chores. Was it because she was black, or because she was not my mother? Had I sensed without words Ma's posture in directing our household, a posture Mattie could not possibly occupy? I've no idea. In the wisdom that comes with age, I'm sure that Mattie grasped the grim reality of slavery that winter. She now had a position, a steady responsibility, rather than an assortment of tasks assigned by her mother. She was now in my father's charge, and the servile character of her life was at that moment sealed forever. I suppose I would have been glum also.

As I've said, Rose was a naturally happy child, and has grown into a reasonably content woman, albeit a strong willed one. Many a morning I gulped my breakfast of cornbread crumbled in cream then gathered Rose in my lap for a game of patty-cake or peep-eye. Wiggly giggly Rose, all warm and satisfying, our hands intertwined in play. What a bright light she was! Anyone would have been drawn to her sunny disposition, a great contrast to Mattie's lumbering about with an old woman's temperament. Rose was my savior that winter. I, being older, was more affected by Ma's passing than my brothers, and was just the right age to be absorbed by the birth of an infant for me to help bathe and dress and diaper, my very own living plaything. Only to have her snatched away too. Rose brought back my childhood, playful the way it ought to be. I am ever indebted to her.

Friday, March 23, 1860

Last night we were struck by a light frost that has threatened for several days. Now the sun is out brightly for a change, and it looks to be warming up. Isaac could find but few browned blossoms on our peach trees, so perhaps we shall have fruit after all.

When 1809 dawned along with my ninth birthday, Pa decided it was high time I should be sent to school. He enrolled me in the common school taught at our church, a Presbyterian one. Most of the new students were younger than I, and I could remember the previous year hearing Ma argue with Pa who insisted I needed a proper education. I rarely heard my parents raise their voices, so it alarmed me somewhat, especially as I was the source of the trouble. Ma prevailed, and I was kept at home that year where she taught me the alphabet and my stitches. When Pa sent me to school the January after Ma died, I assumed it was because Ma was no longer there to teach me, and Mattie hadn't any learning. It was not until years later that I learned that money was the reason for Ma's objection to formal schooling.

Now Pa was a good and kind man, no child could wish for a better father, but all of us have flaws, and Pa's was having not a whit of sense about money. Ma had kept us in check, doing the sums and keeping accounts, and reminding those who owed us. Pa was not possessed by greed, yet he liked to live comfortably, and was embarrassed by the fact that money was involved. He was mortified to approach anyone indebted to him, yet with naïve optimism he blithely bought on credit against a bounty that surely lay ahead. So to school I went, one or two sessions per year, for the next three years, courtesy of a note for ore not yet dug, or a fat sow that appeared to be carrying a large litter. Each session was only six or eight weeks back then, but I did learn to read which I've relished ever since.

Each morning Greene or his oldest boy would haul me onto a horse in front of him, and we would ride the two miles to school. In the afternoons I walked home, unless the weather was dreadful, then one of them would come fetch me. I couldn't get enough of school, so on days when it was not in session, I would create my own. I would set up my pretend classroom in my bedchamber or on the porch, and gather up Rose and my brothers for pupils. I, of course, was the teacher. Jeff and Frank lost interest in a minute, but Rose enjoyed the game as much as I. Before we knew what happened, I had taught Rose to read. In fact we had been admonished at church to teach our little black brethren to read from the Bible, for it would please God for them to do so. Perhaps this was in my mind at first, but it became a minor motive. I had grown enamored of the written word, how a thought or idea or story could be recorded then summoned up at any wish or whim. How convenient! There was no law back then against my teaching Rose this sweet mystery, and no one minded as it kept the two of us out from under foot, and out of trouble. I taught her to write, a bit of ciphering, and other useful things, but it was reading stories that enraptured us, that bound us together for years to come.

Monday, March 26, 1860

Here I have let two days pass, neglecting my journal. Saturday was a busy day. The entire family went into town, as there is much ado in preparation for planting. I escorted the children about while Adie flitted from shop to shop, and Isaac bargained over the price of a plow blade and sundries needed to put his cotton gin in good order. Yesterday, being the Sabbath, I refrained from writing. I have not yet determined if it would be sinful. Contemplation is encouraged on that sacred day, yet this instrument dwells on my past life rather than the fitness of my soul for the one to come, so I'm not certain it qualifies. I will give pious thought to the matter. In any event, we had two preachings yesterday and a social dinner between them, so there was no time to devote to my journal.

Just after my second session of common school, in the waning days of 1809, a new "mother" joined our family. I was not aware of our father courting, and have no memory of when or where he became acquainted with the woman. We children were introduced to her that fall when Pa invited her to our home for dinner and announced that they had decided to marry and planned to do so a few weeks before Christmas. I was completely taken aback. Jeff and Frank seemed to accept the idea with neither enthusiasm nor rancor, as if all it meant to them was a pair of white hands buttoning their drawers rather than black ones. I however, looked into her plain and mirthless face, and wondered how on earth could Pa replace my mother, especially with such a homely sort, tall, broad-shouldered, horsey about the jowls, someone he could not possibly love. He could not have known her long enough!

Well marry they did! On these pages I will refer to the second Mrs. Campbell simply as "Mrs. C.," for I could not, and cannot bring myself to call her Mother. Her Christian and maiden names are unimportant, as her relatives have long since left our environs. I suppose Pa was lonely, and perhaps thought we needed more mothering. After all Mattie was still a child herself, and Cissy had her hands full cooking and washing and raising her own brood. At the time I had no knowledge of a man's need for womanly affection, and it embarrasses me yet to think that Pa may have married to warm his bed.

As you may have gathered by now Mrs. C. was an unfortunate choice for a mother. I never knew her age, but she must have been quite young, as she had no idea what to do with us. She did have affection for Pa, for light rose in her eyes when she gazed at him. But when he was out of the house another persona emerged from her hulking frame. I don't know what sort of preaching Mrs. C. was raised to, but she had latched like a terrier onto the fear of God and an even stronger fear of the Devil. She determined she was meant to save our souls. Each afternoon after dinner she would line up the four of us (my brothers, Rose, and me) in straight-backed chairs in the parlor. There she would preach, or rant is more like it, about the eternal fires of Hell, and how the slightest indiscretion would land us there. She paced back and forth silhouetted against the sunny window, arms wildly beseeching her vengeful God, voice rising to a roaring shout, then dropping to a whisper as she suddenly crouched, her face hovering inches from ours. If we so much as squirmed in our seats she would strike us with a towel she carried for that purpose, snapping it to make a sharp and fearsome sound, smarting dearly, but leaving no mark, at least none that Pa would notice. She may have been crazed, but she was not daft.

It was not long before my brothers lost their indifference to the woman, replacing it with fear. And poor little Rose, now nearly six, had no notion of what to make of the towering white woman. She would sit rigidly on her hands, and bite her lips against sniveling, but no amount of self-control could prevent tears from creeping down her cheeks. Tears to Mrs. C. were a sign of weakness, a sign that one had not embraced the Grace of God. I'm sure she placed us that way, with her back to the window, so that she could see and read every nuance that crossed our faces, and we could see nothing of hers. Even as young as I was I thought her sermons peculiar. If God was all powerful and could create the world any way He pleased, why did He make people so wicked and the path to Heaven so impossible to follow? Did God not want us to join Him at his right hand? Most preachers assured us that He did. If the world worked according to Mrs. C.'s perception, God must be mighty lonely up in Heaven all by Himself.

As I have said she was not daft. When she heard the rattle of the doorknob, indicating Pa was home, she would shake the towel in front of our faces, gently this time. "Go now, shoo," she would say. "You've chores to do. You don't want your Pa to think you're a slothful bunch." Then somehow she would conjure up a smile for her face, and begin dusting the furniture with her supple instrument of torture.

These exercises in discipline are etched so vividly in my memory that it feels as if they occupied most of every day. But they did not. Looking back I can remember chores, and playing games in our yard. Perhaps when we were out of doors she was content to leave us be.

Late in January, school started up, yet I doubt I learned much that session. I sat restless on my bench, toying with my slate, worrying about the others at home. I never asked them what chastisement occurred in my absence. We never spoke of it, as if it were a hideous nightmare, too shameful to mention. Of course we did not tell Pa. Mrs. C. had not asked for our silence, but it was implicit that it was required. Nor did we say a word to Cissy. Mattie must have witnessed this odd religious education, but Mattie rarely talked about anything.

Mrs. C. was not a mad woman in any other way. She did not talk to people who were not there, nor engage in nonsensical rituals. She was perfectly pleasant in the presence of our father, and as far as I know, had complete confidence in the sanctity of his soul. Pa was mesmerized by her, and seemed to adore her in spite of her utter plainness. Perhaps her passion toward him was carnal in nature, yet equally as vigorous as her Godly fervor. I can hardly bear to entertain such a thought! Pa was oblivious to our silent coldness toward her, and her indifference to us. When he was around she smiled at us sweetly and treated us with civility, as if we were neighbors who had inconveniently dropped in for tea. She never held us, soothed us, or showed us any sign of affection.

Frank came the closest to spilling the secret, as he was only four. He asked Pa questions about Heaven and Hell, and why the Devil had to work so hard to get a hold of us if was so easy to do. He was obviously mixing the gentler of our church sermons with the ones in the parlor. I guess Pa expected a small boy to be confused, and innocently gave him simple answers. I don't think Pa ever knew of his wife's private behavior. I never told him, for if I had I would have felt obliged to confess how thoroughly I disliked her for frightening us so. I would not have disappointed Pa for all the world.

Tuesday, March 27, 1860

My hand purely ached after yesterday's session. The memory of Mrs. C. evoked emotions that I thought I had long ago put behind me, but when I began to write, I could not get the words down fast enough. It was good fortune that I began the topic in the evening, alone in my room, for I would have been mortified had Adie seen me scribbling furiously, tears brimming in my eyes. I put down my pen before my lamp and firewood were completely spent, as I was much too weary to finish the tale. I slept fretfully with visions of Mrs. C.'s stony eyes and scowling face looming behind my eyelids, and her rancorous voice ringing in my ears. It is evening again, and I am alone in my chamber. I shall finish the story of Mrs. C., and perhaps rid myself of her poison. I dare not write of her in the presence of others.

When school recommenced that January of 1810, Pa had been married for about six weeks, which seemed more like six years. Each day I would scurry home in a great rush. Admittedly, it was mid-winter, reason enough to go as fast as my legs would carry me, the earth gray and crisp and cold. But I was more moved by fear than weather, fear that I would miss much of the afternoon sermon, a sin surely to cast me into the pit of hell. No doubt the dread she instilled was made plausible by not differing entirely with some of the preaching we heard in church. In those days our neighborhood was not so well populated as to have a regular preacher. We were served by a clutch of itinerants, wandering from pulpit to pulpit, preaching to whomever would listen. People were hungry for religion, and came avidly to hear any sermon they could get. Generally we were sent enlightened and educated Presbyterians of the Old Side (although what had once been considered "old" was becoming "new" again). Those men preached with solemnity, laced with careful reasoning. But some were New Siders, zealously rapt in emotional piety and fervid evangelical revivalism. And there were occasional Methodists and unschooled sorts who followed their own peculiar callings. Those men raged loudly, assuring us that fire and brimstone and Satan himself lay in wait for us, and there was precious little we could do about it, as the nature of man was a sinful one. They shouted and hammered fists into their Bibles, slinging sweat and spittle into the front pews of the sanctuary, praying as if God had gone deaf. It was a spectacle perhaps too intense for a child. I preferred the loving God of our gentler preachers, but who was I, a ten-year-old girl, to question men of the cloth?

By winter's end I began to have more confidence in my own views. I overheard some adults carping about the wilder men in the pulpit, saying they would have sent them packing had we a regular preacher. At least the howling men praised God and shouted hallelujah when a parishioner fell to the floor, speaking in tongues, repenting his sins. To Mrs. C., no amount of redemption was enough for her or her wrathful Deity. My fear toward her turned to anger, and as spring unfolded I began to dawdle coming home from school, reacquainting myself with a loving God's perfect creation. Day by day as the earth softened under my footsteps, I watched green things appear. The haze in the treetops grew dark and full, from faintest buds to fully formed leaves. I marveled in silence as forest creatures crept from their wintertime shelters, and skittered and dashed to feed themselves. Each day as I crossed the footbridge over the creek, I saw the stream gather in size and energy, nourishing new growth. If this was God's work, surely he was a benevolent spirit. The walk lengthened to fritter away entire afternoons as I dawdled as long as I dared. Sometimes I could hear Mrs. C.

shooing the children to their chores as I opened the door, thinking it was Pa coming in. I giggled to myself at the sound of her, the only glee I remember in the presence of my father's second wife.

Occasionally I was confined to the house the entire day, school not being held due to foul weather. Snow was rarely an obstacle, but ice and freshets were. During spring thaws, especially if there was heavy rain, the paths became impassable with mud. I hated those bad weather days. There was no escaping, even to the yard, where I sometimes took Rose and my brothers to tell them about a loving God.

Late in March of 1810 my winter session was done, and once again I was at home all day. Once again I was a captive of the tyrannical authority on hell. Nothing much had changed, although I noticed that my brothers also seemed to harbor more anger than fear. Even Frank had figured out that she was all blather, from the look on his face. Rose was the only one who still trembled, but Negroes are naturally fearful and superstitious.

Then in mid April Mrs. C.'s demeanor changed, softened, ever so slightly. Did she think we were pure at last? Rapt in the Grace of God? There was less energy in her pacing, her arms, her voice. She waved the hated towel, but did not snap it, nor strike us. A few days later she failed to appear at the breakfast table, and Pa said she was unwell, and would keep to her bed for the morning. While Pa blessed our food, I made my silent prayer that she was not carrying a child, as I had seen my own mother ill when a child began. I could not imagine what sort of monster would spring from Mrs. C. If she were capable of breeding an innocent babe, it certainly would not remain so.

She felt better the next day, but worse the day after. On the third day Pa announced she was feverish and he was going to fetch the doctor. I saw how agitated Pa was, fidgety hands grappling with his coat, dread knotting his brow and veiling his eyes. I was sorry for him, but not for Mrs. C., which filled me with a slimy guilt. I decided not to pray, for God would surely see beyond my words, see the unholy wish for her suffering that lay in my heart. The doctor bled her and left some pills, which did no good at all. The fever would not break and turned her delirious. Pa instructed Mattie and me to sit with her whenever he was out of the house. By turns we were to bathe her brow and feet, and send for him if she took a harsh spell. Mattie and I sat with her, an hour or so each, then turn about. That was as much as we could abide at a time.

It was during my watches that I observed another aspect of Mrs. C. She had serious talks with God during her delirium, completely unaware I was in the room. She was terrified, genuinely terrified as if her burning fever emanated from the nearby gates of Hell. She pled with God to forgive her, and shouted at Satan to stay back, stay back! Forgiveness from what I could not ascertain, but surely from some indiscretion in her youth. From her garbled pleas I now think she may have bedded a man, willingly or not, I cannot tell; it would have made no difference to her vengeful God. I was only a child, and did not know the meaning of many of the words whispered through her parched lips, but years later when I remembered them, I concluded that was the sin they implied. I almost felt sorry for the poor woman, for she was indeed a tortured spirit. But not quite. I could not forgive her for what she had done to us, and could never shed my hatred for her.

At last, after about a week of this turmoil, she died. I hope she is in Heaven, not because she deserves to be, but because my God sends only those to Hell who have turned from him, and among all her faults that was not one of them. I hated to see Pa mired in grief again, but was greatly relieved to have Mrs. C. gone from us, only sorry that death was the cause of it.

She was buried near my mother, with a space between them for Pa. Thank goodness they're separated at least by that much. The crowning irony is that her funeral was preached by one of our regular preachers, full of love and hope for a glorious eternity. I realized by then that the preaching for Ma's funeral had been done by a New Sider, or maybe even a Methodist. No wonder he carried on in such a way! I hope Ma did not hear it. I've not yet determined if the dead look down to see what happens on Earth. That is a feature of the Presbyterian faith; some things we are permitted to reason for ourselves.

Wednesday, March 28, 1860

I am on the porch, as it is a pretty day, warming up nicely, and I have more pleasant things to record. Rose came to sit with me, and inquired as to what I was doing. When I told her about journal keeping, she declared it was a fine thing, and she should like to catalog her own memories. I promised I would get her a copybook, but we should keep her journaling to ourselves. In fact she can keep it entirely private if she prefers; I will only assist her if she asks. I know Adie is aware that Rose can read and write, for she learned to do so as a child, long before a law was passed to forbid it. I believe that happened in 1831 in response to

Negro uprisings, some brutally real, but most imagined, or simply feared. In any event our legislators determined that if Negroes could not read, they would not learn of abolitionists, or places where black men lived free. Such folly! Did they think a law would render our black people deaf and mute? No number of laws can keep hope from traveling from place to place, as if borne by the wind, scudded like clouds. Laws do not make people depart from their senses.

As to Adie, she is naïve in many ways. She probably believes Rose gave up reading and writing when that ridiculous law came about, thinks Rose has completely forgotten how. I'll ask her for another copybook, to inventory my possessions or some such excuse; she'll think nothing of it.

Pa seemed to heal more quickly from the second widowing, perhaps because he'd been wed only six months, perhaps because his children emerged unscathed. I pray he never knew why we did, although he may well have figured it out and kept his counsel as we did ours. He never married again. I suppose he feared another loss impossible to endure. In many ways I'm sorry. Pa's natural warmth and exuberance cried out to be shared with a mate. I'm sure somewhere there was a woman to fit the role, if only he'd had the courage to seek her out.

Mattie was once again in charge of us, once again directing us by rote, cleaning our house, washing scraped knees. She did sometimes have smiles or a warm hug, but not many words. I have often wondered what Mattie made of our six months in the mad house, but she never spoke of it, at least not to me.

We had a grand time that spring and summer in our kitchen garden. Pa brought the seed box out from the barn. It was a beautiful thing formed with precise joinery, rectangular, about four inches deep, divided into many small compartments. Each compartment contained seeds and a scrap of paper telling their names. There were tiny ones for celery and dill and lettuce and parsley, larger ones for cucumbers and peppers, fat peas and beans, kernels of sweet corn, and tear shaped seeds for a variety of squashes and gourds and melons. Greene turned up the soil with his shovel, as his mule and plow could not maneuver inside the garden fence. Then Mattie and I got on our knees and broke up the clods and mixed in the manure which one of Mattie's brothers delivered in a barrow.

Pa showed us how to plant. The smallest seeds were strewn in hilled rows below the barest covering of soil, just enough to hide them from the birds. I later observed that we had not fooled them one bit, and hoped we had planted generously enough to feed us all, winged and otherwise. Larger seeds were planted deeper; Pa said the size of the seed determined its placement in the earth. We planted herbs just inside the garden gate where they would be handy, near the lavender and rosemary which had become large and hardy. Cissy used dill, parsley, and marjoram in many of her dishes, and great quantities of thyme and sage would be needed at hog killing time. These were all grown at the left of the gate. On the right we placed the healing herbs, chamomile and comfrey, rue and lovage and pennyroyal; such pretty names they have. Cissy knew how to make the concoctions, and kept us all in good health.

Then we planned out how to place the vegetables. Those that would grow tall were planted along the fence. There we could tie them to the pickets should they need support. The rest were put in rows with ample space between for harvesting. Pa warned us to leave generous paths, for things can grow bushier than one might imagine.

Meanwhile Pa and Greene plowed the fields for barley and oats, field corn and other animal fodder. They also sowed the hardier beans in the field, along with pumpkins, melons, and gourds, things that would grow too large to fit our vegetable plot. The orchards were tended to, dead limbs lopped, and blossoms thinned. Pa had not tried the cotton yet, although he had heard of it. He had too few hands for such an undertaking.

By that time Pa had ceased digging iron ore, as the nearby furnaces had increased their holdings, and were no longer buying ore from local farmers. So that spring we planted and tended and weeded as young shoots sprouted from the soil. Rose was especially helpful with the weeding; little hands are best for the job, and small feet less likely to trample the crop. Mattie and I taught her what to pull, and what to leave. Of course she made some errors, but altogether did a fine job. Before long strawberries woke up in their winter beds, then came peas, and cucumbers, all manner of good fresh things to eat. It was the best time of year as we had all grown weary of turnips and onions and potatoes. The winter diet is a tiresome one.

That was not the first spring I worked the garden, but probably the first I was given true responsibility, and I have gardened ever since. I suppose I remember that spring planting so fondly because the renewal of the earth came when I so dearly needed a renewal of spirit. The rains were plentiful that year; it was altogether a fine spring.

Thursday, March 29, 1860

I asked Adie for another copybook, and before I could invent an explanation for needing it, she had procured one from Isaac's desk. He keeps several on hand for his farm journals. As I had assumed, she thought nothing of it. Perhaps she thinks I am feeble-minded and ought to be indulged. I will leave that thought lie.

My daughters Eliza and Rachel and their families come tomorrow! They don't visit near enough in my opinion, as they live not so far away. Both of their husbands have farms across the river in Mecklenburg County's Hopewell section, only about fifteen miles distant. I suppose it is a chore for them to travel with small children, but they should make the sacrifice more frequently, as I am an old woman. I have only a handful of grandchildren; most my age have at least a dozen, but I am not so blessed. Eliza and her husband, Andrew Wilson have two little girls. I suppose she'll be announcing another one on the way before long. Daughter Rachel is married to Eli Harris and has a small son. She is expecting another in late summer.

They will remain through the Sabbath, so I doubt I'll have leisure for my journal over the next several days, as I intend spending every available moment with my girls and my precious grandchildren. Adie's little ones have been talking for days about their cousins, and have planned all sorts of games to entertain them. Her Matthew asks hourly if it is time to go watch for their carriage. Such a gaggle of small folks we shall have! I am as all in a dither as Matthew!

I have another grandchild, one I will not see on this happy occasion. She is my namesake, Julia, daughter of my deceased son Tom. She has reached her twelfth year, and I regret I have never laid eyes on her nor seen her likeness. I receive rare letters from her, and my fondest wish is to someday make her acquaintance. I know I will love her immediately. I will write about Julia another day.

I should put away my meanderings through history, and help Adie with the preparations. We'll have her children's beds dressed for Eliza and Rachel and their husbands, then decide where pallets should be placed for the assortment of youngsters. So much to do!

Meanwhile I shall sneak the extra copybook to Rose. She shares a shed room on the back porch with Vinia, Adie's nursemaid. When I was invited here to live, I insisted that Rose would not occupy a slave cabin, for she had not dwelt in one for many years, and I was not about to abide a change in her circumstances. Adie thought I was indulging a whim, that Rose would be quite contented among her people. But I put my foot down. If Rose could not be accommodated according to my wishes, then I would continue to live in my own home, no matter how frail or poor I might become.

That was four years since. My husband was dead, Eliza and Rachel were new brides, and the time had come to abandon my beloved farm. I thought it improper to insert myself into the homes of the newlyweds, and brother Frank had no room for me, which I considered a blessing, as I had no desire to live in Lincolnton with a worrisome man. Bless Adie for taking me in! She is a good girl, sweet and generous to a fault, but she often neglects to think things through. Addled Adie, I sometimes call her beneath my breath. Her fondest wish was to please me, but I could not get it through her head that Rose's comfort was as important as my own. She offered Rose the garret, which was never finished out as a proper room. It is oppressively hot in summer, and in winter subject to snow sifting in between the shingles. When I squelched that idea, she was aghast thinking I meant to have Rose share my bedchamber, which was the farthermost thing from my mind. It was Isaac who found the solution. He suggested that Rose live with Vinia whose room had been attached to the house to be near the children. Well, I compromised. It is true that there was no suitable room in the house proper, and I dared not ask Isaac to alter his home again. Two additional mouths to feed was burden enough.

Vinia has turned out to be an adequate roommate for Rose. She's not quite twenty, and being occupied with the little ones, affords Rose a great deal of privacy. Who knows what will become of their living arrangements should Vinia marry, which I expect will happen soon enough. A woman her age not breeding is quite the oddity among Negroes. I suppose Adie, in her short-sighted fashion, prefers Vinia's attention be entirely devoted to her young charges. Undoubtedly Isaac would rather have her producing more hands.

Friday, March 30, 1860

Miss Julia done give me this book to do my writing. I knowed I asked her for it; but now that I got it in my hand, I took a second thought. My writing ain't nowhere up to hers, as I did not practice all these years like she done. Oh I been reading my whole life, but mostly in fits and starts. Master Campbell give me books when I was a girl, and

I have took the time to look back over them when I could. Sometimes letters and such has come to hand, and I try to keep at my Bible. But it weren't much, being I had work to do. So I ain't studied reading and writing like I ought to have, and kept up with how words go. It don't matter, as my children and grands won't never see this. I don't know where they is, and doubts they can read anyway. I watch Miss Julia at her book, plowing the pen cross the page lickety-split. I allowed as how I can't go so fast, needing time to puzzle out words. She say don't fret, just write as it please me.

She told me she took up writing in her book after she went to that lawyer to get her will wrote, and how that man snickered when she told him what to write about me. But she put up a fuss 'til she got her way. She made him write that I was not to be sold, "like a brute beast." He shore didn't want to put down them words. I reckon I is grateful. Lord knows where I'd end up if Master Frank took to sell me. I've seen how pitiful that can be.

She give me this book and show me how to put in the date each time I write. She say an ink pot would call attention, or spill if I stuck it in a drawer, making a mighty mess. So she give me two pencils and a piece of India rubber to wipe out where I go wrong, and it has already come in handy. I think she give me the pencils and India rubber cause I took a second notion about this whole business, and said the part about the ink pot so I wouldn't feel bad. When Miss Julia try to spare my feelings, I can see through her like a windowpane, but she mean well.

Saturday, March 31, 1860

All Miss Adie's kinfolk come yesterday, the whole passel of them. I help out some, but Miss Adie's got her own people, so I ain't much needed. I ain't needed for hardly anything since I come here. I hate that I is a slave, but I don't care for idling neither. Miss Julia done been good to me, good as she know how, but she don't have no idea how it is to be property, and all the goodness in the world can't set that aside. I reckon I love that white woman, but she can be a consternation, and there been times I didn't much like her. If I has to be a slave, I reckon my life's better than most. That much can be said.

I stay with Vinie who tends Miss Adie's younguns. She's a tolerable girl, but acts like I'm highfalutin and I is not. When I first come to this place, this shed room (where I'm told to do my writing) was brand new. Master Isaac built it for Vinie to be close to the white younguns. Matthew was fixing to be borned, and Miss Adie had took to her bed, as she had lost some babies afore their time. Vinie takes her dinner on the back porch, to be close by, but they let her go to the cabin to take supper with her people after the white folk eat. Miss Adie used to have a plate sent to our room for me, and I was mighty lonesome eating all by myself. I asked Miss Julia could I go to the cabin with Vinie, but she say it ain't necessary, cause I don't have family there like Vinie does. I should say that Vinie's family is house servants, not field hands; I would never take my supper with low-down field nigras. I up and told Miss Julia I was going to eat with Vinie's people, and wasn't nothing she could do about it. It confounds me how stubborn white women can be over something that don't make no difference to them. I been going to the cabin ever since. They still think I is highfalutin.

April, 1860

Sunday, April 1, 1860

Master Frank come for dinner yesterday, and there shore was a heap of white folks round the table. I asks to help serve, but Miss Julia say I wasn't needed. She did let me tend the younguns who got fed first, and I tarried with them while the grown folks ate. I wanted to serve so I could hear what Master Frank has to say. He is a persnickety man, and a puffed up no-account scalawag full of foul notions. But he tells who is sick and who is well, him being a doctor, and carries tales about war fixing to come on, and how folks at the North is aiming to slit Southern throats and free the slaves. Now I ain't no gossip, but that is talk I wants to hear. I keep my ears out whenever I can.

After dinner Master Frank go home, but this morning he met the family in town for preaching. I went along as I generally do. Master Isaac don't let the nigras have preaching on his place, but he allows some of us go to town and sit up in the gallery at the white church. I go every chance I get. The preaching is fine, but I specially care for the sociable. Most Sundays there's two preachings, and a heap of time in between to catch up on everybody's doings. Master Frank says they might make us quit mingling between preachings cause some white folks think we is getting ideas. We always had ideas.

There was only one preaching today, so we come home and ate dinner. Then the kinfolk pack up their carriage and leave. They carry some ham and biscuits and dried apples for their supper. I is tired tonight, after all the goings on. It feel good to be tired.

Monday, April 2, 1860

My, what a grand time we had! Eliza and Rachel appear to be in fine health. Rachel is perfectly aglow, and seems to be carrying well, which put my mind at ease. If Eliza is with child, she didn't let on, so I shall have to be patient. The children were a pure joy, and I snuggled them every minute they indulged me. Poor things, they had cousins to play with, and all their grandmother wanted to do was hug! Rose tells me she is writing in her copybook, but finds it tedious as she has forgotten much of her learning. I told her to persevere, that it will reward her in time, and slipped her a book to read to get her into practice. When she returns it I'll find her another. I don't know why she frets about being slow. She has nothing else to do.

I glanced over my earlier pages and realized I've not written about the environs of my childhood. I was raised at Leeper's Creek about ten miles east of the village of Lincolnton. We Presbyterians often name our churches for a landmark, hence Leeper's Creek became the name of our church as well as our community. It was never a village of shops and such, just a collection of farms spread about the countryside, centered on the church. We rarely went into Lincolnton in those days, except to gear up for spring planting, or in the fall to sell what crops we could spare, and buy coffee or tea or spices, whatever we could not grow. Otherwise we managed quite well by trading among ourselves. I don't know who Leeper was, perhaps an early settler long since moved on, or a trapper who named the creek in his wanderings. No Leepers lived among us during my childhood. As I have said, we were generally served by somber and pious Presbyterians. When one of the more animated preachers spoke, urging folks to rise up for the Lord, grasp the rapture, then fall to the floor in submission, we would chuckle behind our hands. Perhaps those who indulged the practice were the true "Leepers."

I was about ten I think when I came to understand one of Leeper's Creek's more eccentric residents, Mr. Brown, Loony Brown as he was commonly known. I had seen him often enough yowling and jangling across the countryside; he was impossible not to notice. It was rumored that his forebears were German, and had once been named Braun, which is no flaw by which to judge a man. It was offered as a reason for his reluctance to attend church, as there was no Lutheran congregation in our midst, although they abounded in Lincolnton and the western part of the county. Most thought the man a heathen or worse.

It was a bright autumn day, and the trees were dressed in vivid gold and red and yellow when Loony Brown made one of his periodic visits to our farm. I heard him before I saw him, shouting and pushing his handcart filled with crockery which clattered noisily as it bumped along the rocky path. I was standing on the porch as he came into view, the fiery backdrop enhancing his strange specter. You see, Mr. Brown carried on a constant conversation with people who were not there, hard-of-hearing people, one would assume from his incessant bellowing. All the while he shook his fists and beat the side of his handcart with a large stick, sometimes beating the mule, who was also not there. I don't remember his words, for they made no sense, only their volume and the urgency in their message delivered to those who existed purely in his mind.

I watched him come up the road howling and haggling with his usual, or perhaps unusual, coterie, jugs of whiskey jangling in his cart, carrying on as if the victim of a mad dog. Frightened, I scurried inside and scrambled under my bed. In a moment the noise abated as he had stopped at our house, and I crept over to the window where I could observe, parting the curtain ever so slightly, hiding my face in its folds. Lo and behold, Pa came out of the barn and shook hands with the loony man. They talked briefly, then Pa gave the man some coins and exchanged an empty jug for a full one. I could tell, for the jug Pa plucked from the wagon had a corncob plug sealed over with wax, and the one he offered Loony Brown did not. I knew Pa drank whiskey from time to time, and I suppose I knew Loony Brown supplied it, but I had never before witnessed the exchange.

Later I asked Pa about the man, for if Pa could do business with him, he must not be dangerous after all. Cissy had told me he was "hainted," had a spell cast over him, a condition I associated with great peril. But Pa told me he was harmless, merely tetched. He said that Loony Brown lived alone in ramshackle cabin deep in the woods where he supplemented his hunting and fishing by keeping a still. He did not grow corn or apples on his little patch, but plucked corn from the edges of fields, and gleaned windfall apples. No one complained about the theft, Pa said; the pittance Loony charged for whiskey was a small price to pay a man to harvest a bit of his neighbor's corn and process it.

Not everyone thought the man harmless. Because of his affliction, one could not tell if he were drunk or not, and many assumed he generally was. He dwelt under a veil of gossip that his lunacy was caused by bad whiskey, a rumor that cost him some customers. And whether drunk or mad, he would surely burn down his cabin while cooking mash, and set the entire forest afire, a realistic cause for worry. But for the most part his jugs were quite popular, and supported his strange and solitary existence.

On another occasion when Loony Brown made his rounds I observed a surprising reaction from Rose. I was in the garden, tending to business, when I heard him approach in his cloud of racket. I wondered if he could see his invisible audience, and did he hear them, for they must be putting up a fierce argument to inspire such a tirade. I stepped around to the front of the house, for I was no longer afraid, but curious. I wanted to see if I could put sense to the harangue. And

27

there on the porch was Rose, arms akimbo, wagging her little hips, her pink tongue stuck out from a smirky face as far as it would go. Shy little Rose confronting the wild man! Loony Brown, of course, took no notice of the child, and ambled his way toward the barn. I could not resist running up to the porch and embracing Rose in a gleeful hug. I could give her no explanation for it, and thankfully she did not ask for one. You see, it was at that moment I realized Rose had at last shed herself of the oppressive influence of Mrs. C.

She had been such a morose child during our religious inquisition. I suppose because of her race and her age she had not recognized the ordeal as the ranting of a woman so fearful and insecure as to be nearly mad herself. It did not help that Cissy filled Rose's mind with haintings and spells and nonsensical Negro Voodoo to explain both Mrs. C. and Loony Brown. I do not know why black people have to be so superstitious when they claim to be devout Christians! I had fretted all summer and fall that Rose would never get over her fears, and would grow into a skittish woman, seeing demons at every turn. But no, Rose was becoming a confident child, healed and whole, and at home in the world.

Monday, April 2, 1860

Miss Julia tell me she been writing bout growing up on the old place, and how it bring back memories, some sweet and some sad like when her Mam passed away. I hardly remember a time afore I stayed all day at Miss Julia's with Mattie. I was just a tiny thing when Mattie took over the white younguns, me on her coattails. Oh, I slept in the cabin with my Mam and Pappy, and kept to the kitchen with Mam when I could. But mostly I stayed at the big house, which was not so big compared to Miss Adie's; she done married above herself.

Mattie told me the first day I walk in that place, I lit up like a fat-lighter torch. Says I got down on the floor, and patted each board to see if it be real, then jumped up bedazzled by the table and chairs, some painted, some polished smooth with wax. I rolled on the floor in a whoop, then hop up again to study the china stacked on the sideboard, pictures on the wall, curtains at the window. I reckon it looked grand compared to Mam and Pappy's dirt floored cabin, but looking back I know it were only middling for white folks.

Mattie slumped into sorrow when we went to the big house, which I thought peculiar amongst such fine things. I couldn't fix a meaning to it cause Mattie had no particular affection for Miss Julia's Mam, no reason

28

to mourn her passing. Not that she was a hard woman, Miss Julia's Mam, but Mattie never worked under her, didn't tarry round the house enough to take a shine to her. Afore she passed it was our Mam that gave Mattie her chores.

I reckon I should put down who we was. Mam and Pappy belonged to Master Campbell, and to his daddy afore that. Mam was born on his daddy's place. Don't know where Pappy come from. They had six younguns, and I was the littlest. Amos was the first borned; he was working with Pappy and Master Campbell by the time I come along. After Amos come Mattie. Next come Joe, then Narcissus, then Caesar who was two years older than me. When I was about three Mam had another baby, but it only lived a few days. She done well to have six out of seven grow up. Broke her heart when they got sold out from under her, all but me.

I asked Mattie why she act so sad living in the big house, but she wouldn't say, not for the longest time. When I was older, she give me her story. The day she toted her pallet up to the garret, was the day she was considered full growed and Master Campbell's slave. After that she hardly saw Mam cept when she went out to the kitchen to fetch the white folk's dinner or carry back the dirty dishes. She rarely saw Pappy between Sundays. She was Master Campbell's property to do his bidding. Oh he never laid a hand on her, to whip her or otherwise, she swore up and down. She said she always knowed that would be her lot, but she took it hard when it happened so sudden like, when the first Miz Campbell passed. Her world turned upside down in the blink of an eye. Mam told me Mattie had spunk before then.

I can't believe I wrote so much! Four days I've studied on writing, and I reckon I'm right pleased at what I have wrote down, if I say so myself.

Wednesday, April 4, 1860

When school commenced in the fall of 1810, I did not go alone. Jeff was seven, and Pa concluded it was time for him to begin his education. Greene (or Amos if Greene were occupied) carried us to school in the wagon as two children were one too many to perch on a horse with a rider. I could tell Pa was unhappy with this arrangement, I assumed because it took a man, as well as the wagon, from the field. In retrospect I can see that was when Pa's foolishness about money began to escalate, though slowly at first. The school session was over in late October. There was no point in holding classes during hog-killing time or when the last crops were harvested and prepared for winter storage, for even small children were needed at home. After Pa gathered his crops and tended to the pork, he made an unusual journey.

He announced one evening that he was leaving the next morning for Salisbury. A journey of nearly fifty miles! He would take Greene with him, and would be gone several days. The crop was especially bountiful and he thought a handsome profit could be made in Salisbury. He had already made several trips to Lincolnton, and I was surprised there was still more business to be done, but I took him at his word. Five days later to the amazement of us all he drove up to the farm in a carriage, Greene following behind with the wagon. A carriage and an extra horse! We children, not knowing the value of anything, thought it was grand.

School recommenced in January, and Greene, grinning broadly, drove us every day in the beautiful new carriage. Pa had thought the wagon shabby, poor man's transport, and Pa did not wish to be considered a poor man. Though he may have been proud and irresponsible, Pa was not greedy. If a neighbor was in need, Pa was right there to lend a hand. And if the church lacked for anything, Pa was among the first to dig into his pocket. We thought this was virtuous behavior, which it was, and had no notion he was incurring debt. Pa signed promissory notes to anyone who would indulge him. He carried an honest demeanor, and was a hard man to refuse.

That spring I was informed that I had completed my schooling. I could read, write, cipher to the rule of three, and knew my stitches. What else did a young lady need? Jeff's education was more important, and Frank was coming up. There was not money for everything. I tried to hide my disappointment from Pa, which was bitter indeed. Maybe I did not need more schooling, but I certainly wanted it. He could tell I was unhappy, and promised to buy me books.

As soon as the crops were planted, Pa painted the house. I suppose the outside needed a fresh coat, and paint was considered a worthwhile investment to protect the wood from weather. But the inside had never been done before. Pa even hired a man to decorate the over-mantle with faux marbling. Yet there was no money to send me to school. Pa wished beyond dream to be of the gentry, not for himself but for his children. He was doing as he thought best for each of us. Jeff and Frank would someday have families to support, and if they were educated, their prospects improved. Pa could not afford to send me to boarding school, even with his reckless borrowing habits. A well appointed house and a fine carriage would do more to attract a prosperous suitor that any amount of time spent in our common school. In his mind that was the very best he could do for me. At eleven I had no interest in suitors; I preferred school.

The trees are nearly in full leaf, speckling Adie's porch. I like to spend afternoons with my journal on the porch, facing east, with the warming sun over my shoulder. If I could see far enough to the east, through the trees, over the hills, I could see the old place which is flooding my memory. Pa's old house lies about five miles in that direction, the place where I was born, and lived nearly my whole life until I removed to Adie's. Even without this memory book, I can close my eyes and rove its every detail. My fingertips still know which windowsills were smooth, and which were rough, where the rain seemed to puddle when driven by wind. There was a slight tilt to the parlor floor, not noticeable to the eye, but as I child I knew which corner a marble would seek and where to look for lost coins. My mind's eye can count each window pane and every scratch in the floor from furniture being shifted about. Tonight while waiting for sleep to come I'll wander my thoughts fondly through Pa's wonderful old house.

Wednesday, April 4, 1860

I pondered more on Mattie after I wrote them last words, and concluded I did not state her case too well. No one is happy being a slave – including them what puts on a show to make white folks think they is – but it's harder on some than others. Some folks take what they is handed from life, poor health, dead babies, being property. They looks to the Lord, and trust he give out trouble and joy as he see fit. Others get the misery. They only see what they ain't got, not what they is. Mattie had the misery. She had a Mam and Pappy that doted on her. She seldom got sent to work the fields. She had plenty to eat and a master who treated her tolerable. Master Campbell never raise his voice or hand to nobody, black or white. But all Mattie could study on was that she was property.

White folks can be purely ignorant. They think we ought to be happy, and they get suspicions when we ain't, which is why there is such bodacious play-acting and grinning. Do white folks really cotton to that tomfoolery? I don't think Miss Julia believe slaves is happy, but I don't know. Sometimes she don't make good sense.

I ain't set eyes on Mattie for nigh over thirty years, and I wonder what become of her. I pray she got her freedom, but I can't conjure how she could of. I feel sorry for folks that gets the misery, all it does is grind them down. Mattie was that kind, and so was my husband. I got no use for the misery.

When I was a little thing, I had no notion why Miss Julia grab me up and treat me like her baby. I figured maybe I was something special, and I reckon I was. Later on she told me it was cause I was the only one that wasn't weepy and long-faced after her Mam passed. It's a good thing I pleased her, cause she kept me out of the clutches of the crazy lady Master Campbell done marry next, and the loony man that sold whiskey. Miss Julia told me Mam's Voodoo was the same sort of foolishness, and I didn't appreciate that one bit. How could she liken Mam to that devil monger or to Loony Brown!

Friday, April 6, 1860

Pa's house was built late in the 1790s as a gift to Ma, his then bride-to-be. My grandfather had settled our land some years before, and he and my grandmother raised their family there in a log cabin. Pa was not their only child. He had a sister who married and moved to Kentucky. She wrote us letters from time to time, but I never met her, nor saw her likeness. Pa had other brothers and sisters, the exact number I do not know; all were born dead or died as children. Pa never spoke of them, being uncomfortable with death. I am writing here all I know on the subject. When Pa and Ma were betrothed, he and his father and Greene undertook the building of a grand house, grand for the time. I don't know when Greene came into the family, or where he came from, just that he and Cissy belonged to my grandfather before I was born. If Pa or my grandfather had written things down, I might know so very much more.

Our house was quite modern for the 1790s. My grandfather had admired many fine places in Salisbury, the grandest city of his acquaintance, and had a firm notion of how the house should be built. He and Pa drew plans, made measurements, and cut timber from the land. When all was prepared, neighbors came to help with the raising. It was a frame house, one and a half stories, topped by a garret. A porch spanned the front of the house with two doors to the inside. One door opened into a large parlor; the other led to Pa's office, a tiny isolated space. I don't know why he felt the need of an office, perhaps he dreamed of joining the gentry class, even back then. I remember the office as a place for Pa's books and other oddments he collected which had no logical place to go. Years later, when the house passed to me, my husband kept it as a proper office. In the parlor a staircase was near the front door, and a fireplace at the gable end of the room. Behind the parlor was the dining room which opened to a back porch. It also opened to Pa's bed chamber, directly behind the office, but not connected to it by a door.

Above stairs on either side of a hallway were two small bedchambers; one was mine, which I would have shared with Jane had she lived, and the other was inhabited by my brothers. They were smallish rooms with dormer windows. Years later they became my children's rooms, and later still I installed Rose in one of them, much to my husband's chagrin. At the end of the hallway a narrow set of steps, perhaps more akin to a ladder than a staircase, led to a long narrow garret that ran from gable to gable. Mattie placed her pallet at one end, under the shutter-like slats that provided ventilation.

On each end of the house was a chimney. One supported two fireplaces, one in the parlor, and one in the dining room. The other, a fireplace in Pa's bedchamber. There was no heating for the office or the upstairs. Pa always fretted that he had been unable to contrive how to build fireplaces upstairs, as he was sure the house would be burnt to the ground by my brothers carrying endless pans of coals to their bedchamber. "I'm sure it could have been done," he had said; "I just didn't know a man who could give me the instructions."

It seems a simple house now, compared to Adie's place, which I will describe at another time, but during my childhood, and to some extent during my marriage, it was fine example of architecture for genteel living.

When Pa and Ma married they went to housekeeping in the beautiful new house, while my grandparents continued to live in the log house about fifteen yards away. I don't remember my grandparents as they were both taken by an epidemic when I was an infant. Then their log cabin became our kitchen. This was a much more satisfactory arrangement for Cissy than cooking in her cabin, where there was barely room to work.

Monday, April 9, 1860

We have had letters! Both Eliza and Rachel wrote they arrived home without incident, and how they enjoyed their brief sojourn with us. Their families, black and white, are in good health, and their husbands are making ready to plant. They don't write near often enough in my opinion, and then such short notes! I've no idea why, as it is such a simple thing to send mail nowadays.

Again I have neglected my journal over the Sabbath, having not yet concluded if it is proper to write on a holy day. I doubt God would be offended, so I may take it up when time permits. Planting season is nigh, and there are several more deep plowings to be done, then hilling and furrowing to prepare the land. Some of the women who usually cook or do laundry have been sent to the fields. So Rose and I will lend our hands to domestic affairs where we can be of use. My journal may be scant for a while.

I have set down our living arrangements during my childhood, and now will continue with the events of my life. Pa kept his promise to buy me books, and that was not all. About the time I completed my schooling, he developed the habit of attending estate sales whenever one was announced. Occasionally he bought furniture, fair pieces but not fine ones, as the better goods were nearly always retained by the family. More often he bought farm implements or tools to keep our place in good repair. Someone's old ax might have a good handle or sharp blade to be combined with the complementary part we already owned, or bits of horse gearing and barnyard things could be refitted into something more satisfactory. But Pa's favorite purchases were lots of sundries. He would bring home crates filled with all sorts of wonders, bought for very little money, or so he said. Nearly every one contained a book or two, sometimes more. Otherwise they held mismatched forks and spoons, chipped plates, broken toys, well worn clothing, anything at all. Most of the books and other oddments found a home among the nooks and crevices of Pa's office, a place that in spite of its small size and cramped shelves, never appeared to overflow its capacity. I rarely noticed Pa reading the books, though he did seem to treasure them, and he displayed the handsomer volumes in the parlor. I devoured every printed word that crossed our threshold.

Every Sunday, as I have said, we worshipped at Leeper's Creek Church. That was our social center as well as our spiritual one. Most families were similar to ours, small to middling farmers with an assortment of children, although most families had a Ma. Not that my mother was the only parent who had died, but it was customary for the widowed of either sex to marry promptly. It benefited the raising of children, and kept loneliness at bay. Pa tried it that one disastrous time, but never again.

There were some in our community who incited gossip, a delicious forbidden fruit nearly as engaging as a good book. Mr. H. is one I well remember. I shall not set down his full name, as some of his relations may still be in the neighborhood, perhaps more relations than I might imagine. I first became acquainted with the H. family the summer of my thirteenth year, for it was then they began attending our church. Mr. H. himself had been around for a year or so, buying land and building a plantation house, outdoing anything for miles around. He had secured temporary lodgings for his family in Lincolnton, so I was unaware of them until his house was completed and they established themselves in our midst. Mr. H. purported to be from a prominent Virginia family; whether that was true or not, I cannot say, as much about him that seemed to be true, proved to be false.

It was said he had his eye on cotton as the up-and-coming crop, and his soil in Virginia had been depleted by tobacco. Land in the backcountry, and Lincoln County was considered such, was plentiful, fertile, and cheap. So he sold his Virginia property and bought nearly a thousand acres in our corner of the world (an enormous holding at the time) and began constructing his little fiefdom. One Sunday not long after the family moved in, I noticed a girl in their company who appeared to be about my age, so I rushed over to her to invite her to share our meal after services. I wanted to make her acquaintance, and assumed she was as hungry for companionship as I was. I had hardly begun to introduce myself when Pa saw what I was up to, and in an uncharacteristic fashion, snatched me away from the child, and told me to get to our pew at once! I asked him why, and he whispered awkwardly that the child was not Mr. H.'s daughter but his servant. I was aghast; her dark hair was curly, not wooly, and her skin was nearly as light as mine. Our church was a small one, and had no gallery for the black people. If the pews were not filled by white families, the Negroes were permitted to sit in the back rows, or on the front steps, or peer through the windows. No one wanted to deny them the Holy word, but they were Negroes, and there were standards. During the service, I turned ever so slightly in our pew and looked back. There I saw the girl sitting cross-legged in the doorway, hunkered to one side of it. Behind her was a woman, black as tar, her hand resting on the child's shoulder. Except for color, they shared a resemblance. Was she the girl's mother?

It turned out that Mr. H. had a large population of Negroes on his place, at least large by local standards, and several were light-skinned children that by the set of their eyes, or cut of their chins, bore a defined likeness to their master. Tongues flew!

Thursday, April 12, 1860

Much ado about here. Planting is in full swing. The air is heavy with the rich aroma of freshly plowed soil, heady with promise. Isaac owns about a thousand acres, and perhaps fifty Negroes. There are probably about fifteen children among them, some are infants, others old enough to feed the horses, gather eggs, tend the garden, or carry water. A dozen men are field hands. They work the crops, primarily corn and that wily mistress Cotton, assisted by older boys and a few sturdy women, maybe twenty souls altogether. I can't imagine the life of a field hand. The work is grueling and their quarters are crude hovels. It purely breaks my heart to see men treated like beasts. Isaac does not appear to be a cruel master, but he doesn't work closely with his hands, as Pa did with Greene and the boys; instead he rides from field to field shouting orders. I suppose that is the only way he knows to manage such a large place. He comes in exhausted at the end of each day, for superintending is as taxing to the mind as labor is to the body. Surely there must be a more civilized way to clothe mankind and earn a livelihood!

I eventually became acquainted with Mr. H.'s amber girl, in that oblique way that blacks and whites from different households can come to know one another. She was indeed my same age, a quiet girl I'll call "Amanda," for I hesitate to put down her true name. Her features were delicately formed like white ones, except for her eyes, almond-shaped, outer corners turning up, framed by long curly lashes, and her cheekbones, high and regal. Her tawny skin was the color of taffy; she was truly an exotic beauty. There was a shyness about her, which may have come from her questionable parentage, if she was aware of it. Mr. H.'s ivory children purely hated her, and the dark Negroes, save her mother, avoided her. There were several other youngsters of her hue, and they were her sole companions. I know this because I befriended Rose to her. Most at our little church did not own slaves, and those who did, had only a hand or two, or like Pa, a small family. Mr. H.'s arrival nearly doubled the number of Negroes who scrambled for the back pews, or hung about the windows and door. I concluded it was my duty to have Rose welcome Amanda into our fold, and beside I wanted to get to the gossip from the inside.

It was immediately rumored about that the dusky children were the offspring of Mr. H. and his Negro women. The fullness of time has convinced me that was indeed the case, but at thirteen I found the idea both appalling and intriguing. As a farm-raised girl, I was completely aware of how life is begun, but the human entry into the equation was mysterious. The rutting in the barnyard seemed appropriate for the animal kingdom, but surely God had designed a more dignified way to people His earth. As I have said, there were few slaves among us, and we lived so closely with them to be bound in a nearly familial way. A true gentleman would no more make overtures to his Negro, than he would to his brother's wife. And should he be tempted, our preachers railed against the egregious sin in a circuitous flurry of language designed not to alarm children, yet promise the wrath of Hell. As further insurance, we all watched one another, keeping the threat of shame at our wagging fingertips should it be needed. Everyone, at least the adults, knew such things happened in wicked places, and certain parts of Virginia held that reputation, but not among us, never!

So I continued to observe Amanda and romanticize that Mr. H. truly loved her mother, or that the whole thing was malicious gossip, completely unfounded. But if it were true, wouldn't the two of them suffer eternity in Hell? And what about poor Amanda? According to scripture, she was also bound for damnation which seemed patently unfair, for surely it was no fault of hers. Mr. H. was oddly regarded in the community. He had been among the first cotton growers in the area, and was certainly the largest. His successful farm spread prosperity throughout the neighborhood. Men eagerly traded with him, then later remarked that his handshake was limp, that his self-satisfied grin was smug, inviting a fist to the face, that surely he gambled and cheated. He was a sleazy character, but he dealt in North Carolina currency, not promissory notes, at least not at first. Mr. H. was an economic godsend, and a social pariah.

His poor wife led an isolated life. Other women hesitated to take up with her, as if her husband's philandering was somehow her responsibility. I saw her often sitting in church, sad eyes peering down into her lap where her hands were clasped. There were bruises on her wrists, which was all that could be seen below her long sleeves, and when her kerchief shifted in the breeze, I noticed old yellowing splotches on her neck. Gradually she was befriended by sympathetic sorts; the sanctimonious remained aloof.

Sunday, April 15, 1860

It is the Sabbath, and I take up my pen. After much prayer I have concluded that God would deem this work contemplative, for in searching my memories, I am discovering the source of my convictions. Planting is well under way, and the pace soon promises to slacken. I welcome that, for I wish to spend more time with this journal, and I have found that I am not so energetic as I once was.

About a year after the H. family entered our realm, Mattie announced a desire to marry. It was a timely announcement, for she was eighteen, and ought to have already been breeding. However we were surprised at her choice for a mate, a hand belonging to Mr. H.! Pa was dumbstruck, having avoided our nefarious neighbor as much as possible. In all fairness, it was a logical choice. As I have said, there were few Negroes in our area, and many of their families were already more intertwined than scripture permits. Mr. H.'s Negroes enriched our community as much as his money did. Well Pa got over his pique, and permitted the ceremony; after all Mattie would never have to set foot on the H. farm. Marital visits among Negroes were always made by the husband. Of course it was not a legal marriage, as they were not allowed, but it was desirable for Negro unions to be sanctified, a compromise we assumed pleased God while obeying the law. We also indulged them their native rituals, brought from Africa it was said. There were few occasions when Negroes from different farms could socialize. Weddings were cheerful and exuberant, compared to church services and funerals.

Mattie's new husband, a broad-shouldered young man with lit-up eyes and a quick smile, was named Harry. Harry came to our place whenever his master permitted, usually arriving on a Saturday evening and staying through the Sabbath. The night of the wedding Harry sheepishly followed Mattie in the back door and up the stairs to the garret; if Negroes could blush, I'm sure he would have done so grandly. I even noticed a grin on Mattie's face. Imagine that! Pa immediately decided that this arrangement would not do, and told Mattie she should sleep in the cabin whenever Harry was on the premises. I was old enough by then to have some notion of the situation; surely the newlyweds had more privacy in the garret than in the two-room cabin occupied by Cissy, Greene, Rose and the four boys. Years later I scavenged my courage to ask Cissy about it. As I grew into young womanhood Cissy became my fount of knowledge concerning female and other delicate matters. She told me that black folks were accustomed to living in such a fashion, after all she got all her babies but the first with "chilluns" in the room. Yet she said it was proper that Pa "seen fit" to protect my sensibilities, and not "give my brothers no notions." I am still offended that white sensibilities are regarded as more fragile than black ones!

Gradually Mattie's time in the cabin surpassed that in the house, whether Harry was in residence or not. We children were growing older, in little need of a nursemaid, and she was more valuable to Pa working with Cissy. The next summer Mattie gave birth to a little boy. We were overjoyed when he proved to be a strong and healthy infant, especially Pa who could see a new hand, perhaps a string of them, to secure his old age.

During those years another infant of doubtful parentage was born on Mr. H.'s place. Then the unthinkable happened. They were sold! Either Mr. H. acquired a debt that was otherwise insurmountable (he was rumored to be a gambler), or Mrs. H. grew a backbone, I never knew which. Without fanfare, along with the other mulatto children and their mothers, Amanda was gone. Gone where, I have no idea, though I've long wondered. I hope to a place where she was not ostracized and shed of the shame that was none of her doing.

I have said the selling of Negroes was unthinkable, which may seem queer nowadays. In my rural childhood where slaves were few, and so very valuable, one was sold only if considered completely intractable, or when the property of a deceased person was divided. This was economics, pure and simple, but it would not be long before I became far too familiar with the emotional onus of splitting families apart. It's no wonder I am so adamant about Rose.

Sunday, April 15, 1860

My, but we had us a bodacious heap of work getting the ground dug up and laid out proper, and putting in the seed! All but the littlest went to the fields, and I done cooked and cleaned like in the old days. Being Sunday, and a peaceful one, I take up my pencil again. Miss Julia say she been pondering on Master H. (she say not to write down his name) and his high-yaller gal she call Amanda, for her name ain't to be set down neither. Them days seem so long ago.

I reckon I was near bout ten years old when Miss Julia told me Amanda look like she need a friend. I tried talking to her in the churchyard, but she a hard one to get close to. Anybody could see how light she was, and folks said that was why Master H.'s darkies didn't take to her. That seemed peculiar to me; there was so few of us back then, we wasn't picky. But now I seen it all. Some dark folks think the light ones uppity, while the tan-faced says the black ones is blue-gums, fresh out from Africa, still half wild. They is all wrong.

Now nobody accused Amanda of being uppity, her being so quiet and shy and all. They say she Master H.'s own child. The black children didn't want nobody to think their Mams had truck with that man, so they keep clear of Amanda and the other light ones. They say Master H. was a mean ogre, forcing hisself wherever he pleased. Them yaller children had several different Mams. The master never gave no privilege to any of them; he just took what he wanted. I didn't know all this at the time, but I come to figure it out.

It was bout two, maybe three years later when Amanda got sold, along with the rest of them suspect children and their Mams. The story got passed around in the quarter who got it from Miz H.'s house maid. Mattie's husband Harry brung it to us. It seem that Miz H. finally got her fill of yaller babies, and got up the gumption to tell her husband a thing or two. She say if he don't get shed of those people, she would have plenty to say about his shady dealings up in Virginia, how he'd sold injured mules and horses as sound, how he'd sold spent land as fertile; oh, she had a long list of folks he owed or cheated. She would allow that he had come to Lincoln County for more than cheap land. He had come to hide hisself where the Virginia sheriff couldn't get at him. Our little patch in the backwoods suited him fine. She also had a list of Virginia plantations where he'd spread his seed, and I don't mean no cotton seed. If he didn't sell those folks, she'd pack up her bags and her younguns and go home to her Pappy.

She'd said all these things before, mumbling like, a-feared cause sometimes he took to beat her. Now she got brave and plumb serious. She had abided his behavior in Virginia where such wickedness was tolerated, and she had nearby kinfolk to take pity. But here she didn't have a kindred soul cept her house nigra. The white womens stayed clear of her, and she'd got to be downright lonely. It was the dead nigra that bolstered her gumption.

A little pickaninny died giving birth to a bone-white baby, the mama only a child herself, maybe bout thirteen. When her belly swole up, she wept to her Mam that the master said it was alright for him to poke her cause she was too young to get a baby. But she did, and it killed her plumb dead. I reckon that was Miz H.'s last straw, every black tongue on the place clacking right under her nose. So she was fixing to up and leave, shouting her husband's catalog of sins to the countryside, and if he laid a hand upside of her, she'd show her Pappy the bruises.

Well Master H. was shook up plenty, and he give in to his wife. Amanda and the entire clutch of suspect Mams and children got sold. Harry didn't know where to. Some said South Carolina, others said Georgia. Tongues quit wagging on the H. farm, and so far as we knew the master behaved himself. If he sired any more yaller babies, he did it a long ways from home.

Mam told me not to say a word to nobody, not even Miss Julia, about what Harry told us. If we got tangled in such a tale, then Master H. would surely sell Harry, and Mattie's marriage would be broke, leaving her babies without a Pappy. I should say that Mattie had lit up like a sunbeam when Harry declared for her, and none of us wanted her misery back. Mam said she'd skin us alive if we so much as whispered, and I believed her! That been so long ago, I'd plumb near forgot it. I reckon I could tell Miss Julia now.

Monday, April 16, 1860

I've neglected to mention my brothers during their formative years. In 1814, the year Mattie was married, Pa assigned me the responsibility of my brothers' supervision. Jeff was eleven that year, and Frank was eight.

Jeff had completed his course of study at our common school. He was an adequate student, cheerful and well disciplined, but glad to see schooling come to an end. He was growing strong and muscular, and was eager to be on the land. Land is lifeblood to farmers, the care and nurture of it the highest of callings. It is hard work, but deeply satisfying when done well, when knowledge and instinct are perfectly mated. Pa was delighted to have his eldest son join him in the family business.

I believe that was the first year Pa talked about cotton, although it would be several more until a crop was planted. Before that could be done, more land had to be cleared, trees felled, stumps pulled, backbreaking, time consuming labor. At last Pa had workers to deal with such an endeavor. Greene must have been about forty, perhaps a bit beyond, yet he was still strong and energetic. Healthy men generally are, and Greene was fortunate in his health. His eldest son Amos was about twenty, Caesar was twelve, a year older than Jeff, and Joe and Narcissus lay in between. So many strong backs to help Pa turn his place into a prosperous farm.

Meanwhile Frank was becoming his own person. Though only eight he had completed several sessions of common school with exemplary results. The tutor sent notes home to Pa stating that Frank was among the finest scholars he had ever instructed. He excelled especially in mathematics and the natural sciences, and Pa should consider sending him to an academy if one could be found within his means. Pleasant Retreat Academy had been established in Lincolnton the year before; Frank's tutor recommended it. He went on to say that he would be pleased to keep Frank with him as long as Pa desired, however, if the boy continued to improve at the current pace, he was afraid that the common school's curriculum would soon be exhausted. He hoped Pa would take this under advisement and come up with a plan for Frank's further elucidation. Not all of this came at once, but in letters scattered over several months.

The news sent Pa into a frenzy of clearing land, and writing away to agricultural agents about cotton. Pa concluded that his younger son was a prodigy, and only by improving his farm could he provide the best education money could buy; perhaps the child should be sent to Salisbury, or Raleigh. Maybe Charleston was the place. It's a wonder he didn't mention Europe! The fact that Pa could afford none of those places was unimportant.

I began to take a keener interest in Frank; after all I had been assigned the task of child care in the family, and schooling was of great interest to me. Heretofore I had considered Frank simply a much younger brother, a pesky child to be avoided. Now he was a project. I introduced him to some of the books I had hoarded away. Among the lots of sundries Pa had brought home was an astronomy text and an atlas. The tutor was right. The boy was a quick study.

I resumed my pretend school, the game I had played so happily with Rose all those years ago. I had not kept up Rose's lessons as I should have, and being ten she sometimes had chores in the kitchen or the garden. But I got hold of her when I could, making a pretense that I needed her help with mending or polishing the furniture. Pa was on the farm, and Cissy was in the kitchen; no one paid much attention to us. Of course my two scholars were completely unequal in their requirements, but this was no hindrance to me. The only school I had known had pupils of varying ages and abilities. It was quite natural to sit Frank down with the atlas while I listened to Rose read from a primer, then listen to Frank recite what he'd learned while Rose reread her lesson silently to be sure she retained it. I had a wonderful time, and both children improved enormously, to my credit if I may flatter myself.

Rose's lessons were not as unusual as one might think. In those days before that absurd law was passed many Negro children were taught to read, especially those owned by Presbyterians, who deemed some reading of the Bible helpful for entry into Heaven. It was also a mark of prestige for both owner and child to have leisure to engage the mind in spiritual pursuits. Even today some pious people teach their Negroes to read the Bible and recite the catechism. Rarely is the law brought into play when a child's soul is in question. I find it a mortal shame that few Negroes in Methodist and Baptist families are given instruction!

Rose tells me she is writing in her journal, and finds it a satisfactory occupation. She has already read the book I slipped her, and now I will search Isaac's shelves for another. Isaac keeps a bulging library to impress his visitors. I find that concept a bit snobbish, but I am thankful he prefers to flatter himself with books rather than horseflesh, as I would much rather read than ride!

Rose also said I had spurred her to think about Mr. H. She revealed that rumors of his misbehavior had circulated the Negro quarters, rumors she had suppressed all these years. I was not one bit surprised, but glad that she obeyed Cissy for Mattie and Harry's sake. Although to my great remorse in the fullness of time it would have made no difference. I had felt sorry for Amanda, sorry that she was sold who knows where, and always wondered what became of her. At least she was sold with her mother; at least she was sold before that slimy scoundrel got her in his clutches, and I wouldn't put it past him even if she were his daughter. Worms have no conscience!

Wednesday, April 18, 1860

The next year, 1815, was like the last. Pa continued clearing land, and inquiring about cotton. He was still all a-stir about Frank's future, and had written for information on various academies. He had set his heart on a place in Charleston, an expensive school, quite in keeping with my father the dreamer. He planted more corn and wheat than ever, and saved back more calves and piglets for breeding stock. We could eat old hens and fish; they were perfectly nutritious. He was set and determined to make a grand profit that year and the next, in order to perfectly situate his brilliant child in school.

It was not to be. His scheme for 1815 went nearly as well as planned, and that winter he purchased a quantity of cotton seed for the upland cotton that held so much promise. In the spring of 1816 he planted it on several newly cleared well-groomed acres. It was a dry and chilly spring, but surely the unfortunate weather would pass. It did not. 1816 came to be called the "year without a summer," one that would be long remembered for its dreadful pillage of our entire known world.

Every day the sky was filled with ominous dark clouds. Not dense summer rain clouds with puffy white crests and smooth liquid underbellies shifting from pewter to nickel to slate, but parched smudgy clouds, ashy and tinged with brown and ocher. They didn't gather into proper cloud shapes, nor give out a drop of rain, but splayed formlessly across the sky like a mixture of dirt and ash swept briskly from the kitchen door. Week after week, month after month the drear continued. No one knew the cause of it. Newspapers reported the phenomenon was sweeping the country with even direr consequences in the northeastern states, and was probably the result of some yet to be discovered force of nature. Dark skies that produced not a drop of rain were unnatural. Many suspected the wrath of God was being visited upon sinners, the first of many plagues to follow. We simply strove to make do as well as possible.

We had planted our kitchen garden as usual in the spring, and when rains did not fall, we watered it with buckets drawn from the well. It was not long before the well became clouded and silty, and we stopped watering to preserve its health. The boys, black and white, had no hoeing to do as the new seeds did not sprout and grow, so they took to fishing nearly every day to keep us fed. At first they fished our nearby creeks; when those dried up they made jaunts to the Catawba, about five miles away. Poor Pa was doubly frustrated. He shared the fears of our neighbors of what would become of us from the lack of a crop, and how far could we parcel out the potatoes and onions and turnips from the root cellar? Those winter vegetables had not been intended to feed us the entire year. And Pa's dreams for Frank were becoming as vaporous as the ever present dust, kicked up from the earth below, wafting down from the sky above.

Rose and I had little to occupy us after the well became fouled. The previous January, when the future still seemed bright, Pa had given Rose to me as a gift for my sixteenth birthday. Of course she still worked at his beckoning, but he permitted her to move into Mattie's old place in the garret. As I was growing into young womanhood, the daughter of a soon to be prosperous planter, it befitted me to have my own personal maid. When she was not needed elsewhere, she was mine, to tend to my wardrobe or do my hair, whatever I wished. None of us expected that she would become entirely my handmaiden, every minute at my fingertips; she was given to me primarily as a gesture to acknowledge my maturity. But as that dreadful year unfolded, there was less and less work to be done. Simple meals of fried fish, johnnycakes, and hoarded root vegetables fed us. Only things that were excessively begrimed were laundered due to meager supply of well water, and gardening had entirely ceased. The animals foraged and grazed, caring for themselves; there was little we could do for them. We even gave up on dusting and polishing, as dust seemed to settle faster than it could be cleaned away. Any task at all was futile.

The bright spot for Rose and me was our reading. That summer we read with abandon. Pa had continued to buy books at every opportunity, and by then he had accumulated a considerable library. Of some of the more popular titles we had more than one copy. I read from one, while Rose followed along in another, then we would turn about. In that way I elevated her ability far beyond the primers we had studied before. By the end of the summer Rose was nearly as capable a reader as I was.

We began each day with a passage from the Bible, then plowed into the secular books. We started out with children's stories, simplified renderings of ancient myths or Greek and Roman history, then delved into biographies of famous men written for young readers. From there we graduated to "The Pilgrim's Progress," some of Shakespeare's plays, and classics like "The Iliad" and "The Odyssey." And poetry, we were fortunate to have volumes full! Henry Fielding and Oliver Goldsmith were well represented. The latter wrote poems and essays and plays, but I remember most his novel, "The Vicar of Wakefield," a long and elegant story we savored for weeks. By midsummer we had discovered a delicious vice, the Gothic novel, although we did not know it by that name. Nowadays I don't consider those books a vice, simply a mindless diversion. Perhaps we should have been improving our minds with more serious literature, but diversion was what we needed that gloomy summer. Stories filled with stormy nights, maidens in peril, and evil villains vanquished at last were just the thing for us. We read "Castle of Otranto," "The Champion of Virtue," "Mysteries of Udolpho," and "The Fatal Revenge". I'm sure there were others; those titles remain with me for we read them over and over.

In spite of our flights of fancy into the imaginary world it was a very difficult time. Everyone in the neighborhood was crabby from the scant monotonous diet, and apprehensive about the future. Would the gloomy clouds ever lift? Men occupied themselves by riding about the neighborhood looking for brushfires which erupted readily in the drought. At least that gave them some sense of purpose. Loony Brown rarely came by to peddle his wares. There was no corn to pilfer, no promise of windfall apples, nothing to cook or ferment or distill behind his shabby cabin. Nothing at all to do but wander the roads with his imaginary ménage, his shouting having given way to weeping and wailing, to baying like a banshee.

Thank goodness for Rose and Frank and our books! While Rose and I read our diversionary stories, Frank continued his studies, and I assisted him as far as I was able. If Pa's circumstances ever improved, Frank would be prepared for any academy in the land. I suppose by spending so many idle hours together Rose and I had become close, nearly as I imagined sisters might be.

Thursday, April 19, 1860

I give back the book Miss Julia got for me, and she promise me another. It was a book of stories by Mr. E. A. Poe. It reminded me of those bodacious dreadful dramas I read with Miss Julia the year the sun didn't shine, them books filled with wicked villains and terrified maidens. I hope she find me another book soon, as I intend to improve my writing. Reading books helps to get the nigra talk out of my head if I set my mind to it.

Miss Julia's been carrying on bout that dreary summer all happy like. I don't recollect it the same way. The January before, when Miss Julia turn sixteen, Master Campbell give me to her. He tell me with a big old smile on his face how privilege I was to be a lady's maid and to live in the big house. I was twelve, the same age Mattie was when she took to the garret. I never in my borned days heard a prison door slam behind my back, but the first time I climb them steep stairs to sleep alone in the dark narrow garret, I swear I could feel one clank in my heart. Just like Mattie, I learn what it was to be a slave. Childrens, black and white, is accustomed to minding and doing what they is told, but when I carried my belongings up them stairs, it come to me like a boom of thunder that to Master Campbell and Miss Julia I would forever be their property, to work for them, and do as I was bid. How strange it dawned that day; all at once I was full growed with a job in the big house, but my owners would never be shed of treating me like a child. Mattie had told me this, but not till that day did I truly grasp what she say. Ain't no white person alive that can cotton to the fact that it is a pure joy and wonder to be the master of your own self.

I didn't suffer miseries like Mattie did. I'd been at Miss Julia's coattails as long as I could remember so the house was familiar to me. And my chores got lighter when that grim summer come. I did love a good story, and I'm grateful to God that Miss Julia taught me to read. When we was reading I felt near bout free. But every night when I trudged up them steps with my lantern, and cozied down in my bed, icy in the winter and stifling in summer, I dwelt on the fact that I was property. Over the years Master Campbell had replaced Mattie's pallet with a cot, and had give her a chair and a little chest to put her things in, but the garret still seemed as barren and dark as a jail. I cried myself to sleep for weeks longing for Mam and Pappy's soft arms, and their warm cabin with a fire crackling in the hearth. When summer came I would have give anything to pull my pallet in front of their cabin doorway to catch the breeze. I never let anyone see them tears, not the white folks, not Pappy, not even Mam.

Miss Julia told me how lucky I was to have my own room, how I didn't have to listen to Mattie's baby fussing in the night, and how crowded the cabin must be with all those boys, and Mattie and Harry, and Mam and Pappy, sharing one room and a loft. Then she mumbled something about being indecently exposed to the marriage bed when Harry had his visits.

I didn't know what she was talking about. I'd slept all my life next to Mam and Pappy's bed. Their soft murmurs of affection made me feel warm and loved all down through my soul. White folks take the strangest notions.

Friday, April 20, 1860

I have another book for Rose to read, one I have recently completed called "Vanity Fair" by Mr. Thackeray of England, so very modern. I do hope she will enjoy it as I did. It is certainly in my nature to see folly in pretentious society; I believe Rose will appreciate it. I've found another book for myself, one by Mr. Dickens. Isaac populates his shelves with thick books bearing handsome covers, all to draw the admiration of his guests. I doubt Isaac has any notion that Mr. Dickens is a raving abolitionist who often spoke on the subject! Adie has little time to read with her brood to tend, however I doubt she would have patience for Dickens had she all the time in the world. I suppose I have blasphemed, being critical of my daughter after she had the kindness of heart to take me in, but she is simply not a scholarly sort. She would have felt kinship with my brother Jeff.

Rose has acted the crotchety old woman lately all because I asked her to starch and iron my petticoats. She never complains in the winter when she can do the job in my bedchamber. But I refuse to have a fire there in this warm weather, so it must be done in the kitchen where the flat irons can be heated on the hearth. She had the audacity to ask if I was too weak and old to do my own ironing! She knows I consider her virtually free, but that does not give her liberty to be rude. She thinks I should wear a cage-crinoline, the new style Adie has adopted. But I fear I could not manage such a contraption with all its slats and wires and hoops, and I would feel perfectly naked without layers of petticoats under my skirt. Certainly Rose understands it would be entirely improper for <u>me</u> to iron in the kitchen surrounded by Negroes. I suppose I could ask Adie for the use of her laundress, but that poor woman already has her hands full. I've no idea what is in Rose's mind!

That dark summer of 1816 finally did come to an end, and our family survived, thinner, and humbler, but living. In the fall blue returned to the skies, gradually, in little shards piercing the gray. It was a cool autumn, drizzly days interspersed with hazy ones, and by winter hazy gave way to bright. In the fall we planted over again, not cotton nor corn, but quick growing lettuce and frost resistant greens, anything that might feed us. And Blessed be the Lord, they flourished. Frank returned to school, bringing home even more notes about his brilliance, and Pa planned once again for his education, but this time with a modicum of restraint. He talked to the headmaster of the Pleasant Retreat Academy in Lincolnton, and made arrangements for Frank to enroll the following fall. That is if he succeeded with cotton this time around.

The winter was blissfully uneventful. When day by day the sky reclaimed its natural appearance, we began to have real hope the plague had passed and once again we ate eggs and slaughtered a few lean pigs. Our hoarding days were over. Never before had I so thoroughly appreciated the aroma of freshly washed linens dried in the sun, or the sweet earthy smell of new mown hay. The boys and men began preparing the land for seed. It was light work as the land had been cleared the year before, and was devoid of stubble as nothing had grown during the barren summer. Cotton seed was purchased once again, although some was still on hand and was perfectly good. It is always prudent to have seed enough for a second planting in case of a late frost or a freshet. Replanting cotton hadn't even been considered the summer before.

The new cotton crop was successful. It was a small harvest as Pa thought it unwise to put much acreage to a crop he was unfamiliar with. However, he made a good profit, which seemed enormous in the wake of the barren year. Even after deducting the toll for ginning and paying to have it carted to the coast, he made more money from cotton than from anything else he had ever raised. The next year he planted more, and though the price per pound fell, his profit was even greater. Year after year that was the pattern for as long as Pa lived; a larger crop, a smaller price, yet an increase in profit. It would have been a completely satisfactory life, if only Pa had come to terms with falling prices. Each year he was entirely surprised when the price dropped once again. In time he built a gin on our land, and he and the boys drove the cotton to market themselves rather than pay for transport. I was somewhat aware of the fickle nature of the cotton market, but not yet fully acquainted with Pa's lack of realism.

In the fall of 1818 Frank enrolled in the Pleasant Retreat Academy. The ten miles to Lincolnton was much too far to ride to and fro each day, so Frank boarded in town, as did most of the students. Frank was twelve, just the right age for such an adventure. Every now and again when there was a recess between sessions, he would come home filled with enthusiasm for his studies and his tutors and the other scholars. He was learning Latin and Greek, and all manner of intriguing sciences. It's no wonder he grew up to be a doctor. Pa regretted that he couldn't spare Greene every Friday to fetch Frank home, and Sunday to return him to school, but when he saw Frank's glowing love of the place, his anxiety eased.

It is growing late, and the next topic I must address is a sad one. So I shall set my journal aside for another day.

Saturday, April 21, 1860

Planting time done come, and I been too busy to write much. Since Miss Julia and I settle at Miss Adie's place, I've been working a heap more during planting time than I used to do. Master Isaac plant more cotton than Miss Julia's husband ever did, which takes a toll on everybody. And my poor old bones is plain weary. Miss Julia asked me to do up her petticoats, and I give her what for. I reckon I oughtn't to have sassed her bout the starching and ironing, but I was plumb fed up and tired. Folks in the quarter is in a stir talking bout a war might be coming, and the Yankees studying to set us free. They says when freedom come we won't have to work no more, just set back and let the Yankees take care of us. I want my freedom bad as anybody, but I don't for one minute think the Yankees going to let us lie back on our haunches. Master Isaac say them Yankees is meaner than any white men we ever seen, lying every chance they get. I don't know who to believe. I wants to be free, but don't want to get mixed up in any war. I reckon the extra work and all this foolish talk has me right frazzled. I spect Miss Julia would set me free if she could keep me here. She is purely flummoxed by that contrary law, for which I don't blame her. Ain't her fault I is a slave. I reckon I ought to do her starching and ironing. Ain't no working on Sunday; maybe Monday I'll get to it.

I been thinking back on when I move to the garret, and looked over what I wrote about it. I concluded that I ought to write down the happy times that come before, for a nigra childhood is mostly a playful one. When I was a little girl I had a fine time romping and carrying on with the white childrens. Jeff was one year older than me, and Master Frank two years younger. Miss Julia was the mother hen, directing and doting on us all. We was just carefree younguns scampering about the yard when we didn't have chores, frolicking, laughing and such – cept when Master Campbell married that old preaching biddy. I come to have a sweet spot for Jeff. He was a cheerful and fine looking boy, and I purely took a shine to him. That was before I learned how black folks and white folks has to be to each other, and before I was told to add "Master" to his and Frank's names. I never let on, thank the Lord, cause I would have been a heap embarrassed, but in my little girl mind, I thought I could grow up to marry Jeff! What a notion that seem now, but then it seem natural as rainfall.

I come to know it was a foolish thought, but I kept a soft spot for Jeff, loved him in a childish way. When I was old enough for chores, and him for school, we kept company in the fading afternoons, feeding chickens, fishing in the creek. Jeff always talk to me like a regular person, like I was somebody, not like property. He didn't care if I called him "Master," and I didn't when we was alone. We shed a passel of tears when his old red dog died whelping a litter too big for her. Every day we fed them pups, and nestled them down in a box in the kitchen, seeing they had a clean blanket and fresh straw. A couple of them pups didn't live, and we cried a heap more, but in the end we hallelujahed when the rest grew strong and healthy, able to fend for theirselves. We figured it was a fine accomplishment, and we done it together.

At summer's end when it was hog gathering time, it was me Jeff took traipsing through the woods rounding up his Pappy's hogs. We'd run and holler, chasing squealing pigs, then herd them into pens for fattening. We filled baskets with feed corn to throw over the fence for them to eat, then we shucked and shelled more basketsful for grinding into meal; all manner of chores seemed less like work when me and Jeff done them together.

I didn't have much truck with Master Frank, him being a bookish boy. Master Campbell was content to leave him at his learning, and didn't send him out hog chasing and such. His chores were light, so he could hunker down with his books. He always had a serious mind, didn't much take to laughing and romping. Later on, when Miss Julia had our little play-like school, she give us different tasks, so we studied quiet-like, not much transpiring between us.

When I moved into the garret I was told we were not childrens no more and we were each to take our proper place. Master Campbell, he try to be gentle, but there ain't no gentle way to tell a person she a slave, though that particular word never come from his mouth. He say his younguns was a young lady and gentlemen, and out of respect I ought to call them "Miss Julia," and "Master Frank," and "Master Jeff." It give me trouble to remember at first, but after a while I reckon I got used to it.

Sunday, April 22, 1860

Today is windy and rainy. We went into town for services this morning, but did not stay for dinner due to the weather. It is now afternoon, and I am writing alone in my room, appropriate for the tale that comes next to my memory.

In the spring of 1819 my dear brother Jeff met with great tragedy. I have said he was not a scholarly sort, but he was the most sunny, cheerful, loving brother a person could wish for. Pa was all agog about Frank's promise in the classroom, yet he was equally enthusiastic about Jeff's destiny as a farmer. Jeff was the boy who would work beside him learning the art and mysteries of agriculture; Jeff was the one who would inherit the land, and perhaps add to it over the years and turn it into a fine plantation. Pa's plans for his sons were very different, yet each boy's calling was equally honorable. Frank might someday be a learned man, perhaps even a leader of men. Jeff would become the steward of the land; nothing to a gentleman and farmer is more important than land.

It was early in April and Jeff, Narcissus, and Caesar were out near the edge of the forest chopping firewood. They had felled a few trees, and were cutting them to lengths for the ever hungry hearths that warmed us and cooked our food. Perhaps Jeff was laughing or talking (as was his wont) and his mind wandered a moment from his work, or perhaps his ax hit a dense knot in the wood diverting it from its course. Whatever the cause, his ax came down hard on the log then bounced and plunged into Jeff's shoe, splitting the leather and releasing a torrent of blood from the gash. I was not there to witness, but all of the boys told the same fearsome tale.

The three of them gasped in astonishment not believing what their eyes saw, then Narcissus and Caesar laid my brother on the ground, and working as gingerly as possible, removed the near severed shoe. The wound, which seemed to be a clean line from the base of his middle toe almost to his ankle, continued to bleed profusely. Leaves were gathered to press into the injury and stanch the flow. One boy's neckerchief was wrapped around the wound, and another neckerchief was tied tightly above the ankle. Narcissus stayed with Jeff, propping his leg on a log, while Caesar ran for Cissy and our father.

Cissy arrived first with a small pail of ashes, a cruet of vinegar, clean towels, and a handful of herbs she had pulled quickly from the kitchen garden. (It was then that I realized why healing herbs were planted so handily by the garden gate!) Cissy carefully removed the neckerchief from the now throbbing wound, all the while fussing at Narcissus for gathering up whatever leaves came to hand. "Common yard trash, what good that do? Got to have the proper herb for the job."

"But Mam," Narcissus wailed, "He bout to bleed to death. We figure any old leaves would stop it till you gets here."

Cissy poured vinegar into a towel and wiped as much debris from the wound as she could, then made a paste from vinegar and ashes and pressed it into the gash, all the while mumbling, "You don't know what be in them leaves, worms or spiders, all kinds of bugs. Some spiders is pisen, don't you know that, boy!" Next she covered the paste with leaves from the lamb's ears she had brought, and tied a clean towel around the entire foot. By this time Pa had arrived, wringing his hands, blanched in the face, for Caesar's frantic cries had convinced him that Jeff's foot had been entirely severed from his leg. Cissy told Narcissus to get the barrow which was waiting nearby in anticipation of firewood. "This boy can't walk on that foot, not one step till it start to heal up."

Cissy's treatment of vinegar and ashes was only emergency aid, only intended to quell the bleeding until she could prepare a proper concoction to speed healing and prevent mortification. Jeff was carted home and helped into Pa's bed (being below stairs, it was the usual place for an invalid); his foot was propped on bolsters, and Cissy went to work. In the kitchen she boiled up the proper combination of herbs, as least proper to her notions, recipes vary. She made one concoction to be used as a plaster on the wound, and another as a tea to promote healing from within. Jeff at first seemed to improve, then his foot swelled and festered. When we bathed it (I was assisting Cissy with the bathing), we noticed pus seeping from the wound. "That be good," Cissy said; "It mean he's throwing out the pisen!" But I think Cissy overestimated herself as a healer.

Pa sent for the doctor who prescribed a different set of remedies, but his were no more helpful. Red streaks crept up Jeff's leg, and two of his toes were turning black. I believe they were also numb, but by this time Jeff was delirious with fever, and his reports of numbness or pain were inconsistent and could not be relied upon. Again the doctor came. This time he suggested amputation, just below the knee. Pa was beside himself. "Half a leg for a few toes gone bad. I'll not hear of it!" The doctor left laudanum for delirium and pills for fever. He told us to bathe and plaster the wound more vigorously, and if more toes blackened the leg would have to come off. There was nothing more to do.

Without going into lurid details, Jeff's fate was sealed. His injury did not improve, and the leg did come off. By that time he had lapsed into such a stupor from the laudanum or the fever, that I doubt he suffered much during the crude surgery performed on our dining table. Rose was particularly disturbed by these events. She wept and flustered about uncontrollably. I walked her far away from the house on the day of the surgery, in an attempt to console her and keep her innocent of Jeff's cries. I thought it was simply her emotional nature that put her in such a state, until she confided in me how dear a friend Jeff had become. I should have known; Jeff was such a cheerful lad and loved by everyone. Rose was certain to be greatly affected, growing up in his spectacular shadow as she did.

The amputation was either useless, or came too late; within days Jeff was dead. At least his suffering was done. Pa blamed himself for not letting the doctor take the leg earlier, but the man had the goodness of heart to tell Pa that it might have made no difference. The first time he was called to Jeff's bedside he was afraid there was little hope, but dared not tell us as we were distraught enough. He had wished to bleed him, but thought he had already lost too much blood to endure the treatment, and aside from the extreme measure of taking the leg, there was nothing beyond salves and the laudanum that he knew to do.

The entire event, from ax fall to death, only lasted about two weeks, although it seemed an eternity at the time. We buried Jeff on the twentieth of April, almost exactly forty-one years ago. Fortunately there was a space for him next to Ma, on her opposite side from the spot Pa had reserved for himself between his two wives. I could not have abided it had Jeff been laid next to Mrs. C., nor could I have expressed my objections to Pa, even though it had been ten years since that horrid woman left us. It was not until years later, after Pa himself had died, that I told my family under no circumstances was I to be buried in any grave that abutted the resting place of that woman. Take me to the far corner of the churchyard if necessary!

Rose was nearly hysterical at Jeff's funeral. I begged Pa to let her sit with us, but he refused. Though Pa treated his Negroes with utmost respect, he could not defy convention. He would have been mortified for our neighbors see us with a Negro child in our pew. I did keep Rose close to me in the graveyard, kept my arm about her, let her tears soak my shoulder. Poor Rose. We were all distraught at Jeff's death, but no one displayed grief as mightily as Rose.

I was about to put my journal away after that sad recount when Rose came to my room and offered to do my petticoats in the morning, and said how sorry she was that she spoke disrespectfully, blaming it on weariness from the extra work. I suppose I was at fault also. The farm has been a beehive of late, everyone doing double duty. I thanked her and suggested they could be ironed in my bedchamber. It is still cool enough for a fire to be bearable if we work in the early morning; yes, I said "we". We often worked together before coming to Adie's. Why not retrieve the old custom? After all, they are my petticoats.

Monday, April 23, 1860

It was a busy morning. Rose and I accomplished our objective and got the petticoats done. Now they are all fragrant, clean and crisp, and put away. It was good to work alongside Rose. I suppose I do get arrogant from time to time and my heart forgets what my head proclaims – that slavery is an evil institution. It is far too easy to go along with the conventions that surround one. I need to be more attentive to my convictions.

The next memorable event of my life was a happy one. In 1821 I met Thomas Henderson, the true love of my life. Thomas hailed from Mecklenburg County across the Catawba River, just a few miles beyond Cowan's Ford. I might never have met him had his sister not married into our community. The Catawba may as well have been as broad as the Atlantic as far as I was concerned. Pa crossed it frequently carrying on his business, but I kept close to home and Leeper's Creek. I was not a worldly child and had no reason to venture. It amuses me now to realize what a sequestered life I led; shallow fords on the Catawba abound!

In the Spring of 1821 Thomas' sister Essie was betrothed to a member of our congregation, he and his family sometimes visited Leeper's Creek in order to become acquainted with her young man and his family. Certainly I have mentioned that sharing dinner after Sabbath services was the hub of our society. I was introduced to Thomas on one of those occasions, and was smitten at once. Our eyes locked and danced in that mysterious way that is instantly perceived, but nearly impossible to describe. What is it about the eyes of those who have fallen (or are about to fall) hopelessly in love? Do they glow, flicker slightly? Whatever it is, I believe that the first moment I set my gaze on Thomas, and his was set on me, we were destined to be man and wife.

I was twenty-one years old, and although sheltered, not unacquainted with men. I perceived most in our church as close as brothers or cousins, awkwardly unacceptable suitors in my eyes. But Pa took me to town from time to time when he had business there, and introduced me to his acquaintances, and Frank often invited the youngest of his tutors to visit our farm. I had met several men who would have made suitable mates, but none that engaged me as rapturously as Thomas did. I suppose having read frivolous novels made me pine for romantic love. I was well aware that marriages were frequently contracted for practical reasons; a young lady sought an economic equal (or better if she was fortunate), a gentleman who could provide and become a good father, a man who attended church, and displayed no bad habits. If love followed – and sometimes it did not – so much the better. In our tiny community my choices seemed hopelessly limited, yet I ached for romance, and in the end was splendidly rewarded.

Of course I could marry no one without Pa's approval, and he would have objected had I chosen someone completely unacceptable. However, it was Pa's nature to kindle my happiness. He might have steered me toward a gentleman of his choosing, but he never would have dictated such a thing.

By June Thomas' sister had married, and he made any number of excuses to cross the Catawba River. First to see Essie, for she was a great favorite and he missed her dearly. Then trading in Lincolnton became his habit; after all it was closer to his family's place than Salisbury, and was becoming a fashionable mercantile center. Of course he stopped at our place on each and every journey, becoming quite a fixture. Pa grew fond of Thomas, and had developed a respect for his father during the family's visits to Leeper's Creek. From their conversations, the Henderson farm seemed to be larger than ours, more acres growing more cotton, worked by more hands. Exactly the situation Pa wished for his daughter. And several months later, after we had declared our intentions, we were invited to visit there and saw that it was true. The only stain on this perfect courtship was Thomas' mother. She appeared cold and distant and aloof. They say love is blind, and it must be so, for in my state of giddiness, I convinced myself the woman was merely shy, and I would come to know and esteem her in time. If only that had been true.

It was a delightful summer with Thomas appearing at our place nearly every week or so. We took long walks through the woods, waded in the creek, giggling like children, rocked on the front porch, and talked endlessly, about what, I have no idea. Just to have him close and hear his voice was a pure pleasure. Sometimes our hands locked as we were walking, and ignited a spark like a tiny bolt of delightful lightning. One afternoon while walking in the kitchen garden, I pointed out that some of our sweet peas and cucumbers looked weak and spindly. He knelt down, pulled a few weeds, then made a small furrow around the plant with his hand. "The garden needs a good weeding, and each plant should be bedded on a slight hill to allow water to reach its roots, and excess water to drain. But weed carefully; you don't want to sever the roots of your crop." Of course he was right. Pa had taught me how to plant several years before when the kitchen garden became my responsibility. Since then he rarely took notice of the garden, after all tending it was women's work. It was the gentleness of Thomas' hands in the earth that struck me so favorably that day, as if the soil were alive and would be injured by a rough touch. I could see that our minds followed the same path. All southern planters value land almost as life itself, but Thomas and I both thought land should be lovingly nurtured, not beaten into shape.

And if I needed proof of his affection toward me, he provided it generously that summer. Thomas thought I was beautiful! He said so, many time with great sincerity. Me beautiful! Imagine that! I did not consider myself unattractive, but I was somewhat plain. My hair was brown, my eyes brown, and my features regular, but in an ordinary way. I had always wished for curly ringlets surrounding my face, or rosy cheeks and wavy lashes, or womanly curves that men find attractive, but was never so blessed. Yet in his eyes I was truly beautiful. I was the happiest girl on earth.

Thomas took me in his carriage to Lincolnton when he had business there, and bought me trinkets or ribbons for my hair. He always took my hand to assist me in and out of the carriage, and usually held it longer than necessary; neither of us wanted to let go. We would stop at Essie's home along the way. Essie was several years younger than Thomas, and a few years older than I; we struck up an easy friendship. She was every bit as charming as her brother. She shared his quick wit, handsome features, and love of learning. Certainly I must have misconstrued the woman who raised her. I had much to learn about them both.

I was so entirely wound up in my own affairs, that I neglected to notice what Rose was up to. You see when Thomas came to visit he was nearly always accompanied by his driver Romulus. At first I thought he was merely demonstrating his affluence, an appropriate gesture for a suitor, although Romulus' assistance was valuable when Thomas had goods to buy or sell in town. It wasn't until late summer that I realized that as surely as Thomas was courting me, Romulus was courting Rose! It was usually Rose who spotted their carriage rounding the bend in a cloud of dust. Then she would come racing into the house billowing with excitement, shouting "Miss Julia, Miss Julia, Master Thomas is a-coming!" And all the while I thought she was exuberant on my behalf! What a silly blind goose I was.

There is so much more to tell, but it grows late.

Monday, April 23, 1860

Well I reckon Miss Julia and I done made peace over doing up her petticoats. Any two folks been together long as we have bound to fuss once in a while, no matter what color they is. I don't read what she write in her book, and she don't read mine, but most every day we talk about what we been pondering. Over the starch bucket she told me she been writing bout Master Jeff and how he died so young with so much promise left undone. I tell her yes'm, I miss that boy to this day, and it purely tore me up when he passed. She say she tumbled to that, but it took her a while. I say, "What you mean? You know we always kept together. I loved that boy bout as good as my own brothers, maybe better."

"I know," she says. Then she tell me that blacks folks always 'display' their feelings more than white folks, and she figured it was a show we put on for our masters, or some notion sprung out of Voodoo and superstition. Then she ask me if we really do feel grief more powerful than white folks. And I say I don't know, cause I ain't never been white. What I don't say is, maybe we got more to grieve about. Then she whisper, "When Jeff was ill I assumed you were overreacting in a typical Negro fashion, but after he died I was not so sure. I never have understood Negro gnashing and wailing." She wrung out a starch petticoat, and made a fine job of rolling it into a tight ball to set by the ironing board, like she was making work to keep more words from coming.

Then I had to say my piece, "I reckon when we is hurt weeping seems plumb fitting. Back then I thought you was the queer one, stiff and dry-eyed like he just gone off for a spell. It wasn't 'til we was grown and had others to bury, that I saw you hunched over crying your eyes out."

She look me in the face with stone hard eyes. "I certainly did shed my share of tears for Jeff, but not in the church, not in public; it would have humiliated me to be seen in such a state." She turned and kneaded that ball of petticoat until the white knots in her hands went soft. "Your grief for Jeff was real, wasn't it?" She mumbled them words like she shamed of herself.

Yes'm, I told her. I truly loved Master Jeff. I ask her did she remember them puppy dogs we raised, and how we done our chores together, and she said she did but hadn't paid it much mind. I boldened up and said, "Master Jeff never treat me like property." I didn't mention that I wanted to marry him when I was a girl; I reckon that's best left unsaid. I could see she had a tear coming, and I had some of my own.

Then she say, "Oh Rose, I never meant to doubt you. Of course you loved Jeff, just as I love you. Look at me, being such a silly old woman after all we've been through!"

"I care about you too, Miss Julia, but I purely hate being property." Not even your property, was words I wished I could add. Then she grab me up, hugging my neck, both of us dripping tears into the starch bucket.

"Rose," she tell me; "I'm sorry I was such a witch about the petticoats. Sometimes I just don't know what gets into me. If I treat you like property, you must tell me, for I don't mean to do that. Promise me."

"Yes'm, yes'm," I say. Poor old white woman got her burden, though it be a heap lighter than mine; of that much I'm sure. Then she say she's fixing to write in her book about marrying Master Thomas, which set me to thinking on Romulus. That shore start out as one happy time.

But I is bone weary with all that washing and starching and ironing and carrying on. I'll put Romulus on my mind while I'm waiting for sleep, and maybe he come see me in my dream.

Tuesday, April 24, 1860

Finally during the fall of 1821 Thomas asked for my hand, and our two families visited back and forth to become better acquainted. We made quite an assemblage when gathered around the Henderson table. Pa and I, and Frank if not at school, joined Thomas, his parents, and others of their family. Thomas had two younger sisters who were soon to be married, but were still in the home. A much younger sister was absent, as she was at boarding school in Salem. Thomas' older brother, his wife and small child were occasionally at the table. They lived on the property, but in a house some distance from the elder Hendersons. Sometimes we gathered up Essie and her husband and brought them along for the feast. Thomas' family was large compared to ours. The size of their family was typical, ours was not.

It was during these family gatherings that I began to have misgivings about Mrs. Henderson; her manner of directing the servants was off balance, out of kilter. She addressed them brusquely, but in our initial encounters the rudeness lay in her tone of voice not her words. I had not yet developed the distaste for slavery I hold today, but even then I loved Rose and considered Cissy almost as a mother. Though I had no deep affection for Greene or Mattie or her brothers, I regarded them worthy of respect and kindness. Even then I knew how to direct servants without demeaning them. Mrs. Henderson did not. In time she revealed a tongue sharp as a chisel, cutting deeply, leaving shavings of human dignity in its wake.

First I must explain that Mrs. Henderson was a woman of great classic beauty. Not schoolgirl prettiness that glows in youth and fades with time, but elegant loveliness that matures into dignity. She was graceful and carried herself with regal charm. It was a complete and utter shock to hear vitriol spill from such courtly lips. One event adheres to my memory in which her veiled crassness erupted into crystalline evil.

We were being served at dinner by an assortment of house servants accomplished in their duties. A pair of Negro girls brought dishes in from the kitchen, curtseying at the doorway upon entering the room.

They were relieved of the major platters by a man-servant dressed in the finest livery. Lesser dishes were taken by several small boys in dark trousers, crisp white shirts, and red silk waistcoats. The entire process unfolded like a minuet, joints presented to the host for carving, one at his right hand, another at his left; vegetables and breads and sauces were placed up and down the table, in order of importance, and in perfect symmetry, all of the servants moving and swaying about one another as if directed by a dance master. All was perfection until a boy laid a sauce at Mrs. Henderson's right hand. She looked at it quizzically, dipped in a spoon, and brought it to her quivery nose, then drew back in dismay.

"You, boy!" Snatching at his shirt collar, shaking him roughly, not even bothering to call him by name, if she even knew it. "Mushroom sauce isn't served in that dish, it belongs in a footed one. Have you no sense about you?" The child, who could not have been older than ten, lowered his head, mumbled an apology, and took the offending dish from the table, shuffling toward the door, breaking the elegant choreography. Meanwhile my future mother-in-law continued her shrill harangue, the child still in earshot. "I never expected niggers to have a lick of sense of their own, but I did think they could be taught proper table service. Mushroom sauce in a soup bowl! That boy needs a lesson he won't forget." Then turning to her husband, "You may take care of him after dinner." It was not a request, but a command.

I sat perfectly astonished. In our home Cissy ladled up food into whichever dishes were clean and convenient, Mattie brought them in from the kitchen, and we served ourselves with no particular formality. If there was a specific container for mushroom sauce, I had never heard of it. I was also perplexed by the poor child's role in the alleged faux-pas. Was not the bowl filled in the kitchen long before it reached his little hands? I prayed Mrs. Henderson didn't intend to have him beaten for his lesson, but I was nearly certain she did.

It was during one of these dinners that the question arose about my grandfather's patriotism and which strain of Campbells had been our ancestors. I believe I mentioned that ugly event early in this journal. It is true that some of Thomas' uncles raised the issue, but Mrs. Henderson voiced it. It was doubly irritating and glaringly plain that she had not been raised in a genteel fashion, and had had no training in dealing with servants. Who was she to question my lineage!

Wednesday, April 25, 1860

I was later to learn that indeed Mrs. Henderson had come from a home with no servants and little grace. Her father had sent her to a tutoress in the neighborhood where proper posture and an elegant stride had been instilled, along with, I suppose, the protocol of sauce dishes. But I doubt she had much reading or writing. She was groomed to marry "up," a deed she accomplished as Mr. Henderson was considered a member of the local gentry. Her natural beauty had surely afforded her greater advantage than the poor imitation of a polishing school.

Thomas and I had an autumn of courtship punctuated by precious few visits to his parents' farm. The event I just described was the most ominous one, which at the time I attributed to nerves on the part of Mrs. Henderson, after all she was just beginning to know us and I would soon be in her family. In fact, I would not only be in the family, but in her household, for Thomas worked alongside his father, and there we would live. It was customary for a bride to join her husband's household, and if I had objected it would have made no difference. Women do as their husbands bid.

I did set my foot down concerning Rose. Pa had consented to her coming with me, and gave her to me as dowry. Of course she had been mine for some years, but this time the gift was binding and in writing. Mrs. Henderson was overjoyed to have another Negro on the property, and insisted she live with a family of field hands. I was having none of that. Rose had lived in my home with me, albeit in the garret, for much of her life, and I would not abide her sleeping on a pallet in a dirt-floored cabin amongst strangers! Mr. Henderson intervened and proclaimed Rose could live satisfactorily with house servants in a well chinked cabin with a board floor, just a few yards from the plantation house. Once his father had spoken, the matter was settled. Besides Rose and Romulus would probably be wed in no time flat. Rose had told me how Romulus had courted her while Thomas and I were courting, And Romulus had told Thomas the same. But if they had never said a word, the way they looked at one another spoke volumes. They needed our permission, of course, but we had no objections. Romulus, being the driver, had quarters in the barn. Well, not precisely in the barn, but a snug lean-to attached to it. It could be improved if they should marry; Thomas would see to it.

In February of 1822 Thomas and I were married in the parlor of Pa's home. With the land idle in winter, the entire neighborhood was free to join in the festivities. A light snow and icy sky were completely eclipsed by the warmth and gaiety around our hearth and table. My dear Thomas understood how shy I was about moving into his parents' home immediately after the ceremony, and had arranged for us to spend several days in a boarding house near Lincolnton, in what was advertised as a very private apartment. After the wedding feast he and I left for that place. I shall not attempt to describe our sojourn there, only to say that Thomas proved to be every bit as loving and gentle as I dreamt he would be. I was pleased to be his wife.

After this idyllic interlude we left for his parents' farm, stopping at Pa's to collect Rose and our belongings. Next to Pa, the most difficult farewell was bid to Cissy. Cissy who had cared for me as long as I could remember, Cissy who had made my wedding dress and it was a beauty, Cissy who had prepared me for the wifely duties of marriage, and from what I now know, I believe I was better prepared than most young ladies. Then Cissy had to part with Rose. Such weeping I had never heard! I promised Cissy we would visit often, as I was in a position to bring Rose whenever I wished. I doubted Pa would take Cissy to the Henderson farm, but I told them both it ought to be done for Cissy's peace of mind.

Thursday, April 26, 1860

April has near bout passed on by, and planting has settled down. Most everybody is back to their usual tasks, and now Master Isaac and his field hands ought to be able to handle the farming by theirselves. Miss Julia give me a book to read a week ago, and I has not had time to read beyond the title which is "Vanity Fair." It's a right fat book, but if I put my mind to it I ought to get it read before the next frenzy that come at harvest time.

I did not dream of Romulus two nights past, as I had hoped, but I did conjure him up in my wide awake mind. I was barely seventeen when Master Thomas come courting Miss Julia. Romulus was his driver, and never in my life had I seen such a bodacious fellow. He was a fine looking man all right, but what I first notice was the clothes he had on. He wore a sleek black coat cut short in front, long and flowing behind. Peeking out from the collar was a gold silk waistcoat, and around his neck he wore a stock with ruffles at the throat. He was dressed bout as smart as his master. When we was introduced, he doffed his beaver hat, and gave me a broad smile. I figured Master Thomas must be the richest man in Mecklenburg County to outfit his driver so. I later come to find out that Romulus was wearing his greeting and visiting clothes, and that most days he dressed more ordinary, but always better than field hands. At Master Campbell's place we was all clothed pretty much alike. I had a heap to learn about the world.

It wasn't long before Romulus got to seeking out my company, and I noticed there was a good man behind them crisp white ruffles. He was long about twenty-five years old, and had been bought by Master Henderson a few years before. Romulus was raised in Virginia first by an old gentleman and then his son who taught him how to keep horses fit and healthy, carriages in good repair, and most of all how to be mannerly around white folks. When his masters die, Romulus and most of the other nigras was put up for sale. Bout that time Master Henderson was getting rich from cotton, and had gone up to Virginia to buy him some more help. When he see how Romulus was trained to take care of horses and behave gentlemanly, he buy him for his wife. She'd be the envy of the neighborhood to have such a person to bow and stoop for her.

If Romulus was unhappy at Master Henderson's place, he didn't let on, but he did allow he had no idea what become of his family, as most everyone on the old plantation was sold off to the four directions of the wind. He got right grim when I asked him that part, and plain did not want to talk about it; I had sense enough to leave it lie. At first I hung back from putting my affections on Romulus. I did not want my heart broke if Master Thomas stopped coming around. But after a spell I could see that Master Thomas and Miss Julia was completely sweet on each other, and by and by Miss Julia was talking bout getting married. She promise me I would go with her when she marry, in fact she been telling me that my whole life. Nigras learn to be wary of such promises. We don't have no say in such things, and white women have little more. Before long their plan to marry was spread all around, and Romulus and I commenced serious courting. Turned out he was dragging his heels for the same reason I was.

Miss Julia and Master Thomas married in the cold of winter, and took me off to live on the Henderson farm. It was the hardest thing I ever done parting with Mam and Pappy, with my brothers, and with Mattie and Harry and their younguns – there was several by then. I got on my knees and thanked the good Lord for three things. First for Miss Julia who had always treat me well and would not let any harm come my way that was in her power to prevent. Second that Miss Julia promised to bring me home to see Mam and Pappy whenever she could. And third for Romulus who had come to love me as mightily as I loved him. If it weren't for them three things, I'd have cried me a whole ocean of tears.

I slipped right in with Master Henderson's black folks like a kitten to a hearth. Romulus being sweet on me caused them to warm up to me in no time flat. Miz Henderson turned out to be one mean woman, but it weren't long before I see everybody laughing at her behind their hands. She just full of squawk and vinegar, they say. She holler and fuss, and send Master Henderson off to beat some poor soul, but he don't never do it. He'd carry the so-called troublemaker back behind the barn and have a talking to, snapping his whip in the air, then he'd grin all sheepish and tell that person not to do no more whatever had riled his wife. My feet had hardly set down on Henderson land when I was told never to let on to no white person, not even Miss Julia, that Master Henderson didn't beat nothing but the air. I reckon that's something else I ought to tell her, now that all those folks is dead. She be pleased to hear it.

Friday, April 27, 1860

I mentioned that Pa gave Rose to me as dowry, but I neglected to tell the whole of it. Pa's generosity could not be contained. First there was a spirited horse and brass trimmed carriage, which was the conveyance that carried us on our brief wedding journey, and then on to the Henderson farm. In addition he presented me a trunk full of fashionable gowns that he had secretly engaged a dressmaker to produce during our courtship. I was to look the part of a proper mistress in my new abode. And finally he added to the silver flatware I had been collecting for several years. It was an extravagant dowry, especially for the daughter of a middling farmer. (Perhaps I should add a note about the silver. The pieces previously in my possession consisted of six teaspoons, every one a different design. They were given to me by my father, one each birthday since my sixteenth year. I regarded them as the beginnings of a hope chest, and as several had belonged to my mother, held them in high esteem. They are delicate, yet simply formed, and have rarely been used. These are the ever same spoons I have willed to my granddaughter and namesake, Julia. She has had so little acquaintance with her paternal heritage, I do hope she will appreciate them.)

I still had little sense of money or the value of things, and I was awed by Pa's magnanimity, but not alarmed. I assumed that his cotton crop, which by that time was in its fifth year, was providing grandly. It was providing well, but not that well. Pa, as usual, was exercising his mighty desire to shower his children with riches, and demonstrate to Mr. Henderson that Thomas had not married beneath himself. Mr. Henderson, of course, made no comment on the value of my dowry, and his wife would have wrinkled her nose had I brought the crown jewels into her home. Poor Pa had overextended himself once again, and I was completely naïve.

In the fall of that year Frank was enrolled at the University of North Carolina. Today one might think sixteen is a bit young for a college man, but then it was not so uncommon. Besides, Frank was a dedicated scholar who had extracted every bit of juice from Pleasant Retreat Academy. I had no notion, and neither did Frank, of the cost of a university education.

I have written little recently about the activity here on Adie's place, as there is nothing extraordinary to comment on. The scurry of preparing the land is over, and planting continues a-pace. Isaac and his hands stay busy from sunrise to dusk, and the rest have returned to their usual duties. That is as it should be. I have become so engrossed in this journal, and the memories it evokes, that I fear I am neglecting my duties as a grandmother. Rebecca and Benjamin are absent in the forenoon, as they are taken to a nearby plantation where they are tutored with a collection of neighborhood children. It would behoove me to spend more mornings with little Matthew, although Vinia has nothing else to do other than chase him about. Just before midday dinner the older children are fetched from their tutorage, and we all dine together, including Isaac if it is convenient for him to come in. After dinner Vinia settles Matthew down for a nap, and Adie and I help the others with their lessons. I supervise Benjamin in his reading and writing, for that is what I enjoy, and Adie instructs Rebecca in sewing. Lately Adie has added piano lessons to Rebecca's curriculum, a skill considered essential for a prosperous marriage. The child is only ten, but Adie believes it is never too early to prepare for the future. Rebecca enjoys her music, so I shall keep my opinions to myself.

In the late afternoons I generally sit on the porch with my journal while the children romp in the yard. Sometimes they scamper up to me for a warm snuggle, and ask what I'm writing. I've shared some tales of my childhood with them, omitting the details inappropriate for their innocent minds. I've told them I'm writing everything down so when they are grown they will have the entire story. Such are my days, one very much like another, yet they are pleasant.

I believe Rose has settled in to a more comfortable routine. When we began this journal business, I thought it best to keep Rose's participation private. I did not want to incite Adie's disapproval, nor rekindle the idea that I am a closeted abolitionist. Whenever Frank visits he re-informs everyone of the fuss I made at the lawyer's office when we wrote my will. This upsets Isaac, for his reputation would surely be in jeopardy if it were rumored that he was harboring a Yankee sympathizer; after all, I live here at his mercy and am not of his blood. When Isaac gets roused, Adie goes into a near tizzy. The entire display is most uncomfortable. My convictions are strong, but I am an old woman, and not one to take a podium. There is no point in discord if it will accomplish nothing.

At first it was a simple matter for Rose to read and write when she could snatch a bit of time. We were all so busy in late March and early April that no one noticed what another did with his scant leisure. But when the schedule lightened it became more difficult. Rose began puttering about the house, dusting, straightening, complaining she had no useful purpose, then when Vinia was occupied with the children, Rose would quietly retreat to their room. Adie asked why she spent so much time there, and I said perhaps she had mending to do, or felt the need of some rest. But Adie heard Rose's mutterings and suggested Rose help out in the kitchen if she wanted to be useful, an idea I firmly rejected, for I knew precisely what the problem was. Rose was as anxious as I to work on the story of her life, and she was keen to bury herself in the books I borrowed from Isaac's library, but not cloistered like a Nun, not always vigilant for the unexpected visitor to her room. My insistence that she keep her literacy secret was frustrating Rose no end.

So I gathered up my gumption and told Adie what we were up to, and that she was not to interfere, for Rose was mine to direct as I saw fit. "But Ma, it's against the law!" bellowed Adie. As I suspected she was appalled that Rose had not unlearned reading when that abominable rule was passed.

"No," I replied, "I believe the law pertains to <u>teaching</u> Negroes, not suppressing those who have already learned." I said this with bold conviction for Adie's benefit. I've no idea what the law actually says. I suppose one would be passed requiring holes to be drilled in black brains to empty out their every thought if that were possible! I continued, "If you truly want Rose to be useful perhaps you ought to have her teach the catechism to your little darkies!"

Then Adie surprised me. She said, "Well, I suppose that would be acceptable if she teaches them only to recite it, but they are not to read, I forbid it." So we agreed. Rose may read and write openly if she wishes, but she is not to flaunt her ability before the other Negroes, nor teach them her skills. We concluded to say nothing to Isaac or Frank. Isaac is seldom in the house between meals, and is preoccupied with his own affairs. And Frank is here rarely. They pay Rose little mind. Nevertheless, I asked her to be discreet in their presence. It would serve no purpose to raise Isaac's ire. I doubt he would evict us against Adie's wishes, yet "Addled Adie" bows to his every whim; I needn't take that chance. As for Frank, of course he knows Rose is literate, after all I taught them together. Certainly Frank is not so naïve as to think Rose has forgotten her lessons, if he thinks on it at all which is unlikely. It grieves me to see how spirited Frank has become about the possibility of war, and the necessity to control every aspect of Negro behavior to prevent insurrection. I wish Frank was a more sensible man.

Saturday, April 28, 1860

Well here I is setting on the porch writing out in the open. Miss Julia tell me she has made new rules, and I do appreciate not having to harbor such a secret. This evening after supper I'll be allowed to teach the Lord's truth to the little black children. Hallelujah! None of Master Isaac's people can read. Those that goes to church tries to teach the little ones, but some things they gets mixed up. It's hard to keep straight what you've learned only with your ears.

Now back to what I was writing. Not long after I go to Master Henderson's place, Romulus asked could he marry me. Master Henderson give his permission, for I reckon he figured I was now owned by Master Thomas, not Miss Julia, and therefore belong to their place. Miss Julia say that not true, for the paper her Pappy had wrote give me to her and no one else. It didn't make no difference long as Master Thomas is alive, but should he die, I was to stay Miss Julia's property no matter what. I wouldn't never belong to the Henderson kinfolk. Miss Julia say not to talk about that unless it come up. So Master Henderson allowed us to jump the broom, as weddings been called since Africa times, and one of his hands who claimed to be a preacher-man presided over the doings. We got ourselves joined the first Saturday night in April; being that it's April now, I reckon that was near bout forty years ago. Master Henderson give us a plumb splendorous feast and even a little corn whiskey. I bet old Miz Henderson grumbled something powerful. After the white folks' supper was carried in the house, they had to serve theirselves while listening to us frolic in the quarter, whooping and hollering long into the night.

I moved into the cabin that Romulus stay in, the one attach to the barn, and Master Thomas and Master Henderson, true to their word, had it fixed up for us. Romulus' little cot was hauled off and a bed big enough for the two of us was brought in. They give me some calico to make window curtains, and bits of crockery to stack in the cupboard. Master Henderson give us a chest for our clothes and bed linens, not a cast-off from a slave cabin, but one from the big house. It was a handsome piece with swirls and flowers painted in green and blue and gold. He say it was our wedding gift. That be the finest piece of furniture I ever seen in a cabin, and I still got it to this day. Those was mighty happy days, as long as I stay clear of Miz Henderson. Romulus was the finest kind of husband. He didn't waste no time in his duty, and on Christmas eve I bore him a baby boy we named Marc. You would have thought we invented the whole business we was so proud!

Sunday, April 29, 1860

Another wet and windy Sunday; two in a row! Yet it is quite chilly for late April, which until now has been unusually warm. We attended Sabbath services this morning, but due to the inclement weather we concluded not to stay for the afternoon sermon. We returned home, had dinner, and I have retired to my room to work in my journal. This morning we had a brief visit with Frank who was on one of his tears, so it pleased me not to linger the entire day in town. I dare say he carries on more than any worrisome old woman I have ever seen. His rant today concerns the Democrat Party, which convened last Monday in

Charleston to nominate a candidate for president. Frank predicts a squabble of grand proportions, although how he figures this is a complete mystery. The meeting has barely begun, and little of the proceedings have reached us. "Take my word," Frank proclaimed. "The southern and northern Democrats are hopelessly severed over the issue of slavery, and those who espouse a middle ground are trusted by neither extreme. It's an ill wind, dear Sister, an ill wind." Then he began to opine about the new party, the Republicans who are to meet next month, and not to count them out. Can the Republicans be taken seriously? I've barely heard of them.

You may be surprised to learn that in spite of Frank's bluster on the matter, he owns no Negroes. Not from conviction, of course, but for convenience. He generally hires from other owners a woman to cook and clean, and a young man to assist in his practice. In January he engages each of them by contract for a year, and the contracts are renewed year by year until he considers the poor souls have outlived their usefulness. Then someone new is engaged. He simply does not want to be saddled with their lifelong care, which is not unusual for a bachelor who does not farm. Frank has no qualms about separating these poor creatures from their families, which I consider cruel exploitation. I rarely encounter Frank's servants, for we generally see him only on Sundays, a day he thankfully permits them to visit their kin. Now on with my story.

It was awkward at best being a new bride on the Henderson place. I thank the Lord it was mid-winter and Thomas had leisure to spend with me. By the time planting commenced I had determined to try to ignore Mrs. Henderson's barbs, although they still cut to the quick. I reminded myself that despite her physical beauty and poise, she was bereft of inner grace from lack of training, no fault of her own. I found it supreme irony that my upbringing, which I considered far superior to hers, was conducted almost entirely by Cissy, a Negro woman Mrs. Henderson would have considered beneath contempt.

In April with Mr. Henderson's permission Rose and Romulus were married. I was overjoyed for them, for they both seemed eager to wed. I stood with the family on the porch and watched the ceremony conducted on the lawn by one of their own. It lacked the solemnity of white weddings, and was imbued instead with joyful and noisy celebration. I took that to be a facet of Negro emotionalism, not a dearth of seriousness or commitment to the sanctity of marriage. After they jumped the broom and were declared man and wife we went inside to our supper while the Negroes continued their frivolity. When our meal was done I retired to my room and watched them from the window.

In the yard, boards were placed across sawhorses to make long tables which were laden with food. An entire ham had been allotted for the feast as well as a goose and a large platter of fried fish. There were numberless pies filled variously with chicken or onions or apples or sweet potatoes and other good things. Although the yard was well lit by smudgy torches, I could not identify the victuals from my window, but knew their assortment from visiting the kitchen earlier in the day. Mr. Henderson had even provided some whiskey, which was permitted the Negroes on only the most festive of occasions. I watched them whoop and sing and dance, all ages joining in. Rose and Romulus were the center of attention, beaming and laughing, their bright teeth glinting in the torch light. Any guilt I may have had over wresting Rose from her family was permanently assuaged. During our supper Mrs. Henderson complained bitterly about the drunkenness that was bound to ensue, and declared that all the outbuildings would surely be burned to the ground by morning. Her husband was unconcerned. The next morning, a Sabbath, dawned bright and clear with the entire plantation intact. Little was required of the Negroes on their day of rest; if any of them suffered from overindulgence, I did not know of it.

It was only two months later that Rose confided to me that she suspected she was carrying a child. I was supremely happy for her, yet my enthusiasm was tempered by the fact that I had been married several months longer than she, and had nothing to show for it. Mrs. Henderson had already commented that a barren woman was a useless creature and a burden. I hugged Rose and congratulated her, and hoped she did not notice my restraint.

Monday, April 30, 1860

I cannot begin to describe how happy I was to be Thomas' wife. As I have said he was the most gentle and tender husband who wanted children as much as I did. Nevertheless, I was constantly frustrated by not promptly producing an infant. Thomas comforted me and held me tenderly. "Be patient my sweet Julia, I'm sure we shall soon have a child, but if we do not, my love for you won't change one whit." He kissed my brow and drew me even closer. God has ordained that women are to bear children, and nurture them for His glory. Month after month my time came, leaving me fraught with bitter disappointment. I did not share this most private information with my mother-in-law, but somehow she seemed to know. Did I wear my failure on my face, or was the woman possessed of supernatural knowledge? She even had the audacity to speak of it. Rose did my personal laundry, and would not deign to reveal my situation, yet month after month on the very day my time commenced, Thomas' mother would say, "Not yet in the family way, I see; such a pity!"

Meanwhile I watched Rose's belly swell and her face glow from the joy of a child within. Not all Negroes are so cheerful in her situation. Presenting their owners with additional human chattel is an onus for some, I'm sure. But for most, the natural inclination toward maternal affection is overpowering. I was delighted that Rose welcomed motherhood. I had seen a shade of the more ominous attitude in her sister Mattie, who continued to multiply at Pa's place. The bloom of being newly wed had faded, and her sullenness had returned. I felt sorry for Mattie, sorry that she could not find more pleasure in life. It would be several more years before I would feel fury on her behalf.

Finally in September I conceived, seven long months after my marriage. Of course it wasn't until October that I had a hint, and November that I was convinced enough to announce the fact. Mrs. Henderson could not be pleased. She said haughtily, "It's about time!" Then filled my head with folklore. An infant conceived with such difficulty was bound to be weak or deformed, probably would not live, might not even be born alive. I was to watch myself, and regard the phases of the moon, and be careful the way I held a knife, or cup, or most anything that came to hand. Even Cissy had no truck with such flagrant superstition. And the woman proclaimed to be of the Christian faith! My intellect told me to ignore her, yet I was young, inexperienced, and frightened by her tirades.

I endeavored to concentrate my life around Thomas, proud as a peacock, and Rose whose time was approaching. On Christmas Eve she bore a son and named him Marc. When Marc was a few weeks old Rose returned to my service, bringing her infant to my room where she tended to my laundry, or brushed and aired my gowns. She let me hold him as she worked. He was a beautiful child, and I can't express the pleasure it gave me to cuddle one fragrant infant in my arms, while another was beginning to quicken within. Was it cold that winter? I have no idea. I was completely preoccupied. Rose and I worked together on light chores in the bedchamber that Thomas and I shared. Dusting, sweeping, tending to our wardrobes and chamber pots. There was not much more to do. I was determined that Mrs. Henderson respect Rose as my property. Every time she announced that she required Rose's services, I politely replied that it was not possible, as she was fully occupied with my needs. Thomas and Mr. Henderson conceded to my wishes, which made no impression on my mother-in-law. Over and over she demanded Rose's assistance, I refused, and Mr. Henderson concurred. In spite of her ornery temperament, she was not one to defy her husband, although she expected to eventually wear him down. The dance continued as long as we lived in her home.

She would have been furious indeed had she known how little Rose and I worked. We spent untold hours cooing over Marc, washing him, changing his diaper napkins, watching him grow from day to day. We giggled over his first smile, the day he turned himself over, when he began to grasp with his chubby little hands, and when he taught himself to belly-creep across the floor. Rose and I talked endlessly, almost girlishly, while she nursed him. I can still see her sitting in my rocking chair, Marc pressed to her bosom, snuffling and snorting like a tiny pig. Those happy hours were only broken by the necessity for me to appear at the dinner table and listen to Mrs. Henderson rant on that my abdomen was not the right size, or shape, that I was too pale, or yellow, or sallow, anything negative.

It was during that winter that Mrs. Henderson was poisoned, or nearly so. It was no amazement to me that one of the Negroes would grind some noxious herb into her food; after all she was terribly cruel to all of them, at least in word if not by deed. I've no idea who the perpetrator was, as so many of them possessed knowledge of voodoo and poisonous substances. The poor soul was violently ill for days, and the doctor was concerned that she might expire. However, she did not, not that I wished for her death in spite of her mean spirit. All of the Negroes were questioned by Mr. Henderson, and their cabins were searched for potions, but no clue was ever found, and the deed went unpunished. Of course Rose and I speculated as to how the old woman had come to be poisoned, and Rose was irate that I assumed the culprit to be a Negro. Who else would have done such a thing! Perhaps it was a novel idea to Rose as poisonings by Negroes were unusual then. One hears about them with some frequency nowadays.

From reading this, one might surmise that my mother-in-law was the only other white woman on the place. I believe I mentioned that Thomas had a brother who lived on the farm with his wife. Their house was elsewhere on the plantation, some distance from the main house. The wife, whose name was Susan, was nearly a decade older than I. They kept to themselves and rarely joined us at the table. Susan had only one child, and was thereby a great disappointment to our mother-in-law. Susan had turned avoidance of Mrs. Henderson into a fine art, consequently I saw her seldom and we never became close. Two of Thomas' younger sisters had married by this time, one a few months before our nuptials, the other just after, and were living elsewhere. Each had a new infant, a fact I was constantly reminded of, and were therefore unable to visit. His youngest sister had completed her schooling at Salem, and had been enrolled in a Philadelphia boarding school. She left the Henderson farm shortly after I arrived, and I had not seen her since. Nor had I seen much of Essie, Thomas' married sister who lived at Leeper's Creek and seemed to prefer to keep close to home. So, yes, on most days Mrs. Henderson was the only white woman in my sphere.

My confinement came in the middle of May, just after planting time when everyone was occupied far and wide nurturing new sprouts. When my pains commenced in earnest one morning, Rose found a little black girl to watch Marc while she went looking for Thomas. It took her some time to locate him, and for him to come in from the field, saddle a horse, and go for the midwife. I suppose there were several Negroes on the property who could have assisted me, but Mrs. Henderson would not hear of it. A widow who lived about four miles of our place was the midwife of choice. She had delivered Mrs. Henderson's other daughter-in-law, and no one else would do. I had so little knowledge, and no experience with childbirth; I dared not object.

After Rose dispatched Thomas on his errand she came to stay by my side. By then my distress was great, and Rose declared the birth seemed near at hand. I could sense her anxiety that the midwife might not arrive in time, but she squelched it with a firm voice as she dispatched Mrs. Henderson to the kitchen for pails of water, both steaming and cool, and a supply of clean linens. If I had not been in such pain I would have laughed out loud hearing my sweet servant barking orders to our common enemy! All afternoon and evening Rose bathed my face and shoulders with cool cloths between agonizing surges. When the pains swelled, she grasped my wrists and commanded me to take hers;

arms locked, I anchored myself against her mighty strength while pushing with all my own to bring forth my child, each time convinced I might expire before the ordeal was over. Between these struggles came blessed relaxation, and Rose stroked my wrists and hands and trembling fingers, and soothed me with her words. "I know how it hurt, Miss Julia, but it soon be over. That child be here in no time. I feel it coming." She crooned as she massaged and pressed my abdomen, "I thought I bout to die when Marc come, but soon as I couldn't take no more, the good Lord brung him out, all satisfied, bleating like a little lamb." Over and over, the waves marched as across a stormy ocean, each more treacherous than the last, day into evening, evening into night. And when I was sure I could bear no more, just as Rose said, the child was born. Did it take courage for her black hands to deliver a white infant from my privacy? I've no idea. But I'm sure it was on that day that Rose and I truly became sisters under the skin; other than Thomas, I have never been so intimate with another human being.

Had I the luxury of reason, I might have been concerned about Rose's inexperience in the process. She had borne Marc, witnessed Mattie's birthings and several others in the quarter (where Mrs. Henderson would not indulge a midwife!), but that was all. I suppose I instinctively trusted her devotion and good common sense. In spite of the uncertain nature of childbirth, I knew Rose would not fail me.

In the fullness of time Thomas returned with the midwife. It turned out the woman was attending another birth, and it took him hours to locate her, then he had to wait until that child was safely delivered before he could bring her to me. It was well after midnight when Thomas arrived with her to greet his little son. The midwife examined me to see that the birth had concluded properly, and carefully looked over the infant and pronounced him healthy. Thomas let the poor woman sleep the night with us, for she was as nearly drained as I. The next morning she examined me and the babe again, found nothing amiss, and Thomas took her home. When he returned we spent the rest of the day marveling over our creation, our baby Tom, named for his exuberant father.

Monday, April 30, 1860

After my baby Marc was borned, I tend to Miss Julia who was carrying a child of her own. We spent most of our days in her room whiling away the time, carrying on over Marc, and talking up a storm. It was a fine winter for us; I reckon frolicking after my baby made us almost like kinfolks. Until that old lady Miz Henderson near bout got herself pisened. Miss Julia allowed she was plumb certain some nigra give her pisen, and that's what tore up her gut. True, the woman was purely sick to death, but I know for a fact that none of us done it. Ain't nobody so brazen to take on the wrath of his master as well the good Lord hisself. I tell Miss Julia that old Miz Henderson done took a fever, or ate something rotten, as I has seen plenty in the quarter near bout as sick, and 'tis a fact we don't pisen each other. Well, she wouldn't have none of it. She say some nigras has a "natural inclination to do in their masters, a proven trait of the black race." I give up trying to argue with her, cause I couldn't change her mind. How she could be so sensible about me, and harbor such notions about other black folks, I will never understand.

Well the old lady recovered, and me and Miss Julia got back to our old selves carrying on over my Marc and her growing belly, but her notion about pisening left a bitter pit in my heart. I love Miss Julia, but sometimes I don't like her much. That's how it is with kinfolk.

When I tell Romulus Miss Julia don't give me no real work to do, he just laugh. I didn't tell nobody else, for that would just stir up trouble. At suppertime Marc and I would go to our cabin, and old Romulus would rock that child in his arms, and prattle on, all high pitched and sing-song. That the happiest I ever see that man be. When planting time come, Romulus was put to the fields, and I could see hurt and gall boil up in him. He weren't no field hand and it made him ill as a hornet to be treated like one. I tell him everybody got to help plant, he know that! And he say he don't see me out there a-hoeing. Well, I says, I gots me a new baby. And he growl, tain't that new. Then I let on how Miss Julia's time bout to come, and somebody has to look out for her, and I should have knowed by then to keep my mouth shut, for every word I say, make it more obvious he is working, and I ain't.

I reckon that's the first time I see Romulus take the misery, and it was a sorry sight. I couldn't figure what it was I was supposed to do. If I spent more time in the cabin trying to be a good wife and Mam, he'd fuss that I was the only one on the place with no work to do. Then I'd stay longer in the big house, and he'd grumble that I was neglecting him to chatter with that white woman. I tell Miss Julia that I was afraid Romulus was taking the misery like Mattie had done, and she tell me to do what I thought best. She need me for a few hours each morning and afternoon, otherwise my time was my own. She'd stand up to Miz Henderson if need be. She say this with a light flip of the hand, like the misery was no worse than a bad cold that runs its course in a week. She have no idea.

Did I say that I brung Miss Julia's baby into the world? I'd seen a birthing or two, but never before did I bring a child all by myself! I can tell you both of us was mighty proud. When little Tom come out all fat and sassy, hollering to beat anything, Miss Julia and I just hugged and cried. After I got her and the baby washed up, and him tucked in her arms, I go downstairs to tell Miz Henderson she have a grandson. That old woman was pacing up and down the parlor, whimpering about the midwife and whatever could be keeping that woman, and I say we don't need her no more. Well she harrumph that a baby come as quick as that must be weak and spindly and she'd send for the doctor. And I say, "No ma'am, that baby all pink and round and has a mighty pair of lungs!" She was confounded and bewildered that Miss Julia and I brought him by ourselves, as if the child ought to have sense enough to wait for the midwife. She'd had enough younguns of her own to know better'n that. Well, she clomp up the stairs and see Miss Julia lying all peaceful like with little Tom by her side. Miss Julia look at the old bat, and smile a smug little smile that say now I'm in charge of my life and won't have no more truck with you.

By and by Romulus got back to grooming horses and carriage-polishing and carrying white folks around. He seemed a speck more peaceful, but me being all caught up with Marc and Miss Julia's baby Tom, I didn't take no notice that it was only a speck.

Later on, when I look back on that time, I figure I ought to had seen the misery coming. Right after we jump the broom Romulus and I was both put to the fields. I was so pleased at myself being a wife, I took sparse notice of how Romulus act. He didn't complain with words, but he put away his broad grin for a jutted chin and steely eyes. When planting was done and I wash his field clothes, he told me to shove them under the mattress where he didn't have to look at them. When harvest come that year, my confinement was nigh, so I was tasked to the kitchen for sausage making. By the time we got to the cabin at the end of the day, both of us was too tired for anything but sleep. I should have seen trouble coming, but I was too tired, too young, and too blind.

May, 1860

Another month has commenced. I indulged myself yesterday reading over what I have written here and am pleased with my progress.

After my precious Tom was born I gained a modicum of self assurance, and ventured more often from my room. I began to sit in the parlor with my mother-in-law, nursing my infant, trying to demonstrate that I was a competent mother. I had desperately hoped that an infant's natural charm would soften Mrs. Henderson so the two of us could aspire to a mother and daughter style kinship. Acquiring such a difficult woman for a mother-in-law was a great disappointment as I had known my own mother so briefly, and remembered her so dimly. As a young girl I had fervently wished to marry a man whose mother would be an affectionate confidante, a pattern for my own motherhood. I would have hated Mrs. Henderson had I any notion that her bitterness gave her pleasure, but it did not, so instead I pitied her when I was able, anytime bereft of a fresh wound she had inflicted.

During my first year of marriage I honored my promise to visit Pa. I went as often as possible with Rose in tow, even after Marc was born. I can't give you any idea of the pleasure that exuded from Cissy upon holding Marc. Mattie's children were a constant presence, but Cissy rarely saw her grandchildren on other plantations. Her sons, like Mattie's husband Harry, had aligned themselves with women on other farms, and as was the custom among the Negroes, men made marital visits; women and children stayed at home. Those unions produced grandchildren that Cissy saw on occasional Sabbaths, never enough to satisfy her.

I sensibly curtailed those visits when my confinement approached and for a while afterwards, as it is painful, as well as dangerous, to travel when the birth is nigh or before one's healing is complete. I desperately wished to introduce our "little stranger" to my father, but put off the visit until I thought it prudent. That is until my "devoted mother-in-law" whom I was trying so hard to win over went on one of her vicious sprees. I had just completed feeding my infant and was swaddling his blanket about him, admiring his contented coos, when from over my shoulder she bellowed, "What ever are you doing?" I opened my mouth, yet before a word could form: "The poor child is starving to death, can't you see how gaunt he is?" She snatched him from my arms, letting his blankets drift to the floor. "Look at him, skin and bones, pale as a fish belly." She lifted poor Tom in the air and placed her ear to his stomach. "He's gurgling, can't possibly be satisfied. I should have known you wouldn't have milk enough, both of you thin as rails." By then Tom had begun to howl from the loss of his blanket, from being waved about in the air. I was too stunned to speak, and she continued her tirade. "I suppose I shall have to find a wet nurse in the quarter. Nigger milk will surely enfeeble his brain, but at least he'll be kept alive."

Now I was livid. I grabbed up the blanket, rose on my newly self-sufficient feet, and wrested my infant from his grandmother's arms. Harsh words leapt unbidden from my lips. I have no recollection of what they were, as I was completely unaccustomed to rough language, and never spoke sharply, even to her. I don't know how long I stood there trembling, clutching Tom to my breast; it could not have been long, although it seemed an eternity.

Rose, always at my hand, witnessed the entire tawdry scene. As soon as I recovered a modicum of sense, I dispatched her to have Romulus prepare the carriage; we were going home. I stormed up the stairs and in no time at all, I had a valise packed for Tom and myself, and off we went. Pa was pleased and surprised to see us rounding the bend with no prior announcement, Rose, Romulus, and me, and our two infants. By then he was well acquainted with Mrs. Henderson's behavior, so the explanation for our unexpected visit was not without precedent. Pa was simply thrilled to meet his first grandchild. In fact he had planned to visit us the following week, and I had saved him the trouble.

About dusk Thomas rode up on his horse, by then having heard of the trouble. Poor Thomas, browbeaten by a difficult mother his entire life; I was yet to learn the toll it had taken on him. He decided we should remain with my father for a few days, then return home as if nothing had happened. After all, the time had come for the child to visit his grandfather. By then Thomas' mother would have forgotten the entire episode, if she had noticed to begin with.

During Tom's first year on earth we visited Pa frequently, and I will be forever grateful that is was a short and easy journey which enabled us to do so. Not all of our sojourns were prompted by Mrs. Henderson's outbursts, but many were. Those interludes with my dear father were a most welcome respite from her difficult nature, and unbeknownst to me, I had not much longer to enjoy his precious society.

Thursday, May 3, 1860

I been reading Mr. Thackeray's book that Miss Julia give to me. There are many things confounding about it, which I reckon would be plain if I lived in England, but I do not. I told Miss Julia that Mr. Thackeray ought to be shamed of hisself writing bout that Black Sambo fellow grinning and bowing and scraping, like he was some old black clown. I thought English folks got over slavery a long time ago. She say Mr. Thackeray was making fun of the so-called rich and cultured class. He made buffoons of all of them, and was depicting Sambo as his pompous employer would regard him. "Depicting and pompous" was the words she use. I do believe my writing is improving, which I credit to reading.

Miss Julia and I have been talking about those fair old days when we flitted to and fro from Master Henderson's place to her Pa's farm, carrying our little first borns. It made my heart proud to see Mam and show off my baby Marc. Mam, she act like she never seen such a child before, her all laughing and squealing. One might conclude I was a lucky slave to see so much of my Mam, but there ain't nothing lucky about being a slave. Nothing at all. Come October, when Marc was near a year old, and Tom about half a year, harvest come and Romulus was back to the fields and not given permission to drive us cept for a rare Sunday now and again. And sure as rain, he took the misery. I was beginning to see that each time the misery come, it was worse than the time before.

Most Sundays Miz Henderson claimed she needed Romulus, being she was denied his service during the week. Then she'd have him drive her to her daughters' places, or somewhere, just make up any old excuse. He'd drive, and she'd sit behind him gussied up to beat all, and rant and carry on about how the "niggers" on her place was the sorriest lot she'd ever seen. Every one of them lazy and good-for-nothing in her opinion, and poor Romulus would sit quiet and listen and boil up inside. Of course he was doing this vile work while the others were having their day of rest. I reckon that was enough to give anybody the misery. On those few Sundays when Master Thomas stomped down his foot and told his Mam that Miss Julia had to go see her Pappy, Romulus drove us, glum as usual, not able to get that old biddy off his mind. Miss Julia and I would carry on cheerful and tickle our babies, trying to get a smile from him, but it hardly ever worked.

Romulus was my special breed of cross to bear, and during them years I come to know why Mam had fretted so over Mattie. There was nothing either of us could do about slavery, but we would have given over our souls to make Mattie and Romulus into happier people. I loved Romulus with all my heart, which just broke in two to see him suffer so. I struggled over that for many a year.

His misery let up a bit once we got to Mam's place, her and Pappy so glad to see us, especially little Marc. Those was some happy days. When Miss Julia's little family got all settled in with her Pappy, she'd give us the rest of the day off. A whole bunch of us would pile in the carriage and go visit my brothers' wives and children. What a sight that was, Master Henderson's fancy carriage filled with nothing but black folks, Romulus driving us, me and Mam and Pappy, sometime Mattie and Harry and their younguns, or some assortment of my brothers. Couldn't all of us fit in at one time, nor could we visit all them places in one day, so we took turns. Romulus was nigh on to cheerful when he drove that carriage full of us! I don't imagine any white family had more fun than we did. If only I could have saved them days in a box tied up tight with a ribbon.

Friday, May 4, 1860

There is little to report of Adie and Isaac's household. The weather has been fine, boding promise for the new crop. The children are in good health and continue as usual with their studies, music, &c. Should the weather hold, I suppose we will spend the entire Sabbath in town (two days hence), and hear more from Frank about the political doings in Charleston and the general discontent. I pray that the prospect of war is a cruel illusion.

Tom's first year was uneventful except for visits to my father and the hurtful taunts of Mrs. Henderson, a topic I've probably exhausted. The next year, 1824, my brother Frank finished his college studies and returned home. He announced that he had obtained a position to study under a doctor in Lincolnton. He had longed to be a physician for some years, and now his dream was to become reality. I'm sure Pa harbored some dim hope that Frank might join him on the farm, now that Jeff was dead, after all the cotton business was growing beyond anyone's expectations. But Pa had not provided Frank's extensive education for no purpose, and took pride in the boy's decision. Perhaps after his training Frank would move back to the family home and be a country doctor. At least Pa could dream.

I, however, did not see Frank being wrested away from city life, if one could call Lincolnton a city, perhaps village life is a better term. I tried to convince Thomas that we should move in with my father. He had plenty of room, and it seemed unlikely that Frank would ever live there again. Thomas' brother was certainly the heir apparent to the Henderson place. But Thomas was fervently committed to his father, and would not be persuaded to budge. This gave me great distress for I was beginning see Mrs. Henderson's behavior had taken its toll on my husband.

Thomas confided to me that he had never been able to please her. From his earliest days she had belittled him, instilled in him that his every move was inadequate: He did not assert himself, was not strong enough, bold enough, ambitious enough, &c., &c. With my own ears I heard her call him a "spineless little twit" over some trifling matter. What a horrible indignity for a grown man to suffer from his mother! The first year or so of our marriage I had been so preoccupied with my barrenness, then the wonderful gift of an infant, that I had not noticed how Thomas was pulled and torn by his parents. Mr. Henderson was an affectionate and delightful man. One could not wish for a more genial father-in-law. But he was a grasping sort of person. He insisted that he needed Thomas to procure supplies and market the cotton, for even then Thomas' innate talent for the business end of farming was apparent. Thomas reveled in the attention. His father's genuine admiration of Thomas' expertise seemed to balance (just barely) his mother's complete disdain. Why Thomas' brother was not party to this madness is a thing I've never completely fathomed. As I have said, his brother lived quite apart from the family. I assume he recognized the macabre performance for what it was and refused to participate. In any event Thomas felt sorely needed by his father, and was sure that if he worked hard enough he would win his mother's praises – which of course would never happen. Mr. Henderson seemed oblivious to his peculiar wife, and seemed to cherish her in spite of her shortcomings.

Saturday, May 5, 1860

I am writing in my room this afternoon, although it is a fine day outside. The year I shall address next was a sad one, and should I shed tears, I prefer my innocent grandchildren not see them. "Grandma needs to rest," I told them. As they seem to think I am older than the moon, they are not surprised. The year of which I speak was 1825.

I had discovered the previous December that I was to have another child, which was joyous news. Little Tom was thriving (despite Mrs. Henderson's assessment), and my own health was vigorous, at least in the beginning. We drove to Lincoln County with some regularity, and Pa, though nearing his sixtieth year, was in fine health and spirits. On each visit he boasted of prosperity, and displayed some new purchase he had made. He owned the finest farm equipment, and every few years he replaced his carriage with a fancier one. His house always wore a fresh coat of paint, and nearly every time I entered it, I spied a new piece of carpet or furniture. Greene, who had been deemed too old for the field, was at work on a pleasure garden. Pa had obtained information from the Agricultural Society about the hardiest species of shrubs and flowers, and was studying an English book on fashionable landscape design. He was sparing no expense in creating an elegant display.

Late one evening in mid-March of 1825, Thomas and I were preparing for bed when we heard a knock at the door. Mr. Henderson answered, and though the voices were muffled that traveled up the staircase, I recognized that it was Rose's brother Caesar at the door. I grabbed a dressing gown and ran down the stairs dreading bad news about Greene or Cissy; Pa would never send Caesar out in the night unless there was some emergency. And there was. Pa was dead. Gentle hearted Caesar was beside himself.

With lowered head and halting words he told us Pa had taken ill three days since, and the following day a putrid phlegm began to fill his lungs, choking and strangling him. "Yesterday he took a terrible turn, and I went to fetch Master Frank and that doctor he work for, cause we was mighty afraid." Then he paused and looked up. Tears were in his eyes. "Those two bled your Pa and made a plaster for his chest, then sat up with him all night long. I asked could I come get you this morning, but Master Frank said to wait a spell cause he thought for sure your Pa was getting better. But he never did. He passed this afternoon." Caesar wiped his eyes with his sleeve, "He didn't suffer too terrible, Miss Julia, didn't have no time to. And now Master Frank is tore up something awful." Poor Frank. He was new to this business of doctoring, and was only beginning to learn how wretchedly death can strike. His spirit was broken by the harshness of Pa's suffering, and his own impotence as a healer.

Thomas and I immediately packed up our little family and summoned Rose from her cabin. We went with Caesar in Pa's carriage to attend the sad duty of arranging the funeral. As we might be gone for several weeks getting Pa's estate in order, Romulus was not permitted to accompany us, much to Rose's distress. After a solemn service at Leeper's Creek Church we buried Pa in his selected spot between his two wives. It pained me to place him as near to Mrs. C. as he was to my dear mother, but I knew that was his wish, and held my peace.

After these mournful details were attended to, Thomas and brother Frank began to delve into Pa's affairs, and discovered more irregularity than we had any idea of. All of us knew Pa had lived beyond his means, but were completely unprepared to discover the gravity of his indebtedness. His desk was filled with unsecured and unpaid notes, some entered into years before. All those gentle people who had been too polite to press Pa for payment would now have to be satisfied. Not that we expected an onslaught of demands, but it was the proper thing to do. We all agreed on that point. I have said that Pa was a generous man, and his desk contained nearly as many notes for money owed to him. Nearly all of them we deemed uncollectible. His debtors were either dead, their estates long ago settled, or so poor we dared not press them. Over the years Loony Brown had borrowed over four hundred dollars. I doubt the man could count to four hundred, and would not earn so much if he lived to eternity. And all this time I thought Pa was only paying for whiskey!

First we arranged for an estate sale. This was the usual manner of clearing away a man's possessions, turning them into cash to meet his creditors and provide for his heirs. That part was easy. None of us had designs on the vast majority of the things Pa had acquired in recent years. We retained enough equipment and livestock to keep his farm intact, yet still sold a number of beasts as well as enough gear to run a small place. Pa's office was raked nearly bare. Most of its contents had come in as odd lots from other men's estates, and went out the same way. Except for the books, those I hoarded. We kept those household things that were meaningful to us, and shed ourselves of the miscellany of furniture, &c. that had accumulated during Pa's recent "prosperity." We even sold his fancy carriage, as the one he had given me as dowry had sat nearly useless in the Henderson barn these last several years; it would suffice, should we need a carriage. It was a very successful sale, yet a mountain of debt remained.

The difficult decisions lay ahead. Which of Pa's remaining assets (meaning land and people) would have to be sacrificed, and could anything be salvaged? It pained us to think the product of his life's work was nothing more than debt. Frank and Thomas made discreet inquiries into the current price of Negroes and the value of the land (Pa's farm had increased from about 300 to nearly 600 acres over the years). We concluded that if we bargained wisely, we could retain some of his assets, but what to sell and what to keep became a sticking point. Pa had provided well for Frank and me while he lived. We should have wanted for nothing. Yet should the debts be met, each of us had a personal desire that could only be realized with the residue of Pa's estate. I wanted badly to keep at least part of Pa's farm so Thomas and I could establish ourselves there. I had had more than enough of my mother-in-law's home, and Thomas, being in a mood to assuage my grief, surprisingly agreed to abandon his father's domain. Surely we could sell enough land to settle the debt and retain sufficient acres for a small farm. Pa had paid for Frank's education; what more could he possibly want? I suppose my condition clouded my thinking, for by now I was not carrying this child easily as I had Tom. Nausea that was mercifully absent during the early months, now raged. I was often light-headed, and my legs were painfully swollen. My deepest wish was to retire to my childhood home and be attended in peace by Rose and Thomas until my child was born.

Well, there was something more that Frank wanted, to attend the new medical school in Charleston. His current situation was adequate, but formal training would be of enormous advantage. Pa's illness had reinforced his desire to become a skilled physician who could be of genuine help to his patients, rather than a country doctor who could offer little more than lancets, pills, and comforting words. Of course Frank deserved a share of Pa's estate. I was a silly goose to think otherwise.

Frank's preference was to sell the Negroes which he thought would settle Pa's debts and pay for his medical schooling. That would leave the farm for Thomas and me, which suited Frank, as he had no interest in the land. At first I was dead set against selling Pa's people. What use was the farm to us with no hands to work it? I could not envision the farm without its people. And deep in my heart I could not bear to part with Cissy. Although she was only about fifty, I hoped no one would want to buy a Negro with so few useful years left. Thomas and Frank suggested we might be able to keep one or two of the boys, and Thomas could buy more hands once he made a crop. They had concluded the people were worth far more than the land, and therefore it was impossible to retain all of the Negroes. Even if we sold the entire farm we would still have to sell some people to erase Pa's debt and pay for Frank's schooling. Then what? I would be left with the remaining people to take back to the Henderson farm, for I would have nowhere else to go. There they would become Mr. Henderson's workers, of no advantage to Thomas and me, and at such a distance, it was doubtful that Mattie or her brothers would be allowed much contact with their spouses. In other words, sold or unsold, their fate would be virtually identical. At least that was the argument made to me, the one I succumbed to.

If only I had been well, not stressed by overwhelming grief, not hobbled by nausea and pain, not embarrassed by Pa's financial indiscretions. If only I had the ability to think ahead. We could have mortgaged the land (to a lender, not by the note of a friend), or rented it for a few years. We could have hired out the Negroes, which would have severed their families only temporarily. But I could not see beyond my own swollen ankles, beyond the here and now, and in the end I reluctantly relented. We did sell about two hundred acres, and we did decide to keep Cissy and Greene. This was not by way of compromise, but because some of the land had to go to make the pennies balance, and the old Negroes had very little value.

I have no words to express how deeply I regret that sorry turn of events, and the stupid decision Thomas and I made that allowed it to happen, even to this day.

Monday, May 7, 1860

I was too stressed and tired to write anything yesterday. We went to services in town, and Frank was filled with ominous news about the Democrat Convention in Charleston. It seems the men abandoned the entire proposition, being unable to agree on a candidate for the coming presidential election. Everyone assumed Mr. Douglas would get the nod, but the man's supporters completely alienated most Southerners, many of whom stomped out of the hall and proceeded to organize their own separate convention. Neither group could form a majority opinion even within their own ranks. Frank said the only thing they agreed upon was to meet in June in Baltimore. I had been under the impression that Mr. Douglas intended to leave the South alone, but Frank reports the man is two-faced and not to be trusted. Had I forgotten his abolitionist ranting over the Kansas matter? Who knows where the truth lies.

Frank says there is heated talk about secession and war, and the North Carolina men are divided on the issue, but he believes the Southern Rights faction will prevail. I can't bear to think of my beloved Country thrown into such turmoil. I believe if we give in to the North's desire to limit slavery in the territories, the despicable institution will surely be ground out of existence. I support that concept completely in my moral heart, but I can't imagine the consequences. What will become of the poor creatures who have not the skills to manage their affairs? What will become of us if they must be paid for their labor? Will cotton become so dear that few can afford it? Then how shall we get our livelihood? Frank has no scruples against fighting to keep the Negroes in their "place." I abhor that idea, but have none to offer in its stead.

I shall take up now where I left off, and perhaps you will begin to see how I came to my "unorthodox" convictions.

Thomas, Frank, and I agreed to sell some of Pa's people. Bitterly I had come to accept this notion, being convinced there was no other way to save even a scrap of the land. All my life Pa instilled in me a respect for the land. To Southern Agrarians the only things more precious than land are family and the Lord himself, and I longed more than anything to raise my family on our own place. Thomas and I returned to his father's home to gather our belongings and prepare for our move to Lincoln Count. We had no idea how long we would be gone, so we left Frank a note giving him permission to sell some of our people in our absence should an attractive offer be made. Frank was still a minor, and needed our consent to enter into a contract. But I never dreamed he would do so without any communication from us. The Henderson farm was not that far away; he could have easily sent us a note, or come himself! But in our absence and without our advice Frank negotiated the sale of our people. All of them, save Cissy and

Greene, which is not at all what we had in mind! And he did the deed in unimaginable haste! How dare he! Mattie was then twenty-nine years old, and the mother of four children. Her brothers, Caesar, Narcissus, Joe, and Amos ranged from twenty-three to thirty-one years, and were strong, well-trained workers. They had been neither beaten nor abused, and showed no rebellious tendencies. They were a valuable lot, and Frank concluded keeping even one or two of them was a luxury we could not afford. He had found an agent who made a generous offer agreeing to sell all nine as an intact group to a farmer not forty miles south of us, perhaps near enough to maintain some modicum of family contact, but there was no promise. Frank felt it was a deal too handsome to refuse. At least we retained Cissy and Greene, and Rose, being my property was not under consideration.

To Frank's credit he did attempt to buy Harry in order to include him in the sale, keeping Mattie's family together. But Harry's owner, Mr. H., asked nearly as much for Harry as Frank would be getting for our four boys combined, a ridiculous amount that would have nullified the entire deal. I'm sure Mr. H. had no intention of selling Harry. It was well known that he resented the poor fellow's marital visits to Mattie, and only abided them because he had had enough wrath from his neighbors. Harry and Mattie's children by law belonged to her owner and would never benefit Mr. H. There was no reason, other than compassion, for Mr. H. to consider selling Harry, and compassion was not among his traits. This was just one shard of the brittle bone that would soon come to stick in my throat.

Meanwhile, Thomas and I were at his parents' home arranging our affairs. Although Mr. Henderson regretted our leaving, he was an honorable man, and concluded it was time to give Thomas the Negroes and other property he was slated to inherit. This was common practice among planters when an offspring left home. The two men sat up late in the evenings figuring out the details, matching the gaps in the remnants of Pa's estate, with what could be spared from the Henderson place. When we finally returned to take up residence in my dear childhood home, we brought a mule, a handful of cows and sheep, a few tools, two bushels of cotton seed, a decent set of dishes (Mrs. Henderson put up a fit, but this was one category Pa neglected on his buying sprees), some cash, and a small Negro family: a man and wife, their two children, and the wife's brother. And Romulus. Thank the good Lord we were permitted to take Romulus into our possession. Again Mrs. Henderson had a conniption, insisting Romulus was her driver, and how would it look, her riding around behind a lazy wall-eyed field hand! Of course, as a married woman she had no property, and Thomas had convinced his father this was the least he could do for me, as I had already lost so much.

On our return I was stunned to find our entire family sold and already departed. Frank was satisfied with the contract he had made, convinced that Mattie, her brothers and children would remain together. He assumed it was our only option under difficult circumstances, having no idea we'd obtained a family that could have been sold in their stead. Nothing could have prepared me for the Negro countenances that greeted us. Cissy and Greene wore looks I had never before seen, red rimmed eyes dully masked, as if sheeted by gauze, lids heavy with grief. Their mouths were flat. Not turned down in angry scowls, but flat as if hammered into grim lines of defeat. And when they deigned to look at me directly, which was seldom, it was with pure hatred. Even Rose distanced herself from me. At first I was chagrined not to see a sympathetic look on any of their drear faces, surely they understood our sorry predicament, understood that it was Frank who had acted hastily without my consent. In time I accepted the fact that they showed me no sympathy because I deserved none. After all, I had been complicit in Frank's plan to sell some of our family as if they were cattle. Oh shame, oh shame! I had never before felt like such a wretch.

Rose and Romulus moved into the cabin with Cissy and Greene, into the space vacated by Mattie and her children, still heavy with Mattie's sullen gloom, which now enveloped its new inhabitants. Our new Negroes occupied the cabin's loft, former home of Cissy and Greene's sons. It was a happy arrangement for neither family, each having undergone severance, neither desiring a fresh alliance. Thomas promised to build a cabin for the new family when the harvest was in; meanwhile they would have to make do. Watching them attempt to do so brought on a new amalgam of grief, guilt and shame. If only Thomas and I had not left Frank with that note; if only we had had a bit of patience.

By this time planting should have been a-pace (Thomas was behindhand due to all the moving), and my confinement was approaching. Thankfully the nausea had passed, but my swollen legs were possessed by persistent cramping, my back ached, and my abdomen clutched in agonizing knots as if trying to expel the infant too soon. On Frank's advice I took to my bed whenever possible, and was attended by Rose with an indifference I had never before seen in her.

The peace I expected to find upon moving to Pa's old place was not to be. My vindictive mother-in-law had been replaced by sullen Negroes, meandering in and out of my realm like wraiths, and a painful uncooperative body that hobbled me at a time when usefulness was so badly needed. I had no idea things could become worse.

Tuesday, May 8, 1860

We soon learned that the agreement Frank struck with the agent to sell our family had been violated. Frank told me the man had been contrary when he came to receive his chattel. The Negroes had been told to collect their belongings which they tied into bundles and piled into crates. And what a set of belongings they were! My ever-generous father had often given them coins to spend and pickings from his odd lots of merchandise, and over the years they had acquired many fine possessions. Mattie had quite a few brightly colored head wraps, some decent pieces of jewelry, and nearly as many petticoats as I. Each of them had pewter plates and cups (not tin), and several stylish pairs of shoes among their collection of curios. Mattie's children had numerous playthings, as many as most white children. Frank said the agent fumed and fretted, complained there was not room in his wagon for nine Negroes (only he used the derogatory word) and so many bundles. Some of it would have to be left behind. Besides, what use did Negroes have for such sundries they couldn't possibly appreciate; certainly their new master would provide for their needs. The fact that our boys were probably better dressed than he must have fueled his ire. Even Frank was offended by the man's behavior, the way he yelled and cursed, shaking his fist while he paced back and forth kicking up dust, terrifying Mattie's children until their eyes seemed about to pop from their faces. But at last room was found, and Amos, Joe, Narcissus, Caesar, Mattie and her children were carted off to heaven knows where. I imagine all of their cheeks were wet with tears, especially Caesar's.

Several weeks later Frank wrote to the agent asking where our family now lived. Even he was beginning to see how deeply Cissy and Greene were mourning, and he may have had a pang of guilt toward Harry and our boys' wives. The agent replied, politely, but coldly; I can almost remember his letter verbatim:

Sir,

I extend my deepest apologies that our recent transaction did not transpire according to your wishes. The gentleman who agreed to *purchase your nine Negroes misrepresented himself, and apparently it was never his intention to acquire them for his own use. The place where he had instructed me to meet him was not the gentleman's farm, but a courthouse some forty miles south of you. He inferred that he gave me those instructions as his farm might be difficult to locate; this I now realize was a scandalous lie. It became immediately obvious that the unscrupulous gentleman planned to auction the Negroes then and there on the courthouse steps. As I had already paid you for them, I had no option but to turn them over to the prevaricator, for I could not absorb such a monetary loss. I have no idea where the man lives, or even his full name; Mr. Jones was all I was given. I would surmise that your Negroes have by now been taken to the South Carolina low country, or Alabama, almost certainly divided among several plantations. I cannot even guarantee that the children remain with their mother. I regret the entire event, and wish I had more pleasant news to render, but the matter is completely out of my hands.*

The letter closed with another flowery apology which was far from contrite.

Frank received this missive about three weeks after Thomas and I returned from his parents' home. He rode out to our place, having decided it was my duty to deliver its intelligence to Cissy and Greene. After all, I had lived closely with them and with Rose, and being a sensitive female would know precisely what to say. Frank was a complete coward, there is no other word for it! So there I was, the newly established mistress of our place, charged with divulging to Cissy and Greene and Rose that we had no idea what had become of their family, and it was doubtful they would ever see or hear of them again.

It was not until then that I understood the true profundity of our deed. I had never before, nor since, experienced such shame. There were no words of comfort to give to our heartbroken Negroes, no words to tell them that through our foolishness we had lost Amos and Joe and Narcissus and Caesar and Mattie and four beautiful children as surely as if we had permitted their drowning in the river. I have described earlier the empty, beaten looks that greeted Thomas and me when we returned to the farm. Those were almost joyful compared to the wailing and keening that now surrounded us. I was furious with Frank for not making more inquiries about the mysterious "Mr. Jones." Irate with him for being far too anxious to get his money quickly and enroll in medical school. Later Thomas wrote many letters, but to no avail. Either the man was not named Jones, or he did not reside in the county where the infamous courthouse was situated. I was so very, very ashamed.

Well, it took three days to get that horrible occurrence written down, and I can still feel the overwhelming shame, as fresh as yesterday. Frank at nineteen was too young and trusting to enter into such negotiations, and too eager to move on with his life. Thomas and I should have insisted the sale be delayed until we had completed our move and were available to participate. But we were nearly as naïve as Frank, and had foolishly written him that unfortunate note. We were all at fault, but I blamed Frank most of all, and could not forgive him for many years. Perhaps part of me never has. Rose tells me repeatedly that I have no notion of how it is to be property. I believe on that occasion I came as close to understanding as I ever will.

Tuesday, May 8, 1860

I been thinking for some days bout the next thing that happen which will be hard to write down. That was when Master Campbell die, and we move back to Mam's only to have our family get sold. I had heard how bleak that be, but till it happen to you, you can't know how it feel. How shall I try to give a notion of it?

For months there was a tumble of things coming so quick upon one another that a body hardly had time to grasp. First Master Campbell die, which grieved me considerable. He was bout as good as a white man could be, treating me almost like one of his own childrens, giving me pretty things, and books of my very own. And I know how much Miss Julia love him, her having no Mam. Me and her had lived so close for so long, it was almost like my own Pappy die. When Caesar came to get us (I could tell he was as tore up as I was), I took it as my duty to go with Miss Julia during her time of mourning, and I went gladly, even if I did have to leave Romulus behind.

Things happen so fast, I'm hard put to keep everything in order. A few weeks before Caesar came to fetch us, I figured I might be having another child, which I craved mightily. I did not tell Miss Julia, who was carrying one of her own, thinking I ought to wait till I was certain. We had had such a frolic with our first babies I was afraid to speak too soon and stir up evil spirits that might be lurking. Besides, Miss Julia would fuss at me for thinking such a thing. Then things come about, one upon another, that I never did get around to telling her.

After Master Campbell was buried Miss Julia and Master Thomas concluded that we was to move back to the Campbell farm, which pleased me to be with Mam and the rest, miles away from Miz Henderson. But my blood froze to think that I could lose Romulus forever, me with a baby coming on who would need a daddy. (Later on it turned out that Master Thomas got to keep Romulus along with a family of Master Henderson's field hands. I wept for joy about Romulus, although I didn't care one whit about the field hands; I believed I was heaps above them.)

Miss Julia and Master Thomas went back to the Henderson farm to collect their belongings and while they were gone Mattie and my brothers got sold cause Master Campbell owed everybody money, and selling them was the only way to get it. That near broke my heart, but Master Frank promised they all be kept together and not too far away so we could see them after the crops was laid by, maybe again at Christmas. The days after the lay by is one sweet time to folks that work the land! As soon as cotton sprouts in the spring, it needs bodacious hoeing every day so it won't be strangled by weeds. We call that chopping cotton, and it's the hottest, most miserable work there is 'til gathering commences. But when the cotton's well up, and the weeds don't stand no chance, we give it one last big hoeing, and let it lay by till picking time. There is other crops to tend, but the work is lighter, giving hands a few days rest in the summertime. Master Frank's words gave me some cheer, but Mam warned me not to set much store by such a promise, a white man's promise ain't worth spit. I figure Mam was moping cause she missed having them all under foot. I prayed the secret child in my belly would make us all feel better before long.

It was one grim day when my brothers and Mattie and her childrens was hauled off. They packed up everything they owned, determined to carry every smidgen with them. The ogre that drove the slave wagon wanted to throw the luggage in the yard, but they squeezed themselves up and made room. They look like a passel of rabbits huddled up in a hutch, eyes wide, faces froze. The little ones squalled. They didn't know where they was going, but they could smell fear. None of us had a bit of faith in what Master Frank had promised, and that driver, he hollered and cussed, and pushed folks around. I never before saw such a low down snake as that.

Miss Julia and Master Thomas were still at the Henderson farm, so I was the only one at home to comfort Mam and Pappy, and lawsy, they shed more tears than I had any notion of. They weeped and wailed and carried on so, that I was tempted to take Mam aside and tell my secret, but she might think I was finding selfish pleasure amongst the misery, so I kept quiet. Come to think she would have been right. Then Romulus and the fields hands move in, and we try to accustom ourselves to the situation, happy to have Romulus home, barely tolerating the new family living in the loft. Pappy tell us to think on summer when the crops was laid by, cause Master Thomas promise to take us to see Mattie and the boys. I figured I wouldn't be fit to go anywhere by then, but I still lacked the gumption to speak up. But Mam didn't look like she was getting happy any time soon, and before long she would be able to see for herself, so I set her down and say she going to have a new grandbaby. Instead of smiling, she just say she wonder how long it be before they snatch it away from me.

Then along come Miss Julia with that letter which was sent to Master Frank, who didn't even have the decency to stick his sorry face in our cabin. And she tell us that her brother was cheated, and the wicked scoundrel that bought our family done sold them off. Nobody knew where they gone. They probably wasn't together. Maybe not even the childrens. I could tell she was upset, words stumbling all around in her mouth. But that weren't nothing next to Mam, who look like she done seen the devil and the hell fires, eyes too parched to make tears any more. Miss Julia say her husband was writing letters to see what he could find out, but she didn't hold out much hope of us learning what had become of my brothers and poor Mattie and her precious children. At first I had trouble blaming Miss Julia cause she always took good care of me. I lashed out that Master Frank done it, and that cheating liar that had swindled him, but Mam set me straight. Master Frank weren't but nineteen years old. Miss Julia and Master Thomas didn't have no business letting him handle things while they was gone. Mam told me the three of them knew all the big men in Lincolnton, and they should have asked for help. They was too eager to get their money to have any thought about what become of our poor family.

I don't know words to give any notion of the misery that set in and hung over us. We went on with our jobs as we had no choice about that. Planting come and Romulus was put to work alongside the field hands as was Pappy, who wasn't too old in Master Thomas' opinion.

We figure that someday our sorrow would grow dim, and I reckon it did a speck, but not much, especially for Mam. She changed forever.

If you ain't property, there is one part of this cruel business you never come up against. When white childrens grow up, 'tis a natural thing for them to marry and leave their Pappy's home. If they is lucky, they live close by, and if they move not too far, they carry on great rounds of visiting, loading up carriages, and traipsing back and forth. They not only gets to see each other, but makes a fine frolic of it. But should they move a long ways off, they writes letters. Every one of them can read and write, and knows where their kinfolks is and how to get the letters to them. What a whoop white folks let out when letters come. They read about what their family is up to, and talk and chatter like they saw them yesterday. They even know when new babies are borned, when the kinfolks die and where they is buried. It ain't like that for us. We never heard a single word about our people. They may as well have been dead.

Amos was almost a man when I was borned. He was a hard working, easy going sort, so I reckon he fared all right, even if times was hard. I reckon he dead by now. Joe and Narcissus was so much alike, I get mixed up in my memory which of them did one thing or another. They was obedient boys, but possessed of a rascally imp that brung on trouble from time to time. Not a heap of trouble, just picayune things. But I hate to think how that imp might have turned to pure devil if they was mistreated. They's old men if they still alive. It shame me to think I got them so muddled together in my head. Caesar was a sweet loving boy, cared about every living thing, cried easy as a woman. I dread to imagine what become of him, possessed of a spirit that can be broke like a twig.

And poor Mattie, who had the misery even under the roof of Master Campbell, the goodliest white man there ever was. I pray the good Lord that she run away and took her babies with her. Nothing but freedom that would cure that kind of misery. I reckon she bout sixty-five if she ain't dead; if her childrens is alive. I pray they is happy.

Wednesday, May 9, 1860

Delivering that horrid news to our dear Negroes left me sickened and depleted. My health being in shambles, I returned to my bed where I worried that the ordeal had weakened me, perhaps to the peril of my unborn child. That thought shrouded me with disgrace; to think I considered my own situation anywhere near as dire as that of my

Negroes. My Negroes! With Pa dead I had come to think of them as such. Had Cissy eroded from substitute mother to mere possession? Had Romulus drifted from Rose's husband to my servant? And Rose? She had always been like family. Was that the family I was born to, or the one I owned? Shame, shame, shame! Everything I said to try to assuage their sorrow, to express sympathy, only seemed to build the walls between us higher and thicker. There was nothing I could do to help them, because I had done absolutely nothing at all to prevent the terrible occurrence. Shame!

So I languished. Thomas was as dutiful as possible, although he was enduring his own difficulty. Planting was in arrears, and he was proceeding slowly with a handful of lethargic Negroes. Greene was old and Romulus had always resented field work, now both of them were even further disabled by sullenness. The field hands from the Henderson place noted this atmosphere, and took full advantage. Thomas was not well suited to work alongside his hands. Not that it demeaned him; he was simply was not as well schooled in agriculture as he should have been, and awkward with the men. At his father's place he had become skilled at conducting plantation business, but not with farming. He was in a complete quandary. At first he hesitated to speak harshly and further injure Greene and Romulus. Yet he could not let the season pass by fallow, for we had only Mr. Henderson's small gift of cash to keep us until the crops could be sold, at least eight months hence.

Little Tom had just turned two. Each morning Thomas arose, washed him and dressed him, then brought me a pitcher of clean warm water and with great despondency left for the fields. By and by Rose sauntered in followed by Marc. The little boys yelped in delight and began a new day racing about, completely innocent of the palpable tension between their mothers. Rose, with barely a word, brought my breakfast, then helped me wash and dress. Frank had insisted I spend most of my time in bed, although he reluctantly permitted me to sit for a while in the parlor or on the porch. Fortunately we slept in Pa's old bedchamber which was below stairs, or I would have been a prisoner as well as an invalid. Rose moved about the house as sullenly as Mattie had in the old days, dusting, sweeping, gathering linens and garments that needed laundering, brushing and airing the rest. As she worked she fixed dull eyes to the floor, or darted them to a far corner of the room, always avoiding my glance. One day as she tucked in my sheet I thought I discerned a new curve in her figure. Then as she stood to adjust the window curtain, a breeze caught her gown revealing her profile, and I gasped, "Rose, you're going to have a baby!"

"Yes'm," she answered without feeling. I was aghast!

"But why haven't you told me? Oh Rose, I'm so happy for you!"

But all she could reply was "yes'm, yes'm" in the same flat voice. I managed to worm out of her that the infant was due about two months beyond my own confinement. Such an odd mixture of emotions. Of course I was pleased that she was also to have a child, but I would have given the world to relive those bright times we shared with our first infants, even under the pall of Mrs. Henderson.

June came and my forays from bed were entirely forbidden. Rose's demeanor softened, at least a bit. I suppose her lifelong concern for me could not completely be eradicated, and the midwife we had engaged was quite concerned about the health of my child. By then Frank was in Charleston beginning his medical education. I'm sure having him at such a remove was beneficial to our Negroes. Poor Rose. I know it was difficult for her to attend to me with my ungainly bulk, especially as hers was increasing. It occurred to me that for months she had worn ample short frocks, pinned loosely at the bodice, not cinched at the waist. Her skirt billowed below the hip-length frocks giving no hint of her shape. I had assumed she was simply not caring for her appearance during the troubling times, which may have been true. How chagrined I was to think that my so-called sister under the skin had been expecting all these months, and I had no idea!

On the tenth of June my pains began and the midwife was summoned. Fortunately she came quickly. I shall not describe the event except to say it was less excruciating than the first, but more troubling as I had carried with such difficulty. I was at last delivered of a baby girl who appeared to be strong and healthy. I named her Jane after my mother and my infant sister who had died so long ago. I hoped Pa knew from his place in heaven that I was keeping the name alive. Over the next weeks I worked to regain my energy and care for Tom and my baby Jane as best I could. Having been confined to my bed, I'm afraid my legs nearly lost all sense of how they ought to operate. All the while I tried to convince Rose to save her strength for her own confinement, but she seemed to think I was snubbing her attention. I clasped her hands when I could and tried to rekindle our old affection, but she remained cool, not rude, simply aloof.

Week after week Jane grew hale and round and rosy, each feature on her tiny face miniature perfection. She nursed heartily, darting her little hands about, behaving in every way like an ideal infant. In early August the cotton was deemed strong, and laid by. The sadness among the Negroes which had lifted somewhat took a dip, for this was the time they had hoped to visit Mattie and the boys, living on a farm forty miles south of us, before the existence of such a farm was revealed as a cruel myth. Thomas overheard Greene tell Romulus how eager he had been to make the journey, and now that the appointed time had rolled around, his heart was like a stone. About the same time a wave of summer colds struck our family. I suppose there was no connection between the Negroes' disappointment and the summer colds, but coming together increased the malaise. All of us, black and white, were coughing and stuffed in our heads and chests, pulling on warm clothes against chills in spite of the summer heat.

One morning Cissy brought in our breakfast and announced, "Rose's time done come. I reckon you all got to tend to yourselves for a spell. That field woman ain't no help. Can't hardly boil water. All she do is get in my way. What I'd give to have Mattie home." I tried to hug her, but was rebuffed. I assured her that none of us were particularly hungry, I would brew a pot of tea if we needed one, yesterday's cornbread would be sufficient for dinner. Could I sit with Rose? Hold her hands? Help her through her pains? She didn't answer any of my questions, just looked down at Jane in her cradle, "That baby don't look good. She done catched the cold?" I picked her up and indeed she was slightly pale and clammy. Her tiny nose was crusted over, and she was breathing shallowly through her mouth. But she was not crying, or showing any signs of discomfort. As Cissy left I promised I would come to the cabin shortly. I chided myself as I washed Jane's face, holding the warm cloth to her nostrils, trying to clear them. All my life I had been dependent on the wisdom of Cissy, who noticed Jane was ill before I had an inkling, who now hated me completely and with good reason.

I wrapped the baby warmly, gathered up Tom and headed for the cabin. Marc was in the yard outside the cabin door, and I left Tom with him. Neither boy was very sick, but both subdued enough to play quietly. Probably a blessing. Inside, I placed Jane in the cradle, the one that lay in wait for Rose's child. I sat on the edge of Rose's bed and took her in my arms. She started to resist, but I held on. This ugly bitterness had to come to an end. I loved her and needed her and I prayed she might return just a smidgen of my affection. She relaxed, and we sat there wordlessly for what seemed an age, then a pain engulfed her. I grasped her wrists the way she had mine when Tom was coming. I'm sure I saw a semblance of thankfulness in her eyes as she locked her hands on my wrists, and we braced against one another with all our strength. At the end of the wave she panted, and managed a weak smile. My Rose was coming back.

Throughout the day Cissy and I bathed her brow and took turns working her through her pains. Between them I nursed Jane and again washed the crust from her nose. She fed weakly, but then none of us were hungry, and all of us light-headed. Both Cissy and I were growing tired, and I prayed we would have strength enough between us to complete the task. Finally the infant presented itself, and Cissy crouched down and brought it into the world. For that I was grateful. As much as I loved Rose, I'm not sure that I had nerve enough, although I hope I would have, had it been necessary. It was a beautiful little boy, so near the age of my Jane! Maybe we could recapture some of what had been lost.

Cissy cleaned Rose and washed and swaddled the baby. By now my head was completely afloat, as if filled with feathers. My hands shook, and I was worried about Jane who seemed more limp each time I picked her up. I told Cissy I would go find Romulus, and I would be back later when all of us had had some rest. Poor little Jane was like a wisp in my arms as I carried her back to the house.

Thursday, May 10, 1860

The next few day passed in a blur. My own health was slow to improve, and little Jane grew weaker. What had begun as a simple cold turned into croup, a grave danger for an infant. Cissy could do little other than bring plasters of herbs for Jane's chest. The poor woman was completely absorbed in cooking for the entire sick family, and tending to Rose and her infant. I was grateful for the herbs, and could ask nothing else. Yet in spite of our careful attention, about four days after Rose gave birth our precious Jane expired. Thomas, who had kept close to my side, was as shaken as I. So many infants are taken during their first fragile months of life, one thinks that parents might be steeled for the possibility. But we are not. Does God send us this plight to keep us humble? It seems a cruelty incompatible with a God of Love. We are told we are not meant to understand His mysteries, and I will confess that infant death has always been beyond my comprehension. Bless Thomas. He was a rock. We shouldered our loss with the same deep intimacy that nurtured our love for one another. Fathers love and cherish their children as fondly as mothers, something I'd learned first hand. I will never believe that "mother's love" is a superior variety. I'm sure we would have perished had it not been for the strength that Thomas and I drew from one another. Bless my precious Thomas.

He and I bathed Jane's tiny body, and dressed her in the crisp gown I had intended for her Baptism. Then Thomas rode to our preacher's home with the sad news and arranged for a churchyard plot for our family nearby my parents; Jane Henderson, barely two months of age, became its first occupant.

The day after Jane died Rose presented herself in my bedchamber. My cold was subsiding, and my head no longer felt stuffed with feathers. Now I languished in pure grief. Without a word she put her arms about me, cradled my head to her shoulder, and began to weep. I can't express how consoling her embrace was. After some time we began to speak, softly, hesitantly, our fingers barely interlocked. Her child was well and strong, which I was glad to hear. She had named him Levi, such a beautiful name. She believed my remorse concerning Mattie and her brothers was genuine, and would try and put her anger away. I promised her that Thomas would continue his letter writing, and perhaps someday we would find her family. She prayed that would be so. Neither of us dared say how unlikely it was to happen.

Gradually a semblance of regularity returned. The cotton gathered in the fall was adequate, though just barely, to meet our needs. Thomas still had many lessons to learn about farming. As promised, the field hands were allowed to build their cabin under Thomas' supervision, and the strain on all of our Negroes was eased.

Levi grew into a happy boy, a gentle one who reminded me of Caesar. As he grew he came to romp in the wake of Tom and Marc, but during those early years his pleasant nature would have made him a perfect companion for Jane.

Well, it has taken near a week to get this dreadful tale onto paper. I have surprised myself in the number of pages I have penned! I wrote from morning to night some days, and on others spent hours in contemplation. Daughter Adie has begun to inquire of my health! Perhaps I shall give this project a bit of a rest, and spend more time with the family.

Thursday, May 10, 1860

These past days Miss Julia and I been scribbling to beat all. I could tell we was writing bout the same things. She done said a word or two, then she holed up in her room like we got the quarantine. I know she feel bad about selling my family, and I come to accept that. Deep down I reckon I forgive her about half way cause women's opinions don't count, at least in no legal way. If Master Frank and Master Thomas took a notion to wrastle down the moon, she couldn't put a stop to it. But I never knew a woman couldn't sway a man, at least a smidgen, if she go about it the right way. I know Mam was right when she say Master Frank too young for business and got the wool pull over his eyes. Master Thomas and Miss Julia was a tad older, but they'd had no truck with sly folks. They was still grieving over Master Campbell, and her feeling poorly. Still it was them that done it, and it hurt to this very day.

Not long after, Miss Julia's baby come. She was a pretty thing, hearty as a colt. I pretend not to notice as I was still feeding my grudge, but I could see how strong she pull on her Mam's bosom, how she looked all around the room, eyes blinking wide and curious, how she hold up her own head when she only a few weeks old. Can't nobody tell me she was born a sickly child. Then we all got the ague. I thank the Lord that all I had was a sniffly nose, cause while the rest of the folks was coughing and shivering my baby come. My bodacious Levi. Miss Julia done put aside her own suffering and come to help me bring Levi. All the time her baby sick near to death, which I didn't know at the time. I reckon that's when my heart told me I still love Miss Julia, no matter what I think about her. My children later teach me the same lesson; they could make me ill as a hornet, but I still love them. In slavery you got to dwell on any love you can find, or you get the misery. Ain't no other way.

Then Miss Julia's baby die, and that was one hard time. Levi was three or four days old when Mam told me. I had wondered why Miss Julia hadn't come to see me after Levi was born, thinking she wasn't finished with the rift between us. When I hear she'd been trying to keep her own baby alive, I done hung my head and went to her. What was done, was done, and it was time to leave it behind.

After we bury Miss Julia's child and made our peace, we settle down. Like he promise, Master Thomas build a cabin for the field hands. That is, Master Thomas give directions, and the others done the raising. I reckon I should give their names, for by this time I bout got over my haughtiness. The man and wife was Sam and Dovey, and Dovey's brother was Fred. Sam and Dovey had two scrappy boys, Little Sam and Bob. They about ten and twelve years old then. They grow up to be mighty fine men, in spite of Master Thomas who had no bent for working with his people.

Mam didn't have no use for the field hands, said they was good-for-nothing. I reckon Pappy had worked crops as much as anybody, but Mam say he used to work with Master Campbell, not under him which was different, and work was easier a-fore cotton came along. Mam looked down her nose at Dovey, scared she might learn to cook. Mam had near bout been "mistress" of Master Campbell's place, him not having a wife, and wanted to keep it that way. By and by, Dovey did get to be a fair cook, but not till years later.

I figure after Levi was borned, Romulus might get shed of his misery. But he didn't. Master Thomas had no call for a carriage driver, most times he drove hisself had he some place to go. Nor did he care about decking out his horses and carriage or other such fancy notions. Romulus knew in his head that the first thing Master Thomas got to do was make a crop if we was to be fed. That wasn't no easy crop, planted so late in the season. But Romulus' heart, as usual, didn't have no sense. He say Master Thomas treat him like he done Little Sam or Bob, like a "boy" with a strong back and weak brain. The misery climb back into Romulus and never did let go.

Monday, May 14, 1860

I've taken a much needed rest from this journal, and today feel I can begin afresh. The weather is warm and beautiful, as it should be in May. We've had decent rainfall of late to feed the crops, but not so much as to drown them. The Lord provides well. Yesterday we were in town for services and took dinner with brother Frank. He had nothing new to report, simply the same old predictions of mayhem. Many of the other men have taken up the worry. I don't know what will become of us!

Frank says our county's iron industry will be quite the coup should war come. I believe I mentioned that during my childhood Pa dug iron ore for nearby forges and furnaces. Over the years those businesses developed into quite a force in Lincoln County, and their owners bought up the iron-rich lands. The business, although still important, has slipped somewhat over the last twenty years or so. The Charleston markets are bloated with inexpensive iron forged at the North, or brought from foreign lands. And the bounty of cotton has eclipsed our local manufactories. Frank is convinced that a huge resurgence is in our future, promising great prosperity. What shall they make? Guns and cannons instead of pots and pans? Disgusting!

Perhaps I should describe Adie's place, and put down some idea of the house we live in. Isaac's farm contains about a thousand acres, and his cash crop, of course, is cotton. Like most of his neighbors he breeds quite a few hogs, for they are our primary source of meat, some sheep, dairy cows, and flocks of chickens. Corn is the largest crop grown to feed the animals and to grind for meal, and there are orchards of peaches and apples. Everyone in Lincoln County grows apples, some have only a few trees, many have orchards. Our county is as renowned for apples as it is for iron. Isaac also raises wheat and barley and most of our vegetables, but we are not completely dependent on our own resources. We are not so far from town, and we can buy almost anything we might need or desire, even food should a crop fail.

Adie's house is a fine one. Isaac had it built just before their marriage on land that belonged to his father. So you can see it is practically new, having stood here only about twelve years. It is made of brick in the latest fashion, and is quite spacious, consisting of eight large rooms, four below stairs, and four above. On the lower floor, facing the front, are a parlor and a study where Isaac maintains his library. Behind them are the dining room and nursery. Both front and back are spanned by broad porches, although about half the back porch has been enclosed for the room adjoining the nursery where Vinia and Rose live. An elegant hallway runs front to back, opening onto the porches. Above are four bedchambers. Adie and Isaac occupy the one above the parlor, it being the slightly largest of the four. Benjamin's room is across the hall from theirs, and I suppose Matthew will join him when he is old enough to leave the nursery. My room is behind Benjamin's, and little Rebecca occupies the other corner. So you can see we all have ample space, rattling around as we do. If Adie had not lost several infants (blessedly long before time for their births), the rooms would be swimming with children.

I am at a loss to say how many Negroes live among us, but I believe they number about fifty. It embarrasses me not to know this precisely, but as they are not my property or responsibility, I've not overly concerned myself with them. I do not know if Isaac mistreats his Negroes, nor do I wish to. I can only say I've seen no evidence of it, and pray he is humane. My attitude toward Rose should extend to all Negroes, and I suppose in my intellect it does. Yet it is difficult to insert one's intellect into daily practicalities. If I dwelt on Isaac's Negroes and how squalidly they live, I'm sure I would be in constant distress. I will pray to be a better Christian, to learn to exemplify the courage of my convictions.

I will try to give an account here of the Negroes I can name. Those who frequent the house are Adie's nursemaid Vinia whom I've already mentioned, Sarah who cleans the house, superintends the care of its contents, and serves our meals, and Echo, our driver and "valet;" that is, he is dressed in fine livery and serves the table when Isaac has guests. He also tends Isaac's wardrobe and helps Sarah with heavy chores. Among those working beyond the house is Lizzy, our cook, who is quite proficient at her job. At least once a week, more often if we are entertaining, Adie confers with Lizzy in the kitchen. Lizzy usually has things well in hand, but it is Adie's duty to make sure. Several other women help Lizzy with the meals, and do the laundry, sewing, mending, and sundry domestic tasks. There are perhaps four old ones in the quarter whose only job is to watch the little children and charm them with fanciful stories. Dovey, who is even older than I, is one of them. She came to Thomas and me from his father all those years ago after Pa died, and Thomas gave her to Adie as dowry. By then Dovey had become an adequate cook, although she was past her prime even then. I suspect Rose enjoys her company although they never did become close. Another old person is a fellow named Marsh. He was inherited by Isaac, and is a great favorite with the children. He's a keeper of the tales handed down by his African-born grandfather to the delight of the little ones, black and white. I've no idea how old Marsh is, but he must be eighty or beyond. I regret to say I've never spent time in his company. Perhaps I should. I cannot name the other old ones.

About a dozen men and older boys work the fields, assisted by those women who are not in confinement. The only ones of my acquaintance are Little Sam and several of his offspring. Little Sam is Dovey's son, and was also part of Adie's dowry. The women who are about to give birth or have nursing infants, help with kitchen and laundry duties, and tend to the children too young for chores. The women who are weak or old, yet still useful, spin and weave, or assist at light tasks. I shall make myself a vow to get to know these people, although Adie will probably have a fit. If war does throw our land into turmoil, they may need an advocate.

Isaac is a good man, and as I have said, I will always appreciate his generosity in taking me in. His farm is successful, and he seems to manage his hands well. His only flaw is vanity, and a keen wish to be known as a gentleman farmer. He looks east with envy toward farmers across the river in Mecklenburg who have become considerably richer and own far more than a thousand acres. He seems not to realize that only a handful of Mecklenburg farmers are so well situated, and those who are have worked their places for several generations. I should not complain, for vanity is a minor flaw for a man to have; that and his pompous library afford me much amusement and pleasure!

Monday, May 14, 1860

I keep busy that next year. Miss Julia done wallow in grief after that baby died, which I reckon was her due, but it did put a load on me. She bout gave up helping out with the housework, which she used to take pride in. Tom was not much over two, and needed a heap of watching, him being big enough to wander all over creation, and too little to have caution. Miss Julia, she try to keep up with him, but I could see sadness creep up out of nowhere and settle behind her eyes, while Tom wander over by the well, or pick up a hoe to swing around, any old dangerous thing. Marc was coming up on three and was a right smart handful, the devil popping out of his eyes. The two of them together kept me hopping. And Levi being new borned needed heaps of tending. Mam was some help, but only I could nurse Levi, and Mam was getting feeble. Her spark never come back after the family was sold.

I hardly got hold of this routine, when I had another baby coming. Miss Julia, she act like she was pleased, but I could tell all she wanted was her dead child back. Levi hardly passed his first birthday when Ezekiel was borned, and Miss Julia was still not carrying. She didn't say much, cause I reckon she thought God was to blame, and maybe she had been blaming him too much and made him angry. Why should I, a slave, be blessed and blessed and blessed while she had only Tom?

Romulus was losing his notion of being a good daddy. He look at his three younguns, and me still young enough to have a heap more, and all he could see was field hands coming up. He couldn't say nothing to Master Thomas, but he give me an ear full. Him going from carriage driver on a fine place to field hand on a middling one just grind him down. Master Thomas holler at him what needs doing, but don't give no particulars, unless he tell Romulus something bound not to work. Then Master Thomas holler some more when the task wasn't done to his liking. Romulus couldn't figure how he was supposed to get anything accomplish. Master Thomas, for all his fine training on the Henderson place, was completely ignorant bout how to farm the land.

He always come up short at having water fetched to the fields for the men and the animals. Every morning each man carried a bucket to where they was working, and after dinner they carried another one. It was never enough. Neither man nor beast can work when they is dry.

Master Thomas worked horses and mules as if one was the same as the other. Horses ain't suited for heavy work like mules is. They is built for galloping and pulling carriages, not for plowing soil that's sun baked hard and not yet broke. The men tried to tell their master that a horse can't work so hard in the heat, specially without enough water. When a horse starts to foam, he should be tied up under a shade tree and watered and allowed to rest. Master Thomas say the hands need to figure out how to keep the horses healthy and busy, but he would not let them go to the well cept at dinner. That's how Master Thomas lost his fine horse, but he blamed Romulus for the poor creature's death! Master Thomas should have knowed how Romulus loved horses, how he would have given his soul to keep one alive. Was he blind when Romulus worked his pappy's horses? Romulus gentled the colts, raising each to be a glorious beast, almost in league with the angels. He raised them from his heart, never touching a whip to horseflesh, and only using a crop as a gentle guide. Master Thomas should be shamed of hisself!

I believe there was only one mule on the place back then. Mules is stout and strong and suited to the task, but they is stubborn, and hard to turn, and refuse to work when they is dry. You can't work a mule to death, but a horse will work 'til it drops, which is what happened, and Romulus got the tongue lash. Horses don't cost near as much money as mules, and mules ain't always easy to come by. Master Thomas was plumb worried about money during them years.

Romulus didn't care one whit bout money. We had food enough and clothes to wear. Romulus had a whole stack of fancy driving clothes he didn't have use for no more. All he could see was Master Thomas hollering "boy this", and "boy that", and then that dead horse. His whole life he had groomed and cared for horses like babies, and now he got blamed cause one was dead. I believe he mourned that horse near bout as much as Miss Julia mourned her child.

Wednesday, May 16, 1860

I cannot say I ever ceased grieving for Jane. Over the years whenever I saw a child about the age she would have been, I wondered would Jane have grown so pretty, so lively, or so demure? I longed to know the person she might have become. But in time life did assume a measure of normality. I suppose God will not permit us to dwell forever on what might have been. I must have lingered in a mist shielding me from the world, for all at once I realized that little Tom was no longer an infant, but a proper boy who was outgrowing his clothing. Rose had become pleasant again, but not so attentive as she once was, as she was completely absorbed in her duties. I doubt Tom was much of a burden to her, for he was attached to Marc, as if the two were tethered. Levi was a joyful child, but like any infant needed care. The next year she produced another boy whom she named Ezekiel. In addition to this flock of children, she had assumed more responsibility in the kitchen. Cissy had slowed down with age, and suffered utter emptiness from the sale of her children. At the time I thought I understood her sorrow, and assumed it would mellow into a benign nostalgia; after all, grown children are supposed to leave their parents and seek lives for themselves. It says so in the Bible. I think after Jane died I began to appreciate Cissy's grief. Her children had not sought their destiny; it had been thrust upon them. They were as irretrievable as my dead Jane.

When I emerged from that foul mist, I determined to become a better wife. I took complete charge of the house, freeing Rose for the children and helping Cissy with meals. I became more attentive to Thomas. He had not had the luxury of turning inward, and had borne the brunt of our tragedy. In addition he was struggling to make a success of our farm. I made sure our home was comfortable and spotless, kept his clothes clean, and his possessions in good order. I did all the cleaning, washing, and ironing myself, everything but beating the rugs, which cannot be handled by a solitary female. In the evenings I fetched our supper from the kitchen, served Thomas, Tom, and myself, and occasionally helped Dovey with the washing up. Afterwards, when Tom had been put to bed, I sat with Thomas and listened for hours as he described his day's work. Perhaps deep in my heart I hoped that if I became the dutiful wife and mother, God would reward me with another child.

It was during those evenings that I began to understand the trouble Thomas was getting into. I had grown up watching my father farm this same land, heard him discussing the daily chores, seen how he worked in tandem with Greene and the boys. Thomas, instead of reporting the daily banter of team work, complained that the Negroes did not obey him. He had to shout to make himself understood, yet they still contradicted his instructions. I had had no interaction with the new family, and assumed they were the objects of Thomas' ire, as he had told me they were a lazy lot. Certainly Romulus was not disobedient. Then one night Thomas came in fuming with anger; Romulus had killed a horse. I could not believe my ears. I had watched Romulus with horses. I had seen him groom them, stroke them lovingly. They ate apples from his hand, and nickered against the soft flesh of his neck. Their ears cocked at the sound of his voice, and I saw the eyes of beast and man lock, and follow one another with the intensity of lovers. Romulus touched horseflesh with the same gentleness in his fingertips as he did Rose and his children. In return horses gave him absolute trust and loyalty. I had never seen another human so at one with a horse. Romulus had killed a horse? Preposterous!

I pressed Thomas for details. He said the Negroes complained of insufficient water, but if he let them go to the well between meals, they loitered and wasted time. He had no time to waste. If he didn't make a decent crop this year and the next, and probably the one after that we would be in debt over our ears. He needed more hands and more animals, and had no funds to buy them. I asked him what task the poor horse was assigned, and he said plowing. Plowing where? That sloping piece of land, where the soil was rocky and impacted. The horse balked and he ordered the Negroes to tighten its gearing; they refused. Romulus wanted to go for water, as the buckets were empty, but Thomas would not permit it. He told Romulus to sharpen the plow blade, and plow a curved furrow over the slope which would be less strenuous. The next thing he knew the horse was dead. Romulus had worked him to death on purpose, out of spite, for not being allowed to have his own way, for being forbidden to loiter at the well.

"Shouldn't the mule be plowing in such a spot?" I asked. Thomas replied that he had only one mule, and it couldn't be everywhere at once. Besides, Romulus was an expert with horses. Surely he should know how to get a day's work from one and keep the creature alive.

Then Thomas drew away from me and I saw a shudder travel his spine. I reached for his hand, and when he turned to face me, anguish I had never seen before distorted his face. He dropped his head and began weeping, sobbing audibly, as if floodgates had unleashed torment within him, and deeply held fears poured out. "I have tried as hard as I know how, but everything I touch fails, and I have no idea how to stop it. Pa made farming look so easy, and I thought I'd learned well from him, but I must not have. I'm terrified of becoming a complete and utter failure." Words sputtered between sobs. "I'm afraid I might lose your farm, and it is yours, Julia, not mine, no matter the name on the deed. I felt privileged to become its caretaker, to use your land to make a life for us, and now everything is falling to ruin, and I am powerless to stop it. I want to be an accomplished man, but I wonder if I'm a man at all. Ma always said I was a weakling who would never amount to anything. Now I'm becoming a disappointment to you and my father as well. I have no idea how to make things right. Help me, Julia, please help me!"

"Go ask your father for help. He respects you, and he'll know where you've erred and what to do instead. Ask him how he taught his hands to do his bidding."

"I can't go to him. I'm too ashamed and embarrassed. Then Ma would get into it, and tell Pa she had been right all along. I could not bear that, Julia; I simply could not."

I caressed his shaking shoulders and murmured words I hoped would comfort. I assured him he had not failed, that he was indeed a man, that there was ample time to make a crop, that I loved and trusted him with all my heart. I had seen Thomas' tender tears of grief when Jane died, but never before such raw and deep anguish. And to think I had vowed to become a dutiful wife so God would reward me with a child. May God forgive my ceaseless pride!

I felt for both Thomas and Romulus. I knew Romulus must be beside himself with grief and remorse. I made a vow to spend more time with Rose, the sort of intimate time we used to while away. And what to do about Thomas? I could not tell him how to run his farm and become the sort of harpy his mother was. I could see her signature all over this sad state, providing a dark underlayment to Thomas' natural good humor. Mr. Henderson had taught his son the broad scope of farming, but not the details. By the time Thomas became a man, the Henderson hands knew what to do when their master said "plant" or "plow" or "harvest." Our hands probably possessed the same knowledge, but Thomas did not trust their intelligence. His mother had carefully taught him that Negroes were stupid and lazy and unreliable. They could not even tie their shoes without detailed instructions. Then, after her vicious tongue had completely flailed the Negroes, she convinced Thomas that he too was a weakling, and a poor excuse for a man. Poor Thomas. He loved the land and genuinely wanted to be the farmer his father was, but he lacked the courage to trust his hands or his own instincts.

I could not tell Thomas what to do, but I could gently give him subtle hints. I would live as economical as possible, and insist we save for another mule. I would suggest he join the Agricultural Society and read its publications. If he would not go to his father, perhaps there he would find the knowledge he lacked. Many men had begun to talk about scientific farming and practice the new methods. Perhaps our hands did need more instructions, but given in a teacherly manner, not as shouted orders. I loved Thomas deeply and would lead him ever so gently.

Should I get to know the field hands better? Or would that make matters worse? I could not appear to them, or to Thomas, to be usurping my husband's authority. I needed to have a long talk with Rose. I trusted her implicitly.

Thursday, May 17, 1860

I ain't been writing much as I ought to, for I am still reading "Vanity Fair". That's shore one long book. I like it better now that I know they is all buffoons set on tricking one another. Plumb full of deception and chicanery. Look at my big words!

I heaved a big sigh of relief when Miss Julia tell me how sorry she was about the dead horse, and how she know Romulus was not to blame. I reckon that's when I figured Romulus had good reason for the misery. I hoped knowing would make it easier to bear, but it didn't. Miss Julia asked should she talk to Dovey or Sam, but I told her that might just stir up more trouble. Then she asked how she could help Master Thomas be a better master. Lord knows, if I had an answer to that one, slavery might not be the miserable state that it is. It seemed to ease her to talk, and I was pleased to hear she believe the horse dying wasn't any of Romulus' doing. Miss Julia and me, we just poor women without any say-so, one free white, one black slave, caught up between the devil and the deep blue sea.

That was one hard time which would have worried me more if I had time for worrying. All the younguns to tend to, and poor Mam getting old, and not caring about much. She took some pleasure in my boys, but not like she ought to have. She ached all over with the rheumatiz, the field hands was griping and complaining, and she figured we weren't never going hear about Mattie and the boys. All this made her so low we would have starved if I hadn't taken over most of the cooking. Pappy wasn't much better. Before Master Campbell died Pappy had started making a pleasure garden. Master Campbell didn't have speed in mind, just growing a beauty spot. This suited Pappy fine. He could dig and hoe and plant when he wanted, then set back and let his imagination wander. Pappy had a good eye for how a bush should be shaped, and where to put flowers. He knew how tall they'd grow, and what colors they'd be. Master Campbell thought Pappy was one smart man. The two of them put their heads together and study that English garden book, both of them just brim full of ideas.

Master Thomas thought Pappy ought to work the fields like everybody else. Pappy was too old for that kind of work. Caused him to grumble like the rest of them. Specially when the rose bushes bout died, and the boxwoods got scraggly. One good thing come of me and Miss Julia talking. We figured she ought to convince Master Thomas to put Pappy in charge of the apple trees, which she did. This helped Pappy feel more like a man. Sometimes he asked Little Sam or Bob to climb up the trees to trim out the top. Master Thomas bout had a fit, said he couldn't spare them younguns from the field, then Miss Julia put her nose in again and say it wouldn't take much time and would make for a heap more apples. Master Thomas, he give in.

Friday, May 18, 1860

Although the Negroes remained sullen, not all was gloom and doom our first few years back in Lincoln County. In spite of Thomas' worry, the crops were tolerably good and we did not starve, nor incur debt. It was not so very long after the horse died that Thomas acquired another mule. Although he never admitted any such thing, I'm sure he felt some degree of guilt. I wish he had apologized to Romulus, but as he was Mrs. Henderson's son, that was unlikely.

Loony Brown was still among us, and we'd hardly settled in when he came by on his rounds. Thomas had met the whiskey peddler during our courtship, and knew the poor demented creature to be harmless. Fortunately for Loony Brown, Thomas developed a taste for his wares before noticing that the corn along the edge of the field seemed to mysteriously disappear. Surely the deer could not be so bold, after all the dogs had been trained to frighten them away. It never occurred to him that the corn had been scavenged by Mr. Brown who always carried scraps to pacify the dogs. Then Thomas was puzzled by the lack of windfall apples. At first he thought Greene was doing a superior job of keeping them picked up. But while Greene was ill one week, Thomas went to inspect, and found not a single fruit on the orchard floor. I decided it was time to explain Mr. Brown's system, and how Pa had thought the small fee he charged for whiskey and brandy was pittance for gathering and processing what was little more than gleanings. Thankfully Thomas concurred.

We were accustomed to Loony Brown, as were Rose and Cissy and Greene. But I nearly keeled over in laughter when I happened to see Dovey observe him for the first time. As always he came clattering and hollering down the road. But he was not the same spectacle he once was, as age had slowed his step, and in the years since my childhood Pa had improved the road, easing Loony's passage. His voice had grown gravely, more otherworldly, and his hair and beard were long and wild and white, enveloping his head and shoulders like a vapor. For all the world he resembled an illustration I had seen of Neptune rising from the sea. And he still conversed vivaciously with his invisible entourage, all the while beating the mule who was not there. Dovey must have heard his approach. I think she was attending a laundry kettle in the kitchen yard, and I was in the garden nearby. She looked up and there he was, whiskey jugs jangling in his push-cart, and him shouting and waving his stick in the air. His white shirt, which hung below the knees of his dark trousers, blended perfectly with the unkempt mane that swirled about him, his wild eyed face like a specter emerging from a cloud. Dovey stood stunned for a moment, then let out a shriek to curdle the blood. Her eyes bulged, and her hands flew to her head as if her hair standing on end was about to unloose her kerchief, flinging it into the air. She nearly sunk to her knees, then caught herself and made a bee line for the kitchen. I heard later that she had dived under the table hollering and moaning about "haints." It took Cissy half the afternoon to calm the poor thing down and convince her that Loony Brown was simply a man who was mad, yet harmless. I doubt Dovey ever got over the fright, for I never again saw her around when he made his visits. I think she developed an ear for his clangy approach, and made herself scarce.

Every now and again Mr. Henderson graced us with a welcome visit. Thomas had the good sense to ask his father for agricultural advice, which proved somewhat helpful, but not enough to engender self-confidence and reliance on his men. Perhaps those are the qualities that cause a few men to become hugely wealthy planters, and others only moderately so. After all, everyone in our neighborhood had the same weather, roughly the same soil, and dealt in the same markets. Thomas provided adequately, and I wanted for nothing; I only wish he could have done so more peacefully.

Mrs. Henderson rarely accompanied her husband to our place. She had a headache, or her stomach was uneasy and she feared one of her people had poisoned her again; there were numerous excuses. I was not interested in her excuses, only pleased she invented them. Our trips to the Henderson farm were mercifully rare, and by God's Grace, it was not of my doing. Thomas was genuinely too busy to leave the farm. The question never arose during planting or harvest, and after the lay by there were fences to build, tools and wagons to repair, never a shortage of chores. "Next year, when I have the place in better order," he had told his father, but next year was always the same as the last.

I did find time to spend with Thomas' sister Essie who lived only a few miles of us. I would perch little Tom on my horse and ride to her place, or she would gather up her children, two of them at that time, and come to us. And of course we saw each other most Sundays at church. As my sister-in-law I expected her to be a kindred spirit, and to feed the hunger I'd had for a sister ever since my own had died. I also hoped she would stand in lieu of Mrs. Henderson who was not motherly to me. At that time she lived up to those expectations, and we delighted in the time we cobbled together. But it was not to last.

Essie regarded her mother much as I did, or so I thought, although she leaned toward pity, and I to contempt. Those differences I attributed to the fact that one loves a mother no matter what flaws she might have. Mrs. Henderson's tirades caused Essie to wince in embarrassment, while I boiled in anger. We had the greatest laugh one day when Essie told me her name, her true Christian name. Mrs. Henderson had a flair for the dramatic, and an intense desire to impress others with her "vast" literary knowledge. When Essie was born her mother had plucked a volume of Shakespeare from the bookshelf, and scanned the pages for the most romantic flamboyant name she could find. She latched onto Desdemona. She had no idea who Desdemona was of course, she simply thought Desdemona Henderson resonated with poetry. And I suppose it did. Little Desdemona was about two years old when someone had the audacious courage to tell her mother that Shakespeare's Desdemona was the wife of Othello, a black Moor. Mrs. Henderson was outraged, but Desdemona had been properly Baptized, recorded on the church rolls and in the family Bible. There was no changing the name of a two-year-old! So somehow "Essie" was extracted from "Desdemona," and Essie she has been ever since. If Essie resented that she had been named for the fictitious wife of a Blackamoor, she did not let on. She only said that Desdemona sounded pretentious. Essie suited her just fine.

Saturday, May 19, 1860

I believe it was the winter of 1826 that Thomas discovered a new way of making money: hiring out some of our people. During those years the iron industry of Lincoln County was blossoming. There were a number of furnaces and forges scattered about, and perhaps I should explain what it was they did. In general the furnaces extracted iron from the raw ore and cast it into pots or skillets or fire dogs or ovens, and also iron bars. Forges heated the bars which were called pig iron and hammered them over anvils into tools and implements. However, there was a great deal of overlapping of those tasks, as a small handful of families, mostly intermarried, owned most of the furnaces and forges and produced whatever was in demand. In addition they farmed like everyone else. Winter and early spring were busy times for the iron works. The intense heat of their fires was less oppressive then, and the springtime rise of the creeks fed their need for water power. The greatest advantage was that Negroes from the neighborhood could be readily hired out when the land was fallow. Unskilled workers chopped limitless quantities of wood and turned it into charcoal. The furnaces had an unquenchable hunger for fuel. Talented Negroes were sometimes trained to casting, forging and blacksmithing.

Thomas concluded to hire out Dovey's husband Sam, their boys Little Sam and Bob, and her brother Fred. Thank goodness he thought Greene was too old for such strenuous work, and needed Romulus at home for wintertime repairs. He hoped that the wages earned by Sam and Fred and the boys would be sufficient to buy another hand, although it might take several seasons of hiring out to accomplish that. It was a forge where they worked, Mount Tirzah Forge, which was located on Leeper's Creek about five miles of our place. Dovey was delighted by that fact, for she assumed her family would spend their Sabbaths at home. But alas, they were not permitted to leave the premises of Mount Tirzah until their contract was up. It was hot and unpleasant work, and I suppose the owner of the forge feared anyone who left his property might neglect to return.

In the spring Thomas was surprised to learn that the iron-master wished to buy Fred. He told Thomas that Fred was intelligent and

115

could be trained to the most skilled portions of the operation, and as Fred was without a wife at that time, certainly Thomas would consider the matter. Thomas was perplexed, for he considered Fred little more than a cipher. In the fields the man was slow and grumbled incessantly under his breath. Otherwise he was a quiet fellow, barely noticed by Thomas. Of course my husband refused to sell him, for we had few enough workers as it was. However he put it in the back of his mind that perhaps he had misjudged Fred, and should consider training him to smithing or carpentry, or some other such trade. But that would come later, when the land was well ordered. Thomas yearned for the day when he might have hands enough to effortlessly produce a crop, and Negroes to spare for skilled labor.

I should reiterate that I loved Thomas deeply in spite of his flaws, which I am sure he absorbed from his mother's milk. His difficulty with the Negroes was mostly wrought by frustration, and rarely overflowed into anger. He never struck them, at least not to my knowledge. I truly believe he never did. He was always loving and kind and good to our little family. He showered us with every bounty that was within his power. He was openly affectionate with us, even to the point of frequently hugging his son, something many men consider unmanly. And we never lacked for any creature comfort he could afford to provide. Every marriage has rough patches; I am convinced our union was more satisfying than most.

In the late fall of 1826 I made the delightful discovery that I was once more expecting a child. Here I was approaching my twenty-seventh year, married almost five of them, and only one child to show for it! I was extremely nervous, taking note of every twinge, and prayed for the Lord's benevolence. Brother Frank lived with us that winter. Just before Christmas he completed his course at the South Carolina Medical College, and we invited him to share our home while he searched in Lincolnton for a suitable house. He wanted a place with ample living space, preferably above stairs, and rooms below for his office and a surgery should he need one. A surgery! What a novel idea in our land of country doctors. In the meantime, I appreciated having him nearby in my state of nervousness. He assured me at length that a slight toothache or case of the sniffles would not endanger my child.

In June of 1827 I gave birth to Adie, the daughter I now live with, who was the picture of health. I thanked the Lord over and over for sending me a robust child. It was a good year when Adie was born. The crops were good, and both the black and white families were healthy.

Thomas seemed to be more successful with his labor, and gaining some self assurance about farming, although that problem was never completely overcome.

Saturday, May 19, 1860

I was a heap busy with three little boys. It was good to be busy. Mam and Pappy settled down some; even Romulus took a better disposition for a while. I think all the baby noises and boy scrambling cheered them up. It's hard to stay low in a house full of younguns. Master Frank come home when he finished his schooling. I still thought him a scoundrel, but it was good to have a doctor close by with Miss Julia expecting another child. The Lord looked over her, and Miss Adie was born sprightly and sound. Not long after Miss Adie come, Master Frank find him a house in Lincolnton, and I for one was not sorry to see him go. Master Frank has never been a favorite of mine, and selling our family was only one reason. I wrote down that he was not much more than a boy when that happened, and if he'd grown into a different kind of man, I might have forgave him. But he never did come to think of us like real people. He treat us like children he can't trust no further than he can spit. He act polite, but his voice sound uppity like he don't mean it. I don't know how he come by such a notion, certainly not from his pappy or Miss Julia, and I already wrote about his brother Jeff, that sweet, sweet white boy that die so young. He never act such a way! Most families got somebody that don't fit in, and I reckon Master Frank was the one.

He was no bigger than a tadpole when his Pappy sent him to school, and even before that he passed his time holed up in his room, nose in a book. Maybe that's where he learn such foolishness. Nowadays I abide Master Frank for the news he brings. I likes to hear how folks is doing, and all his talk about the Yankees coming to whup the South and set the slaves free is of great interest to me. Course I takes a different point of view than the one Master Frank lays out. He is a great scoundrel.

After Miss Adie was born I had my three children to tend to and two white ones. It took all my time. I think that was when Romulus began to slip away from me. He stopped complaining, and got quiet like, drawn up into hisself. When he have his manly needs he take me in silence without affection, just done his business and set me aside with nary a thought like he was hanging his hat on a peg. He paid me no mind 'til he need me again. This all happen slowly, and I was so tired each day from cooking and washing and running after younguns, that it took me a long time to get to worrying, to notice that he had hardly a word for our boys. He come in after work, hang up his coat, and eat his supper. Then he'd say he was bone tired and had to get some sleep. I had to keep the boys quiet which was some chore as sometimes the sun was barely down. Where had their happy daddy gone? Where was the Romulus who had run his gentle fingers over my cheeks and lips, whispered lovey words into my ear, snuggled his grinning face into our babies' flesh?

I ask him what was wrong, but all he would answer is that he didn't want to be here no more. What did he mean by "here?" Here on the plantation, here in slavery, here living in the world? He would not say. Then late in the year 1828 we had us another child, a boy I named Alfred. If I thought he had the misery before, I was sadly mistaken, for now he had the Big Misery, the likes of which I never saw before. Romulus looked at our boys, and all he saw was four field hands coming up, bound forever to Master Thomas. No way out. Never.

Christmas come, and Master Thomas drop by with his gifts. He give me some cloth to make our clothes from. There was a fine white linen piece, to make me a shift and gowns for the little boys, and coarse brown cotton for shirts for Marc and Romulus. He give us several pieces of lightweight wool, and a heavy dense one to make Romulus a coat. Master Thomas, he grin from ear to ear, like he Mr. Bountiful, and handed Romulus a little bag holding a few coins, a tiny jug of Loony Brown's whiskey, and a pair of brogans. Not fancy shoes for wearing at church like Master Campbell would have done, but brogans for working in the field.

Later that night when Mam and Pappy and the older boys was asleep I sat rocking Alfred, who was only a few weeks old and fretful. Romulus, laid low by the warmth from the whiskey and the insult of the brogans, finally tell me what's gnawing out his heart. When he was a little boy in Virginia he had a master who treat him almost like a son. He taught Romulus fine manners and how to read and write and cipher. That master greatly admired the big men of Virginia, and desired to be like them having a servant to make copies of his letters, keep his accounts, help with the farm ledger. That was the mark of a gentleman planter. Romulus figured he'd grow up living better than most white folks. His master died when Romulus was about twelve, leaving him to his son. The son was much like the father, cept he didn't have letters that needed copying. Instead he had horses to race. He was the one who trained Romulus to drive and care for horses. Romulus loved horses better than people back then; he would have been satisfied spending his whole life in a stable. About ten years later the new master die, and his farm got broke up and sold. That's when Master Henderson bought Romulus and brung him down to North Carolina. Romulus figured he spent his whole life sliding downhill. From the promise of being a gentleman's scribe, to a horse trainer, to a driver with some farm work thrown in, to a field hand. What was next, digging and burning iron ore, being hired out to Charlotte where they was working gold mines, the pit of hell for a black man?

Romulus had tears on his face when he said he feared to love his boys, for if he did they would surely be sold away, breaking his heart. It pained his soul that he brought them into the world for nothing but working cotton. He said he wanted to get shed of this place, go up to that Canada he'd heard about, be a real man, a free one, but he didn't have any idea where Canada was exactly, nor how to get there. He said he feared loving me, cause all it did was create more field hands, but sometimes he had his needs and couldn't help hisself, then afterwards he was ashamed. Long into the night I listened to Romulus, him sipping on the whiskey, telling about his childhood when he lived in a brick house with his family. Imagine, brick houses for slaves! Those must have been some rich folks that owned him then. He had a whole passel of family that he ain't seen since the day he was sold, and no idea what become of them. Then he say it don't matter, for his Mam would be mightily shamed to see how low he has sunk.

It frightened me when he said the part about Canada. I never figured Romulus be one to run away, but I had to think about it after that night. It would be nigh impossible for him and me and four younguns to go traipsing off together, so if he took off we'd be left behind. And it was dangerous, which scared me most of all. I loved Romulus, in spite of how ornery he'd become. Folks that run off most always get caught. If they lucky they get sent home and punished. Most have their backs whipped into bloody shreds, and if they live, they gets sold down to the low country in South Carolina and worked by overseers crueler than Satan. From what I hear, that low country make Master Thomas' place look like pastures of heaven. I didn't dare tell any of this to Miss Julia. If the white folks knew they would be even harder on Romulus, never giving him a free minute to hisself. And if he ever did run off, it would be up to me to keep it secret as long as possible, the only power I had over his safety.

Sunday, May 20, 1860

Bless my dear daughter Adie! What an overwhelming joy she was! A fact I must remind myself of when the adult Adie gives me frustration. During the first year or so of Adie's life I was entirely absorbed in my own little world. I was determined that no misfortune would come to my daughter nor to Tom, who had just turned four, and was rapidly becoming a rambunctious little boy. I performed my own housekeeping and child care duties (I was proud of my accomplishments, if I may flatter myself), and nearly lost touch with our black families. It was usually Dovey who brought in our meals and carried out our laundry. In those days I held little regard for Dovey, having taken my lead from Cissy who always considered her a field hand, a low-life, and an interloper in the kitchen. Rose rarely appeared in our house. She was completely preoccupied with her brood of little boys, and had taken over most of the cooking from Cissy. I knew Cissy's rheumatism made her nearly useless, but had no knowledge of how ill and despondent she had become. With Rose virtually absent in my life, there was no one to inform me of how Thomas was getting along with his hands, or any other conditions in the Negro quarters. Blissfully ignorant, I assumed everyone was content and at peace.

Around 1829, I believe that was the year, the year Adie turned two, Thomas purchased three more people. Abel was about twenty, Mary eighteen, and Joe fifteen, more or less. They were siblings, sold as a group, which gave me slight hope that Mattie and her children might be together, wherever they were. At least some slave dealers considered the sanctity of family! I am ashamed to admit that I paid little attention to these people. I was simply pleased that Thomas' burden had been eased, and that there was another female on the place with so many mouths to be fed. Thomas hoped that Fred might take Mary for a wife; it was greatly to his advantage to acquire hands from breeding rather than purchase. Rose had certainly done her share, but Dovey must have become barren. Her younger boy was about fourteen, and as far as we knew she had not since carried another.

The new boys took up residence with Dovey and Sam, and Mary was installed with Cissy and Greene, and Rose's ever growing family. Where they found space, I did not know, nor did I inquire. I was expecting again, and even more deeply ensconced in my own little world. Caleb was born in 1830. He was a plump and cheerful infant, and I was completely contented.

Thomas seemed to be well satisfied with his new hands. If he had complaints, he did not bring them into the house. All three children were thriving and keeping me well occupied. This was the woman I was supposed to be, a God-fearing wife and mother with a well ordered household. I missed Rose's companionship, but we had no time for social exchanges.

Caleb was not past infancy when I concluded another child was on the way. It is uncommon to conceive with a babe still at the breast, but it does happen. By then I had borne enough children to feel confident I could recognize the more subtle symptoms of impending motherhood. I kept my suspicions private until my growing abdomen proved I was right. Fortunately the new Negro Mary was becoming competent in the kitchen, and Rose would be available to me for my confinement. Lawson was born in 1831. Four perfect children. I'm sure I was the proudest mother that ever lived! The Bible tells us that pride goeth before the fall. I was soon to learn that indeed it does.

Sunday, May 20, 1860

What come next is mighty painful to set down. Some of it I never told a living soul, not Miss Julia, not my childrens, not nobody. I work so hard in them days, I ought to have fell asleep the minute I lay down, but I had a heap of worrying to do. Master Thomas had got us three more people, two strong young bucks and a fine girl; that took some load off of Romulus. But it did not fix his misery. He hardly ever took my affection anymore, as if his manhood had dried up like a husk. And he purely ignored our boys, trying mightily not to love them. Him being raised up like a gentleman, and now wallowing in shame that all he could sire was field hands. I know he still loved us. Every now and again the shield of anger would drop from his eyes, revealing love couched in his soul, unguarded for an instant.

The new girl, Mary, was a great help, as I had plenty to do with Miss Julia bringing more babies. Good-for-nothing Dovey never did like to take orders from me, in spite of the fact Miss Julia told her to. I heard her with my own ears! Who else was to run the place with Mam hunkered in her chair all day moaning about her lost children and aching with the rheumatiz? Pappy, he not much better. Did what he had to and not a lick more. But they wasn't lazy, they was old and sick and mired in sorrow. Dovey had no such excuse! All my life Mam told me "lazy good-for-nothings" give us all a bad name, and that's exactly what Dovey was. I reckon she was riled at me running things, her being older than me, and knew that I figured I was better than her, which I was. All that and Romulus getting lower and lower with the misery.

This go on day after day, month after month, till a year or so had passed. Nothing but work and worry. Oh how I missed them old days reading books with Miss Julia, playing with our babies, watching Marc and Tom learning to creep across the floor. That seem a thousand years ago. I felt like an old woman, all used up, and here I was only bout twenty-five years old!

When Alfred was almost two Romulus got me with another baby. I think that was what broke his spirit to pieces. Soon as I told him a child was coming, he began to skulk around like a fox. I'd see him at church going off to the edge of the woods with some men I did not know. They'd stand there huddled under the trees, heads together, whispering. I'd ask him about it, and he'd say it weren't none of my business, and to keep my mouth shut. Sometimes I saw one of the men sneak a piece of paper from his pocket, and they'd all study on it, half hidden in cupped hands, like it was real important. Could those other men read? It oughtn't to have surprised me, but it did. I didn't know Romulus could read till that dreadful night when he told me about his sweet childhood. Back then it wasn't no deep dark secret that a black person could read (that come later); I reckon we didn't talk about it cause we didn't have any use to. We didn't have no time to do any reading.

One day when I was shaking Romulus' coat out to air, a paper dropped from his pocket, a folded up scrap like those men had been studying. It had only a few words strung together by lots of lines, some curvy, some straight. Then I heard Romulus coming, so I stuck it back before I had time to figure what it was. Later I looked for it, but it was gone. Lo and behold, after a week or so, it turned up under the mattress. Didn't Romulus know I beat the mattress every now and again? That weren't much of a hiding place. It took a while to make sense of that paper scrap, cause it had words I didn't know and had to sound out. It slowly come to me that the wavy lines was creeks and rivers. A little snaky one was marked Leeper's Creek, and a fat one said Catawba River, then I knew I had it figured out. It was a map. The straight lines was roads sprinkled along with words that I puzzled out to be names of towns and farms. No wonder I'd never seen them in books before. It was a map leading to the middle of the state where the Quakers lived. The word "Quakers" was underlined three times. Everybody knew about Quakers. How they'd hide runaways and help them up to Canada. Romulus was planning to run off, all by hisself I reckoned, cause he hadn't told me a bit of it.

I folded up the map and put it back where I found it. Mattress beating could wait for another day. If we got bed bugs, so be it. I couldn't let on I knew. I took to watching Romulus more careful. Sometimes he'd sneak out in the middle of the night, and climb back in bed afore daybreak. Don't know where he went. Odds and ends of his clothes disappeared, and the box where we kept our coins shifted from one place on the shelf to another. Was he taking it down to count them?

Must have been about January Romulus took up this sneaky business. Most of the men and big boys was over working at the furnace. I reckon that's why nobody else noticed his peculiar comings and goings. It end up one Saturday night in March when he snuck out of bed and never came back. At daybreak I pretended to be asleep as long as I could, for I knew what had happened as sure as if he'd told me with his own breath. I knew he was gone and feared I would never see him this side of the pearly gates. I pressed my face in the pillow to muffle the weeping that was coming on, and when I did my hand brushed against a folded piece of paper. He'd left me a note.

Monday May 21, 1860

This story too big to set down all in one day, so I continue. When I found that paper by the pillow, I balled it up in my fist, jumped out of bed and scurried down toward the privy. That was the one place I knew I folks didn't dawdle for long, and I shore didn't want no witnesses. Nobody was there, so I sat myself down behind a nearby tree and uncrumpled the paper. Romulus had wrote:

My Beautiful Rose,

With the heaviest heart a man can endure I take up my pen. When you read these words I will be gone. I love you more than life itself Rose, but I cannot abide to live in slavery another day. I have told you some of my woes, but there are more. I have failed at preventing myself from loving our sons no matter how I try. I cannot sleep forever by your side and not take you to my bosom. Surely the Good Lord did not put me on this earth to populate it with slaves. My heart is shattered.

All this winter Master Thomas has made the threat of hiring me out to the furnace. I told him I preferred not to go. He turned a threat into a bribe by promising me a fair portion of my wages. I then told him I would not go. He accused me of being insubordinate (in foul words learned from his mother, no doubt) then gave me a scowl that surely meant trouble would follow. I once admired Master Thomas when we lived on his father's place, but now I do not. I suppose the elder gentleman was a good manager of men. His son has never mastered the skill. I had hoped when his money worries diminished, that my lot would improve, and that I might live out my days training horses and grooming a son in the craft. I know now that is not to be.

I hope to soon find a safe place, a place of freedom and perhaps plenty. When I am situated I will make arrangements for you and the children to join me. Should you be approached by a Quaker lady or gentleman, pay careful attention and do as they say. Please keep my absence a secret as long as humanly possible. No one will inquire of me on the Sabbath. Perhaps I can be considered "ill" for the next several days. I pray that no harm comes to you from my rash action. I trust that the ally you have in Miss Julia will protect you. Take care of my fine children and remind them always of my love for them. When they are older perhaps they will understand, although I pray that by then we will have long been reunited. If my effort should fail, please seek out any opportunity that might arise for my sons to learn a trade; seize it, for that is their only hope for a contented life.

Forgive me, my dear love. My heart is shriveled and dead. I have no other choice. By the grace of God and the kindness of Quakers, may we live together once more in the future.

With undying love forever,

Romulus

What beautiful words! I never knew 'til that morning that he had been so perfectly schooled by his old master in Virginia. I have kept his letter all these years, hidden away in my possessions, and copied it here word for word. I pray that he found freedom, but doubt that he did, as no Quaker ever come to get us. I reckon he's gone up to Heaven, which is finer than Canada from what I hear.

I must have been some sight setting under a tree in my night dress, bawling over his sad letter. I was soon chilled, clad as I was, and ambled back to the cabin, numbed by the news. I told Mam and the boys that Romulus had took his traps and gone off in the woods, an ordinary thing to do on a Sunday. Pappy asked why he wasn't invited, and I say I don't know. Romulus woke up early; maybe he didn't want to bother nobody. Then I dressed and go to the kitchen to fix dinner for the white folks. Mostly we gets Sunday off, but it was my turn to cook; folks got to eat no matter what day it is. Sunday meals were plain fare, so I put some ham on to boil, washed a mess of collards, and fixed a pan of biscuits. I reckon it was good that I had an easy and solitary task, for my mind was a spinning with concocting a lie, and I had tears to hide.

Monday was harder. I told Marc that his daddy had business to tend to and we was to pretend he hurt hisself, and would be off his feet for a spell. He promised to keep the secret; being nine I could count on him. I told Mam, Pappy, Levi and Ezekiel that Romulus was puny and had gone to Dovey's cabin cause it was quieter there. Sam and the men were all at the furnace, so it truly was a quieter place. I didn't say anything to Alfred who was barely three. Nobody would be poking at him for information. Then I went up to the big house and told Master Thomas that Romulus hurt his leg while trapping on Sunday, and would be laid up for a piece. He asked should he send for the doctor, and I said no, he just turned his ankle bad and ought to be off it a while. Then I allowed that I needed some time to make Romulus comfortable. That was a powerful act of lying. I had to turn my scared rabbit face into a sad one, pretending Romulus was hurt, and hide the hate for Master Thomas that was boiling up in my chest.

I sure was glad Miss Julia didn't come to the door when I went up there, for she would have known I was lying to beat all. The thought of it set me to shuddering. But I wouldn't be able to keep clear of Miss Julia for long, cause I was once again working mostly in the house. A few months before, she said she needed me, cause her baby about to come, and Caleb nigh a year old. By that time Mary did most of the cooking, and Mam abided her just fine. Dovey's chores of laundry and mending and gardening kept her out of Mam's way, and all of us had become more peaceful. But it was not like the old days. I'd been pent up with worrying about Romulus, him skulking about, and acting so peculiar. Miss Julia had been noticing I was not my old self. I'd let on that my stomach was giving me fits with the baby I was carrying (Lord forgive me), and her younguns was a handful (that part was true). Then her baby Lawson was borned, and a few weeks later Romulus up and run off. I was afraid if she'd come to the door that morning she would see what happened sketched all over my face.

About mid-morning, after making a pretense of nursing Romulus, I was back at the house, face to face with Miss Julia. She could see my eyes was red, and I told her I didn't get much sleep with Romulus moaning in pain half the night, and my stomach heaving in the morning. I hated to lie to that woman. She didn't deserve such a thing, and I had never practiced lying. She believed me because she trusted me, and I felt so ashamed. This story held up 'til Wednesday afternoon. It was warm for March and Miss Julia and I decided to set out on the back porch and give her baby some fresh air. Dovey was hanging laundry out to dry, when up comes my poor innocent Levi, and asks Dovey as big as you please how long his daddy would have to stay at her cabin. "What you mean, boy?" she says "Your daddy ain't at my place."

"Sure he is," said Levi. "He got to be, cause he ain't been at home since he got hurt." Both Dovey and Miss Julia turned and stared at me with four eyeballs boring through my skin like hot pokers. The time had come to tell the truth. I prayed to God that four days was ample to get to the Quakers, and that the Quakers had taken my beloved in.

Wednesday, May 23, 1860

Early in March of 1831, my son Lawson was born, and I reveled in the perfection of my situation. I suppose that was a prideful sin, a precursor of what was to follow. Tom was almost eight that year, and a great help with his new brother. Adie at three and a half thought herself to be a splendid little mother. How precious she was! Caleb was only fourteen months old when Lawson made his appearance. A few months before, dear Rose had once again become my house servant, as I could hardly be expected to care for two infants by myself. Rose seemed despondent, though not disagreeable, which was a complete puzzle to me, for I assumed she would have been delighted to leave the heat of the kitchen for the comfort of my home. She said the child she was carrying was causing a weak stomach, and my children were troublesome. I've no doubt that was true, but it was audacious of her to say so! Rose always was one to speak her mind. I ignored her mood, as I was overjoyed to have her help and companionship, and was convinced that we would soon have our happy household back again.

Lawson was not quite two weeks old, when the ominous year began to unfold itself with the revelation that Romulus had run away. Romulus of all people! I had considered him a trusted servant, and had never heard a word to suggest otherwise, except for that odious horse incident several years before. Even my mother-in-law respected Romulus. A Negro recipient of her esteem was certainly a saint among men.

On a Monday morning Rose reported that her husband had injured himself while trapping in the woods, and would have to be off his feet for a few days. Thomas and I did not question her explanation for his absence from his chores. Rose had never before lied to us, and Romulus had always been a reliable man. It never occurred to Thomas to go to the cabin to see for himself. It was an innocent comment made several days later by one of Rose's children that alerted us to the truth. I suppose I should have noticed Rose's nervousness, but with a newborn, I was aware of very little else.

Rose and I were sitting on the porch with my infants when her little boy inquired of Dovey as to the whereabouts of his sick father. The lie was obvious in an instant. Dovey assumed, as I had, that Romulus was laid up in his own bed, and Rose had told the residents of her household that he was recuperating at Dovey's cabin. I was completely astonished! I immediately took Rose inside where we could speak privately. Poor Rose. (I say "poor Rose" now; at the time I was livid at her deliberate deception.) It was dreadfully awkward for her to relate the truth to me. Her eyes would not meet mine, and her fingers fidgeted with her apron. She told me in halting words that Romulus had been unhappy for years, that he had been raised by an elegant gentleman, that he had spent his youth in relative ease in a brick slave house receiving an education to rival that of most white boys. She told me he had later been trained to groom and train race horses, that his job as Mrs. Henderson's driver was a cruel demotion in his eyes. She told me how deeply Romulus detested the field work Thomas required of him, and how furious he had been when Thomas forced him to work a precious horse to death. The death of that horse could have not been more mournful than the loss of one of his sons; it was an abscess on his soul that would not heal. Except for the horse incident, I had heard none of this. Nor did I know that Thomas desired to send Romulus to Mount Tirzah Forge, and threatened punishment when he rebelled against the idea. Rose told me that Romulus had had "the misery" for years, and had grown quite adept at keeping it hidden from his masters.

Poor, poor Rose. She was obviously sad and embarrassed and angry. She loved Romulus and was fearful for his future. She was also fearful that she might be punished for his deed. I've no idea why she harbored such a notion. For all of Thomas' ineptitude with the Negroes, I don't believe he was ever cruel. I asked why she had kept this from us for so many days, and she replied she was afraid Romulus would be caught and beaten. I promised her Thomas would do no such thing, but what if some other man did the catching, she asked. Of course she was right. A runaway is like a fox before hounds; no wonder she was so agitated. Then I asked if she had any knowledge of where he might have gone, or whom he might have consorted with. She told me point blank that she did not, and I did not believe her. In my ire, I started to press, then hesitated. What purpose would it serve? Any plan made by Romulus four days since had either been accomplished or altered. I loved Rose and could not break her heart further. A pact between a man and wife is inviolate, even among Negroes.

It astonishes me yet that wisdom penetrated my anger, perhaps it was intuitive. It certainly occurred to me that his plot might include Rose and their children. If there was the slightest possibility that she was planning to join him, I could not risk alienating her and push her to do so. I cherished her too much. She was such a pitiful waif, I could not believe she was plotting to leave me, yet I feared that was the reason for her unease.

We never saw Romulus again, nor heard anything of him. It is likely that he perished, or was captured and sold far away from us. Thomas published a notice offering a reward for his return, but an unscrupulous man could earn far more by selling him than by collecting Thomas' reward. I doubt if he communicated with Rose. She never left me, nor gave me any reason to think she might. I'm sure if she had heard of his death or capture she would have told me.

Rose never married again. Some time after Romulus ran away she told me Dovey's brother Fred was trying to court her. But she was not interested. What if Romulus should come home and find her with another man? Besides, if she couldn't have Romulus there was no one else she wanted. Fred, rebuffed, married Mary, just as Thomas had hoped he would.

Thursday, May 24, 1860

Rose mourned for Romulus as if he had died. And as with a death, the demands of living asserted themselves, bringing some sense of order. My sympathy for Rose was genuine, and she seemed to accept it as such. In no uncertain terms I informed Thomas that she was to receive no blame, ill-will, or censure of any kind for Romulus' disappearance. I reminded him that she was my property, that I trusted her, and needed her confidence in return. I did not threaten to withhold my affections, although he may have assumed so. In any event he took my concern seriously, and complied completely.

In late March the men returned from the forge, and preparation for a crop began. Rose and I resumed our old pattern as much as possible, with so many little ones to care for. Tom was old enough for school, and went to the one held at Leeper's Creek Church, just as I had done so many years ago. Marc had chores with the men. With Adie and my babies, and Rose's three littlest ones, our house was filled with scurrying and laughter, sniffles and bumped knees, all of the busyness that accompanies children. We were content.

In two months time an epidemic invaded our community, an epidemic of measles. Tom was the first to be infected, then Alfred fell ill. Thomas sent Little Sam to fetch my brother. Frank was not a frequent visitor to our place. In part because he was a very busy man. There were other doctors in Lincolnton, but none with his education. Also I think Frank was still embarrassed, perhaps even remorseful, for selling our black family, and dreaded facing Cissy and Greene. Rose generally scowled at him openly with great abandon, which completely befuddled Frank for he had never encountered such behavior from a Negro, and had no idea how to respond. However, children were ill, and for once Rose welcomed Frank into our abode.

Frank prescribed sweating. He instructed us to apply mustard plasters to the children's chests, and smother them in blankets. We heated bricks in the fireplace and placed them in pans under the children's beds. As often as possible they were to drink a scalding tea brewed from snake root. Lastly he told us to bathe their feet in water as warm as they could bear, and draw the curtains keeping the room as dark as convenient to protect their eyes. One by one the rest of the children fell ill. We had our hands full with nursing, which especially taxing for Rose as her confinement was approaching.

Cissy, distrustful of doctors, especially Frank, inserted her own opinions, which were welcome, as Cissy had been remote for such a long time. She approved of the plasters and the snake root tea, but thought the blankets and hot bricks excessive, as it was dreadfully hot, and all of us were sweating copiously. She told us to open the curtains to let in fresh air. "But Mam," wailed Rose, "what about their eyes? If they live they'll be blind!"

Cissy harrumphed. "Tie a neckerchief round they eyes. No use for the whole fambly stumbling in the dark. Master Frank sold my younguns to get hisself some learning, and didn't get a penny's worth of sense!"

Cissy was always adamant about fresh air, no matter what the ailment or the season. Doctors feared it as a malicious source of contamination. Doctors are changing their thinking nowadays. I believe the prevailing theory is that Cissy was right.

It was nearly a month before the measles left our environs, and it took my two littlest lambs in its wake. Lawson died the twenty-fifth of June, in the third month of his tiny life. Caleb succumbed two days later, not yet a year and a half of age. If there was any consolation in this wretched event, it was that all of the others were mending, and I did not have to choose between nursing one mortally ill child, and attending the funeral of another. It pains me to say that I did not mourn those two as I should have, enveloped by numbness and utter fatigue. But over the years I have longed for those children, yearned to have their baby fists grasping my hair or gown, yearned to take in their freshly scrubbed fragrance, and fill my arms with soft baby flesh. I have mourned them now, not with the sudden overwhelming grief that followed Jane's death, but with a slow deliberate release spanning decades.

In July, Rose was delivered of her fifth and last child, a daughter she named Patsy. I had insisted that Tom engage a midwife for Rose's delivery, as Cissy was too hobbled by rheumatism to be of any use. It was the midwife who brought little Patsy into the world, but I pulled Rose through her pains, and soothed her between them, an old familiar task that gave us both comfort. Rose wept when she first held her infant daughter, wept that the ordeal was ended, wept that Romulus might never know his precious female child, who was not destined for the plow.

Friday, May 25, 1860

Telling Miss Julia the truth about Romulus was one hard thing to do. I told her how low he'd sunk since his childhood, and how he hungered after them good old days. I told her how shamed he felt, siring one field hand after another. I told her he'd always had a gloomy streak, just like Mattie did. But I held my peace bout the Quakers, the map, and the letter he left me. My heart tell me Miss Julia would do me no harm, but I was mighty afraid seeing her so angry, and was shamed of my deceitfulness. I already wrote that Mam and Pappy despised "lazy, good-for-nothings," and would have whupped me for being one. They held the same opinion of lying.

I wasn't so sure about Master Thomas. I never heard of him beating anybody, but he sure knew how to rant and holler, and work a person till they felt like they'd been beat. I prayed that Miss Julia wouldn't let him get after me, and thank goodness he didn't. Lord knows what I might have done. I never had the gumption to fight back at a white person, but if Master Thomas had called me up, I might have clawed his eyes out. I plumb wanted to kill that man, for he had run Romulus off as sure as if he chased him with a pack of wild dogs. Miss Julia must have give him a good talking-to, cause he never said one word to me bout Romulus. He didn't say he was angry, or sorry, not nothing.

I reckon Miss Julia come to see my grief. At first she was all het up, eyes steely, huffing and puffing and carrying on. Then her shoulders slumped and softened, like she tumbled to the notion that I had no blame in what Romulus done. She say she'd ask Master Thomas to offer a reward, but we both knew it wasn't likely to fetch him home. Whether he was alive or not, my heart was heavy like he was dead. Miss Julia done buried a heap of her family, and knew how grieving cramps up a heart. The old affection we used to have crept back between us.

Then the measles come. Every one of our younguns, black and white was sick to beat all. Miss Julia and I had all we could do making plasters, heating bricks. Master Frank come and told us what to do, and for once in my life I was glad to see him, and glad he had gone to the doctoring school. Not that I forgave him, but it was about time we got some use of the money he made from selling our family. We'd brought all the sick younguns into the big house, pallets scattered every which way, otherwise we never could have took care of them. Miss Julia and I would flit from one child to the next, whoever needed us, bathing, nursing, soothing, no matter whose child it was, no matter what color the skin. Each of us fluttered over the child who was ailing the worst, and rejoiced when it was better.

Master Thomas, he help too. He tended the black ones and the white ones alike, just like his wife. In the evenings, he'd come in all hot and tired, and help with the nursing, giving us some rest. He'd bathe the children's feet, kiss their hot faces, stroke their hands, and tell them stories. He'd sit up half the night, his soft voice lulling them to sleep. Miss Julia always said he was a fine daddy, but I hadn't seen it before. She told me how he fretted over their baby Jane, and how grief struck him down when she died. I wasn't in the house much back then, as Levi had just been borned. I would never have believed that Master Thomas could be as tender a Pappy as my Romulus, had I not seen it with my own eyes. I got a little respect for Master Thomas that summer, but it was a tainted with hate, for I could not put aside that he was the man that run Romulus off.

The measles passed and all my boys got well, but Miss Julia's two littlest died; half her younguns gone in two days time. Oh my, you wouldn't believe the sorrow that come over us. Little Caleb who had barely begun to toddle around, and Lawson not much more than a newborn. Even Mam and Pappy joined in the weeping. And Master Thomas, he just as tore up as Miss Julia. I never saw a white man shed so many tears. He was indeed a fine daddy, and I felt sorry for him in spite of what he done.

Them babies hadn't been buried but a few weeks when my Patsy was born. Miss Julia helped the midwife bring her, just like in the old days, and we was like kinfolk again. Miss Julia hadn't spent time in the cabin for a long while, so I reckon that's when she noticed how terrible Mam and Pappy was ailing. I had told her they wasn't well, but it took her own eyes to see how bad it was. Old Mam was near bent over with the rheumatiz, and her mind had near bout left her. She'd sit in a corner and mumble on this thing or that, half of it pure nonsense. She'd rallied up a bit when the younguns was sick, cause making plasters and herb concoctions was her specialty, but when the measles passed, she sunk back down. She was a pitiful sight to see. Pappy wasn't much better. He complained that he hurt in his chest, and had trouble catching his breath. Most mornings, if he could get up the energy, he'd go out to the apple orchard, cause that was his job. But he didn't do no work. He'd sit under a tree and doze the morning away, then come in at dinner time. After dinner he'd sit outside the cabin door and watch the children play.

Miss Julia was plenty upset. She offered to call Master Frank, which was the one thing that roused Mam's attention. Wasn't no way Mam was having him come and doctor her! So Miss Julia went to town and ask her brother for some medicine. She brought back laudanum for Mam's pain, and foxglove for Pappy's chest. It didn't do much good. Mam seemed to ache less, but her mind got more addled. The medicine for Pappy helped for a while.

Late in August Mam went to bed one night, and in the morning she was dead. At least she died peaceful without a struggle. We buried her outside the churchyard wall, which was where the black folks lay. I hunted the largest fieldstone I could carry to mark her place. Pappy was beside himself with grief. I don't know how long they'd been married, but my brother Amos was ten years older than me, so it must have been nigh on to forty years. Mam had been gone about three months when Pappy died. Could be his medicine didn't work good enough, but I think he plumb give up. Wasn't no use living without Mam. I was mighty sad to lose them, but glad their suffering was over. I sure do envy them all those years together, loving each other.

Saturday, May 26, 1860

Writing bout Mam and Pappy dying reminded me of a strange and frightful tale. It was winter, and Pappy was barely cold in the ground when Master Frank come by with the news. It was a tale about Nat Turner, a black preacher-man in Virginia, who took it upon himself to kill all the white folks. It was in the newspapers, Master Frank said. Nat Turner hatched himself a plot, then gathered up a bunch of slaves to put it in motion. They set out on a killing spree, racing from farm to farm, slaughtering every white person they could get a hold of. Master Frank says nearly a hundred people was murdered, most stabbed and hacked to pieces! The butchering happened in August. The sheriff rounded up Nat and his gang and by November had hanged them every one.

Here is how the tale gets strange. This rampage didn't happen on some big low country plantation where I hear slaves is treated the worst, but in a country place of small farms, not much different from how we live. And Nat professed to be a preacher-man! Master Frank says Nat claimed the Lord told him to do all that slaying, and that he read the directions in the Bible. I never heard such as that! He also tell us that white folks is trembling in their boots all over creation, scared their slaves might take such a notion. I can't imagine anybody I know getting wrought up in such an evil scheme, nor where in the Bible those instructions might be. I concluded that man was tetched in the head. I pray that Romulus never got mixed up with rabble like that. And this is the frightful part. It was bout that time that some white folks commenced to get mighty jittery around nigras. Maybe they always was and I never noticed, but I truly believe Nat Turner caused white men to fear black men. Black folks have always feared the white man, most for good reason. Nowadays folks of both colors is wary of one another, slinking around with suspicions high; that don't bode for nothing but trouble. Now I got no use for slavery, but killing all the white folks ain't the answer. Lord knows what got into that deranged man!

Sunday, May 27, 1860

We attended services today in Lincolnton. Two sermons, morning and afternoon, separated by a social dinner on the grounds. Frank has no news to report. He still carries on about our government. If the western territories are formed into free states, slave owners who already live there might lose their property, and the Southern States, being outnumbered, will be stripped of any power they have in Washington. He worries that war will surely follow. At least he claims to be worried; his demeanor looks more like excitement in my opinion. The entire concept of war is dreadful to me, no matter what issues are involved. I fear Frank will be disappointed if this conflict is settled without violence. As much as war distresses me, I can offer no answer for the preservation of our nation; there seems to be no compromise acceptable to all. Should we elect a president content to leave the South alone, the poor slaves may never be free. An interfering president will incite rebellion; I see no other way.

After Rose's little girl was born Cissy and Greene's health began to decline dramatically. Rose had said they were unwell, but perhaps I was too overwhelmed by the epidemic of measles and the deaths of Caleb and Lawson to comprehend. I was particularly distressed to see how vacant Cissy had become. As a child I was convinced she was the fount of all wisdom. I loved her deeply, and wished she could forgive me for the loss of her children. But she could not; I understood, but it was difficult to accept.

Frank sent medicine for her pain, which seemed to be constant. We assumed this from the anguish that crossed her face when she moved, and the ever present moans that fluttered her lips. The medicine seemed to ease her ancient body, but the spirited, opinionated, sometimes haughty Cissy never came back to us. Perhaps there was more I could have done to end our estrangement. I had apologized endlessly, but she would hear none of it. I had hesitated to hug her, thinking it would be an affront in her icy state. Did I misjudge? I had not told her how much I cared for her, for fear she would think I was fawning to regain her favor. I regret it now. Late that summer she died in her sleep without reconciliation. I never told her how honored I was to have had her as my "mother."

Greene lingered on for a few months. Frank had concluded his heart was giving out, and with Cissy's passing it fizzled into oblivion. I wept for weeks upon Cissy's death, which was natural enough considering how she had mothered me, and how anguished I was over our unreconciled estrangement. But I had not expected to grieve so completely for Greene. We had never been particularly close; I valued him for the love and comfort he showered on Cissy and Rose. Looking back, I suppose that was precisely the point. May God forgive me for taking Greene for granted, for not embracing him with the dignity due a man.

My children missed him deeply. Greene had spent his last years with children, black and white, telling stories, brushing away scrapes and bruises, allaying fears and disappointments. A better grandfather did not exist. I suppose that is how children react to death, a missing more than a mourning, but equally filled with grief. At last the year of 1831 was done.

Perhaps God thought He had dealt us tribulation enough to humble us, for the next several years were happy ones. Thomas acquired more land, buying adjacent acreage as it became available, and became more adept at the intricacies of farming. His hands began to work more like a team, albeit not an overly contented one. Fred had married Mary, who to Thomas' joy began producing little black babies.

Rose began spending most of her time in my home. As we had convinced ourselves that Cissy and Greene were free and at peace at the foot of God's throne, we rekindled our old camaraderie. Raising children and enduring illness and death bind women together. Men can work side by side their entire lives, and may never have an inkling of the experience. We began to see more of my sister-in-law Essie after the measles and the passing of Cissy and Greene. Babies and duties at home had kept us from visiting as often as we wished, and of course no one traveled during the epidemic. Her household was attacked as were most in the neighborhood, fortunately all of her children survived. A dark side of Essie emerged after we resumed our relationship, an aspect that distressed me no end. I suppose her mother's influence was mostly to blame, but she did admit on one occasion the Nat Turner rebellion had shaken her to her roots. But that is a tale for another day.

It is late, and my lamp is spent. Tonight I will forget Essie, and reflect on the good years that came next in my life. Farewell for now.

Monday, May 28, 1860

What a glorious spring day! We have been blessed with decent rains of late, and in the night another comforting shower fell. Today the sun is bright and the air is washed clean. Soon summer will set in bringing oppressive heat, heat that often foments tempers and unrest. I pray to God for our conflicted Nation!

We received letters from daughters Eliza and Rachel today. They and their families are in good health, and plan another visit, at the end of this week or next, weather permitting. I hope they will remain for a while, as Rachel's confinement is approaching, and her travel will soon be restricted. When her time comes, I plan to go to her; surely Isaac will permit Echo to drive me. A woman needs her mother when a new child comes, especially with a three-year-old in the house. Her husband's people live nearby their place. His mother is a genial woman and a great comfort to Rachel, unlike the hussy I acquired upon my marriage. But there is no substitute for one's own mother, at least that is what Rachel wrote in her letter nearly begging me to come. I am so pleased to be wanted, and am eager to comply.

After the deaths of my sons and the loss of Romulus the 1830s progressed as a time of contentment, punctuated by very few dramatic events; happy scenes tumble through my memory. We began to see more of Essie and her family, and my social life expanded pleasantly. My children were past infancy and with Rose's assistance I had leisure to spend in town, as well as time to devote to the work of our church. I joined the Sabbath School Committee whose mission was to educate poor children who had neither time nor money to attend common school. Their fathers were laborers who could not spare them from the farms or the iron works on week days. My assignment was to teach reading and writing on Sunday afternoons to a group of children Tom's age and younger, that is if I could convince their parents to let them come. Most parents were eager to grasp the opportunity, but some were downright obstinate. They either considered the school a charity, of which they wanted no part, or feared their children once educated, would abandon their parents' way of life.

I so enjoyed teaching the little ones. In spite of poverty, their minds hungered for knowledge. Many had never seen a book save the Bible, and some of their parents signed their names with an "X." Imagine, having to affix an X on an important paper, trusting the person who desired your signature to read the document to you, honestly and without chicanery! I swelled with pride thinking I might help their children avoid the handicap, and it pleasured me no end to see their eager eyes drinking up words and their stubby pencils spill them back onto paper. The whole experience reminded me of my "pretend" classroom of so many years before when Rose and Frank were my pupils. Perhaps God designed me to be a teacher.

I also served in the Missionary Society. Our task was to raise money to help support an assortment of pious men who had gone to The Territories to bring salvation to the Indians. I considered the goal admirable, for those poor souls had not rejected God's plan, but were simply unaware of it, yet the method of obtaining the objective was unpleasant. I felt nearly like a beggar going from house to house pleading for money. We often went in little groups of two or three which made the task more bearable, but there was not enough money in Lincoln County to convert all the Indians that roamed the western lands. And there was competition among various congregations as to who could raise the most money. I could not imagine that God would pit his servants against one another in such a way, and when my next child's arrival became apparent, I gracefully exited the missionary work.

Eliza was born in the fall of 1833. Of course I was anxious, considering I had lost three of my five children, but Rose constantly reminded me that those deaths had all resulted from illness, not from any weakness of mine. Eliza was a beautiful child, although I've never seen an infant who was not. From the beginning she was a quiet thing who seemed to take in the entire world with wide and curious eyes. She was about a month old the night Thomas and I watched in awe, Eliza cradled in my arms, as nature sent down a most spectacular shower of falling stars. Star after star swept across the night sky, bursting into sparkles of light streaking toward the horizon. We, being educated people, were aware they were not actually stars, but meteors. Yet we did not know what composed them, where they had come from, or why they were visited upon us in such profusion that particular night. I feel sure that Eliza absorbed the sight, for she was to become a child in whom knowledge and wonder are perfectly aligned.

Tuesday, May 29, 1860

Miss Adie told us her sisters is coming for a visit, so I been helping Sarah get ready. Sarah is Miss Adie's house servant, so I stay around her most every day. She's married to Echo who drives Master Isaac's carriage, and serves the table when company come. Sarah and me been cleaning and scrubbing floors, then we'll have to shuffle beds and set up pallets. Seven extra people is a heap to fix up for. I don't mind working with Sarah. She don't complain, in fact she don't say much at all. She don't work so fast that I can't keep up, but she ain't lazy either. I reckon in that way she remind me of Mattie, moseying around without saying much, eyes giving no idea what's in her mind. In another way she remind me of my child Patsy. Patsy would be about Sarah's age, if she was still living. But first I need to write down what happen next, after Mam and Pappy was buried.

That Angel of Death leave us be for a while. I reckon he done took enough. When Patsy was two Miss Julia had another baby girl, Eliza; she's one of them that's coming to visit. It was 1833, and not a hard year to remember, for that was the winter that the stars fell. I believe everyone alive that night saw the spectacle in the sky. The white folks, at least the ones I know of, said mother nature was putting on quite a show. But some of the nigras was plumb certain that the last days was a-coming, and readied themselves for the judgment. White folks think this superstition, but it's not; it's hope. They don't have no idea how joyful a slave would be to have that glorious day roll round, and go sit by God and not have to work no more. Now falling stars is unusual, and most folks has seen only a few. That night they came by the hundreds, maybe hundreds of hundreds. It was something!

By the time Eliza come along, more children didn't mean so much extra work. That's cause the others was big enough to be of some use. Marc was beginning to work in the fields, which I'm glad his daddy never had to witness, and Levi and Ezekiel had chores. So I only had Alfred and Patsy to tend to, and Alfred was bout big enough to take care of hisself. The white children was even less bother. Tom was at school most days, and had his own chores when he come home. Adie was six and was all over me helping with her baby sister. Miss Julia took to church work, so some days it was just me and the younguns in the house.

I still missed Romulus, but I had given out hope that Quakers would come calling and offer to take me to him. The missing grew softer as the years rolled by. When I see him in heaven, I aim to ask if there was anything I could have done to ease his misery.

Miss Essie come by more often, and sometimes me and Miss Julia gather up our younguns and go to her place. Now I hate to speak ill of a person, but the more I seen of Miss Essie, the less I cared for her. Master Thomas had his problems working his hands, but otherwise he was tolerable; he seemed to be trying mightily to get shed of his Mam. But Miss Essie, she was a fruit that didn't fall far from the tree. Oh she acted like a good woman, once upon a time, but something happened to change her, and I got no idea what it was. We didn't see much of her when we was bound up in so much trouble, Romulus going off, the measles, and all the dying. Something evil come over her when I wasn't paying attention. Miss Essie was a sly one. At first she didn't speak in that ugly tone that came so easy to her Mam, but I could see she'd come to share that old woman's opinion of black folks. In her mind we was all stupid and no-account, no better than the mules in the field and needing just as much fussing at. Many times I heard her sass her younguns' nursemaid, and saw the poor creature shrink into her skin. When she talked to me that way I glowered at her, which I doubt she even noticed. Miss Julia noticed though. I could see her spine straighten up and her jaw set tight.

I felt bad for Miss Julia. She wanted nothing more than to have her husband's sister for a friend. And they were for a while. Miss Essie was smart and laughed easy, and them two women would have got along fine if they didn't have to deal with black folks. But they did, and the cleft between them grew as broad as the sea. I never could figure out why people like Miss Essie owned nigras. What use did she have for "ornery good-for-nothings," especially the one raising her children?

Wednesday, May 30, 1860

Adie's house is all astir in preparation for our guests. I can't wait to see Eliza and Rachel and their precious children. I suppose that puts me in the perfect frame of mind to continue writing about the happy years.

Cotton was good to us during the early 1830s, and our farm began to prosper. Thomas benefitted greatly from his foray into scientific farming, which led to his keeping a farm journal recording daily and seasonal activity and weather. He had never been a stranger to hard work, and spent nearly every daylight hour on the land. Sharing knowledge with his Negroes, instead of issuing orders to them made him less awkward with his hands. He became more confident and cheerful, and therefore a better husband and father, as well as a better farmer. He had a natural bent for finding the best cotton markets, and drivers willing to transport our crop at a favorable price. He quickly acquired a reputation for accurately representing the condition of his cotton; if it was moldy or poor quality, he said so. And his bales were always free of bracts or other trash. The factors were confident there would be no nasty surprises in Thomas' crop. Although the price of cotton continued to decline during those years, Thomas (as opposed to my dear father) understood that increased production and honest negotiation were the key, not expecting things to change.

He was also liked and respected by our neighbors. He was more than generous to anyone in need, and bore a gracious persona that compelled men to please him. Therefore we were never cheated and prospered from our modest farm. Although he had increased his acreage over the years, and acquired more mules and equipment, our place was by no means a grand plantation.

In 1834 we purchased another black family, Louis and Cindy, and their children Washington and Mose who were twelve and ten, and Sally who was seven. Thomas made a great display of how diligently he strove to buy an intact family knowing how important it had become to me for parents and children to live together. Later I learned through Rose that Cindy had two older boys who were not offered in the sale. I never broached the question to Thomas, assuming that my gentle trusting husband had been hoodwinked, and was unaware of them. It was not in his nature to prevaricate; I doubt he could have carried it off had he tried.

At long last Thomas considered himself a successful planter, which he was, and his confidence soared. He consented, with much urging from me, to appoint Sam to the position of slave driver which meant that Sam, not Thomas would direct the men in the fields, and this turned out to be a wise decision. Sam had been trained by Thomas' father, and well understood the requirements for making a crop, and Thomas was relieved of the chore for which he had the least talent. Sam literally came alive with the added authority, and summoned up energy and enthusiasm that we had never seen before. Thomas no longer had any use for the opinion of Negroes learned at his mother's knee, and peace billowed over our household.

It is said that when one door closes, another opens, and through this unfortunate aperture strode my sister-in-law Essie. As I have said Essie became a frequent companion during this time due to our children being more manageable, and both of us having more household help. Which was the irony of the thing. In the fullness of time I began to see that Essie, though lacking her mother's rough edge, had thoroughly absorbed her insolent manner toward the Negroes. I offer no apology for Essie, for I cannot. Like most Southerners she held the belief that the black skinned were created to serve us, and needed considerable assistance in managing their affairs. But I'm convinced that in her deepest heart she also considered them inhuman in every respect; every one a liar, cheat, and malingerer. Had she been more guarded when we were newly acquainted, had I been blind, or had her heart truly hardened? Her embarrassment and disdain toward her mother seemed to have disappeared, and the old woman's abhorrent philosophy became acceptable. I was completely puzzled for in all other ways she remained as sensible and affectionate as her brother. At first there were only sharp glances or uncalled for reprimands. Then reality unfolded.

I remained mute for the longest while, for she was clever and bright, and I so enjoyed her company. Aside from my church associates, I had little other female companionship. When I first noticed her disagreeable behavior, I told her quietly that I thought her chastisements unnecessary, careful to speak out of earshot of the poor victim. When this failed I tried to acquaint her with more positive methods of management. Of course Negroes needed instruction. How else would they know their duties? Nearly all of them can be taught gently and kindly to be productive workers. The truly incorrigible – and there are bound to be a few in any mass of humanity – can be relieved of household responsibilities. I tried to explain this to Essie, and to show her by example, but it was of no use. Essie had taken to bullying, and little did I know that a bully is often forged by fear. The more time we spent together, the easier it became for her to unloose her reserve, and the more difficult for me to abide it. But abide it I did until I saw little Adie mimic her aunt's behavior. (Tom, being in school, was witness to little of this, which was a blessing. Tom had become an impatient boy with a keen sense for injustice, and in his eyes, injustice abounded, which is a topic for another day.) It was when I heard Adie, who had just reached her seventh year, order Rose around with the voice of a harpy that I truly became alarmed. I tried to limit my time with Essie, and arrange for my children to be otherwise occupied when we did visit, but there were lapses. She would come to my home unannounced, for which I cannot fault her as over the years we had developed an informal camaraderie; we were family after all.

I struggled with myself on Adie's behalf; she was always the literal child with no sensitivity for nuance. I did not want to deprive Adie of her aunt's company (as I had her grandmother's and I bore guilt for that). Yet I could not tolerate my child imitating unpardonable behavior. I tried to explain that her aunt was generally a good woman who had incorrect ideas about Negroes, and that in our home no one was to be treated with disrespect no matter who they were. Poor Adie was confused. She saw that both Essie and I issued orders, but she could not discern the difference in our manner. Nor could Adie understand that treating Negroes differently from white people was not the same as treating them badly. "If they are as human as we," she asked, "why don't they share our table and have nice bedchambers in our house?" I told her that each family deserved its own house, and she quickly pointed out that our black people were not exactly housed as individual families. Then I said that a certain decorum must be maintained in order to delineate the roles of master and servant. I could not believe I had uttered such a thing! I had fallen headlong into my own trap.

It was probably a year or two later when calamity resolved the situation. It was a midwinter Sabbath, and Essie and her family had come to our home for dinner after services. It was too cold for anyone to be out of doors, therefore impossible to shelter my children from Essie's outburst. She had a small child at the time who was obviously unwell. The poor thing's nose was stuffed, and he constantly wailed and tugged at his ear which was red and swollen. Essie asked the child's nurse to quiet him (asked is too mild a word, barked is what she did). The poor woman gathered up the child, who could not be consoled, and carried him toward the parlor. As we were all seated around the dining table, I suppose she thought getting him out of earshot was the best she could do. Essie rose from her chair, grabbed the woman's arm, and roughly swung her around. "Not in there!" she shouted. "You know niggers aren't permitted to sit in the parlor! Were you under the impression I'd sent you to dust the furniture?" The poor woman's eyes grew as large as saucers, and she snuggled the crying child to her shoulder, burying his head below her chin. "I ain't got nowhere else to go," she replied, which was true. Was she expected to take the sick child into our bedchamber, or out in the cold? Essie was livid. "Don't you sass me, you black hussy!" With that she raised her hand and struck her servant across the face. The sound reverberated around us, sending a snarl of shame and revulsion to the pit of my stomach. The room became quiet as a tomb, everyone struck dumb. I saw Essie's handprint emerge red on the girl's tawny face, and realized she had not snuggled the baby for its comfort, but drawn it toward her to protect its tender head. She had been hit before, and perhaps often. I was appalled.

Thursday, May 31, 1860

I wrote late into the night, and still could not get this evil story out. So I will complete it today, then set my journal aside until our guests have left. To think I began yesterday to tell a happy tale.

To this day I can hear the smack of Essie's hand against human flesh. I sat perfectly astonished for what seemed an eon, the cruel slap echoing in my ears; at that moment I knew I had completely lost the sister I had so hoped to cherish. Then Essie's husband scurried out of his chair and took the child in his arms. "I'll take care of him," he said as he danced the baby around the room. Thomas was next out of his seat. With a hand to her elbow, he guided his sister into our bedchamber whispering, "Calm yourself, Essie; you must get ahold of yourself." and they left the room. Essie's husband leaned toward me, flustering to find words. "Poor Essie. It's her nerves, don't you know. She can't cope with the Negroes anymore. That old Nat Turner business scared her senseless, and she won't let it go. She has convinced herself that if we lose one iota of control, the Negroes will rise up and slit our throats. Please don't judge her harshly, Julia; she's not a wicked woman, she's scared as a little rabbit." His voice trailed off as he carried the child to the parlor, jiggling the lad in his arms, eyes darting from my face to the floor. Did he really believe fright excused Essie's behavior? That stunned rabbits are capable of violence? I'm sure it was shame I saw in the poor man's eyes.

Thomas and Essie remained sequestered for at least an hour, maybe longer. I never inquired about their private conversation. If he had any sympathy for his sister, and the bond of blood is tight, I did not want to know about it. I concluded long before they ended their tête-à-tête that Essie would never cross my threshold again.

Rose and I attended to the assaulted Negro, whose name I'm afraid I never learned. Essie appeared to have a new nursemaid nearly every time we saw her, as she flung them aside one by one for the slightest offense. I'm not sure how many people her husband owned, but it wasn't an endless supply. Even I was aware that after a passage of time, a previous reject became the newest trusted servant. I don't know if I had seen our current victim before or not. I had tried to become oblivious to Essie's nursemaids, for otherwise sympathy would be required, a sympathy that would interfere with the sisterly affection I so wanted to nurture. Now there was no choice.

Rose had dampened a cloth from the water pitcher and was bathing the face of the woman who was now seated at our table. (Essie would have boiled had she known!) I knelt down beside her, tried to hold her trembling hands, tried to embrace her slumped shoulder. But she shrugged away from me. I was white, and there was one thing the poor Negro was sure of: white hands were used for beating. I fetched her a cup of tea, and tried to soothe her with a soft voice. Rose assured her that I would not harm her, and at last pent up tears coursed down her face. There were no sobs, however; she had turned stoicism into an art.

Finally Essie and her family left our house with no attempt to reconvene our dinner. Thomas and I sat down to a cold and silent repast. When we were done, I spoke. "Your sister is never again to enter our home. There will be no exceptions. Tomorrow you are to go to her place and tell her so. I will not abide an argument." To his credit Thomas did not offer one. A year or so later Essie's family joined the migration to Alabama where fertile land had been opened for settlement, and plantations were sprouting like dandelions. Essie wrote to Thomas from time to time, but gradually the letters dwindled, then ceased altogether. I've no idea what became of them, nor do I care.

I have been rereading portions of this journal and it astonishes me how every aspect of my life has been encumbered by slavery. I was born into this infernal situation as surely as Rose was, although my suffering has been of the soul, not of the flesh. How could I be so ensnarled in a system I detest? Why am I so powerless to change it? If brother Frank is correct, and war is inevitable, please Lord, make it merciful for our poor bound brothers.

As I mentioned, I intended here to give an account of happy years, and I will, for they did exist. I will put this journal away for a while and enjoy my grandchildren who are due to arrive tomorrow. Then I promise to proceed along a more cheerful vein.

June, 1860

Wednesday, June 6, 1860

I ain't wrote for a week being busy getting ready for the kinfolk, then busy tending to them. They come Friday last. Mostly I helps with the littlest ones, Miss Adie's Matthew and his three cousins. I ought to be the story teller to the younguns, old as I am, but I don't know the tales like I should. There weren't any old ones around when I was coming up, and I reckon I didn't pay no attention when Pappy took my boys to his knee. I was just grateful for his help. So I rounded up Matthew and his cousins and took them over to Old Marsh's cabin and listen to him go on about the Africa times. Old Marsh's Grandpappy come from Africa on a boat, and he told Marsh all about the beasts that roam the forest over yonder, and how they play tricks on one another. Now I don't believe in talking lions and terrapins, nor hares and foxes hatching plots, but it's a pure wonder to hear Old Marsh, his voice rising and falling to fit the mood, his big black hands and gnarly knuckles drawing pictures in the air. I listen careful, cause someday Marsh bound to pass on, and my time will come to spin the stories.

Matthew being Adie's child has knowed Marsh all his life, and runs right up to him, jumping in his lap and hugging his neck. The cousins was shy at first, but it don't take long to warm up to Marsh. Sometimes Miss Adie's other younguns come along. Benjamin pretend he too big for stories, but he gobble them up just the same. Rebecca come with us once, but mostly she say she's a young lady now and must practice her piano. Children oughtn't to be so eager to grow up; they'll get their share of troubles soon enough. Surely a heap of them lies ahead.

Miss Julia told me she been remembering the last time Miss Essie come to her house, and how shamed she felt when that poor girl got slapped. I plumb near bout forgot it. Oh I remember Miss Essie alright, and I remember how mean and spiteful she was. What Miss Julia don't know is I seen her slap her girls around more times than I can count. Whenever me and her nursemaid would be in the yard with the little ones, Miss Essie would come see how we was doing. She'd always find some excuse to push or shove or shout or slap. She never hit me cause she knew she couldn't get by with that, but it hurt me all over to see those girls suffer, just like I'd been hit myself. Miss Julia never come out to check on us. She knew I'd ask her if we needed something.

After Miss Essie went back inside, the girl would tell me how it was on their place, and I thanked my stars that woman didn't own me. And it wasn't just one girl, but one after another after another, each one of them with the same sorry tale. If they had scars, they didn't show me, but I doubt that Miss Essie, for all of her meanness, had that much strength.

I reckon it's time to help the younguns with their supper. They is such sweet babies; remind me of their Mams when they was young. The affection of children makes slave life near bout tolerable, and I've had it easier than most, working in the house. I always looked down on the field hands, but I envy them one thing. They got each other. I never had many of my own kind to gossip with. I hate what Miss Essie done to her girls, but I did enjoy their company.

Sunday, June 10, 1860

Eliza and Rachel and their families left this morning. Ten wonderful days I had with my grandchildren! We did not attend services today, as we helped with packing, loading the carriage, and assembling their dinner for the road. God understands, and will forgive us, I'm sure. My sons-in-law must be prospering, for Eliza's husband Andrew stayed the entire time, and Rachel's Eli left only a few days ago. The children were a delight. It was especially poignant to be with them at this time, as I've been writing about their mothers as children, and there is so much more to tell.

But first I shall report current circumstances. Last Sunday brother Frank came home with us after church and spent the entire day. He brought newspapers dense with political news, and I'm sure he wanted Andrew and Eli's opinions. Some men are at last being nominated for president, and Frank feels certain this election will determine the fate of the country. About a month ago a convention was held by a group calling themselves the Constitutional Union Party, who are mostly Northerners wishing to distance themselves from the Republicans (Black Republicans they are sometimes called, not that any of them are Negroes, but for their abolitionist sympathy). The Constitutional Union Party nominated Mr. John Bell of Tennessee, who happens to be a slaveholder. From Frank's description their ideas offer the best chance of compromise between the North and South, as they seem content to leave the Southerners alone, hoping that slavery will someday die a natural death. But Frank gives them little chance of winning the election. They are mostly doddering old men, remnants of the tired old Whig Party, with no capacity for stirring up enthusiasm.

A week later the new Republican Party met, and caused quite a stir. The newspapers called it a high spirited affair, riotous is probably a better word. There was a grand melee of shouting and jostling, people crowding together to hear and be heard. Never has such prodigious disorder been seen at a political event, and they are generally rowdy affairs. The convention was held in Chicago, a new city of the West with a reputation for wildness. An enormous pavilion called the Wigwam was built for the occasion. Some said it was filled by six thousand souls, the galleries alone holding half that number. Others estimated thousands more were in attendance. At one point foot stamping and jumping onto tables caused the building to shake, and people feared for their lives. There was even a telegraph system installed within the pavilion, which is why we have news in only a few days. I am completely amazed!

Very few Southerners attended the event, and those who did hailed from border states where slavery is not unanimously embraced. Many Republicans are ardent abolitionists, and the rest aim to at least keep the territories free, thinking that will lead to the death of the system. I tend to agree somewhat with the latter point. Instant abolition will surely invite chaos; a slow demise of slavery would at least let the nation prepare for a free black workforce. However I kept my peace. It solves nothing to stir up a family argument.

After two days of platform building and administrative matters, names were put up for the Republican nomination. Everyone expected Mr. Seward from New York to take the prize, although he is reputed to be a disagreeable fellow. To everyone's amazement Mr. Lincoln from Illinois was nominated! None of us, save Frank, had ever heard of the man. Some say he's an abolitionist, others a moderate. It remains to be seen.

In a week's time the Democrats will meet in Baltimore after festering all summer from the debacle in Charleston. Frank is certain the Republicans will prevail in November if the cotton state Democrats and those at the North refuse to set aside their differences. He puts on a gloomy face, but I am still convinced that he is excited about the prospect of a war.

The next topic of discussion was a local one. Now that the Republicans have pushed abolition to the forefront, Frank asked my sons-in-law how poor Pinkney Helper was faring in Mecklenburg. Mr. Pink, as he is always called, owns an elegant hotel at Davidson College in that county, and is unfortunately a brother of Mr. Hinton Helper, an embarrassment to the South, and perhaps the entire human race. Several years ago Mr. Hinton wrote a book, or rather a diatribe, called "The Impending Crisis of the South – How to Meet It." At first glance it appeared to be abolitionist propaganda, for it did advocate the dismantling of slavery. But a closer look showed that Mr. Hinton Helper despises Negroes, considers them lower than beasts; the man vilifies slaves and slave owners with equal ferocity. His idea was for the underclass of poor whites to take up arms and eradicate the entire plantation system, slaughtering all those connected with it, black and white. The man is plainly a lunatic, and was not taken seriously. He became a laughing stock, not the John Brown style martyr he wished to be, and mortified, slunk off to New York.

Last fall some Republican congressmen got hold of Helper's foul book, and published a shorter version, leaving out the more odious parts, and distributed it thinking the discovery of a southern abolitionist would help their cause. Instead it caused a mighty uproar which did nothing but deepen the divisions in Washington.

Mr. Pinkney Helper, whose hotel clientele are Davidson College visitors and parents of students, is very well respected by his community. When that horrible book was printed, Mr. Pink refused to discuss politics or his brother with anyone. A wise man, he was, but his reticence did not prevent curiosity. Andrew said he has not spoken to Mr. Pink since the Republican nomination became known, but he doubted that the furor of last fall would recur. "Everyone knows Mr. Hinton Helper is a mad man, and that no lucid thought has ever crossed his brain. The entire town pities Mr. Pink; he is undeniably a gentleman." Eli added that the college library has several copies of "The Impending Crisis," but he doubts they have ever been borrowed. I feel sorry for Mr. Pink, and perhaps a certain kinship with him. Whether he opposes slavery, or is disinclined to air the family's soiled linen, I have no idea. Yet he is certainly in an uncomfortable situation, one with which I completely sympathize.

Quite a day it was; I've never in my life heard so much politics discussed all in one day! The rest of the week was spent in a more homely fashion, catching up with my daughters, and playing with the grandchildren. Rachel is healthy and expects her child in July, but when in July is anyone's guess. Isaac has agreed to have Echo drive me to her place when the little stranger arrives.

Sunday, June 10, 1860

This one quiet afternoon, all the kinfolk done gone home. Last Sunday Master Frank come to dinner, and as usual, I keep my ears perked up. I ain't figured out what all the meetings and conventions is about, but I do understand if things don't go a certain way, the white folks around here will be plenty angry. All them gentlemens pretend they don't want no war, but I can see fire in their eyes, and know they is just itching for a fight. They reminds me of Mr. Thackeray's book that I is still reading, but I'm getting near the end. One of the buffoons he write about is Mr. Rawdon Crawley, a haughty pompous fellow full of tricks and slights, say one thing, mean another. Mr. Crawley resemble Master Frank in some queer way. When I'm reading "Vanity Fair" my mind sees Master Frank whenever Mr. Crawley wanders cross the page.

The black folks here don't pay a bit of attention to the politics, least none that I hear. I asked Sarah and Vinie what they think, and they just shrug their shoulders, say it don't make no nevermind. I didn't ask nobody else, as they wouldn't give me an opinion if they had one. I feel powerful lonesome sometimes. The house nigras give me the snub cause they think I'm too dark to be one of them, and the others act like I was high yaller, which I is not. I got nobody, save Miss Julia. I reckon Miss Julia is why they don't cotton to me, not cause of my warm mahogany skin. Romulus loved my color. He say my velvety cheeks were soft like rose petals; he whisper that the prettiest flower that ever bloom was his sweet Mahogany Rose. And when he kissed my soft cheek, he say it look and taste like the richest molasses. I love that ornery old man.

Not a one of them (cept Dovey and Little Sam if they bother theirselves to remember!) knows that my Romulus run off. And none, including those two, knows how I grieved him. Most don't know I had younguns or what become of them. What a strange conundrum the good Lord give us. Us that work in the house gets the best food and clothes, and the easiest work. But we don't get much free time, babies fuss when they please, and white folks need waiting on night and day. Them that works the fields, as low down as they is, at least gets to frolic together.

Oh, what a blue afternoon this is turned out to be. Master Frank's carryings on makes me wonder what will become of me if the slaves get freed. Miss Julia say she and her girls will take care of me, and I pray the good Lord they will. Freedom wouldn't be much use at my age. Got no family to go live with, no way to earn my keep. I shore do miss

Romulus. I remember how contented Mam and Pappy was before Master Campbell die, before the family got sold. I'd expected Romulus and I would spend our old age that way. What a prize I would give to live with him in the soft comfort of an old, well worn love, him shed of his misery. I reckon heaven be like that.

Monday, June 11,1860

As in all families, my children were different one from another, and I shall pause here to paint a word portrait of each of them as they grew into adulthood. I have written about Tom, the great miracle of his birth and his early years. Yet in spite of the best mothering I could muster, he became a troublesome boy, and none of us could turn him. He was an active and rambunctious child, his mind set on a mule-headed course, a fertile field for growing a short temper laced with impatience. At first I thought his behavior was simply boyish, but then notes began to come home from school. Tom would not complete his work. Tom would argue when he was corrected. Tom would storm out of the classroom at the slightest provocation. He even had the audacity to call his tutor an ogre when he disagreed with him. Several times Tom was threatened with dismissal, but we managed to calm our son, and smooth the tutor's feathers. Somehow we managed to get him educated.

Perhaps Thomas overly indulged the boy. Thomas was determined not to be constantly critical, as his mother had been, and he praised Tom's every accomplishment, ignoring every flaw. Tom grew up completely assured his notions were always right, even when they were not. Thomas rarely contradicted his son, and Tom took it as a personal affront when anyone else did. I suppose, he got his keen abhorrence of injustice from me. I have written about Essie, and how irate I was over her outrageous behavior, which was not the only time I expressed such an opinion. While I muttered in frustration behind closed doors, Tom perceived problems as needing to be solved, punishment meted out, justice served!

His actions were equally audacious. He climbed rotten trees, swam in rain swollen creeks, rode horses far too fast over precarious paths. I will have to implicate Marc too, in this flight from reason. The two of them were healthy, robust, and as surefooted as goats. Of course it was wise to become intimate with nature, and confident in their ability, but I do wish they had added a modicum of caution, though I'm not sure caution comes naturally to the Negro race. Perhaps I should have made some effort to separate Tom from Marc when he reached school age, but I could not cleave Tom from Rose's son. My sense of fairness and customs of propriety always seem to be in conflict. Tom never broke a limb, nor severely injured himself, but he certainly worried his mother no end! Thankfully, these characteristics were tamed by maturity.

I have also written about Adie. Such a sweet, kind, and generous child she was, but as I have said very literal minded. She would sit absolutely perplexed when one would make a play on words or engage in jest. And to some extent she still does, although she quickly takes part in the laughter when her husband is the jokester. She never was a scholar, which is no handicap for a female, and she compensated by becoming a bubbling friendly girl. She did (and does) have one unfortunate habit: whatever comes into her head, comes out of her mouth. I have tried to teach her to think before she speaks, but to no avail. I remember once when I was compelled to correct Rose for some minor error, and Adie blurted: "Don't fuss at her, she's just a black nigger; she doesn't know any better!" I was appalled! Fortunately Rose took the whole matter with good humor.

Later on we sent her to the Moravian boarding school for girls in Salem. She is the only young lady of my acquaintance who was not completely charmed with the place. She remained only one session, highly unusual. One of the teaching Sisters sat me down, and said with great sympathy, that not all are meant to be scholars, and God has His own plan for each of us. She felt sure that Adie had been blessed with vivacity for a purpose God had yet to reveal.

She eventually grew into a spirited young lady with a flirtatious eye. She attracted young men by the score, who swarmed around like drooling puppies, and she reveled in the attention. She had affection for any number of them, falling in love at the drop of an eyelash. Frank invited her to stay with him in Lincolnton whenever she wished, and she ensconced herself in village activity. I doubt there was a gay event in the entire county she didn't attend. The teaching Sisters at Salem proved to be right. The society she so enjoyed introduced her to Isaac Lowery, and I believe they've made a fine marriage. Her naïve nature is still with her, as she is incapable of a deviant thought, and she bows cheerfully to Isaac's every whim.

Eliza, as I have said was born in 1833, and she proved to be the exact opposite of her sister. She was a shy, quiet, scholarly child. Early on she had a keen interest in matters of nature and science. Had Frank's talent skipped over a branch of the family tree? Or had the explosion of falling stars she observed as an infant left an indelible impression? She is also a lover of music, and has a fine talent, which I hope she will impart to her young daughters. She attended the school at Salem for the usual two years, and afterwards was engaged as a piano tutor in the neighborhood. She was such a shy thing that I was afraid that would be her life, a spinster piano teacher. But alas she did marry Andrew Wilson.

In 1837 we had another gift from God, our dear Rachel. Many women are not eager to have yet another child late in their thirties. But having lost three children, and having only three living ones, I considered her truly a blessing. A mother should not say that one child is more comely than another, but Rachel was (and is) a beauty. Adie and Eliza were fine looking children and have become handsome women. I flatter myself to think they resemble their mother! Rachel however inherited my mother-in-law's regal classic features, and graceful poise. Thanks to a merciful God the resemblance ends there. I am not being boastful in describing her thus. Throughout her life perfect strangers have commented on her beauty. Like Adie she is lively and gregarious, and had little fondness for schooling, though perhaps more ability. Unlike Adie she is naturally tactful. Rachel attended Salem for two years, where she enjoyed the social life more than the intellectual. She had barely finished school when she met Eli Harris. She married him the next year at the age of nineteen!

Tuesday, June 12, 1860

Last week I got to thinking about my Patsy while I was tending to Miss Eliza's little girls. Patsy, she sure was a sweet one. She was borned right after Miss Julia lost them two boys with the measles, so she didn't pay Patsy much mind as a baby. But when she began scrambling around behind my coattails, Miss Julia took a pure shine to her, said she resembled me when I was a youngun. She had the biggest eyes of any child you ever saw, and long curvy eyelashes that could charm fleas off a dog. She laugh and smile at every little thing, and had a hug for everybody, black and white. Pappy come to love her those last few months he was alive; poor Mam, her mind had plumb left her when Patsy come.

Eliza come along when Patsy was two, and when they was old enough she helped Patsy with her reading. I'm proud to say I taught my daughter her letters, but didn't have time enough for real studying. Childrens got to read most every day to stick it in their mind. By then it was against the law, but Miss Julia say she don't care. She said that law that wasn't fit to be on the books. I'm glad that at least one of Miss Julia's girls was bookish; Adie and Rachel was frolicky girls; they didn't have much use for learning.

During them years Patsy was a pure joy and comfort with her sweet girl charm. My boys was not so easy to raise. Marc was a trouble. He and Tom coming one on top of the other was raised like brothers, so it weren't no surprise they acted the part. Now Tom, and God forgive me for saying so, was a wrong-headed one. He knew more ways of finding trouble than you can shake a stick at, and he dragged Marc along on every caper. He'd stand up and sass a man, which was a naughty thing for a white boy and plumb dangerous for a black one. The good Lord heard from me powerful often when those two was coming up. Miss Julia, she fretted bout the trouble Tom got into, and had the bodacious gall to blame my boy! I knew better than to set her straight. She wouldn't have listened to me no how.

When Marc was bout fourteen him and Tom went off romping in the woods one day, said they was going fishing, fishing for mischief if you ask me. Why else would they go down to Loony Brown's cabin? I reckon they was looking to buy whiskey, have themselves a spree out behind the barn. I'd seen Marc act stumble-footed once before, and told him flat out to stay away from that tetched man. He swore up and down he never drank no liquor, and didn't even know where Loony Brown lived. I doubted that last part! Well, that day when they got to Loony's cabin they found it burned flat to the ground! Reckon everybody figured he might burn his place down, cooking mash day and night, him with no more sense than a spider. But it come as a shock to the boys. Marc told me that fire was fresh, cause kettles and things was hot, and smoke was hovering all over. He wanted to run home straight away, but Tom said they should stay and explore, make a full report to the sheriff. I figure Tom was really hunting for whiskey, cause once before Master Thomas had found one of Loony's jugs hid in Tom's room; Marc allowed he didn't know nothing bout it. I believe Master Thomas actually punished his boy for once! Anyhow, those boys commenced to poke around the embers, pushing things hither and yon with a pair of sticks they cut in the woods. Marc said not much was left mongst the ashes, iron pots, tools, heaps of jugs, eerie bits of furniture that ought to had burned, but didn't. What the boys did find hid in the ashes was Loony Brown! Dead and burned under the rubble of his cabin, his wild mass of white hair singed off, his face black as a coal.

That put the fear of the Lord in the boys, and they hightailed it and run like the devil was chasing them.

When they got home, scared and trembling at finding a dead man, Master Thomas sent for the sheriff. What happen next was as predictable as nightfall. The sheriff asked Tom a few questions, then he got hold of Marc. He asked Marc over and over did how did the fire start, and would not believe it when Marc say he didn't know. He had convinced hisself that Marc had gone to rob Loony Brown, having a mind to sell whiskey in the quarter. The sheriff figured Loony Brown caught him in the act, and either tried to stop him, or frightened him with his queer behavior. Whichever, Marc must have knocked over a kettle of boiling mash, or maybe throwed it at the addled fellow, which set the spirits alight, and sparked the whole cabin to burning. Then he accused Tom of covering up for his "nigger" friend, said he ought to know better. Well that raised Tom's ire. That boy might have been full of the devil, but he would not cotton to false blame. He stood up to the sheriff and called him a name that embarrassed me to hear. He said neither he nor Marc would do such a thing, and the sheriff could take his foul notions straight to…, well you know where. Marc didn't say nothing, just stood there with his head hanging, his fingers twisting in his shirttail. I know, cause I was there. Well the sheriff must have figured he didn't need a row with Master Thomas' son, so he act like Marc was the sassy one. He hollered some more, then hauled Marc all the way to Lincolnton to the jail, where he was tied to the whipping post and beat. They kept him in jail all night. Sheriff said it was too late to carry him home that evening, but I didn't believe that for a minute.

The next day they brung him back, limp and bleeding, all the spunk whupped out of him. The bile done raised up in my throat when I saw the sheriff leading my boy to the cabin, his hands tied behind him with a rope. The sheriff hollered for me to come outside, then he cuts Marc's hands loose and shoved him toward me. He tell me to keep control of my boy, and don't ever let him, the sheriff that is, see Marc in trouble again, or he be beaten like a man next time, fifty lashes at least. Then he allowed that Master Thomas bound to sell my boy if he can't be kept out of trouble. I stood there, nodding my head, saying yes sir, yes sir, cause that's what he want to hear, biting my lip hoping that vile white varmint didn't see the tears bout to blind me.

I brung Marc inside and slowly peeled off his bloody shirt. My heart plummeted at the damage I seen. Gashes up and down his back, red and looking bout ready to fester, poor boy trying not to sob, but I could hear him, and feel his shoulders quiver. I laid him on the bed on his belly, and rummaged through my pots and jars to make a salve. I pound up some chamomile and lavender with a pinch of sage, then bind it into a poultice with honey. I smeared it onto every wound, trying to be gentle, but I could tell his pain was powerful. Then I go to the yard and gather up a mess of lambs ears, and press the leaves all over his back to hold the salve in place and bring on the healing. That poor child sleep on his belly for weeks, and I cried every night, tears of aching and anger and pure humiliation. I ain't never had a child hurt so bad, which pained me bout as much as him, and no one in my family had ever spent a night in the jail, which shamed me to the core. I made up my mind it would never happen again, not if I had any say-so! Marc never blamed Tom for this ugly business, but I did. I also blamed the fact that Marc was a black boy, borned into slavery, through no fault of his own.

Levi, Ezekiel, and Alfred had little truck with mischief. They was fine boys, no more trouble than younguns ought to be. They didn't latch so closely to white children. Adie, Eliza, and Rachel was girls after all, and younger than them. Little boys, after they gets a certain age, have no use for littler girls, specially girls that think they is rascally dirty things. When my boys was old enough to work, I could see their Daddy's nature come over them, and it like to break my heart. They never did have the misery bad like Romulus; they was more like Mattie, steeped in sadness that hung on like a fog. When they got to be big boys they was tasked to the fields. By that time Sam was the boss man, so they didn't see much of the white folks. Master Thomas never paid them much mind, and neither did Miss Julia. She was all over them when they was babies, but when they outgrew their cuteness the white folks lost notice of them.

Wednesday, June 13, 1860

When describing the diverse personalities of my children I alluded to Tom's errant behavior entwined with that of Marc. I shall set down now one particular incident that caused Thomas and me to take a hard look at our son and his association with Marc. I believe the year was 1836, when Tom about thirteen, and Marc a year older. According to Tom, he and Marc were scampering about in the woods, as they so often did, when they happened upon a frightening and bizarre scene. They found poor old Loony Brown burned to death in a fire at his cabin. He described an eerie scene, the rubble of the cabin shrouded in gray smoke, surrounded by white mists rising from the forest floor. We had had several days of steady rain, and the earth and trees were saturated as if dressed in wet flannel. Mercifully the forest did not burn.

They came running home to report the event, and Thomas sent for the sheriff to investigate. What exactly there was to investigate, I could not fathom, as all of us had expected for years that the deranged fellow might one day burn his place to the ground. But it roused suspicion that Loony had not fled to the woods and escaped the conflagration. Instead he became its victim.

The sheriff decided to place blame, and he placed it squarely on Marc. At the time I did not doubt for a moment that Marc had gone to Loony's to buy whiskey, and had cajoled Tom into going along. After all, it is well known how much the Negroes enjoy their whiskey. They often pooled their coins and sent one of their number to make a purchase from Loony, in spite of the fact that it was explicitly forbidden. So I made no objection when the sheriff accused Marc of that offense and carted him off to town. Surely he would not persist in accusing Marc of setting the fire which had obviously happened before the boys arrived. If I'd only had a notion of the consequences that would ensue.

It was about noon of the following day when I, being in the yard, saw the sheriff ride up with Marc perched before him on his horse, the boy slumped over nearly double, his face fairly buried in the creature's mane. The sheriff alit, snatched the limp boy from the steed, and headed toward Rose's cabin, the sheriff yelling for her in a rude coarse voice. I could see the back of Marc's shirt, caked with blood, and his hands bound behind him. I was horrified! I knew Marc would receive some punishment, but it never occurred to me that it would be so brutal. Rose came to the cabin door, and stood meekly nodding at the man who continued what appeared to be a tirade, although I could not hear his words. He finally left, and Rose draped a soft hand on her child's shoulder and led him inside. I started toward the cabin, but hesitated as I reached the door. I could hear Marc sobbing softly, and Rose murmuring soothing words, a private encounter between mother and child, an intimacy that should not be intruded upon.

Later I returned to the cabin and asked what I could do, but it was clear Rose did not want my help, considered it interference. In fact she seemed to think Tom was responsible for the entire episode. I tried to apologize, smooth over the ugliness, but it was obvious Rose confused my awkwardness for insincerity, and wanted nothing to do with me. I was bitter at the time for being rebuffed, but in hindsight I have more understanding. I had said not a word when the sheriff carried Marc away. I had stood silently and let the sheriff and my husband concoct a case for Marc's guilt. I did believe that Marc had gone to Loony's for whiskey, inducing Tom in the caper, even though Tom denied that Marc led the venture, or that he planned to buy spirits. He said repeatedly that while roaming in the woods they both had the idea to spy on the lunatic purely for boyish amusement. I never for a minute believed Marc set the fire, accidentally or otherwise, yet I did not stand up to the sheriff's insistence on casting blame, and my husband's failure to interfere. I had been raised to be a dutiful wife who never contradicts her husband in the presence of others. I hope I am bolder now, yet had I acted differently, the outcome would have been the same. My humble female opinion would have not had the weight of a feather.

It was then that Thomas and I concluded that Tom needed further schooling, preferably away from the plantation and away from the influence of Marc. So we enrolled him in the Pleasant Retreat Academy, the school brother Frank had attended in Lincolnton all those years ago. It was not considered as fashionable as it had been in Frank's day; newly opened academies had taken that role. That suited us fine. Tom, as I have said, was not the scholar his uncle had been. An old fashioned school that meted out a fair amount of learning with firm Christian discipline was what Tom required. So he spent the next several years in Lincolnton, boarding during the week with Frank. Of course this did not sever the friendship between Tom and Marc, which is not what I had intended. After all, they had been companions since birth. Tom did learn the proper stance of white men toward black and vice versa, and the nature of duty, responsibility, and respect that each should have for the other.

Rose and I eventually repaired our rift, as we had so many times before. I truly loved her, and do still, yet I must constantly remind myself that she was born a Negro, and is not responsible for the shortcomings of her race. I must temper the frustrations that often confound me with compassion and good will. God grant me grace.

Thursday, June 14, 1860

Late in 1836 Mrs. Henderson's health truly began to fail. She had complained for years that her Negroes were poisoning her (which I had long since stopped believing), and Thomas had often made trips to

Mecklenburg to comfort his "ailing" mother. But it was then that her symptoms changed. The new affliction did not resemble poisoning, nor a veiled attempt to garner attention; it bore all the marks of impending death. The old woman was somewhere around seventy, although I never knew her true age. Convinced that her suffering was genuine, the children and I joined Thomas to go to her and pay our respects. I steeled myself for a journey that was bound to be unpleasant on many fronts. First, and least important, was my own condition. My child Rachel was due soon and traveling had become uncomfortable. Of greater importance was my intense dislike of the woman. Though it had been fifteen years since I married Thomas and took up residence in the old harpy's lair, I had never gotten over the indignities I suffered there, and had avoided her company whenever possible. Lately she had developed a new grudge against me. In addition to my complete inability to raise children or manage a household, and my unsuitability to be Thomas' wife, she considered it entirely my fault that Essie and her family had pulled up stakes and moved to the West. If I had not insulted Essie and criticized the way she managed her "niggers," which was far too lenient in Mrs. Henderson's eyes, her dear devoted Essie would still be living in our midst.

The most disturbing aspect of the journey was taking my children to her, yet it had to be done. I had kept them nearly sheltered from her realm, but I could not deny her their presence as she lay near death, nor could I deny my children their own flesh and blood. Tom was fourteen and Adie nearly ten. They had been told their grandmother was a difficult woman molded by a harsh childhood (not true!), who deep in her heart loved them in her own curious manner (ha!). Did they remember how Cissy's mind had crumbled in old age? (Tom did, Adie barely). Well Grandma Henderson's mind was weak and old too, but in a different way. It could cause her to say things she didn't mean, sometimes unkind things, poor woman. She couldn't help it. Eliza was three and a half, and I doubt she took notice of Mrs. Henderson's behavior, or my explanation of it. Bless God for the innocence of youth.

When we reached the Henderson farm we were ushered into my mother-in law's bedchamber, where I encountered a visage I was ill prepared for. Evil had taken flight, and a pale wraith had landed in its stead. Her elegant beauty had dissolved. Her lips had shrunk into a withered crack between the dusky hollows of her cheeks, the limpid pools that had once been her eyes had nearly dried up, leaving a pair of black stones in viscous pits.

She was in a delusional state induced, I'm sure, by her medications. There was the ever present laudanum for aches, pains, &c. Foxglove to stimulate her heart, and spruce syrup to ease her breathing. I almost felt sorry for the old biddy, seeing her so limp and frail, translucent skin tautly covering a sack of bones, nestled among the bedclothes. She slept a great deal, occasionally falling into slumber in mid-sentence. When awake she was sometimes lucid, more often in a world of her own.

She nearly always recognized Mr. Henderson who was beside himself with anxiety. Usually she had no trouble placing Thomas. (Thank Providence! He might have blamed me for limiting our association with her.) Sometimes she saw me as Julia, Thomas' wife of fifteen years; other days I was Julia, Thomas' new wife (or second wife?); "How pleased to meet you, my dear." I'm not sure which "Julia" was mother to my children. They were brought to her chamber, but no preparation by me could have inured them for what ensued. She told them of pretty Angels dancing around her bed, tossing their halos one to another as if in a game of graces. Then, "Look! Look through the window at the lightning! Can you see it? There's a red flash; and there, a yellow one framed in purple. Oh my, a fresh bolt breaking every second; are they not spectacular!" Her bony finger drifted before her face, indicating one window, then another, her eyes glassy and gaunt. "Look over there at the stars, silver and gold, spiraling through the trees. They're floating into the room now, spilling through the window, bursting like Chinese crackers; catch them, dear children, catch me a handful of stars, catch them like fireflies! My, what a show we have! Let me take your hand, sweet child; no no, not that hand, the other one, the one without the talon. Now that's better." She sighed sweetly as she reached for my child, her gnarled hand with its long nails curved like miniature scimitars.

On each visit to her chamber we were treated to a different scene; I cannot give you any idea of all of them; what I am writing here is a mere sampling. Glorious supernatural fireworks were sometimes interspersed with dark and evil gargoyles that scampered around the room, swaggering, sidling monkey-like with their long arms swaying to and fro before them. They leapt upon her dressing table baring their rancid teeth, then crawled beneath her bedclothes where she gathered them in her arms and lovingly kissed their slimy lips. On other occasions she viewed the wicked creatures as monsters and writhed in horror at their presence. I had never before been subjected to so macabre a performance.

My children were wide eyed and horrified. Each time we left her presence I soothed them and said that illness caused the strange illusions. I assured them the God understood her malady, and did not hold her accountable for the dissipation of her poor savaged brain.

Mercifully in a few days Thomas determined there was nothing more we could do to ease his mother's distress, and as Mr. Henderson had his other children close at hand, home we went. She died soon after, just days after Rachel's birth, and I was genuinely in no condition to travel. I sent my condolences to Mr. Henderson by way of Thomas, and praised God that I did not have to attend her funeral, for there was no way I could have mustered a single tear.

Friday, June 15, 1860

Rachel was born in February of 1837. It was an easy birth, as is often the case for a woman who has borne many children. She was the seventh from my womb, and the last, as God must have ordained that our family was complete. By spring I was occupied with my usual duties which I will now describe. Our plantation had grown, and along with it our population of Negroes. I have mentioned that Fred and Mary had married and begun a family. By that spring I believe their children numbered three. Surprisingly, Louis and Cindy had had another child since their purchase several years before. I hadn't expected any more from Cindy, for she appeared to be even older that I. Abel and Little Sam had both married girls from a neighboring place, and when their master moved to the West, he agreed to sell those girls and their children to us. The man needed money for the venture, and I'm sure it was an easier journey with fewer women and infants in tow. It was men required in the West where land was to be cleared. If I remember correctly, Abel's wife had three small children, and Little Sam's wife had two. The health of our families was good; we had buried none of them since Greene.

About twice a week I made the rounds of the cabins; Thomas had built several more to accommodate the increase, yet I must confess they still lived in crowded conditions. Among my duties was to inquire of their health, and send for a doctor if needed. Negroes disdain doctors, so I was careful in my questioning, and observant with my eyes. If a Negro could hide an illness, he would do so, to the point of near death. I remembered Cissy's confidence in herbal cures, and noticed that

Cindy was similarly steeped in the lore. I let her tend to the sick ones, and rarely called for a physician until her remedies were exhausted. Gradually I earned Cindy's trust, and was then given better information as to the health of our families. It turned out to be a good system, trust running both ways, ensuring a robust cadre of workers.

I also assessed their provisions. Every week a ration of pork and corn was allotted to each family, along with foodstuffs of the season. They ground their corn into meal for their bread. They cooked their midday dinners in the kitchen along with ours. Those who worked in or around the house took their dinner together, while some of the children carried food to the fields. Each family prepared and ate breakfast and supper in their own cabins. The cabins were surrounded by small plots they used as they pleased. Most raised chickens, or vegetables which could be eaten or sold. We were often the buyers of this bounty, which made not a whit of difference in their total provisions. To determine their rations I noted the contents and conditions of their plots, and took into account what they raised and what they sold. Earning a few coins brought a sense of autonomy benefiting their dispositions, so we indulged them.

I took stock of their clothing and linens, which was never done during my childhood. If Cissy's family needed anything, she would tell Pa, and he would provide. I kept a ledger listing the shirts, trousers, blankets, &c that had been given to every individual and on what date. That way I could replenish their belongings fairly, and in a timely fashion without waste, or set the women to weaving, as they produced much of their own cloth. Thomas had impressed upon me that unnecessary provisions for Negroes was a loss of income to us. Pa must have rolled in his grave at such a notion. But Pa left behind a copiously supplied black family, and a mound of debts. And Pa did not have so many to provide for.

I suppose my ledger book was a symbol of how slavery had changed during my life to that point, and an omen of things to come. I believe Thomas owned thirty people then; I have made a list of a sort on a scrap of paper, and that is the number I ciphered. I am ashamed to admit that I no longer remember all of their names, especially the children. When I was young Cissy and Rose were dear as family, even Mattie and Greene were more familiar than most white people of my acquaintance. By the late 1830s I was awash in a sea of black faces; I could put names to them then, but few character traits. Today it is much worse. I can name only a handful of Isaac's Negroes, and I doubt if Adie is better informed than I. Are we about to tear our nation apart over a race of simple people valued only for the ease they provide us, and not as human beings? How very sad.

Friday, June 15, 1860

I forgot to write down something Master Frank say when he was here last. I heard him tell the other men that the Yankees might take us to a place across the sea called Liberia. He say the abolitions been sending black folks there for years, cause once they get them free, they can't find much use for them at the North. So they puts them in boats and totes them back to Africa where they come from. Then he say something else that got my attention raised up. That the Quakers been doing that for years and years, rounding up black folks that "pretends" they wants to be free, and shipping them to Liberia in the heart of blackest Africa. I wonder if Romulus is there? I always thought he'd be in Canada, if he's alive. I never had any idea about Africa.

This week I learned things about Miss Adie's place that I never heard one peep of in the four years I been here. Sarah, Miss Adie's house maid that I help sometimes, is laid up in the bed. So Naomi was took out of the kitchen to do house work, and there was a heap to do when all the company left. I wrote down that Sarah don't say much, well Naomi can't keep her mouth from flapping. Oh she works good enough, but she mutters about this and that every step she takes.

Naomi says some of Master Isaac's field hands is fixing to run off. They got a plan of when to leave and where to go. They even has a map to show them the way. But they can't read, so the map don't have words on it and Naomi don't know how they figure to follow it. I keep my mouth shut about the map Romulus had, and how I reckon it led him nowhere but to the graveyard. Then she say one of them men stole a pistol and got it hid away. He plans to shoot Master Isaac if he catches them running and tries to haul them back! I couldn't believe what I was hearing. Shoot a white man! If they do that they might as well turn the gun around and shoot theirselves, cause there's no getting away with killing a white man. Why they wants to run, I ask her, keeping my voice cool like this was idle talk. She say cause Master Isaac beats them, beats them hard with a big old cat, which is a whip made from a fat rope with its end splayed into nine strands, each one knotted all up and down its length. A cat like that can do a heap of damage. I say I never heard such a thing. She say she ain't surprised. According to Naomi, Master Isaac only whip his field hands, never the women or the ones what work around the house. He carries out this punishment out behind the gin house which is too far away for Miss Adie to see, or hear any hollering, although they hardly ever holler cause it makes them look weak. Everybody on the place knows if they whisper one word to Miss Adie, they'll get beat worse or sold.

All the time I been here I had no notion! I reckon I had noticed that the field hands look stooped and low. I figure they had the misery for which I don't blame them, for 'tis mighty hard work on a place big as this one. Otherwise, I never give them a thought, as I am an old woman of the house, and they is young men of the fields. Naomi says they all have scars streaking down their backs. She's done her share of bathing and bandaging gashes, some deep down to the bone.

Vinie never said a word. But I don't think she trust me cause I belong to Miss Julia. And Sarah don't say much to anybody, not that I knows of anyhow. Now I know why I feel so lonesome amongst Miss Adie's people. They all got this big secret that I ain't privy to. How I must look to them, setting on the porch chattering away with Miss Julia when I got free time, which I has plenty of. No wonder they treat me like I is highfalutin!

Well, I didn't let on to Naomi how surprised I was at all this news, act like I expected as much. I tell Naomi that Miss Julia didn't have a notion, which she don't, and I promise to say nary a word to her or nobody else. It ain't in my plan to stir up a nest of snakes! I feel sorry for Miss Adie, all these wicked shenanigans going on right under her nose, and she being a slight simple minded. She believe everything her husband tell her. If he tell her horses can fly and the sun rise in the west, she'd take it as gospel.

I can't tell Miss Julia. It would make her ill as a hornet to know Master Isaac act so mean. She'd be bound to let on she know, even if she didn't mean to, her claiming to hate slavery in the first place. I reckon anger would glow in her face like an ember, then come busting out. Then what would happen? Master Isaac would go on a rampage, that's what, and I can't be responsible for that. If there was any chance at all that Miss Julia could fix things, I'd tell her in a minute, but there ain't. I hate setting on a mean shameful secret. The evil part of slavery just slips and slides over everybody connected to it, no matter where they fits in.

Sunday, June 17, 1860

It shore is one hot afternoon. I chose to set on the shady end of the porch to write in my book while Miss Adie and Miss Julia has gone to visit a neighbor lady who is mighty bad sick. Master Isaac's gone who knows where. There is two huge oak trees out in the yard a piece, and a leafy maple draping its branches over the porch roof. Every now and again a breeze stirs up, so this is a right pleasant place to set. God willing, this peaceful scene will keep my mind away from all that whupping that I wrote of, cause I can't do nothing about it. Now I will get on with the story of my life.

After Marc got in that trouble over Loony Brown and the fire, Tom was sent off to school. He come home from time to time, and he and Marc would go fishing and such, but they never was like boys again. Like Miss Julia and me, they kept their affection, but as they growed up they took their places as a black man and a white one. About that time that mean old Miz Henderson die, and I for one was not sorry to see her go. They say she was right pitiful at the end, as the devil had took her mind. Then Rachel was borned. When Rachel come Adie was about ten and Eliza was three or so. That's when Miss Julia decided it was time to train my Patsy to be a "ladies maid" to her daughters. Patsy was only six, so thank the good Lord Miss Julia didn't make her live up in that infernal garret where I used to stay. Our pattern didn't change for Patsy and me, as we had always come together to the big house when we brought in the breakfast, and go home to the cabin at supper time. What change was Patsy's duties. Before, she was just another child playing around. Now she was taught to brush the white girls' hair, and keep their clothes pick up and put away.

Over the next several years Miss Julia give Patsy more and more to do. Watching over Eliza and Rachel as they growed from babies to little girls, sewing and mending, helping me with the polishing and cleaning. Miss Julia taught Patsy the proper manners for a house servant, saying "ma'am" and "sir" to the white folks, and how to curtsey like a lady, holding her shoulders back and her spine straight. I worried for a piece that Miss Julia was grinding my child down to be a dancing monkey, but bless the Lord she didn't take her lessons so far as that. When Miss Julia look at Patsy she see me as a little girl, and remember the fun we had before either of us knowed she owned me. And it was Patsy's nature to aim to please. Truly in her nature to light up with her big wide grin, showing off a whole mouthful of shiny teeth. We all learn to act cheerful to please our masters cause that's what we got to do to get along, to stay clear of trouble, to get full rations and warm clothes. It don't matter if we mean it as long as white folks think we do. Patsy was different. She wanted everybody around her as happy as she was, black and white. She was one sprightly child.

Back then it seemed like my life was split in two, cause my boys was growing up in a world I had little part in. When Marc turned fifteen he was considered a full hand, and all four of my boys was working from dawn to nightfall according to their ability. They worked under Sam, in the fields, in the barn, at the gin, wherever needed, seeing a white face only when they pass Miss Julia or Master Thomas in the yard, or when I drags them to church, which wasn't often enough if you ask me. They hardly ever spoke to a white person cept to say howdy. Marc took up with Tom whenever he was home, which got to be more and more seldom. My boys was growing up as field hands, with no idea of living any other way. Slavery was all they knew.

Patsy and me lived among the white family from daybreak to dusk. Daytimes we hardly saw a black face outside each other, lest we get a peek at Mary or Cindy, whichever one brung in the dinner. After the white folks ate, we'd carry the dishes to the kitchen and have us some food. By then the others had eaten and was back at work. Sometimes I had to peer in the looking glass to be sure who I was. I'd go to the cabin at night all sorry for myself for missing out on mingling with the black folks, then shamed when my boys came in, aching to the bone, misery coming over them. What a whimpering soul I was.

By and by, after Adie come home from boarding school (which she didn't take to), Miss Julia insist that Patsy and I call her "Miss Adie," and her sisters Miss Eliza and Miss Rachel. It took us a spell to get accustomed to the change, but Miss Julia give us a look whenever we get it wrong, so we learned. I reckon she was about Adie's age when her Pappy told me to call her Miss Julia cause she own me. I never did understand why white folks set such store on words, but I did what I was told. I chuckle to myself reading over this book. I mostly wrote Adie, Eliza, and Rachel for them as little girls, and added "Miss" for when they grow up. I never did get to saying "Master Tom"; I reckon he was too much like my own child.

It was a terrible thing to hear what Naomi said about Master Isaac beating his hands, and I reckon it bound to be true. My bones has long felt wickedness lurking over Miss Adie's place, hanging thick in the air and slimy on your skin, like a swamp vapor you can't see or clutch in your hands. The black folks treat me like I'm not one of them, the way they act polite, then turn away, rolling their eyes. I should have knowed what was wrong, but I was too pent up in Miss Julia's white world to have any notion. I mostly takes my supper with Vinie and Sarah and Echo after the white folks been fed. Every time I go in their cabin they smile sweet, then fidget like I interrupted a private talk. All this time I reckoned they thought I was highfalutin, but that weren't it at all. It was the secret about the beatings they was hiding. They wasn't about to breathe a word to me, living almost like a white woman.

I aim to hold my peace. Ain't no point in me telling that I know what a monster their master is. They may let me in their cabin, but they won't never let me feel like I belong there, or like I'm one of them. I'm wise enough to know that much. I wonder if they got more secrets. Could be, as they shore kept a powerful big one for four years. How many families do you suppose Master Isaac has split apart? I wonder did he ever kill a man?

Monday, June 18, 1860

After Rachel was born I decided it was time to train Patsy to attend my daughters. Not that they needed a maid of their own, after all Rose was perfectly sufficient. But I had to think of Patsy's future. It was my duty to give her every advantage at my disposal to prevent her from being relegated to a hot kitchen or, heaven forbid, the fields. The appropriate skills would go far to guarantee her a household position, especially if I were unable protect her interests. Should I die, she might be sold; life is replete with uncertainties. I began teaching her proper English and terms of respect. I cared not a whit whether she called me "Julia" or "Miss Julia," but if she ever came under the control of another white person it would make a great deal of difference indeed. I taught her to brush my children's hair and care for their clothing. As she grew she learned to polish silver and shoes, mend with the skill of the best seamstress, and create the most elegant coifs. I also determined that she should be literate, even though it was illegal by then. However, I was sure God desired her to read His Holy Word.

It was a gentle task I set myself, molding Patsy. As I have mentioned before, she was the image of her mother as a child, so pretty and cheerful, such a pleasure to have around. I'm sure her nature revived the comfort I found in Rose after my mother's death and during my father's disastrous second marriage. I had hoped my girls would embrace Patsy in the same manner, but they did not, at least not then. They enjoyed her well enough as a playmate, but took her for granted as a servant. Having one another, they were not so hungry for companionship as I had been. I satisfied myself that kindness and respect toward Patsy was all that I could ask of them; the misfortunes of my childhood I would not wish on anyone.

I was disappointed that Adie did not make Patsy a project as I had done with Rose; there were four years between them just as there were between Rose and me. But Adie did not have the inclination or sense of deprivation to do such a thing. Later on it was Eliza who took the role, which should not have surprised me, as Eliza has more of my temperament than the other girls. It was Eliza who would teach Patsy to read.

About the time of Rachel's birth an economic depression began sweeping the nation, but by a stroke of luck our corner of the world suffered less than most. Every year the price of cotton continued its fall, and good markets became hard to find. Thomas, like most of our neighbors, compensated by planting larger crops, and through his efforts we kept the wolf from the door. However it was gold, not cotton, that benefited our section of North Carolina. Some years before, gold had been discovered about forty miles east of us, and by the late 1830s the gold fields had spread yielding prodigious quantities of ore, especially in Mecklenburg County. Lincoln County boasted a few small deposits, none on our property, at least none we discovered. The found wealth filtered itself throughout the area. Many who had little or no cash had nuggets in their pockets, so trade was not nearly so difficult as it was in the wide world beyond. Merchants gravitate toward hard money, so we rarely lacked for anything.

We kept Tom at the Pleasant Retreat Academy for three years; then he joined his father on the farm. When Adie was fourteen we concluded to send her to the Salem Female Boarding School operated by the Moravian Church in Salem, North Carolina. Its academic reputation was stellar, and its discipline was gentle yet thorough. Adie had not done well in our common school. Though lively and high spirited she was not the rowdy Tom had been; she seemed simply unable to absorb the information placed before her. Perhaps the Moravians would be able to open her mind. So in the fall of 1841

Thomas and I took her to Salem and enrolled her there. It was a delightful place with an aura of piety and promise. We left her with great confidence that we had done the right thing.

Her first letters home were cheerful, but quickly disappointment set in. She didn't understand her lessons. The teaching Sisters were patient, but had to divide their attention among all the girls. She asked her classmates for help, but they quickly became exasperated and began to avoid her. My sunny, happy, frivolous girl was at her wits' end and wanted desperately to come home. Thomas and I insisted she finish the term, and we exchanged letters with the Sisters who taught her. Their assessment was always the same. Adie was pleasant and charming, but some girls are not meant for schooling. Early in December, the session being over, Thomas and I went to fetch our sad little girl. We spoke with the Inspector (the gentleman in charge of the school) and several of the Sisters. All had the same advice. Adie had social gifts that were the envy of many girls, but her mind was not suited for academics. Poor Adie, I felt so sorry for her, sorry that she would miss the great joy that books and learning have given me.

Adie had hardly reached our doorstep when her vivacity returned. She even had hugs for Rose and Patsy. All giggles and squeals, she rushed Patsy upstairs to teach her the latest hairstyles. Over the next few months we watched her friendly nature grow to include a flirtatious streak, the young men at church always gathering in a clutch around her. Thomas and I lost our fear that her lack of schooling might limit her choice of a husband, we now feared that she might be swept up too soon; she was not quite fifteen!

That winter Thomas' father passed away. Mr. Henderson had developed a pneumonia that took him mercifully and swiftly. We had barely received news of his illness, when one of his Negroes came to tell us he had died. Thomas, the children, and I went to Mecklenburg to hear his funeral and see him buried. Our association with the Henderson clan diminished after that. Thomas and his father had exchanged letters over the years, and visited back and forth. Otherwise our acquaintance with the family was slight. Thomas had never been close to his older brother, in fact the man and his wife were almost reclusive. Essie, by then, had stopped writing, much to my relief. His other sisters, well trained by their mother, remained convinced that I was socially unsuitable. They occasionally sent short bland notes, and I responded in kind. I would miss Mr. Henderson, for he had been a kind, gentle man. I wish I had been able to spend more time in his company, without the dreadful encumbrance of his wife.

Monday, June 18, 1860

Nathan done gone to the woods! What addled notion gets into a man to make him run off, times being so dangerous! Oh, I know why he done it, which don't make it less foolish. All them years ago when Romulus took off, I reckoned he could traipse through the woods night after night, and see nary a soul. But times is different now. Patrollers out all night long looking for folks whether they'd run away or not, any black person what seems out of place is a rabbit for their traps. We never used to see patrollers hereabouts, being a piece from town, but nowadays they is more plentiful. All Master Isaac got to do is say the word, and they'll be here in a trice, thick as flies on fatback.

I reckon I ought to write down who Nathan is. He is the son of Little Sam and grandson of Sam and Dovey. Little Sam was bout twelve years old when they come to Miss Julia's place after her Pappy died. Little Sam grew up and married a woman on a neighbor's farm and started himself a family. By and by Master Thomas bought Little Sam's wife and younguns; one of them was Nathan. That was a long time ago; I reckon Nathan is now bout twenty-five years old.

When Miss Adie got married, Master Thomas give her Dovey and Little Sam. Dovey come here to live straight away, but Little Sam was more like a promise than a gift. Master Thomas still needed him on his place. After Master Thomas die, Miss Julia sent Little Sam and his family to Miss Adie's where they rightly belonged. That was about six years ago, and that was when Nathan got his first taste of a cruel master.

Poor Miss Julia, her being ignorant of Master Isaac's wicked ways, has wrought this whole mess. She's bound to ask me do I know why Nathan run away, and I'll tell her, "No Ma'am; don't nobody tell me nothing," which was true until Friday last. I reckon Nathan couldn't take the beating any longer. Don't matter much whether he gets caught or not; either way he bound to end up dead. Don't know if he was the one hiding a gun, and I doubt anyone will tell me, but I plan to keep my ears clean.

I spect Miss Julia will call up Little Sam and ask him what he know, and he won't have nothing to say. He knows better than to tell a white woman how Master Isaac treats his hands.

I ought to be writing down the story of my life, which was what I set out to do when I got this book, although Miss Julia tell me to write whatever I want. Learning all the ugly things that goes on here has got me off my course. I will go back now to where I left off, when my Patsy was a girl.

If I give the impression that Patsy and I lived a sad life taking care of Miss Julia's girls, it was a wrong one. I had deep regret bout my boys' lot in the world, but not about Patsy. She loved doing up the girls' hair, and playing dress-up in their clothes. All of them would borrow Miss Julia's ribbons and hats, and strut around like little queens. Adie was too growed up for such, but Patsy and Eliza and Rachel had a fine time. Bout the time Adie went off to Salem, Eliza commenced the little school at the church, where she took to learning like a bee to a flower bush. Flit from one book to another like she couldn't take them in fast enough. And when she come home in the afternoon, she practice her lessons by sitting Patsy down and reciting. Before we knowed it Patsy could read. I reckon those girls had as much glee playing school as me and Miss Julia used to do. Miss Julia, she was as proud as punch. I had taught Patsy her letters, and Miss Julia had give her a lesson now and again, but Patsy didn't think much of it until Eliza come home from school just busting to tell somebody all she learn, and Patsy plumb caught the fever.

Patsy take to everything that same way. Miss Julia teach her bows and curtsies, and Ma'ams and Sirs, and how to talk proper (which is a lesson I reckon I missed) and Patsy act like she up on the stage performing for the white folks. The more they eat it up, the more charm she give them, having more fun that a cat with a string. It's an attitude, I suppose, that you is born with or not. Slavery ain't no good for nobody, but you can't help what you get borned into. It's a pure gift to be like Patsy and not take the misery. If only she had stayed a precious child.

Tuesday, June 19, 1860

I have just been informed that Nathan, Little Sam's son, has run away. I pray to God that he will not be captured, for it will surely be the end of him. Not that I believe for a moment that Isaac would harm a trusted servant, but the patrollers who generally nab runaways can be notoriously cruel. And Heaven forbid the fate that would befall him should he be caught by a slave trader! Poor Nathan, what could he have been thinking! But I suppose like most Negroes, he is incapable of thinking more than a day into the future. My instinct tells me to inquire of Little Sam for the reason. But I've never been close to the man, and have no confidence that he would confide in me. I'm sure Dovey knows nothing; she never has seemed to have one iota of sense.

After Tom completed his schooling and began working alongside his father, restlessness began to creep over him. It was a gradual change that was perhaps fed by adventurous tales of the West. In the 1830s young men began leaving our area in droves for new land in Alabama and Mississippi. Virgin forests were being cleared revealing fertile soil, perfect for cotton. Perhaps it is the nature of youth to strike out for new raw land, away from their fathers' sedate plantations. This was especially true in families where many sons might have to divide the family holdings. But not for Tom. He would have been the sole inheritor of our place; yet wanderlust is a powerful temptress, one whose siren song cannot be ignored.

I'm getting ahead of myself. Thomas had determined to groom his son Tom to be a planter. By this time Thomas' accommodation with his Negroes was well developed, as he directed their tasks on a broad scale, and trusted them with the details. When Tom joined his father in plantation work, it was running like a fine clock. I was so proud of my husband! When we married I knew his joyful carefree sprit enveloped a competent man, and it had been a long struggle for that man to emerge. Now he was skilled, confident and eager to school his son. Over the next five years I watched lessons unfold. I would often catch Thomas and Tom deep in the study of our farm journal, Thomas explaining why he had selected a particular field for this crop or that, why and when crops should be rotated or fields left fallow, where the best markets could be found, which cotton factors were shrewd and which were honest. Gradually Tom's voice began to predominate in these encounters, and Thomas became the listener, proud of his son's accomplishments.

Thomas began to pay Tom for his work. That is each year when the crop was sold, Thomas would designate a percentage of the profits for his son, a bounty that increased year by year. Thomas encouraged his son to salt away most of his earnings, as he would someday wish to build his own home and start a family. A man who is paid once a year learns to mete out funds carefully. At least most do. My poor father never grasped the lesson, which is perhaps why Thomas ingrained it so carefully in his son.

By 1843 Tom had a fair nest egg, and wanderlust settled in. I suppose it was abetted by Tom's character. He never was one to sit quietly when he felt an itch under his skin. His childhood impatience had been tamed, not obliterated. He talked frequently with people whose kinfolk had made the move west, and listened raptly as letters from the West were read aloud, filled with glowing reports from the new land. It was more fertile than our piedmont, and could produce more bales to the acre. The southwesterly growing season was longer, consequently a late frost or spring deluge was less perilous, as a damaged crop could be replanted. River transport was nearby to most, making the farm-to-market journey cheap and efficient. We were yet to have railroads, and our rivers were too shoal-ridden to be very useful. Our trip to market was a long and arduous overland ordeal. Thomas could not convince our son that there was any good reason for remaining in the Carolinas.

Tom read newspaper accounts of the West, as well as letters from those who had tried the venture, and he learned where there was land for sale. When he was nearly twenty-one years old he concluded it was time to leave us. Texas had become the new frontier, and it was to Texas he was bound. As a mother I was distressed at the proposition, for Texas seemed as far away as the moon. Have I mentioned that my son had no sense of caution! Tom promised he would visit each winter or when crops had been laid by, although it might take a year or two to establish his place. And the stagecoach could take us west to see his progress at any time. I tried to control my maternal misgivings, although I will admit there were many times I fretted silently. I feared that the miraculous tales from the West were exaggerations, and that I might never see my son again. Thomas, of course, was not so emotional as I, simply disappointed. He had planned for so long to take his only son as his business partner. He gradually accepted that it was not to be, and in the end wished his son well.

Then the unthinkable happened. How could I have been such a naïve goose to think that the loss of my son would be the only torment I would have to bear! Tom's savings were not nearly enough to support this expedition, or so his father insisted. His inheritance would have to be given him in advance. Thomas and Tom concluded (outside my presence, of course, and much to my horror), that Rose's four sons would become Tom's property and accompany him to Texas. Thomas was adamant that he not go west without the necessary manpower. I was livid. I knew Rose would be devastated by the plan. It was no surprise to me that Marc might be included in the caper, as close as he and Tom had always been. But all four of them! In all fairness Rose's other boys were of an age for the venture; strong young men were ideal for breaking new land. Levi was eighteen, Ezekiel seventeen, and Alfred fifteen. Nevertheless they were Rose's children, and I had no intention of seeing them separated from her. I could still see in my mind's eye the downtrodden, defeated faces of Cissy and Greene when their children were sold. I had no desire to ever witness such an ordeal again!

We had other Negroes. Surely there were some who could go with Tom, anyone other than Rose's sons. Perhaps Little Sam and his family would suit. But Thomas would not hear of it. He needed to keep the adults who were skilled at their jobs (skills dearly bought!), he couldn't possibly send women or children, and the few others who were strong young men were not so closely aligned to Tom and might run away. There would be plenty of opportunity to slip away on a journey of that sort. Only Rose's sons would do.

Thomas insisted that this was a gift, not a sale, which made all the difference to him. But not to me. A separation was a separation, and among Negroes with no voice in the matter, either sale or gift was deplorable. I was livid!

Wednesday, June 20, 1860

Over the last months of 1843, details of this wild adventure were put into place. Thomas decided which wagon he could spare, which tools, how many bushels of seed, &c. I, with no pretense of good cheer, got Tom's clothes in order, saw to the mending, counted out spare sheets and blankets, parceled out pots and pans. Rose was at my side every step, and was terribly distraught. Poor thing. One minute she was sad, the next angry, then anguished. She grieved all over again about losing Mattie and her brothers which was not unexpected, then re-mourned the loss of Romulus who left us thirteen long years ago. I could barely remember hearing his name cross her lips. It surprised me to hear her go on so. I knew she had affection for the man, but had no idea it still ran so deep. Rose had said Romulus had become despondent those last years with us; I had assumed their ardor had cooled, and that played some part in his dour mood. Although Rose had explained it at the time, I was apparently too dense to fully understand. It was Thomas' treatment of Romulus that caused him to desert his wife and family. My husband had humiliated hers, stripped him of his dignity. Now Thomas was once again playing the role of insensitive despot. I became more livid!

Then I hatched a plan. The thing that saved Rose when the rest of her family was sold was my ownership of her. I had the paper that my father had drawn up to prove it. If I owned Rose, then I owned her children. A female slave's children belong to her owner. It was a simple matter of law, at least so I thought. I would go to Thomas and explain that Rose's sons were mine, to do with as I wished, and I wished them to stay with us. So There! At first Thomas was perturbed. I could see him squirm with this new information. He thought for a while, the turnings of his brain nearly visible. Then he went to the locked compartment of his desk, and drew out the yellowed paper my father had drawn. "Aha!" he said. "This document concerns Rose and only Rose. It does not mention her increase; her future children were not included in your dowry. Those boys are mine, and I have every right to give them to Tom."

"No, no, no!" I rarely raised my voice to my husband; this was an exception. "The law is clear. Slave children pass through the female line. I own Rose, therefore her children are mine."

"You are misinterpreting the law. Slave children do pass through the female line, which means simply that Romulus' owner has no claim to them. Even though Romulus was mine, I have no claim through his parentage. However, any property you had before our marriage, or acquired since, unless legally excluded, is mine as long as I live, and mine to give to whomever I please. You have a document excluding Rose from my estate, but it does not extend to her children. They are mine."

Thomas and I rarely went to bed angry, but we did that night. I was furious. To add to my frustration Marc was eager to make the Texas journey, and the other three were beginning to catch his enthusiasm. It was only Rose and I who were against the idea. The next day I wrote to my brother Frank. Though he was a physician, he hobnobbed with lawyers and politicians at every chance. He ought to have some knowledge of the law, or at least know who to consult. Frank wrote back, agreeing with Thomas, but promised to inquire of one of his lawyer friends. I guess we put him on a fence. Though his inclination was toward Thomas, both of them being male, I was his sister, flesh and blood. A few days later he appeared at our farm. The law was clear.

Rose was mine, but not her children. As a female, I owned nothing, not even the clothes on my back, unless I had a paper that said otherwise. Livid, livid, livid!

So in the waning days of 1843, Tom, Marc, Levi, Ezekiel, and Alfred left for Texas, to what fate, none of us could imagine. Tom and Marc were almost like children again, giddy with expectation for a grand adventure. Levi, Ezekiel, and Alfred were nearly as excited. I cannot say I blame the boys. Any young man would be caught up in the idea of going to Texas. But all of them were so lacking in experience and judgment, so ignorant of the harsh ways of the world. Rose and I wept until our tears were spent.

Tom promised to take care of his charges, and to write letters reporting their progress. None of the black boys could read or write. Rose had meant to teach them, but had little time before they were put to work. It had never occurred to me to teach them, as they were bound for the fields, and Thomas had no use for literate Negroes. At least they could sign their names and read a Bible verse or two, a rare accomplishment for field hands. I suppose I had hoped as our circumstances improved, that one of them would be placed in the footsteps their father should have left, training horses, driving an elegant carriage, attending Thomas' personal needs, serving in the house. But we had all become slaves to cotton, the insidious mistress of the land.

If there was any salvation in this horrid affair, it was that Rose did not blame me this time. She saw that day by day I fought with every sinew of my being to keep her sons at home. I was her ally, purely and totally. Any rift that had ever formed between us was absent the day Tom's wagon lumbered over the horizon.

I had one more battle to wage. Because Thomas had offended me so deeply, I prayed he would honor my request. As Tom's room was now vacant, I insisted Rose and Patsy be installed there. Not in the garret, not on a pallet in the hallway, but in a proper room of their own, a highly unusual residence for servants. Patsy was twelve, and quite competent at her duties toward my girls. Thank the Lord it had not occurred to Thomas to send her to cook for our vagabonds; however, she had no experience in the kitchen, and the subject never arose. Thomas was well aware that daughters with a ladies' maid would attract desirable suitors. A servant living in the house was usual, but in a bedchamber, nearly unheard of! Thomas dared not cross me again concerning Rose. So into the house they came, never to inhabit a slave cabin again.

Thursday, June 21, 1860

Miss Julia say she been writing bout when all our boys left for the West. I sure did hate to see mine get mixed up in that foolishness, but I didn't have any say-so. Neither did Miss Julia. All the years I lived under her nose, I never saw her get so riled up at Master Thomas as she did over that business. It did beat all. She thought she figured out how she could turn him, but it was all for naught. It was one bad day when them younguns tossed their belongings into the wagon, and set off down the road. At least Tom promised to write letters.

I don't know what I expected for my boys, as I had learned not to expect much. I suppose I hoped they would marry girls on our place or nearby, and I would help raise up a heap of grandchildren. Inside my heart I always knew I could lose them, but I never conjured they would go all at once. That's what hurt me so much. Without no warning to speak of, all of them gone in a trice. It was one bad day. I know I'd grumbled bout being crowded in the cabin, and them being under foot, hungry morning and night, and clothes getting tore up faster than I could mend. But I didn't mean nothing by it. Just grumbling bout ordinary things, like a mother bound to do. I hope the good Lord looks over them.

At least they wanted to go. Marc was downright eager from the first, and his brothers come round pretty quick. I reckon that made my grief a little easier, knowing they was happy to get to new land. I had no idea how far Texas was, cept it was bout as far as Canada, only in the other direction.

I stay angry at Master Thomas for a mighty long time. Whenever I see him, I scowl, and he put his eyes down, pretend not to notice. He knowed he done wrong by me, but he weren't sorry. He done what he thought best for Tom; Lord knows he couldn't have gone off to Texas by hisself. But he could have hitched up with some other white folks. Seems like there was bunches of them heading west back then. But for all my anger I couldn't fault Master Thomas on one point; he was looking out for his child, which is exactly what I was doing for mine. All folks, black and white, wants to do right by their younguns; but when a white man's purpose bumps up against a black man's, the white man always wins.

After the boys left, Patsy and I moved into the big house. Miss Julia figure her husband owe her something, so she put us in Tom's room, directly across from the girls' room, and Master Thomas, he don't say nothing. It changed me being in that room. It was not one bit like staying in the garret. The walls was smooth, painted bright blue, and fitted tight to keep out the wind. Sunshine poured through the windows. Course I'd known the room all my life, but it was different living among fine furniture instead of just cleaning it. It made me feel like a lady, almost a free lady. What little truck I had with the others on the property bout come to a stop. Not living in the cabin, not having my boys working among them, cut me apart. Miss Julia said Patsy and I could eat in the dining room after the white family had finished. But most fine days we took our plates out on the back porch. Sometimes we ate in the kitchen with the black folks, but not very often. I purely looked down on the field hands, and thought I was some better than the rest. But sometimes I missed their company.

Another thing come from living in the house. A good thing. I missed my boys something powerful, but it would have been a whole lot worse if I'd stayed in the cabin. Stumbling over their beds, seeing their empty chairs at the table, finding a shirt or cup or any old thing they left behind. It was bad enough without all them things to call up their memory. Every now and again I thought I heard Alfred's voice calling out "Mam," or that little chuckle that Levi had, or Marc snoring in the night. Ezekiel like to sing them old spiritual songs, said it made the work go better. I swear I sometimes heard his singing coming up the path from the field. But when I looked up half expecting to see him, of course he wasn't there. It was all a trick in my mind. No wonder Mam got so low when Mattie and my brothers got sold. I was sad then too, but I had Romulus and Marc and a whole life ahead. I reckon if I'd stayed in the cabin my spirit would have left me like Mam's did.

Friday, June 22, 1860

I have received a letter from my granddaughter Julia which I shall copy into my journal while it is close to hand. She is twelve years old, and lives in Lexington, Kentucky, where her father operates a fine mercantile business. Of course he is not her actual father, my son Tom was, but she considers him such. I am perhaps getting ahead of myself again, and I shall put down shortly how Julia came to be in Kentucky. For now I will record her letter.

My Dearest Grandmother,

I now take my pen in hand to write to you how I am getting along. My mother reminds me it has been some months since you have heard from me, and that you are always interested in a letter from your granddaughter. Papa's business has been quite profitable of late. Lexington seems to be the center of society in Kentucky, fine people coming in everyday to buy bonnets or laces and silks for ball gowns. Every week there seems to be a ball somewhere.

I suppose the greatest news from our corner of the world is the selection of Mr. Lincoln as a candidate for president. We've only just gotten the news, so I am not able to inform you how many it suits hereabouts, but I can tell you it does not suit my father! He speaks of "that man from Illinois" with great disdain. This turn of events is of special interest to us as Mrs. Lincoln, the former Miss Todd, is a native of this place, and has relations here. I cannot imagine what they must be thinking. Papa says the Todds can be a quarrelsome clan, and could not be collectively pleased about anything. I suppose I shall be hearing more as the months roll by.

My school is in recess, so I have little to occupy me. Sometimes I help Papa in his store, making sure that all is neat and tidy. It is astonishing how ladies who appear to have fine manners can rummage through cloth and ribbons and other sundries, leaving a complete jumble behind them. Otherwise I tend to my needlework. I have stitched a plain sampler, and am now working on an ornamental one. Some of my friends say that samplers are horribly old fashioned, but I find the work pleasing.

Mama said to tell you that I showed excellent improvement in my last school session. I find school interesting, but am happy to be in recess. I enclose herein a likeness of myself. A gentleman in town has a photography business, and getting one's picture made has become the thing to do. As you have never laid eyes on me, I thought you would be pleased to see what I look like. Do I resemble your relations? I would love to have a likeness of you, if you would be so kind as to send me one. And of your other grandchildren, my dear cousins I have never met.

I have asked Papa to take me on the stage to visit you, but he says there is not time as his business is very demanding. Does the railroad go to your place? Perhaps when I'm older Mama will let me take the cars to North Carolina. I hope to see you someday in my life.

Your ever affectionate granddaughter,

Julia Henderson

My precious Julia, what a lovely girl she is! I can see Tom in her eyes, maybe a bit about the mouth. And Thomas had the same arch to his brows. Oh what I would give to see the child in the flesh. I shall write her to say there is no railroad in Lincolnton. They are laying rails to connect us to Charlotte, proceeding at a snail's pace; at least we can get there by the stage. In any event the cars from Kentucky could not get her easily to Charlotte. It is not possible to cross the mountains by rail. One must travel far to the north or south and go around them.

I've never thought about having my likeness taken. I'm sure someone in Lincolnton is in the business. I'll have to ask Adie. Adie's Rebecca is only two years younger than Julia. Wouldn't it be wonderful if the girls could know one another.

Friday, June 22, 1860

Tom was good as his word, and afore long letters started coming. Miss Julia let me read every one of them, and I read them over and over, till I bout knew them by heart. I wish my boys could write, for good as Tom was, he didn't write what I wanted to hear. When he mention my boys he told how much land they cleared, and how they was building a cabin, all of them sleeping in tents till they got it done. He don't say nothing bout whether they is happy. He did say it was right warm for February, and they was mighty busy trying to clear land and build all at once. And that lots of folks had lost their raising on the road to Texas. There was a bunch of rough folks out there, scrabbling and fighting to beat all. So far he'd stayed clear of it and hoped to continue. He said my boys was in good health, and all five of them was working sunup to dark.

Then as time go by he wrote he had his crop in the ground, only a few acres that first year, but they'd catch up. Ezekiel had a bad cold, but got over it. All of them got the dysentery before the well was dug. Every little scrap he wrote bout my boys I tucked in my memory. Their place was nearby the Sabine River, and was a pretty piece of land. He did write that my boys told him to say "howdy" to their Mam. Miss Julia got a whole long letter and I got a howdy. Course most of what Tom wrote was for Master Thomas. Miss Julia weren't no more interested than me in how many bales they planned to make, or what price they thought they could get for it. But that's the way men folk write letters, most all about business.

The next year I heard even less about my sons, cause Tom got something else on his mind. He met hisself a woman. She must have been something, cause he go on and on about her. Her name was Jane, and to hear him tell she was quite the beauty. What I wanted to know, was if my boys found someone to be sweet on, but if they did, Tom didn't let on. Now that's why I wish my children had learning. Miss Julia, when she write to Tom, she ask about my boys, cause she knowed I wanted some news. But Tom could never think of a thing to say, cept they'd been sick with this or that, and was now in good health.

Meanwhile Patsy and me cozied in to living with the white folks. Miss Adie was preening herself to be a high styled lady, and she did like to be treated like a queen. Patsy took pride in doing up her hair and fixing her clothes. Patsy had a true gift for gussying up a gown, changing the ribbons, or adding a scrap of lace, gathering flounces here, letting out there. With Patsy's fine sewing Miss Adie looked like she never wore the same gown twice. A heap of beaus was calling on her, and she always looked like she just stepped out of the fashion book. Patsy would stand by the parlor door and giggle and grin when those boys told Miss Adie how fine she looked, cause Patsy knew it was all her doing.

Miss Eliza didn't care nothing bout clothes, long as she was covered up. She and Patsy spent hours buried in books, or roaming round the countryside looking for Indian arrowheads, or spangley bird feathers, any old curiosity. Those two got along happy as larks. I swear I don't think Patsy knew she was property. Rachel was still a little thing, just coming into girlhood. Mostly me and Miss Julia took care of her. But she liked for Patsy to fix her hair and pick out her clothes. Even as a little thing you could see she was going to take after Miss Adie.

But it didn't last. I got a bad thing to write down about my Patsy. I reckon I'll put my book away now and ponder on how to tell it.

Sunday, June 24, 1860

All yesterday I studied on how to put this next part down. I reckon about a year after the boys went to Texas I come to notice that Patsy was losing her cheerful nature. She was fourteen, and got me thinking of how Mattie took the misery at bout that age. But I couldn't see any reason for Patsy to carry on so. Nothing around her had changed that I could see. Master Thomas hadn't moved her to the garret, and didn't holler at her to do this or that, Master Thomas hardly paid her no nevermind. He tend to the farm business, Miss Julia tend to the house. Miss Adie pleased as punch how Patsy get her up all fancy, and Patsy just love to puzzle on how to make a dress over nine different ways. She and Miss Eliza had heaps of time to do as they pleased. I couldn't see no reason for Patsy's smile to disappear, for the sadness to creep in behind her eyes. I ask her bout it, and she say she just tired, that's all. Tired my foot! That girl didn't do a lick of work to get tired over.

Next she took to keeping to herself, staying clear of me as much as she could. It's plumb natural for a girl that age to feel clumsy bout turning into a woman, so I tried to keep my mouth shut. By and by I start to notice that she was carrying a little weight where a girl her age oughtn't to; her belly was round as a little melon! My Patsy! She ain't never said a word to me bout any boys. She hardly had the time of day for the ones on our place, me and her living in the house like we did. Oh she'd go out to the kitchen now and again and chatter with the women out there, or she'd carry the girls' clothes to be washed, and help out with the ironing and such. But I never saw her have any truck with men folks.

Well, I concluded to keep an eye on her for a spell; maybe I was scared to ask questions, cause I purely dreaded to hear the answers. I watched like a hawk for a week or two, but didn't see nothing unusual cept that round little belly. So I gathered up my gumption and sat her down to have us a talk. It was a heap worse than I thought.

I reckon she had got weary of pretending nothing was wrong, that her trouble would just pass over like a mist. She mumbled on about nothing in particular for a while, then she buried her head in my shoulder and started to bawl like a baby. And the whole ugly business poured out of her in wails and sobs, her clinging to my gown, then weeping in her hands, then clutching that poor helpless belly. My Patsy had been raped! It was a boy from another farm what took her, one she had met at church. He had took a shine to her and tried to be friendly, but she wouldn't have nothing to do with him. He was owned by a no-account white man struggling to make a farm with only two hands. White trash, Patsy called him. When Patsy allowed to that scrabbly black boy that she didn't have no time for him, it baited him like a dare. He flirted, then taunted and teased every Sunday out in the churchyard, but all she do is look down her nose. She reckoned she'd find herself a fitting mate when the time come, meanwhile she had no use for a raggedy boy belonging to white trash. She told him as much to his sorry face which riled him up like a hornet. He grabbed her arm and yanked her close, and through clenched teeth, spit slinging in her face, said he'd teach her a lesson she wouldn't never forget. Then he drug her off through the woods, his nails gouging her poor arm. She say she didn't holler at first, her mouth dry and froze by fear, then they was too deep in the woods for anybody to hear. He throwed her to the ground, bruising her back against a rock, cussing and yowling bout how good she thinks she is, and he'd show her what she was good for. He pinned her down and yanked off her underclothes, ripping her britches. Then he shoved his thing in her which felt like a hot poker and a slimy snake all at the same time. She say she'd never hurt so bad in her life, and never been so shamed. Poor Patsy.

When he'd had his way, he snarled that she needn't act so prissy anymore cause she was ruined and nobody else would have anything to do with her. She was his whenever he wanted. He left her in the woods, cut and bruised, dirt and leaves clinging all over, her privates throbbing and bloody. When she near bout finished trembling and sobbing, she took herself to the creek and washed as best as she could. Then she slunk home and began to keep to herself.

He got her twice more. One Saturday when we was all in town shopping, he come up by surprise and took her in the shed behind the miller's. I hadn't paid no attention at the time. Younguns is always scattering here and yonder in town, especially when they got a little money to spend. Another day he caught her at the edge of the woods picking blueberries. She said she fought like the devil, but he was as strong as he was mean. I reckon I noticed that she begged off from church when she could, and clung to my coattails when I made her go. Should have struck me as strange that she avoided me at home, and hung on like a leech at church.

She had managed to keep shed of him for a spell, and figured he was done with his wickedness, when she started to suspect he had got her a baby. No wonder my pretty girl had lost her happy smile.

Well, I cried bout as much as she did, and told her it was not her fault, and we would take care of the baby who was bound to be precious no matter who its Pappy was. Lord knows I'd seen plenty of good babies sired by the meanest men to traipse the earth! Wasn't nothing else we could do. Nobody gets punished for raping a nigra girl, not nobody, black or white. I told Miss Julia what happen, and she told Master Thomas. We loved and doted on Patsy best we could, but I knew nothing would make her feel better till that sweet baby grinned in her face.

Monday, June 25, 1860

I did not attend services yesterday, as I was feeling out of sorts. Not ill exactly, but tired to the bone. The rest of the family went, and if Frank had news to report about the state of our Country, I've not heard of it. Adie, of course, is not interested. It would never occur to Isaac to relate political information to me, for I am a woman after all, and an old one at that. Or maybe he fears I would make some comment about slavery, that contemptible system that supports him so well. Adie's little Matthew had been bounding about all day like a Chinese rocket. My head aches, and the heat leaves me breathless!

Tom began to write letters as soon as he reached Texas. He bought a fine piece of land near the Sabine River, which he felt confident he could turn into a profitable cotton farm. His letters were mostly filled with agricultural information, for Thomas' benefit I presume. He was avid for his father to take pride in his accomplishments. Tom's neighbors were all farmers, yet there was plenty of good land still uncultivated. He felt sure he could acquire more acres after his crop was sold, and that someday he would have a large and splendid holding. He was an optimistic man. The next year a lady named Jane began to creep into his letters. She was a native of Kentucky, and had gone to Texas with several brothers and their wives. It was unusual for a single woman to be included on such a venture, but not unheard of. Tom wrote that Jane had grown bored with frivolous parties and endless social engagements in Lexington. She liked to ride horses, and had an endless thirst to see new places. She had concluded to help her sisters-in-law establish new homes and raise their children, the sort of useful work that pleased her. And she felt a calling to take God's word to the heathen Indians.

She and Tom had become acquainted at the little church in their neighborhood. It was a Methodist Church, the only one for miles around. Tom said many of the bachelor farmers didn't bother with church, and Jane was impressed by his spiritual interest. I suppose church was such a habit in our family, that it never occurred to Tom not to go. Every letter he wrote seemed to be filled more and more with news of Jane. How pretty she was, how resourceful, how hard and cheerfully she worked. On Saturdays she held catechism lessons for the Indians, and a few actually attended, perhaps drawn by her sweet nature. I wrote back that I would be pleased to meet Jane, that they should take the stagecoach and come for a visit. He replied that he could not leave his farm until it was better established; it sometimes took several years to get a place in order. I inquired about our black boys, for Rose was eager for news of them, but all Tom could write about in any detail was Jane and the farm.

After about six months of this, he announced that he and Jane were to be married. It would be a December wedding, and he would be honored if we could attend. Thomas said no. Of course stage fare would have been expensive for the five of us, and I'm sure we would have had a revolt on our hands had Thomas and I gone leaving the girls at home. However I don't think Thomas even considered the expense. I think the idea of riding by stage to Texas completely overwhelmed him. He had rarely ventured beyond Lincoln and Mecklenburg Counties, except to take his crop to market, and then, of course, driving his own rig.

As it turned out it was just as well that we did not go to Texas. That summer we learned that Patsy was expecting a child, having been assaulted by a young buck in the neighborhood. Poor thing, she was not yet fifteen. I know it was not her fault. The owner of the perpetrator had a sullied reputation, and had surely neglected to guide his hands in moral principles. Yet I could not help but consider the innate lust of Negroes, as they seem to multiply so handily. I hate when thoughts like that come unbidden to my mind, but nevertheless they do from time to time. I'm sure Patsy fought the man off with all her might, which proved ineffective; she was a slight girl after all. At least it would be a black child, and Thomas would not be suspect in the deed.

I was uncomfortable explaining this unfortunate occurrence to my daughters. Adie was puzzled that a man could force himself on a girl. Shouldn't Patsy's refusal have been sufficient? I explained to her that the attacker was a very bad man. "Well, he should be punished!" she said. I replied that was unlikely as his master probably wouldn't see it that way. In fact Thomas had no intention of confronting his master, for he knew it would have no effect except to invite animosity.

Eliza was completely shocked. But her affection for Patsy was nearly as deep as mine for Rose. She was a loving sympathetic companion throughout Patsy's tribulation. Thank the good Lord for our sensible

Eliza. Rachel was only about seven at the time, old enough to know Patsy was to have a baby, much too young to understand any more.

I've written quite a bit for a woman as weary as I am. I think I shall take my supper in my room and retire early. Perhaps a good night's sleep is what I need.

Tuesday, June 26, 1860

Patsy moseyed bout fall into winter like she's waiting on the hang-man. I didn't make her go to church, cause she didn't want nobody to see her; I doubt she even wandered off the property. Miss Julia tried to bring out her smile with fat apple pies, trinkets from the store, but Patsy shied away from her. She was too ashamed. Bless the Lord for Miss Eliza; she would not stand still and let Patsy mope. She'd drag Patsy up to the garret where they'd rummage through them boxes of books that Miss Julia's Pappy bought all them years ago. Some were the same stories I read as a girl. Then Miss Eliza made a production of sewing baby clothes, digging through the scrap basket, looking for crisp linen, bits of lace, pieces too small for big folks clothes, but too precious to waste. Every week Miss Eliza have some new plan to pull Patsy out of her blues. She was only twelve, but wise beyond her years. I reckon she gets her smarts from her Uncle Frank, but thank heaven, none of his orneriness.

As Patsy's belly got bigger, her soul shrunk up like a raisin. I worried and worried over her. Some days she'd hardly eat a thing, and others I catch her feeding on some odd thing. Setting out in the kitchen with a bowl of cornmeal, shoveling it in her mouth with her hand. Not cooked or nothing, just plain old cornmeal. I'd heard bout women eating strange things when they carrying a baby. It's a powerful bad sign.

Miss Julia had decided when Patsy's time come, she would have her baby in the cabin we used to live in. She didn't want her daughters hearing the hollering. At first I got my ire up at being pushed out of the house, but I concluded to go along. Miss Eliza had been such an angel, and she was far too young to hear a birthing. Mary and Fred was raising their younguns in the cabin by that time. Mary had been the cook for many a year, Fred had been trained to blacksmithing. They was bout as high up as house servants.

Patsy's time came too early. Not that we knew exactly when to expect the child, but Patsy didn't seem near big enough, and she was carrying way too high. At first I hoped the pains would pass away; lots of women has pains early on that don't amount to nothing. But after they linger a spell, I figured we better get ready. I tell Miss Julia to send for the midwife, then went out to the cabin and tell Mary it was time to get the bed ready. We got some boil water from the kitchen, and a passel of clean sheets and towels, then I went back to the house to help my child to her birthing bed. Her pains was powerful, which they always is the first time. Between them I mop her brow and we talk soft and low. I try to soothe her, then she tell me something that gave me a fright. She said she ain't feel the baby moving the last few days, maybe a week. She figured it had growed big and took up all the space, didn't have room to wiggle no more. She'd be glad when it was born and could kick to high heavens. I just say yes, I suppose that's so. I couldn't tell her what I feared; she didn't need a worry on top of the pain.

The midwife never did show up. Them women can be mighty hard to find, flitting from one birthing to another. Half the time once they gets tracked down, the baby is already hollering. Mary and me and Miss Julia done the best we know how. Patsy pushed and hollered 'til she was so limp and tired she liked to faint. We pull and tug at her, dash cold water on her face, shout and beg. I can't say how many hours went by. We was bout in a panic, and sent a boy to town for Master Frank, and finally when it looked like Patsy plumb give up the struggle, a tiny blue-black child come slipping out of her. We tried to breathe life into him, for it was a boy, but he wouldn't come to. I reckon Patsy was too spent to notice that the child didn't cry, I don't think she noticed he'd been born. We laid him beside her, and tried to bring the cord.

I reckon Patsy had fell out by then, cause she wasn't helping at all, and didn't seem to hear what we was saying. Miss Julia and I press on Patsy's belly, try to squeeze her womb, while Mary tug at the cord. Not pull, just nudge gently, trying to coax it to let loose. That dead baby was the tiniest mite I ever seen, but somehow he'd manage to cause Patsy to tear. She was bleeding something fearsome. Miss Julia keep on squeezing, and I grab a towel and press it hard against the bleeding. But the cord was in the way, and it needed to come out. I never been in such a mess in my life, and I would have shrunk from the gruesome sight, had Patsy not been my child. I don't know how Mary and Miss Julia abided it. Finally the cord break loose, and slid out from Patsy's limp body. Then come a gush of blood like nothing I ever seen. All three of us lift Patsy's legs and pushed pillows underneath her, and pressed towels against her to stop the bleeding. She was breathing in tiny gasps, and her face turned pale around her lips. She moaned and whimpered, but she was still out, and thank the good Lord, didn't seem to have any idea what was going on. I prayed that Master Frank hurry up. We needed a doctor bad.

The bleeding slowed a bit, but it would not stop. Patsy's breaths grew weaker and weaker, and the ashy circle around her mouth spread wide. I took her sweet hand and it was cold as ice, her fingertips limp and dusky. While the others kept working on the towels, I rubbed her hands, and pulled the blankets up close about her shoulders, and over her lower parts as best I could. Her breathing seemed to ease, and I thought I saw color return to her fingers, but I reckon I was seeing what I wished for. It wasn't long before her breath was gone. I slip my hand under the blanket, and could not find her heart. My precious Patsy was dead.

Master Frank came in before long. He peeled back the covers, one corner at a time, and examined my poor dead child. His hands were as gentle as if she were living, and he kept her covered as much as he was able, as if trying not to embarrass her. Then he took the baby and study its tiny body, tapping here and there with tender fingers. I'd never seen him be so respectful. I reckon he had a kindly side after all, at least when doctoring. When he was done he placed the child at Patsy's side, and crooked her arm around him. He smooth back her hair, and turn her face slightly toward the child. They look like they had peacefully fallen asleep. Then he pulled the blanket up to cover them.

Master Frank said we did everything right. If he'd got there sooner, there probably was nothing he could have done to save Patsy. The baby looked to have been dead for several days. A baby born early, especially a dead one, can cause dreadful bleeding. Girls as young as Patsy have trouble giving birth, their hips not yet grown to womanly proportions, and their wombs immature. I never heard Master Frank talk so doctor-like before, and I was grateful for his words. Then he tell us to go wash ourselves, and he would send the soiled linens to be laundered, and clean away the blood. When he was done we could wash Patsy and her child for the laying out.

Miss Julia had a way with the preacher. His funeral for Patsy was as splendid as those for white folks, and he preached over her again at the burying. Black folks hardly ever have gravestones. But Miss Julia got one for Patsy, ordered it from Charleston. She asked me what I wanted it to say, and I had to think on it a while. She ask me did I want to name the baby and put his name on the stone. I thought that a good idea. She and I wrote down this and that on scraps of paper, trying to find the best words. You got to be sure before you set words in stone. Here's what was carved on Patsy's marker:

PATSY

July 24, 1831 – January 19, 1846

Beloved Daughter and Faithful Servant
Whose Glorious Smile
Will Forever Adorn God's Heaven

Her Infant Son Romulus
Precious Child Who Never Drew Breath
January 19, 1846

Thursday, June 28, 1860

I have not written for several days due to a weakness in my right arm. I found it difficult to grasp my pen, my hand being nearly numb, and when I did, it would hardly perform as I wished it to. I loosened my clothing so blood can flow freely through my veins, and asked Adie for an extra bolster for my bed. I have heard Frank talk about patients with similar complaints, and he generally thinks they suffer from too much blood in the brain, or fits of apoplexy. I am determined not to give in to either condition. Loose corsets and sleeping with the head well raised are often recommended, and appear to have helped; today I am nearly recovered except for persistent weariness. I have said nothing to anyone, for I do not want Frank to be brought in. I've heard him speak about such cases, and although he does not bleed near as frequently as he used to do, I fear he would recommend it. I will not abide being blistered or bled, especially about the head!

After Tom and Jane were betrothed, his letters were filled with glowing reports of his bride-to-be, and she added chatty post scripts detailing marriage plans. I felt I almost knew Jane from her notes, replete with sparkle and enthusiasm. The wilderness of Texas was no elegant setting for a wedding, but she seemed determined to make it as cheerful as possible. Her parents, like Thomas and I, were unable to make the journey west, but her brothers, sisters-in-laws, and the little church community provided the proper atmosphere, a fine mixture of festivity and piety.

I generally kept my correspondence cheerful, although I did report the unfortunate attack on Patsy. Her brothers deserved to know. On the last day of 1845 Tom and Jane were married, and less than a month later I had to relate the sad news of Patsy's death. As I have said, Patsy's exuberant nature completely disappeared when she discovered she was with child, and the melancholy that replaced it was equally extreme. Rose and I did all we could think to do to boost her spirits, but it was only Eliza who had any success. I'm sure Patsy's mind was filled with dreadful gloomy thoughts, which are well known to injure an unborn child. Patsy also ate poorly and neglected to take any exercise at all. None of this bode well. Patsy was probably a month shy of her time when the poor infant, unbeknownst to any of us, died in the womb. When her pains began I sent Fred for the midwife, then Rose and I took her to Mary's cabin where we had decided she should give birth. Patsy's ordeal was slow and relentlessly difficult. After hours of little progress she lost consciousness, and was unable to expel the baby or assist in any way. I sent another of the Negroes to town for Frank, as Fred and the midwife had yet to make an appearance. I cannot express how frightened I was. Surely Patsy would die if we could not free the child from her body.

Finally a tiny dead infant emerged. Patsy still breathed, but was yet unconscious, so it was up to us to deliver the cord. I cannot described the copious bleeding that ensued. The cord at long last was brought forth, which only increased the problem. We did all we could to stanch the bleeding, but it was to no avail. Patsy died never knowing she had given birth to a stillborn son. Before long Frank arrived and convinced us the situation had been hopeless from the start. With uncharacteristic sympathy he explained that delivering a dead infant is often difficult, and Patsy's youth made the situation worse.

We buried Patsy and her child, and I determined to buy a proper gravestone for them, unusual in the Negro cemetery. I only wish I could have done more.

Thursday, June 28, 1860

Miss Julia has been poorly. I ask her how she feel, and she say she's fine, just tired, probably from the heat, and it is one hot summer. I can tell she's ailing from more than the weather cause I knows her too well.

But I ain't going to press her. I have not heard one more word about Nathan that run off. I can't ask Miss Julia if she hear anything, cause I know she feel guilty, Nathan being raised on her and Master Thomas' place. I wish I could give her some peace, but I don't aim to say nothing bout the meanness that go on here. I don't dare. It's plenty dangerous.

There is a dank air about this place almost like a stench. Everybody in the quarter is tensed up like something fearsome is bout to happen. I tried to sidle up to Naomi, see if she'd tell me anything, but for once she ain't talking. Did somebody warn her to keep shed of me? Wouldn't surprise me none. I'm still hankering to hear if Nathan was the one that stole the gun, or was it somebody else. It scares the living daylights out of me to think a good-for-nothing field hand, riled up with hate, is walking around toting a gun in his pocket. I take my supper with Vinie and Sarah and Echo like always, and they try to act like everything's peaceful. "My, this be one hot day! Have some more sweet peas, they come from my own garden," and such like that. Then they talk about how old Marsh got the rheumatiz, and this one's baby is feeling puny, and somebody else bout to jump the broom. Just ordinary gossip. I ask if anything been heard about Nathan, and they say, "Naw, not a word, reckon he got away or got sold off somewhere." Not so long ago such talk would lead to how miserable it was to get sold off, and how they got to toe the line when the master's watching. But no more. They just stop talking, like the walls got ears.

I wish I could get clear of this place. Meanness hangs in the air like trouble been put on to boil. Mam would swear somebody's practicing Voodoo, casting spells. I never had no truck with Voodoo. The preacher say not to mess with such a thing, cause it's the instrument of the Devil, but I don't know. Maybe the old ones knew what they was up to. Won't be too long before Miss Rachel has her baby, and me and Miss Julia is going to her place to help out. I pray we can stay there a good long time.

I suppose it could be ain't nothing going on, and it's what I learned about Master Isaac that makes me so fidgety. Every time he walk in the house I try to find some excuse to scurry off to my room. Should he happen to set eyes on my face, I'm certain he'll see etched all across it that I know what he's been doing. Miss Julia ain't asked why I disappear whenever he come in, but it won't be long before she notice. She'd have figured it out before now if she weren't so wore out. I pray that baby don't tarry, cause I got to get away from here.

I done finished reading "Vanity Fair." When I read bout them bodacious fancy people I could imagine Master Frank and Master Isaac all over the pages. I can see Miss Adie in there too, not one of the scheming folks, but one who gets the wool pulled over her eyes. But not Miss Julia, or Miss Eliza. I don't know bout Miss Rachel, but s'pose I'll find out when she have her baby. If Master Isaac can be a secret tyrant, I reckon her husband could be one too. Lordy I hope I ain't jumping from the frying pan into the fire! And that Black Sambo character, bowing and scraping and acting happy-like to be serving the fancy folks. I swan he be just like Echo! I reckon I will ask for another book. I need something to take this mean skulky mess off my mind. I asked Miss Julia if she could get me "Uncle Tom's Cabin." I hear that the abolitions praise it to the skies. She say it won't be in Master Isaac's library. Though he buy books for their pretty covers, even he know better than to have that one around! She said she'd buy it for me if she could find it in Lincolnton, but she don't think anybody there would be selling it.

July, 1860

Sunday, July 1, 1860

The citizens of Lincolnton have grown very afraid of the Negroes. I attended services this morning, and upon looking up, saw the galleries packed with many more black faces than usual. Most Negroes are now prohibited from holding services on the various plantations, and encouraged to attend our churches where the lessons are strictly controlled. The preaching of late is thick with sermons on absolute obedience to one's master; which means we are to obey God, and our servants are to obey us. It is feared any unsupervised assemblage of Negroes might lead to plots of uprising and murder, or talk about freedom, or the spread of abolitionist propaganda. Rumors already abound about Negroes poisoning their masters. Many families go straight home after services, rather than stay to socialize. Every effort is being made to prevent Negroes from having contact with those of other plantations. Such folly. Negroes communicate as naturally and broadly as birds singing from the trees!

I feel so isolated at Adie's place. I hear nothing except at church. (Though I've no shortage of opinions from Frank which are far from unbiased.) I correspond only with my daughters, who write mostly about their children, and my granddaughter Julia who is but a child herself. I've heard not one word to engender fear on Adie's place, yet the white family seems to have become more remote from our black families, auguring a tacit distrust. The isolation I sense is palpable, as if invisible walls quietly erect themselves in the night, one by one, at an imperceptible pace, until each race is set apart from the other. I've still no idea why Nathan ran away. He has lived here for some years now, therefore I think a remnant from his raising on our old place was not the cause. I'm convinced Thomas learned to get on peaceably with his people. Yet there is always a niggling doubt. It can't be that he was mistreated by Isaac? Yet who knows what occurs behind those invisible walls.

And speaking of Frank's opinions, I received an earful this morning. It seems that the Democrats behaved no differently in Baltimore last week than they did in Charleston in May. The convention convened June 18th, and the first several days were spent reviewing credentials, &c. When the balloting was to commence, most of the Southerners, primarily those from the cotton states, walked out. Those who remained selected Stephen Douglas for their candidate, who Frank contends is secretly a brash abolitionist in his cloaked black heart. Those who left the assemblage, including a few from the North and a number from border states who joined their cotton state brethren, considered themselves the true Democrat Party and proceeded to hold their own convention. They nominated John Breckenridge of Tennessee, a stalwart Southerner pledged to protect states' rights and the institution of slavery.

One would think Frank would be pleased at this turn of events, having a Southerner on the ballot, but he is not. He says with a somber cast to his face, that the Democrats, split apart as they are, cannot prevail, and Mr. Lincoln will surely be elected. He opined the South will not sit still for such an occurrence. "I'm afraid," he said, "that the South will feel compelled to leave the Union, and the North will do all in its power to prevent them from doing so, even if it means war." I know I detected a tinge of excitement beneath his somber facade. It is easy for a man far too old to fight to become excited by war. Frank did not even bother to pretend that the Southerners are united on this issue. He says the papers report a great deal of squabbling. If they cannot reach accord among themselves, how can they possibly expect to convince the North, by peaceful means or otherwise, that we should be allowed to conduct our own governance? I see no good coming from this at all! It makes me weary; I fear I am coming down with the blues. Independence Day is three days hence. Such mockery!

Sunday, July 1, 1860

After my sweet Patsy died, I come to miss my boys more and more, cause they was the only ones I got left in the world. By that time all Tom could write about besides farming, was his new wife and how they was fixing up their cabin, chinking it good, polishing the floors. His Miss Jane had set herself to sewing curtains, and making a real home. I ask Miss Julia could I write to him, and maybe he'd say more bout my sons. She say yes, so I did. He obliged to say they was well and working hard. They was clearing more land and fixing to plow. Miss Jane must have figured I was inquiring as a mother, not a farmer, and she took it on herself to write a letter to me! Well, not a whole letter exactly, but a note tacked on to the bottom of one she wrote to Miss Julia. It began: "My Dear Rose," then she say Marc is a cheerful worker, and had a lady friend. He hadn't asked to marry her yet, but they expected he would before long. Levi is a quiet one, but don't complain. Ezekiel had a sickly winter, but now that warm weather had come, he was out in the sun and fresh air and growing stronger. Tom was careful not to work him too hard, so as to preserve his health. Alfred was also looking at a young lady, but she didn't appear to be looking back. Their community was small, with not many black folks, and most of them was men.

Miss Jane says she was asking Tom to buy her a woman, cause she surely did need help cooking and fetching for all them men. Before Tom married Miss Jane he lived with my sons in a little cabin, with Ezekiel doing the cooking. That place weren't fit for a woman, so Tom and the boys raised up another cabin for the newlyweds. That was the one they was chinking and sewing curtains for. I never would have guessed such a thing from Tom's letters. He never give a hint what the living arrangements was; all that time he and my younguns was living in the same house! Anyway, now that there's a mistress on the property, Ezekiel figure it ain't his job to cook no more, cause that's woman's work. But Miss Jane thought Ezekiel was plain embarrassed bout his cooking. All he know how to do was to fry.

She say Tom had bought a brood sow as soon as he got to Texas, and they got hams in the smoke house. Traders come through from time to time so they didn't eat too bad. Well, praise the Lord, Tom got hisself a wife, for she was just what I needed to hear about my boys. I decided to write her back, and ask her to read my letter to my younguns. I don't reckon Tom had read them the letter I wrote; I don't reckon it even crossed his mind.

I been worried bout Miss Julia lately. She sometime sleep half the afternoon away, and as far as I know she ain't wakeful at night. I seen her rubbing one of her hands with the other, like it's got the pricklys, and sometimes she don't seem to remember things like she ought to. I don't mean to say her mind is leaving her, cause she is quick with most things, but little things that ought to be plain as the nose on your face can purely escape her. Like she ain't got me a new book to read, and I asked her twice. Miss Adie don't seemed to have noticed nothing, but it takes a powerful commotion to get her attention.

However today she seem better. This morning we went to church, and been sitting on the porch since dinner, talking and writing in our books. At church she got all riled up over Master Frank's news, he allowed the politicians can't do nothing but fuss with each other. They is all a bunch of scoundrels in her opinion. I reckon being riled up is a good sign. I purely hope Miss Julia don't take ill before Miss Rachel's baby comes, cause I do need to leave this place.

Wednesday, July 4, 1860

Today is Independence Day, and if there are any celebrations in our neighborhood, I've not heard of them. I'm having another good day. I experienced more weakness, in fact my entire right side was sluggish. It has blessedly passed, old age I presume, after all I'm halfway through my sixtieth year. We all slow down; it's to be expected. So I shall now attempt to move along to the end of my story, for I've no idea how much time God has ordained me to live. I'm now writing of a time, my dear daughters, when you were becoming young ladies, and I'm sure you have your own memories.

Tom's wife made a great improvement in our communications, and I began to have some idea of life on the frontier. She wrote with glee about their new cabin and their little community. Having her sisters-in-law close to hand was a great blessing, for western life is difficult for women. Tom, with the help of Rose's sons, built them a new cabin prior to their marriage, and when they moved into it, Jane proceeded to turn it into a proper home. She also took time to write letters to me, and Tom's scribblings became mere postscripts to her newsy pages. She took pity on Rose when I permitted her to write to them inquiring about her sons, and on several occasions added notes especially for Rose. Why had I not thought earlier of suggesting that Rose write her own letters? How could I have been so stupid?

It was not many months later when Jane wrote to say she was expecting a child. At long last I was to have a grandchild! But my heart ached as they lived at such a distance. I wanted more than life itself to be able to wrap my arms around a grandchild. I, more than most, know how important it is to embrace an infant and emblazon its image in one's mind and heart, for that is all I have of three of my own children. Don't think for a moment that I ever forgot precious Jane, or Caleb, or Lawson.

When Jane's time neared, I begged Thomas to let me go on the stage to Texas. I could take Rose with me. We would be perfectly safe. "Imagine what a great benefit I would be to Jane, and what a grand reunion Rose would have with her boys," I told him. The boys had become men since she saw them last. Thomas would hear none of it. "Travel is not safe," he said. "We hear of highway robbery every day." I'd heard no such thing, and felt surely he was inventing the entire matter. "Besides," he went on, "the child is due in the middle of winter; you know how dangerous that can be. A stage can become stranded, leaving all aboard to freeze to death." There was no arguing with him. How my practical, sensible Thomas became like a worrisome old woman on the issue of travel is something I never understood.

On January 10, 1848, little Julia Henderson was born. Imagine, my namesake born on my birthday! What a strange coincidence it was. Again I begged Thomas to take me to the West, or at least let me go and take Rose along. To no avail.

Thursday, July 5, 1860

Meanwhile our family at home increased, not an increase by birth of course, but one by marriage. I believe I mentioned earlier what a social butterfly our Adie turned out to be. After she returned from Salem, her life filled with engagements. When she was at home there was a steady stream of beaus vying for her attention, and whenever possible, she spent time in Lincolnton. She was always welcome to stay at Frank's home which made it convenient for her to attend any number of balls and other gay affairs. She made friends with young ladies whose fathers were upstanding prosperous men. It was in this circle of friends that she became acquainted with Isaac Lowery. His father, who has since passed away, farmed the land on which we now live. Isaac's parents married late and Isaac was their only child. His mother had died before Adie and Isaac met, and the elder Mr. Lowery followed not long after they were wed. But I get ahead of myself.

When Isaac first came to call on our daughter, he presented himself as a well mannered, well dressed young man. He had completed his education at the University of North Carolina, and was helping farm his father's land. It was a fine plantation, larger than ours, but not mammoth. Isaac seemed sensible and settled. Adie was a bubbly flirtatious young lady, who rarely met a young man who displeased her. She would hover around a beau like a butterfly, until another more interesting one came along. Thomas and I had ceased to worry that she would marry too young, for she was nearly twenty-two when Isaac entered her realm, but the other worries still nagged us. Adie was a vivacious child, nearly boisterous in her joie de vivre. Many young men were attracted to her nature. But as I have said she was literal minded, and far from an intellect. I'm afraid some of her suitors became bored after a brief acquaintance. Which never bothered Adie, for she was ever ready to flit to the next flower.

It was different with Isaac. When we met him and saw how smitten he was with our child, we were overjoyed. It is always a mystery what attracts one person to another. It soon became obvious that Isaac found my daughter irresistible, and her affection for him remained firmly fixed. Month after month Isaac continued to call, and one by one the other suitors drifted away. When his proposal of marriage was offered Thomas and I could not have been happier.

They were married late in the summer of 1849. By then she had reached her twenty-second year, and had assumed a maturity we had never imagined for our flighty, naïve little Adie. The ceremony was held at our home, and I can promise you I was nervous about the prospect. As I have said Adie had learned to travel in heady social circles, which had always been Isaac's milieu. I was afraid our old-fashioned little farm house would seem puny to our invited guests. I should not have fretted. Rose and I cleaned and polished, arranged what flowers we could find that time of year. The wedding was lovely, and every guest seemed at ease and happy to be included.

After the marriage Adie moved to this place which is about halfway between our old farm and town. She enjoyed being closer to Lincolnton, and other young people in her set, as she still does. Isaac is not flawless, he's a bit pompous and self satisfied, yet he is a good man and adores my daughter. I am blessed that all of my daughters have made good marriages.

Friday, July 6, 1860

Three good days in a row. Perhaps whatever ailed me has passed, and I shall live to a ripe old age after all!

For nearly two years after little Julia's birth my argument with Thomas about visiting the West continued. The only break occurred during the planning of Adie's wedding. Tom and Jane wrote letters telling us all about Julia's progress, when she smiled and crept, and when she took her first steps and uttered her first words. Each letter begged us to come west, replete with great detail of how settled and civilized their neighborhood had become; how different it was from the rough wilderness of four years before. Thomas didn't believe a word.

I wrote to them pleading that they come east. After all, Tom did promise to visit when he left our place, and he had not. Tom had one excuse after another, the crops, the livestock, &c, &c, &c! Would this dance never end!

At long last, Tom wrote that they would soon be on the road to Carolina. The letter came in November of 1849. He wished they could join us for the Christmas season, but was afraid that finding a market for his crop might occupy him until mid-December. When that was accomplished they planned to take the stage and hoped to be at our house in time to celebrate the common birthday of little Julia and myself. Of course I wished they could come for Christmas and stay through the birthday season, but any visit at all was more than joyous news. Another letter followed with more exact timing, instructing us to meet the stage in Lincolnton on January eighth.

I pray I didn't neglect the observance of our dear Lord's birth that year. Although I'm well beyond believing that every lapse of religious duty invites God's wrath, one never knows the mysterious workings of the Lord. I did spend a great deal of time that holiday season preparing for the visitors. I made sure the house was spotless, the silver and brass polished, the rugs beaten, and the windows washed until they gleamed. I asked Thomas to move his most recent correspondence and other important papers to the desk in the parlor, and place a cot in his office for Rose. Tom and his family would need his old room upstairs, the one I had installed Rose in four years before, and I was not about to send her back to the cabin. Thomas outdid himself with cooperation. I carried a small grudge that he had not allowed Rose and me to go to the West, and was disappointed that Rose's sons were not coming with Tom. Someone was needed to look after the farm, after all, and between traveling and visiting this jaunt would last nearly three months. It would be planting time when Tom got home. Thomas, well aware of this, dared not cross me.

I also gathered up playthings for little Julia, rummaging through crates in the garret for dolls and toys that had belonged to my girls. And of course they had to be washed, or mended, or polished. A bit of fresh paint was required to brighten the smile on a porcelain doll, or make a stack of alphabet blocks like new. I planned menus. All of Tom's favorites, and fancies I thought would please Jane. What was she missing in the West? I gambled on cakes and pies with plenty of spice, and a plump goose.

Eliza was sixteen that year, and had entered the school in Salem that fall. I had written and made arrangements to extend her Christmas recess by a few weeks so she could join our festivities. Eliza was an excellent student, curious and dedicated, and was permitted to begin her winter session a bit late. She promised to read extra books and write essays over the holiday, which she did. She would have done so in any event.

The time came and we met the stage in Lincolnton, but they were not on board. We were not alarmed, for the stage can be quite irregular due to the weather, or the amount of mail to be carried, or the number of passengers boarding and disembarking at a myriad of stops along the way. We stayed the night with Frank and the next day we were again disappointed. On the tenth of January we made a third trip to the stage coach office, and I was most apprehensive; not that I feared disaster, but I was eager to be with the little child on our common birthday. Again they were not on the stage, but a letter was, a letter written by Jane's brother:

My Dear Mr. Henderson and Lady,

It is with sadness and remorse that I must take pen in hand and inform you of the great misfortune that occurred on yesterday. Regretfully, your dear son Tom is no longer among the living. He and Jane were happily anticipating their visit to North Carolina, and busily preparing for the journey. Tom had gone to the village for necessary supplies, and on his return was violently thrown from his horse. It appears the poor creature stepped in a hole left by a burrowing rodent, and lost its footing. Knowing Tom's enthusiasm for seeing his family once again, I imagine he was riding at full gallop.

A passerby found Tom lying in a rock filled ditch, his life and breath having left him, and the lame horse whinnying and hovering nearby. The man came to our place for assistance, and we quickly retrieved Tom's lifeless form and brought him home. From the peaceful expression on his face, I would venture to say the poor fellow expired instantly, and did not suffer. He will be buried in our Methodist Churchyard on the morrow.

Jane is distraught with grief, so I took it upon myself to relate to you this unfortunate news. When she is able, she will undoubtedly write herself. Tom was a fine man, esteemed by all who knew him. I was honored to have him as a neighbor, and rejoiced when he came into our family. He made Jane a fine husband, and I have never seen her more contented than during the brief years of their marriage. It is our ever abiding belief that Tom now resides at the foot of the throne of Our Lord, and has entered into an eternity of heavenly bliss, where we will surely meet again. Tom was a faithful member of our congregation, and a true disciple of the Lord. I hope this will bring you comfort.

        Please accept our deepest sympathy.
            Yours respectfully,
                Henry Jackson

P.S. Your grandchild is in good health.

The letter had been posted on the very stage that was supposed to have carried my dear son and his family. I cannot tell you the grief I experienced. Death is always traumatic, under any circumstances at all, but coming at the heels of such eager anticipation was nearly more than I could bear. Thomas took me home, and I suppose put me to bed, and I suppose gave me nourishment, and love, and comfort. I have no memory of it at all. My mind was a blur for weeks, perhaps months.

Thursday, July 6, 1860

Miss Jane kept up writing me notes bout my boys. That was not near as good as seeing them, but a sight better than Tom had done. When she write that she was due to have a baby, Miss Julia begged Master Thomas to let us go out there to help her. He was having none of it. Miss Julia keep on begging, to help with the birthing, to see the new child, to see the little thing growing, then walking and talking. Nearly two years she beg, but all he say is no. By and by they gets a letter saying Tom and Miss Jane and the little girl they had named Julia was coming to us. I was glad they was coming, but more than a mite disappointed that we weren't the ones traveling, cause Tom wouldn't be bringing my boys. They had to mind the farm. White folks talk a smart piece how they care about family, but when the family's black, the farm always comes first. As I have wrote many times before, you don't have to be whipped to be miserable in slavery.

Well lo and behold, Tom and them never made it to our place. He got throwed from his horse just as they was fixing to leave, and died plumb on the spot. Miss Julia took it mighty hard. We was all grieving, but I ain't never seen a body mourn like she did. She took to her bed a-weeping, and wouldn't see nobody cept Master Thomas. She hardly touched a bite of food. I feared she might join him in the grave if she didn't get hold of herself.

Bout the time she start to perk up a bit, we got letters from Miss Jane with news I didn't want to hear. Seems that she concluded to go back to her people in Kentucky. She needed money to carry her and the little girl back east, and to live on once they got there. So she had decided to sell the land and the people what belonged to her now with Tom dead.

I can't say how many letters transpired revealing bit by bit this bad news. Each one made my heart sink lower and lower. So I will just give here the end result. Miss Jane's brothers declined to buy her property, as they had about as much as they could handle, and no money to speak of. She found someone to buy the land, but he couldn't afford more hands. She wrote that the market for nigras was "depressed" in their neighborhood, and had to sell my children to a "speculator," which meant a slave trader, the lowest form of life that ever roamed God's green earth. By that time Marc had married the woman he'd been courting on the next place over, and she was about to have a youngun, one he would never see. Miss Jane wrote that I shouldn't fret about Marc leaving his wife, as she was a "most unattractive Negress." Tom had bought his wife a woman to cook, and Levi was sweet on her. I never did hear if he married her or not, I only know he wanted to. She got sold off with my sons, but only the Lord knows if they got to stay together. The last letter that come from Miss Jane before she left for Kentucky said "her people" had left in good health with a dealer who had a reputation for being fair minded and she believed they would be kept together cause she had sold them as "a lot." I know that kind of talk from a slave trader don't mean a thing. Could be some man would want all of them, but I know they was sold which ever way brought the most money. Miss Jane figured they'd end up in Mississippi where the "demand for Negroes was high, a favorable place to make a new family," she said. I just pray to the Lord they didn't end up down by New Orleans working sugar cane. From what I hear that's the worst place on earth for a black man.

Miss Julia come out of her grieving, and I sunk into mine. I heard Miss Julia and Master Thomas quarrel bout how he wrote the paper giving my sons to Tom, and how it wasn't done good enough to protect them. I confess I didn't pay much attention, for I could only see that what was done, was done. I wanted somebody to blame, but I didn't know who. Should it be Miss Julia's Pappy who didn't write the paper concerning me to include my children, or Master Thomas for whatever mistake he made on the paper he give to Tom, or the good Lord in

Heaven who made our skins black. I didn't think I ought to be blaming the Lord, but it was hard not to give Him some responsibility.

Wednesday, July 11, 1860

I've had another spell of weakness in my right hand and arm. Then my right leg seemed to want to join the game! I will keep this to myself as long as possible. Today I feel much improved, which I pray is good sign. There is still tension on Adie's farm, but I shall admit I have not paid much heed. Trying to hide, as well as endure, my malady has fully occupied my mind.

Over the winter of 1850 I slowly emerged from grief. Not that it was ever shed, but gradually it became manageable. Thomas was my anchor. Many a night he held me close and let me weep, and kissed my tears away. He rocked me in his strong arms, and listened, and listened, and listened. He was grieving too, or course, and echoed my words, yet he set the depth of his sorrow aside to lift me out of mine. All the while he protected me from the everyday worries of home and farm; I cannot express how deeply I loved my Thomas, nor how thoroughly bound we were to one another.

Jane wrote frequently, and I could see she was recovering her life at the same rate I was. By summer she had forged a plan, which I suppose should have been no surprise to us. She intended leaving Texas and returning to her parents in Kentucky. Being alone with her thoughts had brought her to several conclusions. She did not wish to raise Julia in Texas. The rough edges had not worn off the place after all – I suppose what we had heard earlier was Tom's wishful thinking. Texas overflowed with ruffian bachelors, most of whom had no qualms about settling disputes with knives, and who used foul language with abandon. It was not a fitting place to raise a child, nor for her, should she chose to remarry. The hard work that had once been a challenge had become drudgery, and produced little reward. Each day she worked her fingers raw, yet still they ate poorly and lived like paupers. She dearly missed the comforts of her childhood. What had begun as an adventure had become coarse and disagreeable.

She had also become disillusioned with her Indian mission. The sparse attendance at catechism sessions had never increased; in fact, it had diminished and often no one appeared at all. In the beginning she had given beads to the Indians, or broken bits of jewelry, or mirrors and other pretty things to coax them into the church where she could pique their interest in the Lord. She had gradually become convinced that they only wanted the trinkets to adorn themselves, and had no interest in Christian salvation. She suspected some listened to her holy message only to ingratiate themselves to white people in order to obtain whiskey or guns. The Indians had their own gods, heathen though they were, and had no intention of giving them up for the white man's religion. She felt a failure, having saved not a single soul.

We learned all of this in a series of letters over the spring into summer as her ideas began to fall into place. It all seemed quite wise until the next part of the plan was revealed. She planned to sell her land and her Negroes, for she needed money to travel to Kentucky, and secure Julia's care. She had no desire to be a burden on her parents, and would remain in Texas until she could go home financially sound. I don't mean to imply her idea was unwise, it was actually a mature stance to take. But Rose's sons were not hers to sell. At least Thomas didn't think so.

"They were part of Tom's inheritance," Thomas protested. "As he predeceased me, they revert back to me. A man can't inherit property while the one who bequeathed it still lives. They were his to use, not disperse; Jane has no right to them. The laws are clear!" Had my carping about keeping Rose's family together hit its target, or did Thomas simply want his hands back? I had not the courage to ask. He wrote to Jane kindly explaining that the Negroes were not hers to sell, and offered to pay the stage fare to bring them home. Jane disagreed, politely. Thomas wrote a more assertive letter. Jane held her ground. Thomas offered to sweeten the stage fare with a small loan. Jane declined, her politeness diminished. Thomas wrote an angry letter. Jane replied that the deed had been done. The four men and one woman had been sold to a speculator who would do all in his power to keep them together. Thomas was welcome to bring a suit, but she was certain he would not prevail. She said a lawyer had examined Tom's deed, and the property was clearly hers to dispose of as she wished.

The paper Thomas had penned deeding ownership of Rose's sons to Tom did not use the words bequeath, or inherit, or will, or testament. We had kept a copy, and it simply transferred ownership of the boys from Thomas to Tom. Nothing more, nothing less. How stupid could we have been! One would think that after our previous experiences with the gnarly laws governing Negroes we would have had the sense to consult a lawyer. I suppose it never occurred to us that Thomas would outlive our hardy, strapping son.

Poor Rose was devastated. I could see sadness and anger mingle in her eyes. She held little hope of ever seeing her sons again, or hearing of their situation. She was especially stressed by Marc's abandoned marriage, and the broken promise of a grandchild. At least she didn't blame me for this disaster.

Thank the Lord, Thomas did not instigate a lawsuit. I'm sure it would have made no difference as far as the Negroes were concerned. Their fate was sealed the day they left our farm with Tom. We never saw them again. This unfortunate turn of events hardened Jane's heart toward us, and a lawsuit might have severed our connection entirely. I cannot say I blame her, although I did at the time. After the ugly spate of letters, she and little Julia left for Kentucky, and I heard no more from her for several years. I wrote to her brother in Texas who did not answer my inquiry. And I wrote to "Mrs. Jane Henderson, Lexington, Kentucky." Whether she received the missive or not I never knew; mail is often irregular, and I had no precise address. Finally when little Julia was about five, Jane began a correspondence, chilly at first, but a correspondence nevertheless. I hear from her once or twice a year, and her letters have grown cordial, but never warm. Julia's own letters are my chief delight, from her first childish scrawls at the age of seven to the present. What a dear child she is to write to an old grandmother she has never met! Jane married a merchant who provides well for her and my granddaughter, for that much I am thankful, however she shows no interest in bringing Julia to Carolina.

As long as Thomas lived I begged to go to Kentucky, and as usual he refused, "There is no safe road over the mountain, we hear of stages falling from cliffs every day!" Where he heard such nonsense I'll never know. Since Thomas' death, I have had neither the courage nor the where-with-all to go on my own. I am old, and I must contribute to my maintenance here at Adie's place. Should I live so long, perhaps Julia will be permitted to come to me.

Wednesday, July 11, 1860

I been worrying bout Miss Julia. One day she shuffle around and act confused, then the next day she seem her old self. I ask should we send for Master Frank, and she squawked don't you dare say a word, and not bother Miss Adie neither! So I keep quiet. I'm setting out on the porch keeping her company. She's writing in her book, pen rushing cross the page to beat all, and I ain't got nothing to say, cause I can't fix my mind on anything cept her and the people round here nervous as turkeys in thunder. She do seem better today. I can't tell if she's writing so fast to get her words down before the next spell comes, or if she truly is her old self. Lord have mercy on her. I dread what might become of me if Miss Julia passes. And this is a two-part worry. I can't imagine being without that woman. I can say in my deepest heart that I love her, and would grieve for her like I done my own blood. Oh I know we've had our differences, but we've mostly got past them. She has took good care of me, but more than that, she ain't let anybody get in her way and treat me poorly. Which is the second worry. Miss Adie, she act kindly, but sometimes she don't have the sense of a knot on a log. If Master Isaac send me to live in the quarter, she won't say nothing, and I shore couldn't abide living amongst folks that don't give me a lick of respect.

So I'm setting here trying to put down any old words, long as Miss Julia keeps writing. It's mighty hot, but July generally is. The corn been laid by, and is near ready for pulling. The garden looks peaked, we need us some rain. The beans are still bearing some, but their leaves is beginning to curl. Miss Adie has two little boys watering her rose bushes. They each got two buckets and yoke, and giggle and cavort across the yard from the well to the garden. Miss Adie sticks her head out the door from time to time, hollering at them to slow down cause they's splashing water all over creation. They step easy till she gets her head back inside, then they take up their game again. If Miss Adie had a speck of sense, she'd let them boys do chores with all the fun they can manage. Otherwise they'll turn into soured old men itching to run away. Although I reckon that don't matter here with all the evil that Master Isaac done sowed.

I got out my pen knife and sharpened my pencil while I was watching the younguns run round. I never heard nothing bout my boys. Marc would be near bout forty by now, Alfred past thirty, and Levi and Ezekiel in between, that is if they still alive. I reckon I'm bound to have grandchildren. I wish I could see them dancing and squealing, carrying buckets of water for roses. I sharpen my pencil real slow while I think of what else to write. Now Miss Julia has put down her pen, and is reading over what she wrote. "I would give anything to see little Julia, my heart just aches for her," she say. Then she reach down in her writing box for the likeness the child sent to her bout three weeks since. "Isn't she the prettiest thing! Rose, do you think she resembles Tom?" I reckon I ain't the only one not knowing grandchildren. But at least Miss Julia knows who she is, where she live, and what she look like.

Saturday, July 14, 1860

I felt stupid and confused yesterday and the day before. Today the cobwebs have been swept away, at least they have in my perception. I'm almost afraid to speak to Adie for fear of giving myself away. Rose has noticed, and I've sworn her to silence. Tomorrow is the Sabbath and I plan to feign a headache, reasonable in this hot weather. I doubt I could fool Frank, should we encounter him at church, although he may be too wrought up in politics to notice.

Thomas and I had only a few short years together after our beloved Tom died. He kept abreast of our farm, and I concerned myself with our daughters, but mostly we devoted ourselves to each other. He was greatly chagrinned over the blunder he made failing to secure Rose's children. His remorse was so profound that I completely forgave him for letting them go to Texas with Tom. I had long before forgiven him for his part in selling Rose's brothers and sister. After all I was as guilty as he in that matter, and we were both so young and ill informed about the ways of the world.

When Eliza was not quite eighteen she completed her studies at Salem and came home to us. She had excelled in all her subjects, and would have enjoyed further schooling, but being a girl there were no options. Colleges were for men. She had no practical use for her beloved natural sciences, although she continued to read and study for her own edification. Salem had unlocked another of her talents, a love and mastery of music. Thomas had purchased a piano when Adie was a schoolgirl. While Adie played woodenly without enthusiasm, Eliza learned to tease song from the keys like an angel. She took pure joy from her accomplishment and spread pleasure among all within earshot. Eliza began giving lessons to the young people in our neighborhood, which turned out to be a great advantage. She was somewhat socially withdrawn, and music connected her to the families of her pupils and helped her overcome her shy nature. Our Eliza, whom we feared might flounder in solitude, blossomed.

In 1853 we sent Rachel to Salem. Rachel, although not as scholarly as Eliza, never gave us a moment's worry. She was every bit as gregarious as Adie, yet unlike Adie she was graceful and naturally tactful. Never did a blunder cross her lips. I have mentioned before her elegant beauty. All of my girls are fine looking, but Rachel possessed a countenance that turned every head in a room. And because of her inner grace, she gave the impression, which was an honest one, that to her it mattered not at all. That year was among the happiest of my life, for everyone in my orb seemed content. Even Rose. I suppose she had convinced herself that her boys might be together, and were able enough men to have made the best of whatever situation they encountered. She remarked more than once that they were cheerful when they marched off to Texas, and a cheerful Negro is bound to please his master and invite humane treatment.

Monday July 16, 1860

I had my "headache" yesterday as planned, and did not attend church. Although it was not so much an ache as a dizziness and a sharp pain behind my eye. The right one. In fact I sometimes need to shut that eye to focus on my journal. Adie has noticed nothing, and Isaac has paid me little attention since the day I moved into his home. I feel an intense desire to get the last of my story onto paper; I do not know if my eagerness is due to my queer state of health which wavers to and fro, or to the fact that I've brought my history nearly to a conclusion and have only a handful of pages remaining in my copybook. I could ask Adie for another, but it fits my sense of order to put it all in one volume if that is possible.

I've said before that pride goeth before the fall, and perhaps once again the Lord had a lesson for me. Had I indulged in self-satisfaction? Rachel was thrilled to be at Salem. I have said she was not a scholar, which is perhaps an exaggeration. It is true she did not crave learning more than breath as Eliza had. But she was at least an average student, not frustrated at every turn like Adie. And she reveled in the company of so many girls from fine families from around the countryside. Eliza had as many piano students as she could handle, and her talent was becoming well known. She was asked to play for nearly every important occasion for miles around. Adie was living her dream. She was the mistress of a plantation grander than she had dared wish for, and had been blessed with two fine babies. Rebecca was born the year after she married, and Benjamin came along two years afterward. Thomas' farm continued to prosper. With fewer mouths to feed, and the education of our youngest well under way; we were beginning to feel well-to-do ourselves. Sinful pride!

It was the summer of 1854 that the epidemic of dysentery reached our environs. The previous summer some cases were reported, mostly to the east of us. Winter generally squelches an outbreak of the vile disease, and that year was no exception. I cannot say if 1854 was hotter than usual, or if the morning fogs and mists were more sultry. In any event the epidemic reestablished itself in monstrous proportions. It is common knowledge that the illness is spread by gaseous mists rising from fetid and low lying wetlands, and is made especially malignant by a roasting sun. In 1854 dysentery accosted our little community with extreme vigor. Rachel was on her summer recess from Salem, so both my unmarried daughters were at home. Nearly everyone of my acquaintance fell ill.

I will not try to describe the horrific nature of the disease in lurid detail, but will only say that the bowels are seized in excruciating pain and are loosed with incredible violence. These attacks are accompanied by aches and malaise beyond anything I have ever known. Many in our family, black and white, were afflicted, as were many in the neighborhood. There were a fair number of deaths, and bodies were buried with little ceremony. Funerals were brief, and they were sparsely attended. The ill of course could not leave home, and those who were well were afraid to. When the coolness of autumn returned some families supplemented those brief and unsatisfying services with more fitting ones.

Most of this despicable season has faded from memory; I can only say that those who were least ill tended the others. All of us, black and white, took our turns as givers and recipients of what meager care we could muster. We had no energy for concocting medicines, and though we sent for Frank, he did not make it to our place, for the village of Lincolnton was equally afflicted. So we bathed one another's feet and brows, and tried to keep our bedchambers clean, a hopeless proposition.

In time the malady left us, taking with it my beloved Thomas. He breathed his last on the eighteenth of August, in the sixty-second year of his age. At the time of his passing, being nearly helpless, I simply wrapped his body in bed linens, and had one of the Negroes cart him to the cemetery. I pinned a note to his shroud stating who he was, and when he had died, and requesting he be buried in our plot next to our children. I trusted the preacher to find some box to lay him in, and inform me of the time his funeral would be preached, for I was far too weak to cope with these details, my own illness having just passed its bleakest phase. Rose seemed in a way to recover. My daughters were weary from nursing, and afraid they might yet be attacked. Thomas was laid to rest as I wished, with Jane and Caleb and Lawson. Finally by the middle of September the ordeal was over, and a proper memorial service was held for him. In addition to Thomas we lost several of our Negroes. Sam who had become as kindly and trustworthy as Greene had been, was my keenest loss; he was not much older than Thomas, and in the leisure of his life, the happiest time for a Negro. One of Fred's grandchildren died, and Cindy succumbed along with one of her offspring. There may have been another death among the little ones; the entire season has been obscured in my brain.

This grim episode has left me weary and sad, for I loved Thomas more than I can say. We had our differences over our long years together, and he was not perfect, but none of us are. I believe we were bound to one another that day our eyes first locked, thirty-three years before his death, and in that stream of time our love and affection deepened and ripened a thousand fold. Few women are blessed with such a satisfying marriage. I can honestly say I am not overly alarmed by my current malady. To be joined with Thomas and our blessed Lord would be a joy indeed. I only hope I can last until Rachel's child is born and launched into a healthy infancy, then perhaps my earthly obligations will be discharged.

Monday, July 16, 1860

Miss Julia been talking bout Master Thomas and that fretful summer when he passed. I reckon that mean her journal is near bout done, cause ain't a lot has happened to us between then and now. I had almost come to care for Master Thomas, for he was good to his wife and children, which is the most you can expect from a white man. Except for Miss Julia's Pappy, and her brother Jeff. Those two been gone a mighty long time, and I miss them still. If it weren't for them I would have come to believe that all white men was the spawn of the devil. As I said, Master Thomas was good to his family and come to earn my respect, but I never let go of the hurt he caused when they sold my family, or when he hounded my precious Romulus, driving him away, or when he sent my boys to Texas. Miss Julia loved him, and I purely cherish her; I was sad for her at his passing.

When the dysentery come lots of folks took sick. Living in the house as I did, I had grown unaccustomed to the cabins, but that summer whenever my own gut was still, I sashayed back and forth, from the house to one cabin then another tending to folks, helping them tend to each other, stench hanging on us like a curtain of filth. I ain't never seen such before, and hope never to again. Soon as one dead person get wrapped up and sent to the graveyard, there was another passed away. I hope the dysentery didn't go to wherever my boys was.

I hear a rumor that two more has run away from Miss Adie's place. Two big strong boys. Being beaten is harder on strong ones, I reckon it rankles them something fierce not to fight back. But if they tries it, all they get for the effort is more lashes. I hate that Master Isaac is such a tyrant, and wish I had never heard of it. Even though he never touch a house slave, least not that I knows of, it makes me powerful afraid. I hope them that run off is the ones with the gun, and that they took it with them. I don't want to be around should any gun get shot.

Miss Julia's bound to hear bout the running away, and it pains me mightily to play ignorant if she ask me the cause of it. I hate lying to that woman, cause it is pure sin, and she got the right to know. If I told her bout the beatings, it might get us off this place in a trice, but not without one heap of a ruckus. If she ask why them boys run off, I'll keep playing dumb, but if she ask directly do Master Isaac beat his people, maybe I should own up. If I got that much gumption. This is one sorry muddle.

I wish Miss Rachel's would get on with her birthing! If Miss Julia and me could get to her place I would feel safe. Least I pray I would. I keep reminding myself that I don't know what go on over there; could be it's just as bad. But her place is smaller. When there's not so many people cooped up together, folks act like they got sense. I pray the Lord Miss Rachel and Miss Eliza's husbands aren't wicked like Master Isaac, who is the worst I ever seen. I've lived long enough to abide that field hands get raggedy clothes, sorry victuals, hard labor, ugly words, and general orneriness. But whipping is something else. Not even a beast deserves such. I pray never again to see bloody gashes, or ridged up scars. Lord help us.

Friday, July 20, 1860

Adie inquired of my health. I suppose my spells have become noticeable, even to her. Drat! I told her it was the heat, and all I need is rest to build my strength, for it was during a similar hot season that her father was taken, and I should not exert myself and become vulnerable. That turned out to be a wise ploy. The summer of dysentery is not a topic she wishes to remember or discuss. I can't imagine why we have not heard from Rachel. I suppose the child is late arriving, although I cannot say for sure that I was told precisely when to expect it. My mind is becoming muddled. I have trouble remembering the smallest things. Which is not quite true. I can remember the past with clarity; it's what I ate at breakfast, or when to expect Rachel's confinement that eludes me. Old age is a grand curse!

After Thomas died I briefly considered giving Rose her freedom. He would never have permitted it, but as a widow it was my decision to make. If only the laws had not been written by men intent on perpetuating slavery, thus making manumission nearly impossible. In order to free Rose I would have had to arrange for her to live outside of North Carolina, and as I had no relations so situated (save my granddaughter I'd never met); where could she have gone? Was I to send her unaccompanied into the great unknown? I would also have to post a bond of a thousand dollars to ensure that she remained in that other state. Where was I to find a thousand dollars? Impossible! Besides I could not, and cannot, bear the thought of parting with her. With Thomas gone she was more precious than ever. If only she could be free and still live with me, not as a slave, but as a fond companion. Therefore I've endeavored to treat her as if that were the case. A few other slave owners have made that same accommodation, keeping slaves who live virtually free. I've explained this to Rose. I hope she understands the bind I am in, but one cannot be sure. She always makes such a fuss about being property.

When our household returned to reasonable health, Rachel returned to Salem for her final session. Thomas had left us adequately provided for, and I had every confidence I could harvest our crop and have it sold. Dovey's son Bob was by then the manager of our hands, and had proved to be good at his job. Frank offered to procure an overseer should I need one. I declined as Thomas for many years had trusted his Negroes to farm the land, although I did tell Frank that I might need assistance when it came time to send the cotton to market. That was where Thomas excelled, and I was completely ignorant. We did find a market and made a profit, but not nearly so handsome as Thomas usually made. It was then I began to wonder how long I could keep on with the farming. It is not unusual for a widow to run a successful place, but they rarely prosper as their husbands had done. It was time for me to consider the future.

In the spring of 1855 Rachel completed her studies and returned home. She had cultivated a fine group of friends, many from Mecklenburg County, not far from where Thomas had grown up. She and Eliza became close that summer, in spite of their differences in temperament. In fact their differences may have bolstered their companionship, for they traversed their social milieu as complements, not competitors. Among their young crowd Eliza sought out the serious bookish sorts, while Rachel gravitated to the outgoing, fun loving ones. It pleased me to see them enjoy each other so much, Rachel trusting her older sister's experience and wisdom, and shy Eliza relying on Rachel to forge friendships. Before long young men came to call, in twos and threes, sometimes more, for they knew I had two available daughters. By the end of summer only a pair of suitors was left in the pack. Andrew Wilson had attached himself to Eliza, and Eli Harris to Rachel.

The two gentlemen were friends and lived nearby one another in the northwest corner of Mecklenburg County. They were both farmers, however Andrew had studied the law, and planned to supplement his income as a country lawyer. He concluded there was a great need for his business, for most men had little interest in traveling twenty miles to Charlotte unless they were required at the court house. In fact he hoped to do well enough to give up farming altogether. Andrew was also an avid reader, a lover of music, and possessed a curious mind. He and Eliza were a perfect match.

Eli was farming land adjacent to his father's place. His father had given it to him when he reached his majority. He was looking to develop a plantation, as well as a stable of race horses. He had a long way yet to go, but he was young and bristling with enthusiasm. Rachel would make him the perfect wife, charming, graceful, and beautiful.

What a whirlwind of entertainment they envisioned, balls and horse races, all manner of gaiety, precisely what they each wished for.

Betrothals were announced, and the weddings were nearly simultaneous. Eliza and Andrew were married early in December of 1855. Late January, in 1856, Rachel wed Eli Harris. The only flaw in their beautiful weddings was presented by nature. December was bitterly cold, and January brought snows the likes of which I'd never seen before. Many who wished to attend the festivities were prevented. Both daughters are still in the infancy of married life, but their unions seem to bode well. They are filled with joy whenever they visit here, their husbands have been nothing but attentive and gracious to me. Dear Lord, I am not displaying pride, merely happiness.

Sunday, July 22, 1860

I declined to attend church again today, and I think that fact alarmed Adie more than my weakness. She insisted on bringing Frank home after services. He looked me over, and to his questioning, I outright lied about how dysfunctional my right side becomes on some days. After all, it is perfectly fine on others. My handwriting on this page is nearly as neat as the first one I penned. I convinced Rose to stand by my story, and blessedly, she did. He left some pills to thin my blood, for I would not consent to bleeding, although he offered to do so. Thankfully he did not insist. He promised the pills contained no laudanum, nor anything else to muddy my brain. I will try them for a few days, but if they impair my thinking, I will desist.

There is not much more to tell, my dear daughters, for I have brought my life's story nearly to the present time. The fall before the marriages I made a pitiful crop, and getting it to market was delayed by many weeks, the roads being impassable due to snow and ice which would not melt. I'm sure the distraction of hosting two weddings also played its part. Yet the situation was more complex than that. My Negroes did as well as could be expected, but some of our acres were worn out, and I had little additional land to exploit. And again, I was completely unsavvy at market. I had had no experience at cunning, and did not recognize shrewdness when it was propelled against me. Frank was little help in spite of his good intentions. He was a physician after all, and unfamiliar with cotton markets. My neighbors offered assistance, which was beneficial only to a point, for they also had crops to sell. No one wished to see a poor widow starve, but it was only natural that they should consider their own families first. I suppose I could have persevered, but I was tired of this business, business I did not care for, and knew I was unsuited for.

Rose was my constant companion. Without her sweet presence my life would have been dreary indeed, for I was the only white person on the place. Not that I harbored the slightest fear or distrust toward the Negroes, but I grew melancholy from isolation. I traveled occasionally to town, but with little purpose. There was not much shopping to be done; with a lifetime of accumulation I needed little beyond sugar and tea and coffee, &c, supplies that could easily be maintained by shopping every few months. When I visited old friends I felt almost an interloper, for they were busily engaged with family. Church was my sole comfort, the tiny Leeper's Creek Church that had salved me so well for so many years. I had always loved it deeply, and still did, yet it seemed hollow when it became my only source of companionship.

About that time Adie suggested I move to her place. She had become aware of my distress, for I would stop to visit with her on my forays to town. Even my simple Adie noticed I was becoming blue! I thought long and hard before accepting Adie's invitation and consulting Frank about selling my farm. In spite of my dissatisfaction, it wrenched my heart to leave my precious land. I had great attachment to the house I was born in, and had lived in my entire life, save for the appalling three years under my mother-in-law's roof. Yet I had to let go. My land was nearly as exhausted as I, my resources had run low, and I was lonely, a sensation I had not encountered in my entire life.

Frank found a buyer for our place, which fetched far less than we expected. I'm sure our combined lack of business acumen worked to our detriment. Yet it was sufficient to cede a small portion of Thomas' estate to each of our daughters, which was what he would have wished. The remainder was placed under Frank's management for my upkeep. I did not wish to be a burden to Isaac, and so far I have succeeded. Each daughter selected a few bits of furniture, carpets, dishes, &c. Eliza and Rachel took the lion's share, as their households were newly established. A few of our people had already gone to them as dowry, and I had made a special gift of the piano to Eliza. I took my bedroom furnishings to Adie's, along with other sentimental things. I divided the remaining Negroes among my daughters, keeping families together as much as possible. I included a caveat in the deeds returning their ownership to me should any of my daughters predecease me. I do eventually learn!

In May of 1856, just over four years ago I moved into Adie's home. I have been happy here, but I should like to see more of my other daughters. I will ask to spend a good long time with Rachel when her little one arrives. And after that, the good Lord willing, perhaps I will visit Eliza. She is established in her marriage now, and I'm sure I would be welcome. I would not deign to say I have a favorite among my children, but Eliza and I share common views and a love of learning. Although she named her first daughter Annabella for her husband's grandmother, it was her love of music that guided her choice for her second born. She is named Constance, in honor of Mozart's wife (Constanze seemed a bit too German, so she chose the English spelling). Eliza's husband has a fine library, while not as extravagant as Isaac's, contains more of interest to me. He may even have a copy of "Uncle Tom's Cabin" that Rose has been asking for, although I suppose that is too much to expect.

Yes, I think I will speak to Eliza once I reach Rachel's place. They live not so far apart, and I'm bound to see a great deal of her. I think Rose would be happier there also. Poor Rose has hinted that she is uncomfortable here. Since Nathan disappeared several others have run away, and the uneasy aura that surrounds the Negroes has thickened. Rose has said nothing, but I can see her spine stiffen, and agitation stir her eyes whenever the subject comes up. She also avoids Isaac, though she denies it. I know Rose as well as I know myself, and I have watched her satisfaction decline. I cannot bear to see her so on edge. It would be good to be in the home of a country lawyer. I'm sure we would have more to discuss than crops and the hateful possibility of a war, bound to rip our nation to shreds! God bless our poor beleaguered Country!

Monday, July 23, 1860

I am stupid and confused again. Have Frank's pills been the cause? I'll give them up if this continues. Worry grips me from every quarter. I am in a sour quandary over Rose. She's more furtive and nervous than ever, as if waiting for a trap to spring. She's never been a social companion to the other Negroes, but her indifference has turned to avoidance, a strained avoidance as if laced with fear. Whatever can be bothering her? As close as we've lived, I often felt I could read behind her eyes, anticipate her every word. Now all I see are murky clouds and a dark anguish, yet when I ask, she denies her skittish behavior, then quickly changes the subject. The next thing I know she is asking have I heard from Rachel, and says how anxious she is to get to her place. Perhaps I'm seeing trouble where none exists. My poor uncooperative body is surely playing tricks on my mind! I am so weary; I can barely move my pen across the page. Nor do I see much use to do so; not much use for anything at all.

Thursday, July 26, 1860

I know I have more to say, and I shan't give up! Frank's pills seem to be helpful after all, and I am now expecting a complete recovery. With the exception of little Julia, I've not yet written about my grandchildren. Each one deserves a long page at least. And I should put down more about Kentucky. Although Julia's letters come only about twice per year, taken together they present a fine portrait of her childhood and environs. I'm sure my North Carolina grandchildren will want to know more about their Kentucky cousin. Perhaps they shall meet her someday; what wonderful fodder for conversation her sweet letters would be! I will ask Adie for another copybook after all. What was I thinking when I said my tale was complete? It must have been my lethargy that caused me to write such a thing.

And I need to say more about Rose. I need to tell you, my dear ones, in person, as well as in these pages, how adamant I am that she not be sold. She is as dear and perfect as each of you. The paper that proclaims my ownership of her is anathema in God's eyes. In His perfect vision no one can possibly own another person. I've been far too quiet on the matter living here in Isaac's home; I've been cowed to fit his and Adie's expectations, and it has been a most uncomfortable fit. Oh, that I had the courage of my convictions!

Dear daughters, I beseech you not to disregard my wishes. I have loved and protected Rose since she was an infant, as you can see from these pages. I know you have affection for your own servants, and would never mistreat them. But none of you has experienced lifelong intimacy with a Negro as I have. I love Rose nearly as I do you, yet my responsibility to her extends miles further. For unlike you, Rose lacks the luxury of a husband or laws to guard her interests. In its stead, she and I have formed an uncommon bond, as strong and unyielding as if forged from steel. When my time on earth has ended, and I have newfound confidence that will be some years hence, please keep Rose in peace and earthly comfort for the remainder of her days. I ask no more.

August, 1860

August 17, 1860

   Miss Julia done died two weeks ago. She'd been poorly for a spell, and two days before she passed, the ailment that had plagued her now and again attacked like a cruel beast. It came on her in the night and must have caused a mighty struggle, for I found her in the morning sprawled crosswise on her bed. She was half propped against her bolster, one arm grasping weakly at the air, one helpless leg slipping toward the floor. I hollered for Miss Adie, and we tugged and shifted her limbs to make her more comfortable, and piled pillows around to support her, and there she remained, for a day and a half. She was unable to move one whole side of herself, and not a word would come past her lips, though we could see by the pleading in her eyes she had something to say. I ask her this thing and that, and she'd nod, or shake her head a mite, then she'd squeeze my hand with her good one. Master Frank came, and said there was nothing he could do. He said she'd had a fit of apoplexy, which he had feared was about to attack her. The last time he'd come by she looked like she was ripe for it. Early in the afternoon of the third of August, she shut her eyes and fell into a sleep. She seemed peaceful as a lamb, and I pray the Lord that she was. I sat with her throughout the afternoon and into the night, holding her hand, praying she would get her rest, and come back to us. About ten at night, with me and Miss Adie and Master Frank by her bed, she took her last breath, and passed to the other side. Lord have mercy on her soul.

   Miss Adie, she carry on something fierce. Oh she was missing her Mam alright, for she truly did love her, but she was also scared half to death. She was afraid something she'd done had made Miss Julia sick, or that she should have sent for Master Frank sooner even though her Mam told her not to, or that one of the nigras had put pisen in her food. Now that surprised me. Not that one of Master Isaac's sorry darkies would stoop to pisening, but that Miss Adie would suspect such a thing. I didn't think she had any idea of the evil stirrings round her place. She may be smarter than I give her credit for.

   Morning dawned and Echo was sent cross the river to tell Miss Eliza and Miss Rachel their Mam was dead. Then Miss Adie and I bathe my poor mistress, and dress her in her prettiest silk gown for the laying out. She look like an angel. By and by Miss Eliza and her family got in. She told us Miss Rachel wouldn't be coming as she done had her baby the day before Miss Julia passed, and was getting someone ready to fetch us when Echo arrived with the sad news. Miss Rachel had a little boy that she name Thomas for her Pappy. The Lord giveth, the Lord taketh away. I wonder could Miss Julia look down from the throne of God and see that precious child?

The day of the funeral all the carriages line up to take Miss Julia to the burying ground at Leeper's Creek. Master Frank, Miss Adie, Miss Eliza and their families piled in the carriages, and a few neighbors joined the caravan. Miss Adie allowed some black folks to go. Me, of course, and Dovey and Little Sam cause they was raised at Leeper's Creek. She also took Sarah and Vinie to tend the younguns. Echo and two other men were the drivers. When we got to the grave I was pleased to see Miss Julia would be put to rest next to Master Thomas surrounded by her three babies lost so long ago. Nearby was her Mam and Pappy, but no corner of the new-dug plot touched the grave occupied by her Pappy's second wife, in fact it was a slight piece away. I remember how Miss Julia ranted bout that crazy woman, and vowed she could never rest buried by her. I had promised myself I would make a fuss if the grave had been dug in the wrong place, and I hope I would have had the gumption, but thank the Lord I didn't have to say a word, for a funeral ain't the time to raise a ruckus.

After the sermonizing, we come home all long faced and bleary-eyed. Lizzy and Naomi had fixed us a feast to beat all. It went on for days, the eating and carrying on, and that is when I got to be itchy under my skin. I didn't belong with those black folks, and with Miss Julia gone, I didn't fit with the white ones neither. Master Frank read Miss Julia's will to the family. There wasn't much property, just like Miss Julia had said when she wrote it last spring.

I fetched the six silver teaspoons for Master Frank, as he said he would send them to little Julia. I was the only one who knew where they was kept along side of her Kentucky address. Miss Eliza proposed to write a letter to the child, to send with the teaspoons, and I told her the story of them as best as I knew. Some had belonged to Miss Julia's Mam, others her Pappy had bought for her birthdays. The first one he gave her when she was sixteen, the same day he gave me to her. Miss Eliza wrote it all down, to put in a letter to send it to Master Frank to enclose with the spoons. Master Frank had been keeping Miss Julia's accounts, and told us there was money enough for Bibles for all the grandchildren, even the one who had just been born. He would buy the best ones he could find, leather bound, and see that each child got one.

No one had any interest in Miss Julia's old mare. It was a sweet old creature she loved to ride back at the old farm, but hadn't had much use for since we come here. As it was not needed elsewhere they concluded to leave it where it was, here at Miss Adie's. There was also no argument over me when Master Frank read that Miss Julia had instructed that I not to be sold "like a brute beast." I am too old to be of much value, otherwise I reckon Master Isaac would have raised a fuss. Miss Adie and Miss Eliza promised to keep me in comfort, and was sure Miss Rachel would agree. I prayed to the Lord that the three of them would figure that I had spent my share at Miss Adie's already, and the other two deserved a nice long spell of my presence.

The next day the two daughters and me began going through Miss Julia's belongings, sorting out her clothes and such. The finer things was set aside for the girls to divide after Miss Rachel's confinement when she could be there with her own opinion. They did conclude to give me Miss Julia's petticoats being they was far too old fashioned for them to wear. They prefer new-fangled cage crinolines that make their skirts poke out like splayed barrels. Miss Julia's petticoats swish and sweep with grace, and I was pleased to have them. They bore her scent and more memory than I can recount. I been sewing and washing and starching and ironing her petticoats my whole life, often as not the two of us working side by side. I will cherish them. They let me keep a passel of her books. (If they disapproved of my reading they didn't let on!) Some were those frightful tales we pored over when we was young girls that summer the weather was so peculiar. I reckon I might read them again, for they'll surely light up memories to ponder in my old age. There was also newer books she had bought or been given over the years, some I had read, others would be a future pleasure. They give me a few trinkets including a lock of Miss Julia's hair which I will have put in a bauble to wear around my neck. There were other locks that had been put into jewelry, one from Miss Julia's Mam, and some from her dead babies. Her girls will divide them up, as they should, them being from their family. I have a piece of Patsy's hair tucked away, but I never had it put in a locket. I reckon I ought to see to it.

While we was at this task, I looked through Miss Julia's secretary and found the journal she had been writing these last few months, and a small bundle of letters from little Julia along with her likeness. I concluded to trust them to Miss Eliza. Miss Julia had carried on a lot about that particular daughter recently, I reckon it was cause she was writing about her. She told me both she and Eliza prized books and learning more than fashions and fancy things, and neither of them had any had any use for slavery. I had my own fond spot for Miss Eliza, she being the one that brought a smidgen of delight to Patsy when she was so low afore she died. I took her aside and give her the letters and journal, and told her all her Mam had said about her. I allowed I'd be mighty flattered to stay a right long spell at her place if she'd have me, that I would make myself useful with her little girls, and she say nothing would please her more. Thank the good Lord.

I have been at Miss Rachel's bout a month now taking care of her and her childrens. Miss Eliza brung me here after we sorted out Miss Julia's things as best we could. I did not write all this long piece in one day, for I only have little snatches of time now and again for myself. It runs a body ragged caring for a newborn with a three-year-old under foot. I reckon by now September has come on. Miss Rachel don't keep a calendar around, least not that I knows of. It's more peaceful here than at Miss Adie's. Or maybe I just don't see any commotion cause I'm too busy with younguns to spend much time with Miss Rachel's people. There's not so many here as at Miss Adie's. Master Eli who is more occupied with raising horses than growing cotton, seems to treat them well as far I can tell. My beloved Romulus used to think caring for horses brought out the gentler side of folks, and I spect it does. It aches my heart that Romulus ain't here to tend those fine horses. The misery would have left him like a vapor.

I been told I shall stay here through Christmas time, then at the New Year I will go to Miss Eliza's. That's a good plan. By Christmas baby Thomas ought to be settled into his new life, and I will have the deep part of winter to get better acquainted with Miss Eliza who remind me so much of her Mam.

The pages in this book is nearly full, just a handful left to write on. I reckon I'll save them until I have something important to put down. It's foolish, I suppose, to wish my children could read this, and my grandchildren if I have any, and if they is alive.

April, 1869

Well we had us a war, a bodacious frightful one. But I reckon it was worth all the terror and bloodshed, cause now the black folks is free! It has been a powerful long time since I wrote in this book; I near bout forgot I had it! I found it a few weeks back, and have read over the pages, and will now try to set down here what has transpired in my life since before the war.

I stayed with Miss Rachel helping her with her baby till after Christmas that year, and on New Year's day Miss Eliza come to get me. I am pleased to say I been here at her place ever since. Miss Eliza is a good one to talk to. She read Miss Julia's journal that I give her, and she had lots to ask me about her Mam and the old days. She didn't know about all that history, and was mighty pleased to learn it. We talked when we got the chance, week by week, until a few months go by. Then I get up the gumption to ask her could I stay here for a good long time. I told her how uneasy I came to be at Miss Adie's, how the other nigras always looked at me sidewise, and she say she'd be pleased to have me. By then she was expecting another youngun, and I had made myself mighty useful taking care of her two little girls. I never said one bad word bout Miss Adie or Master Isaac, and never made no mention of the beating he done. I wouldn't be surprised if she figured it out, cause she is one smart woman. I also thanked her over and over for how she cheered Patsy during her last sad winter.

We had just got comfortable with one another when the war come. All the white men hereabouts went off to fight, leaving the women and children to fend for theirselves. At first most of the nigras stayed on the farms, so I can't say the white women had to do much fending; they just gave orders, like their husbands had done before. All of us, black and white, had been taught to fear the Yankees like they was the devil hisself. It ain't easy to work when you figure Old Scratch bout to come round the corner, swishing his wicked forked tail. Yet in the quarter we prayed that that was a vicious lie, that the Yankees was fine folks who would come to set us free. We planted and tried to keep on as usual, but they was mighty hard times. We raised all our food, so we was tolerably fed, but it was nigh impossible to sell any cotton. When clothes wore out and dishes broke we learned to make do. No finery was to be had, even if there had been money to buy it. This was not such a burden to Miss Eliza, cause she didn't care much for finery anyhow. Miss Rachel didn't fret much neither. Oh she and Master Eli had enjoyed the rich life a plenty, but they bout busted with pride over their "noble sacrifice for the glorious Southern Cause." Miss Julia always used to quote the scripture: "Pride goeth before the fall," and I reckon Miss Rachel should have took note. I feel sorriest for Miss Adie. The war was hardest on her, partly cause her simple mind can't fathom beyond the here and now, and partly cause of Master Isaac's wickedness of which she was completely blind.

When the war come we get bad news every day, bout some man or other that's been killed; half the time we learn that news was not true; the ones thought to be killed is alive, and others we thought safe, was not. That was what scared the daylights out of us, not knowing what was true, and what was not. I don't mean a bunch of lying was going on, just confusion and fear. This go on for four long years, and every day the news came grimmer and grimmer, and the white folks got poorer and poorer. Not long after the fighting started, Mr. Lincoln, who had got to be president, declared that the slaves was free. Lots of folks run off, but they didn't have nowhere to go, and couldn't scratch a living in the woods. So mostly they come home, those that the patrollers didn't catch and tear up limb from limb. It turned out Mr. Lincoln's "proclamation" didn't make no real difference, freeing slaves in the South where white folks didn't consider he was their president. They had a Mr. Davis instead.

The slaves, they get mighty low. They figure they fixing to get free any minute now, but their hopes was dashed again and again as the war drug on. Some continued to run off, and many got caught, and the rest got plumb ornery for which I can't blame them. As I have said before, not owning yourself is a powerful cross to bear. Most hardly worked at all which they could generally get away with, all the masters off to war, and no cotton markets. Everybody was snarly and fidgety, waiting for the end to come. It wasn't so bad for me. Taking care of children ain't a bit like plowing. I mentioned that when I come here Miss Eliza was expecting a child. She had another little girl not long after the war commenced, a little girl she named Julia, after her Mam. A smiling little baby can wrap its tiny fat fist round your finger, and eat up your heart. Don't matter who is the president, or is there a market. Babies is just babies. And babies named Julia is the most precious of all.

At long last it was over and the Yankees prevailed. Master Isaac got his leg shot off, and come home limping on one good leg and one wooden one. I reckon that made him powerful irritable, cause he do like to stomp his foot. Master Andrew got shot in the arm, the left one, which made it weak and near useless. He laugh, saying a lawyer only need a right hand cause that's the one he swears with and writes with, that was good enough for him. Master Eli, Miss Rachel's husband, didn't come home at all. He didn't get shot, he got sick. They say soldiers on both sides was dying like flies from the dysentery or fevers or putrefied wounds, most anything. A camp of soldiers is no healthy place to be. I doubt Miss Rachel will find herself another husband, cause there is hardly an unmarried white man anywhere around. She have plenty of company though. There is white widows a plenty.

Hooray for freedom, is what the black folks thought. There was shouting and cheering in every quarter. But first the Yankees figure they got to teach the Confederates a thing or two, as if they hadn't suffered enough, and us along with them. Them Yankee soldiers riding back to the North stopped at every farm they come to, stealing and burning to beat all. A little rag-tag bunch come by here, and Miss Eliza as polite as she can be offer to feed them what she had, which wasn't much. We had come to making do. After that they pretty much let us alone. Miss Rachel was treat real bad. I reckon they could see that she didn't have a husband around, but she did have a fine stable with a few prize horses left, precious few compared to the old days. So the Yankees steal Miss Rachel's horses, slaughter her hogs, and burn down the stable. They didn't eat hardly any of the hogs they killed. Most was wasted. It was summertime, and there was no way to bleed and gut and salt and smoke them afore they spoiled. My dreams was dashed about Yankees. I had prayed for saviors, and got marauders instead.

Poor Miss Adie suffer most of all. Not just from the Yankees, but from Master Isaac's field hands whose hearts had been filled with hate. This happen afore their master got home. When they heard the Yankees had won and set them free, they went on a rampage, disguised as a jubilee. The cotton had just been planted, what there was of it, and was starting to sprout. Those men was mighty tired of the lash and abuse their master dished out, so they gather up all Master Isaac's horses and mules and proceeded to trample every inch of his farm. They galloped up and down his land, row by row, acre by acre, throwing up mighty clouds of dust like the Apocalypse had arrived. When they were nearly done, the sky opened up, and a torrential rainstorm poured down. Lightening flashed and thunder chimed in with the singing and shouting of the black men, as if God had sent fireworks and drums to bolster their celebration. The dust succumbed to a sea of roiling mud. As far as the eye could behold, the land looked like the great Red Sea had opened, for red is the color of our clay soil. And like the slaves of Egypt, having ruined everything in their path, they rode off to the wilderness and was never heard from again. Old Marsh and Dovey was dead by then, which was a blessing, cause I don't think they could have abided such terror. Miss Adie said some of the men had guns, and there was a heap of shooting and tearing things apart during the melee. They rummaged the smokehouse and storage rooms, stealing all they could carry, then gathered up their women and fled. Miss Adie, scared clean out of her skin, had locked herself and her younguns in a room above stairs, and prayed for their lives.

After Master Isaac's nigras left, the Yankees came, but there was not much left to plunder. They burned the barn and a smokehouse and some other outbuildings. They was about to fling a torch on the big house when the younguns run out on the porch a screaming. Seeing little ones, they lost their nerve and run off. As soon as they left, Miss Adie gathered her children and Echo, who had declined to participate in the rampage, and headed over here. She told us this story in shrieks and sobs, still in fear of their lives. Surely another band of Yankees could not be far behind, and with the farm purely pillaged, there was nothing left but murder to satisfy their vengeance.

It was all over when Master Isaac got home. He was one angry man with his war lost and his place in shambles. He ramble around hollering and shouting, trying to stomp the ground with his wooden peg leg, but it pained him like the dickens, which fueled his maniacal rage. All his people gone cept for a few women and old ones, everything he worked for ruined. I reckon his hands had every right to be so hateful, but they didn't need to take it out on Miss Adie, poor thing; she don't deserve such. I is pleased, however, that Master Isaac got his comeuppance for all his evil ways. I don't feel sorry for him one bit. He still ain't right in the head, act like he been to the devil and back.

The war led Master Frank in another direction, him being a doctor. It humbled him. He was sent to a hospital to treat wounded Confederates, but things never stay straight in a world scrambled up by war. Before long he was tending whoever was hurt, no matter what side they fought on, binding wounds, sawing off arms and legs, applying maggots, in the midst of a sea of rotting bodies and discarded limbs. A purely disgusting business that would not let up. He come to see that boys is boys. It don't matter whose flag they carry, or where they come from, all of them holler in pain and dread, and all of them cry out for their Mams. Now Master Frank won't say he was wrong in supporting the

Southern Cause, but he does admit that war is more brutal than he ever imagined, and wished we had never come to it. Master Frank is a changed man.

After the marauders went home another brand of Yankees was sent to take their place. Their job was to see that the now freed slaves got money and land and mules, and that the Confederates were punished as traitors. But there wasn't much money or land or mules to give, so that part of the promise was broken. Oh they tried. Tried to set up black farms and schools, secure passage for some of us to the North. I reckon they had no idea how many we was, and was purely overwhelmed. Some of them is still here, but I don't know what good they do. One thing never changes. Those big men in Washington bicker with each other, just like always, and we just scrabble to get by. Lots of the young nigras has gone to the North. Some has got their own land hereabouts and are trying to farm, but it ain't easy with most every plow and scythe broken and busted by the war. Some have gone back to work for their old masters. They is supposed to get paid now that they is free, but not many old masters have money to pay with. So the white folks feed them and clothe them, like they always done, and call it wages. We are a free people, we do own ourselves, and that is one big difference when one has the leisure to sit and ponder. Maybe someday when we're not hungry and raggedy and bone tired it will make the difference it ought to.

Most old darkies, like me, have stayed on where we was. Our old masters believe it's their duty to provide for our old age, just like they did in slavery. Oh there is some progress for the black folks, but it comes slow as molasses, and is sometimes hard to see. I concluded to do my part by teaching the little black children to read and write. There are only two on this place, as Master Andrew gets his living by lawyering, and has "employed" just one small family to tend to the garden and the chickens and the pigs, and help Miss Eliza with the housework. But there are others around the neighborhood. So each morning I go out to one of the cabins that is empty now and conduct my school. You cannot imagine how hungry those little folks are for learning. I don't need to remind them that reading and ciphering are the tools they need to get them off this poor ravaged land, and into trades where freedom will count for something. Paper and pens, not cotton, are the coinage of their future.

It was this teaching business that caused me to find my journal. When the war was going on, and especially when it was fresh over, we was all fearful of Yankees raiding and stealing. So we took to hiding what was of value to us. Then we'd hear tales and get nervous, and move things from one hidey hole to another. That's how my books got shuffled around, hither and yon. Not that the Yankees had a yen for books, but out of shear meanness they destroyed things of no use to them, that might be cherished by us. Them books meant all the world to me. And this journal remind me of happier days, sweet Romulus, my darling Patsy, and Miss Julia, may God keep and rest their souls. I pray my precious boys are still alive.

When I stared teaching, I scrabbled about the garret and every other little hidey nook I could think of, and turned up a few books, enough to get us started. Most of them was the old stories from my childhood. By and by my scholars took to giggling at fiendish villains, fair maids and moats and such. Where was the other books? Miss Julia had a bunch from teaching that Sabbath School when Tom was a boy, and some that come from Master Isaac, and others bought in town. Whenever Master Frank went to Charleston, she'd give him a list, and he brought home what he could find. I searched high and low and couldn't find a trace of them. I'd bout figured they was lost forever. After all, we had gone through Miss Julia's things in such a scurry after she died, maybe they never got put in the wagon when I left Miss Adie's. I was too busy with Miss Rachel's baby to give it any thought. When I first come here, I figured I'd be sent back to Miss Rachel after a spell. Had I brought all my luggage, or left some at her place? Then the war come, and the idea of books plain dropped from my mind.

Well you know how it is, you always find what you're looking for when you is looking for something else. A few weeks ago I was picking in the scrap bin looking for some bits of wool to piece into a quilt. In these hard times since the war, pieced quilts is what we been making to keep ourselves warm. And lo and behold, beneath the scraps of cloth was a clutch of my books. I had completely forgotten the hiding place, under torn and raggedy clothes, things Yankees had no use for, and wouldn't bother to burn. They chiefly burned what they thought would deprive us. Then I discovered a box of Master Andrew's war uniforms, and underneath them, more books, including this journal. So I sat down and read it, and concluded to write what is written here.

I have set my life in writing in case any of my kin who are now free, should come in search of me when I am dead, although I pray daily that some of us might meet while still in the flesh. Could Mattie or my brothers be among the living? Amos, the oldest, would be about seventy-five. All these years I have prayed that Romulus got to Canada or Africa. Surely folks in those lands know that we are free. He would be near bout as old as Amos, and it is truly a foolish notion to think I might see him this side of the grave, but I never did give up hope. How old would my sons be? I calculate they'd all be in their forties, young enough to go traipsing the countryside. Maybe I have grandchildren somewhere! It's been four years since the war, but it can take time to piece a life together.

Which brings me to the last thing I need to state. My name is Rose Campbell. Most of the freedmen have taken the name of the first man who owned them. Although some have chosen something else, anything else if that man was cruel. I doubt if any of Master Isaac's old slaves bear the name Lowery. Taking the name of our first owner makes it easier to find our kinfolk, for so many of us were ripped apart during slavery times. Surely if my sister and brothers are alive, they would search for me as Rose Campbell, and as I live not so far from the old place, there is a meager hope that we might be reunited. I gave this matter lots of thought, cause my sons might figure me for a Henderson. They wouldn't remember Master Campbell, but I told them about him, how generous he had been, and how he had secured me to Miss Julia. If my sons have a lick of sense they should remember the name Campbell. I've no idea where any of my kin might have gone, so please dear merciful God, let them come looking for me!

I am among the fortunate, bearing Master Campbell's name with pride, for he was one true gentleman. Mam and Pappy respected him, and as far as I know were never belittled working at his direction. Pappy and my brothers plowed and hoed alongside him, no one's task exalted over another's. And when he prospered, the black family benefited with the white one, as if we were all of a color. We could have got over slavery without a war if more white men were like Master Campbell.

Now I shall conclude, for my pages are nearly filled. I have promised this volume to Miss Eliza, for I trust her to follow my wishes. She, like her mother, despised slavery, and is pleased to have it in the past. But like her mother, and all white folks I imagine, has no idea how it was to be property, even if well treated. She has my permission to read my words, and share them with anyone else who might care to learn about the old days from the pen of a slave. When I have left this world she has promised to keep this copybook for my family, should any of them appear at her doorstep. On her death I trust her to leave it in good hands along with Miss Julia's journal, which I have read many times with great pleasure. Surely someday children of slaves and those who owned us will want to know about life in the South before the war.

AFTERWORD

On the 16th day of March in 1808, seventy-eight year old Annabella Morrison drafted her will. A handful of her words grabbed my attention: "…concerning my said old faithful servant Rose, my will is that she shall not be sold (like a brute beast) but shall be kept by my said three daughters in as easy circumstances as the nature of slavery will admit…" Those words took root and began to grow in my imagination resulting in the fictional tale of Julia and Rose. I borrowed heavily from Annabella in constructing Julia's will; the opening paragraphs are nearly identical. Both Annabella and Julia were widows who had moved with all their worldly goods into a daughter's home. Each willed six silver teaspoons to a granddaughter and namesake, child of a deceased son. Each arranged to have pocket Bibles bought for her grandchildren. Each had three surviving daughters who were left clothing, a mare, and her "old faithful servant Rose." Every word in Julia's will directing Rose's fate was taken from Annabella Morrison. She was my inspiration.

Here the assimilation ends. Annabella and the Rose she bequeathed were real women. My Julia and Rose are imaginary, and although their experiences are firmly rooted in history, theirs is not Annabella's history. I advanced their lifetimes half a century to accommodate the story I wished to tell. Annabella gave birth to ten children (several of whom died in infancy, like Julia's), and she left a dozen grandchildren, more characters than I wanted to deal with. Annabella's husband was a leader and political activist in their pre-revolutionary community. I chose to depict a more ordinary family on a middling farm that grew to prosperity during the cotton years. Annabella's husband secured the real Rose to her in his will with the words: "I do bequeath unto my dear and loving wife Annabella Morrison the negro wench called Rose, during her widowhood or natural life and to be at her own disposal at her death." In other words, should Annabella remarry Rose would not become her new husband's property unless she willed it so. Eerily, I did not discover this will until long after I had secured the fictional Rose to Julia by a similar act of her father.

I did borrow two small thing from Annabella, just for fun. One of the witnesses to Annabella's will was James McWhirter. I know nothing about the real James McWhirter, but I had a gentleman of the same name witness Julia's will. And I gave Julia a granddaughter named Annabella, supposedly named for a paternal great grandmother.

Annabella Morrison lived in Mecklenburg County. I moved Julia and Rose's story to neighboring Lincoln County, a more rural place. *Annals of Lincoln County, North Carolina,* by William L. Sherrill was a valuable source for the county's history. I hope I have depicted it accurately. The western part of the county, including the town of Lincolnton, was settled primarily by German Lutherans and secondly by Scots-Irish Presbyterians. By the 19th century the eastern portion of the county, hugging the banks of the Catawba River, was predominantly inhabited by farmers whose Scots-Irish ancestors had migrated down the Shenandoah Valley a generation or two before. The Battle of Ramsour's Mill in the Revolutionary War was real, and was brutally bloody. Many brave men perished there. The iron industry of the county was hugely important in the early 19th century. There were many forges and furnaces, most operated by the much interrelated Forney, Davidson, Brevard, and Graham families. Vesuvius Furnace and Mount Tirzah Forge were part of their enterprise. Apples were always important in local agriculture; orchards still dot the countryside. The Pleasant Retreat Academy operated for many years; the building it occupied still stands. Also still standing is the Salem Female Boarding School in Winston-Salem, North Carolina. It has been in continuous operation by the Moravian Church since the late 1700s, and is known today as Salem Academy and Salem College. The Medical College of the State of South Carolina was established in Charleston in 1824.

There is a Leeper's Creek, a tiny stream that meanders through much of Lincoln County, and Mount Tirzah Forge was on its banks, but exactly where I do not know. There was no Leeper's Creek community or church, at least none that I could find. My purpose was to create an appropriate setting for Julia and Rose's mythical families, not to document a real one.

The anticipation and fears of an impending civil war were rampant during the summer of 1860. I relied heavily on Bruce Catton's book, *The Coming Fury,* for the descriptions of the political maneuvering during that infamous season. Mary Boykin Chesnut's civil war diaries tell us that the incessant squabbling among Southern leaders continued throughout the war. Hinton Helper was indeed a wild and raving malcontent, and his gentlemanly brother Pinkney kept a hotel in Davidson, North Carolina. The building still stands across the street from Davidson College. Catton's book and *The Plantation World Around Davidson,* by Chalmers Davidson provided details about their interesting lives. Other real people, such as Nat Turner and Abraham Lincoln should be obvious. Julia and Rose, their families and acquaintances are purely imaginary.

There is nothing imaginary about slavery. In spite of its cruelty, not all who were entrapped by the system suffered equally. Early in the 19th century on small backcountry farms, slavery was relatively benign and paternalistic. The worst brutality occurred on enormous coastal and river plantations. As cotton produced prosperity, the nature of slavery ominously changed, and physical abuse became more widespread. I have used many sources to acquaint myself with the wide variety of circumstances and attitudes engendered by slavery, many of them first person accounts of the black and white people who experienced them. All of these sources tell us that the most universal, pervasive, and demeaning aspect of the institution was the loss of personal autonomy.

Julia was not the only Southerner dismayed by the albatross slavery became, and Rose was not alone in being kept in relative comfort. A small but significant number of slaveholders were frustrated by laws that made it difficult, if not impossible, to free one's slaves. John Hope Franklin's essay "Slaves Virtually Free in Antebellum North Carolina" (*Race and History; Selected Essays 1938-1988*) was very helpful.

Julia's belief that Negros were superstitious, childlike, and degraded was commonplace in the antebellum South, and few people of that time, even in the North, would have considered her to be biased. Our ancestors were products of the times in which they lived. It is simplistic, and perhaps unfair, for us to judge them by modern mores. However some people did make the leap, and Julia's distaste for the institution of slavery was an admirable step in that direction.

The rebellion of Nat Turner had a riveting effect on the nation. In the North the abolition movement gained new energy. In the South it spawned fear and strengthened laws to control slaves, including the 1831 law in North Carolina prohibiting teaching slaves to read, a law that was often ignored where religious education was concerned. However other laws, customs, and practices limiting Negro travel, assembly, and emancipation became nearly draconian. A Negro abroad, especially at night, was considered a runaway, and his papers, if he carried them, were considered forgeries. It is perhaps an irony that Nat Turner was most likely an unbalanced man, rather than a crusader for liberty. He proclaimed that God had told him to kill all the white people, and he seemed to have no plan to escape to the North or reorganize society once that goal was accomplished.

Other details are a blending of the nature of the times with specific events. Epidemics, illness, and death were constant companions. Epidemics of measles were frequent, and varied in severity. The 1854 epidemic of dysentery is documented in local records. Medical treatment consisted of bleeding, blistering, purging, amputation, and massive quantities of opiates. The slaves preferred herbal remedies and generally distrusted doctors. The westward migration from the Carolina piedmont during the 1830s and '40s was significant, the frontier advancing from Tennessee to Alabama to Mississippi to Texas. 1816 was truly a "year without a summer" caused by the enormous volcanic eruption of Mt. Tambora in Indonesia which spewed an ash cloud that circled the northern hemisphere. The parched and cloudy summer was widely recounted, although its cause was unknown at the time. There was a dramatic Leonid meteor shower on November 13, 1833, which was readily observed in the piedmont of North Carolina. Educated people recognized "falling stars" as a natural phenomenon that occasionally occurred en masse. Others saw it as an omen of Judgment Day. The winter of Eliza and Rachel's marriages was unusually snowy and cold; other weather events are simply typical for the time of year.

Rose's literacy was unusual, but not an anomaly. In the Carolina piedmont many slave children were taught to read Bible verses and the catechism; Presbyterian Churches encouraged it. A few Negroes from various places in America went on to acquire serious literacy as evidenced by the number of narratives written by slaves and former slaves in the nineteenth century. Rose's imaginary journal could have easily fit into the mix.

The bond that developed between Julia and Rose was uncommon, but not unprecedented. White women living on plantations were often isolated from white female companionship, and frequently became close to their Negro house servants. But rarely did they become as completely intertwined as Julia and Rose. Their bond, though it bore imperfections, that were shaped and shaded by their circumstances, and viewed differently by the two women themselves, was nonetheless impenetrable, unshakable and possible.

ACKNOWLEDGMENTS

I am ever grateful to those generous 19th century people who gave us their stories in their own words telling us how they spoke, thought, and lived. They have become some of my closest friends, as I feel that I truly know them. That gratitude extends to the historians who preserved and interpreted those stories, and put them in context.

When I began this project, I was not sure if readers would accept a literary slave, or a close mistress and slave relationship. Or accept me, a white woman, having the audacity to write from a slave's point of view! My dear friend Martha Matthews read an early draft and gave me the confidence and encouragement I needed. Without her input I might have abandoned Julia and Rose. I wish Martha had lived to see the book completed; I think she would have been pleased.

For many years I have been immersed in a large regional history community composed of people who love to share their research and considerable knowledge. Gleanings from their work, augmented my own research, gave me the basis for Julia and Rose's experiences. Because I too wanted to share, I turned those experiences into a story. For that I am indebted to more people and sources that I can possibly name.

There are a few who can be named whose specific contributions helped me turn the story into a book. Mary Kratt and Jim Daniel were more recent readers. They are both astute historians and writers who offered valuable suggestions. Amy Rogers, my sharp-eyed editor, pointed out flaws, and helped me strengthen several characters to get them up on their feet. Publishers Richard Griffin and Maureen Ryan Griffin led me through the process with their literary, artistic, and technological skills. Several books by Kay Moss on healing, herbs, and cookery of the period provided perfect authentic details. And Barbara Jackson lent me a hand, or rather a pair of them. Thank you, all of you; without you this story would not have been told.

I greatly appreciate the help and encouragement of my family. Scotty, Jim, and Doug are my best cheerleaders. But most of all, my gratitude goes to my dear husband Jim. He is also a historian, researcher, and writer who gave me many excellent suggestions. I turned over a myriad of technical and computer problems to him, and they were instantly solved. His love and support are ever present, and as Julia said of Thomas, "He thinks I am beautiful. Imagine that!"

About the Author

Ann Williams has been immersed in regional history for over thirty years. She has a particular interest in antebellum plantation life, and the families, black and white, who worked those plantations. She has researched farming practices of the period, especially cotton farming, and the extensive collections of family papers of several large Mecklenburg planters. She has used a variety of sources to study slave life especially books and papers written by slaves or former slaves. Using this information she has written detailed accounts for local historic sites. Along with her husband she volunteers at historic sites doing research, giving tours, and doing first person interpretations in the personas of those who lived before.

She is the author of *Your Affectionate Daughter, Isabella,* a documented story drawn from family papers about the experiences and adventures of the Torrance family, owners of a fine Mecklenburg plantation. And she is co-editor of *A Life in Antebellum Charlotte, The Private Journal of Sarah F. Davidson, 1837,* which portrays Charlotte in a pivotal year of its history.

Ann and her husband Jim have lived in Charlotte, North Carolina since 1969. They are the parents of three grown children, and have four fabulous grandchildren.